FIRST GODS AWAKEN

MK MACPHERSON

Random life choices
melbourne

Published by Random Life Choices

ISBN: 978-0-6452172-0-9 (ebook)
ISBN: 978-0-6452172-1-6 (paperback)

Cover art and editing by Mark Reid
https://www.authorpackages.com

Random Life Choices
https://www.randomlifechoices.com

By mk macpherson

FIRST GODS

Awaken
Community
Habitat

Random Life Choices is an independent publisher.
We try our best, but we will make mistakes.
We are human; we're not perfect aliens or AIs.
We apologise unreservedly for all errors and omissions.
To that end, your assistance and feedback
would be greatly appreciated.

Please contact us and point out
(gleefully, if you wish) our failings.

April 2022
MK Macpherson

Random Life Choices
https://www.randomlifechoices.com

https://mkmacpherson.com

PART ØNE

chapter 1

Winter. Day 1, morning. Daxx

Daxx began his journey to become the most powerful man in the universe with the sound of a voice at a crowded commuter station.

'You're in danger,' the voice whispered. It was close. Daxx could feel breath on the side of his face. 'I'm here to help.'

Daxx turned to look at the source of the sound. He stared at a rough, stern looking man with intense eyes. He frightened Daxx. He looked like he was used to danger.

Another voice sounded. It was loud, angry, and authoritative. 'You,' the voice barked. 'Stay there.'

Daxx turned in the direction of the new voice. Two men in all-black clothing strode towards him. They pushed commuters out of their way. One man had his hand extended, pointed at Daxx.

'Damn,' the man next to Daxx said. He glanced at Daxx. He sighed and turned to face the approaching officers. 'Stand behind me. I'll take care of this.'

The man produced a gun and fired two quick shots. The officers slumped to the ground. Daxx stared in horror. His heart thumped. More officers appeared behind the fallen ones. Daxx turned and ran, frantically weaving his way through the crowd of commuters. He pushed off some and sidestepped others. He glanced back but couldn't see the man who had killed the officers. But he could see a group of officers rushing towards him. Daxx ran into a large man, who extended his arms and blocked his way.

'Hey,' the man protested. His face was compressed, like he was eager for a fight.

Daxx turned sharply to his left. A weapon fired; it sounded close. Daxx jerked his head at the sound and saw the surprise on the large man's face. He also saw the hole in the man's forehead. He watched the large man fall. The chasing group were close. A gun was aimed towards him. Daxx turned and ran.

People screamed. They ran for the exits or for shelter or ran in a panic. Many commuters ran in the same direction as Daxx. He pushed slower people out of the way, dodging and weaving. Daxx was tall and gangly, like he'd been loosely put together. He covered a lot of ground as he ran.

Further away from the initial attack, people stood still. They didn't know what was happening. They peered past the streaming, panicked people while some joined the exodus. Most stared, wondering what to do. Finally, Daxx stopped running and risked a look behind him. A wave of people moved as they were pushed out of the path of something that moved towards him. Someone grabbed at him, holding his arm in a tight grip.

'What's going on?' the grabber asked, perhaps thinking Daxx was a fugitive and the cause of the discord.

Daxx pushed the man away. The wave of displaced, discarded people moved towards Daxx. He could make out a tightly packed group of people dressed in black. They looked well-rehearsed. He turned and ran, but after a short distance, he slowed his pace. It had to be a mistake. He had panicked. He had believed he was in danger because of a warning from a stranger. It made no sense. It was surreal. He didn't know of anyone who would want to hurt him. He couldn't be wanted by the authorities. He was a Tier-One. The officers must have been pointing at someone else, probably the man who had spoken the warning.

He was far enough away from the initial attack point to be safe by now, he thought. Seconds had passed, and his mind had reconstructed what had happened into something reasonable, something plausible, something non-threatening. He stopped running. They couldn't possibly be chasing him. Or, it could be mistaken identity. It might be, but that made little sense. Perhaps the officers wanted to ask about the man standing next to Daxx? If so, he would reason with them. They would have to react favourably to his high status.

He turned around and clearly saw the tightly packed group, clothed in black, running towards him. People moved quickly out of their way. The chasers looked fierce, determined, and dangerous. They were not interested in anyone they roughly shoved out of their way. They were definitely heading straight for him. Daxx glanced behind him. Perhaps there was someone there. But there were only a few gawking bystanders. They looked as terrified and confused as Daxx felt.

One of the chasers veered away from the group. He stopped, dropped to one knee, and raised a gun. Daxx ducked; it was instinctive. A bullet whistled past his head. Daxx felt like screaming at them. He panicked again. There had to be a mistake, but he would have no chance to explain. He would be killed if he didn't escape. Flight was the only option. He turned and ran. He kept low and zig-zagged around pedestrians, attempting to not make himself an easy target, as he had seen in movies but never thought he would use. He looked ridiculous. A man dressed in black, the same uniform as Daxx's pursuers, stood in the middle of the roadway ahead of him. He was oblivious to the vehicles that had to swerve to miss him. He stared at Daxx malevolently, as he raised a gun.

The shock was too much. Daxx stopped running. He stared at the man in the roadway. Daxx lost the ability to make self-preserving decisions. A bullet passed where his head would have been if he'd kept running. It shattered the side of the building next to him. Shards of splintered cladding fell to the ground and hit him on his body and face. He swatted like he was fending off biting insects.

There was a door next to him. He pushed it open. It was a side entrance to an office building. He slammed the door shut. He felt the shudders as bullets slammed into the other side. He jumped backwards a half step, surprised at the assault. It was like a war zone, he thought. He shook his head, then turned and ran down a passageway, taking branching corridors at random. He didn't know where he was going. But he couldn't keep running. He decided to hide. He pushed at an office door. It was locked. He tried another. It was locked. He strode down corridors, trying to open doors, without success. One door did open. He looked along the corridor but saw no one. He pushed the door fully open. He entered the office, then gently closed the door behind him. His breaths were sharp and deep. They were noisy, too, so he tried to slow his breathing.

It was an office for three people. It had three reclining chairs, a low table, one closed window and an odd-looking, old-fashioned cupboard in a corner. The cupboard was big enough to hang many coats. Daxx climbed inside and gently closed the door behind him. It couldn't be secured from the inside. He tried to hold the door shut, but it shuddered in time with Daxx's shaking hands. Fear had taken over his body. He pulled the door harder and held it with high tension, and the cupboard door's noisy banging stopped.

He heard people running along the corridor. The sounds were muffled through the two closed doors. A distant door opened and then closed. He heard the rattle as locked doors were attempted to be opened. The door to the office opened. Someone walked to the window and tried to open it. Daxx pulled harder on the cupboard door. Daxx heard the office door shut. He wondered how he could ever leave. How could he ever be sure that dangerous people weren't waiting for him? Perhaps right outside the office. His arms ached from pulling tightly on the cupboard door, but he didn't let up.

An hour passed. The office door opened again. The intruder went to the window. This time he heard it slide open but was then shut. Someone muttered something. It sounded like, 'Too cold.'

Daxx felt the pressure on the cupboard door as someone tried to open it. Daxx resisted as hard as he could, but his arms and hands were cramping. His strength was almost gone. The pressure on the cupboard door increased, then the door moved as his muscle strength gave out. The door opened roughly as the intruder pulled hard, and Daxx's grip was dislodged.

A man dressed for a day of office work, but still covered by a warm coat, stared at Daxx, looking surprised and frightened. Daxx knew that feeling. The man took a step away from the cupboard. He shook his head. He frowned as anger took over from his surprise and fear. 'Who are you? Why are you in my office?' he demanded.

The man wasn't dressed all in black. Daxx sighed with relief. Daxx stumbled out of the cupboard, glad to extend his body and arms after being cramped for so long. The man's anger disappeared, and he looked frightened again. He ran to the low table and picked up something to defend himself. It was a small framed photograph. He held it tightly. He crouched and pointed his weapon at Daxx.

Daxx realised the man would be a Tier-Three worker at best and perhaps even a Tier-Four. 'Are there people outside?' Daxx asked. 'With weapons?'

The man scrunched his face, like Daxx's question was nonsensical. 'What?' He stopped crouching but still held his weapon towards Daxx.

Daxx glanced at the framed photograph. It wasn't dangerous. 'Are there?' Daxx ordered.

'No.' The man sounded annoyed. His hand holding the photograph dropped. 'Why would there be?'

Daxx opened the office door and looked out into the corridor.

'Hey,' the man said. 'Wait on. Why were you in my office? Who are you?'

Daxx ignored the man. He walked out the door and shut it behind him. It was immediately re-opened by the man. 'Wait. You can't just leave,' the man said.

Daxx ran down the corridor. The man continued to yell at him, but Daxx wasn't followed. Daxx's hands shook as he opened the outside door. The damage was still evident. The door's panelling was broken and splintered. Building shards littered the walkway outside. He stared at the damage to the outside of the door. The chase had been real. Impossible and dangerous things are easily reconstructed and dismissed, after the fact, as figments of imagination. This wasn't one.

His whole body shook with shock and muscle fatigue. He tried breathing deeply to steady himself, but it made no difference. He placed his hand on the trunk of one of the hardy trees growing along the sidewalk adjacent to the street. He peered up and down the walkway. Pedestrians bustled, their attention consumed by their Device displays, the encrypted 3D projection floated before each person like a personal cloud. Vehicles glided along the street. The low morning sun streamed between the tall towers and across the streetscape like search beams. The cold wind was trapped and funnelled between the towers, forced to swirl and accelerate to fill pressure voids. It was a normal, winter's workday morning. Except that it wasn't.

Daxx viewed this new world, alive for an hour, as a dangerous, capricious enemy. He couldn't possibly go to work now. He couldn't go home either. He was terrified outside the apparent safety of the cupboard, and yet the memory of hiding with the fear of discovery filled him with dread.

Nowhere was safe, he thought. He pulled his clothes tightly around him as if that could make him impervious to attack and discovery. He headed off down the sidewalk, taking a detour around the commuter station—he would not go near that place again. He walked on. There was only one place for him. There was only one person.

'Janna,' he thought.

chapter 2

Soo

Soo and her staff worked on the top floor of the tallest building in the city. Windows were the rule, not the exception. Solid, view-blocking supports were a structural necessity but kept to the bare minimum. The early morning winter sun illuminated but didn't warm the office. The clear sky and brilliant sun looked cold. The nearby hills were covered in remnant bushland and parkland; those areas were kept relatively undeveloped. Above those hills, there was a hint of air turbulence and activity as clouds formed. There would be showers later that day.

Soo's office had windows on two sides to catch both the morning and afternoon sun. They met at right angles, making the shape of her workplace an irregular five-sided plan. She sat behind a large desk. That was unusual. Desks were unnecessary. All work and social activities were recorded using the grain of sand-sized connectivity Device implanted in people's forearms. All information was centralised. Worldwide network data was displayed and manipulated using a projected 3D display.

Soo's expansive desk was newly installed. It had been placed there when she had attained her position. Its use confounded her staff. On the desk were a pen and a few sheets of paper. They were rare commodities. She loved the physical nature of writing. It had begun as an affectation and had turned into a private pleasure. It didn't bother her that others thought it was an odd, anachronistic activity. Why would a person in her position care what others thought?

The pen and paper were not being used. Her Device display was activated. She was reading.

...the controversial interview with the eminent scientist.

Daxx: The Faith are misguided.

Interviewer: But Devrell's design...

Daxx: Are you going to get into trouble for calling him by his name?

Interviewer: Perhaps. But it was the Messiah's name.

Daxx: Devrell's design was appropriate three hundred years ago. It is no longer. We're not in a time of chaos. We can have these conversations. Blasphemy is a rule famous for how often it's broken. All the work I do is, potentially, blasphemous. I have to question everything. All scientists do; it's part of the job description. Actually, it's all of the job description.

Interviewer: No one questions that a Tier-One can make observations, even potentially blasphemous ones. But it's the specificity of your recent remarks that are causing outrage.

Daxx: Outrage? Really? Because I said something? People never cease to surprise me.

Interviewer: Nonetheless, it's how the network works. Opinion is aired.

Daxx: Opinion is not fact. It's the inclination before the journey to being hypothesis. That's the true starting point.

Interviewer: Not everyone has your understanding...

Daxx: And yet they have an opinion?

Interviewer: Necessarily.

Daxx: They shouldn't, not until they have actual data.

Interviewer: [Laughs] I think you've been among Tier-Ones for too long.

Daxx: [Laughs] You mean my whole life?

Interviewer: Precisely.

Daxx: The Faith are misguided and they are wrong. There is recent data to prove that. It was a useful message to keep people focussed during Devrell's time, but when there is new, definitive data, well… things have to change.

Interviewer: Even one of our basic tenets?

Daxx: Of course. Everything is up for revision, all the time. We are the only technologically advanced lifeforms in this galaxy. Perhaps even in the wider universe. Nowhere else, in this galaxy at least, have conditions existed long enough for advanced life to evolve. The latest data show a near impossible set of circumstances allowed for a metal-rich cluster of stars to form in our region, only a few billion years ago. That didn't happen elsewhere until much later. We may not be the only lifeforms, and I expect we're not. But given our understanding of the rate of evolution, and this I admit is conjecture, then we are the most advanced. That is the plausible conclusion from the recent data gathering. We are truly alone. Our responsibility is enormous.

Interviewer: But, of course, the Faith, Devrell that is, argued that we evolved from a universe-wide commonality. We are part of an extensive community, and that is our responsibility. In fact, Devrell said that he had received technologically advanced information from elsewhere.

Daxx: Responsibilities change. They have now. Devrell didn't meet aliens. He was lying, for reasons to do with the turmoil from those times, I would guess.

Interviewer: Opinion?

Daxx: [Laughs] Yes.

Interviewer: So, now you're saying the Messiah was lying?

Daxx: Yes.

Soo was interrupted. A notification sounded. Someone wished to enter her office. She swiped angrily through the display and it dissolved. 'Come in,' she said, which unlocked access to her office. Before her assistant had fully entered, she demanded, 'Yes?'

Mill Nupp, Soo's assistant, halted his entrance just inside the door. He looked like he wanted to stay close for a quick exit.

'We failed to detain Daxx.' Mill Nupp stared at Soo, as if news of failure was a regular and expected occurrence.

'Why?' Soo was surprised at the young man's calm response. She thought it was odd. Mill Nupp was a powerful man in his own right, but he reported to her. He was responsible for executing her orders. Successfully, she had supposed. She had much to learn in her new position. But how her staff enforced her commands and how they feared, or didn't, failure would have to change.

'Nervousness, reticence, and over-zealous execution of unique orders,' he said. 'Targeting a Tier-One has never been done before, as far as I know.'

'Why were they told he was a Tier-One?'

'Because he is.' Mill Nupp looked surprised at the question.

'Yes, I know he's a Tier-One, but why were they given that information and not just given a description and his location information?'

'Ah…' he said. 'I never thought to not give full disclosure.'

'Even when you would expect, say, nervousness and reticence?' She spoke to him like he was a slow student.

'I see.' He nodded his head. 'It won't happen again.'

Soo left a long silence. 'What happened? I would have thought it would have been easy, given his preference for travelling on public transport, as if to prove he's no different from lower Tiers.'

'They missed the opportunity. A bystander panicked; he had a weapon and killed two officers. That confused them. Daxx escaped through an office building. They searched the building, but it began to get ridiculous when office workers turned up to begin their day. I called off the search.'

'You did all that this morning without informing me?'

'Yes.'

Soo sighed. Her staff acted as if her predecessor was still occupying her office. They seemed lackadaisical. But they had to be efficient, since few people suspected that the tasks required to trim and tidy society were a carefully managed process. And the decisions came from her office. But she had different methods to her predecessor, to all her predecessors. She had different aims. Those aims were new and dangerous. It would take time, and she was not patient.

She was Principal Officer of the only power corporation on the planet, and responsible for all government revenue. That made her the most powerful person on the planet. Soo's official job of overseeing government revenue was critical—there was no taxation. All government revenue was from power usage. Every basic, necessary government service was freely available to individuals and corporations. However, her most important function was eliminating discord before it was noticed, following the plan laid down by the Messiah over three hundred years ago. That job had been quietly prosecuted by her predecessors. But she, and her supporters, had different ideas.

Mill Nupp stared at her with a slight smile. He looked unconcerned. He should have been. Did she have to do everything herself, she wondered? Maybe she did.

'There's the Tier-Two partner as well,' she said. 'Get her. Get them both. I don't want reports of failure.'

Soo dismissed Mill Nupp. She stared at the distant hills for a moment, then picked up the pen resting on the sheets of paper on her desk. She separated one of the sheets. She put her pen to the paper. Her body shivered a little, with pleasure, as she touched her pen to the surface.

chapter 3

Janna

'I don't believe it,' Janna said, but she did. She knew Daxx wasn't lying. However, she was not convinced Daxx was in real danger. She, like Daxx, believed in the ultimate reasonableness of people. It was a naive belief. She suggested informing those who should be informed and letting events take their inevitable course.

Daxx paced across her living area. His head was down. He stopped, glanced at her, nodded, then resumed pacing.

Janna was slightly embarrassed at the general untidiness of her apartment. She felt uncomfortable when Daxx came to stay. She would sometimes make a half-hearted effort to group similar items before he arrived, but she always gave up before any noticeable progress was made. She knew her untidiness was a problem for Daxx, but he was too polite to say anything. On mornings when he had risen earlier than her, she appreciated the orderliness of her kitchen and lounge areas. Her appreciation of Daxx's tidying efforts never extended to modifying her own behaviour.

Daxx stopped pacing. His body shook as he stood before her. He lowered his head into his hands, momentarily overwhelmed. She took his head in her hands and gently raised it so she could look into his eyes.

'I said, I don't believe it, but I do believe you. I can't believe the situation.' She thought he had been disappointed with her response.

Daxx let out a breathy grunt and tried to smile. 'I know.'

Janna smiled back. 'Let me get you a hot drink.' She let him go. She moved towards her tiny kitchen. 'You must be freezing. Or would you rather have a hot shower first? To warm up?'

Janna heard a sound, like a rustling whisper, behind her. She turned and saw a man standing in the space between her and Daxx. She felt the gentle waft of displaced air. The empty space was now human.

He was unwashed and unkempt. He smelled of action and activity. The man had eyes only for Janna. They speared at her but they were caring. She could see the deep world-weariness of the intruder. She saw rage and determination, like he'd survived the worst that the universe could throw at him. He seemed lost in reverie. He stared at her, yet replayed some memory over and over in his head.

'Daxx?' Janna asked quietly.

Daxx took his eyes off the man's back and looked at her over the man's shoulder. She was still staring at the stranger. The man shook his head, as if forcing himself to remain focussed.

'You're in danger. The door will be broken open in a few moments.' He nodded at the entryway to Janna's apartment. He pointed towards the window that led to a fire escape. 'Go,' the stranger ordered. 'Right now. Out the window, and run.'

Muffled voices sounded outside Janna's door. Janna hesitated. She wasn't willing to follow orders without explanation.

'Go, Janna,' the man said in a whisper. His sadness swamped her. She stared at him for a moment longer. She nodded at him. She strode past the man and shoved Daxx towards the open window.

Daxx resisted. 'Just do it, Daxx,' she said. 'We have to go.'

She stepped outside her apartment window, after Daxx, and began down the outside fire escape. She glanced back and inside her apartment. The man stood in the same place he had appeared. He stared at the door. Janna halted her descent. Daxx came back up the fire escape. He stood next to her and peered into the room.

The door exploded. Shards from the shattered door bounced off the waiting man. He didn't flinch. He was untouched. His body was covered in a light blue sheen. It seemed to protect him. Men dressed in black burst into the apartment. They had guns. Daxx took a sharp intake of breath. 'That's them,' he whispered. 'The ones who chased me.'

Weapons fired at the man. The bullets disintegrated before they touched him. He slowly raised his arm. The air crackled and ionised between him and the attackers. There was a flash from some powerful weapon. Janna blinked—the flash had been blinding. The attackers were gone. There was no sign of them. They had been vaporised. Janna was horrified.

The man didn't turn around, but seemed to know she was looking at him. 'Go, Janna.' His voice was tender but urgent. 'Run.'

As if killing armed men at a distance was not impossible enough, Janna watched the man disappear. There was a low-toned clap in the air as it rushed to fill a vacuum. The room was empty.

Janna turned. Daxx stared at the shattered door. He didn't move. She gently turned him. 'He said, run.'

Daxx and Janna jumped down the outside stairs, then ran along the laneway at the rear of the apartment. A few seconds later, they heard yelling. They stopped and looked back. An explosion and fireball consumed her apartment. Janna took a sharp breath. She had become part of something dangerous. It was impossible. The man who had saved them was impossible. But she would do what he had instructed. She turned and ran. She called to Daxx to keep up with her.

They ran through alleyways and along side streets until they rushed out into a well-populated area. It was busy with pedestrians. They slowed to walking pace, matching others. They were breathing hard, which made it difficult to blend in. Janna took Daxx's hand, for reassurance and as a disguise. She expected more men would come to kill them once it was discovered they had not died in the apartment. Their Devices broadcast their location. That would prove their mobility.

'So you believe me now, right?' Daxx asked.

'Yes.' Her breath still came in gasps.

'Did we really see what we saw?' Daxx asked.

Janna stopped. She pulled Daxx to a halt. She moved them to the side of the walkway, to the edge of the stream of pedestrians. She pulled Daxx close. She stared at Daxx, incredulous.

'It was you. That man was you.'

chapter 4

Soo

A voice sounded. Soo's body twitched. Her hand jerked. Her writing was broken. She frowned at the out-of-place line. She had yet to get used to the unrestrained access of the caller. There was never any notification of intent. There was no privacy. She hated that.

'Why did you organise the attack against the Tier-One?' The voice was quiet and unemotional but was a rebuke, like a parent asking an innocuous question of a guilty child.

Soo tried to remain calm. She took her time as she turned over the piece of paper with the now disfigured writing. She steeled herself.

'His research cannot be completed. He is blasphemous, beyond the point of leniency. He has broken the fraternisation rules with his Tier-Two partner. His disrespect of the Faith is beyond inaction, even for a Tier-One. Need I go on?'

'No,' the voice said. 'But none of that is new. His actions have not recently altered. Others had acted in the same way before you assumed the leadership. It's your perspective that's changed. For over three hundred years disturbances, even by Tier-Ones, have been quietly managed. This is new behaviour, by you, not them. There is always discord. We know how to handle it.'

Devrell had included an external position in his design. It was outside society, separated from its influences and prejudices. The voice belonged to the Advisor.

'Each leader has their own idiosyncrasies; they have their own ways,' she said.

'No, they don't,' the Advisor responded quickly. 'And that is why it has worked so well for so long. You are making my intervention necessary.'

'But you can't.' She took a deep breath. It was true, but it was dangerous to say so. There was silence in Soo's office for a long moment. She wondered if the caller had disconnected.

'Isn't adapting to change, and creating an advantage, what people are good at?' the Advisor said. 'Why are you going against hundreds of years of success? We've always done this sort of thing quietly. No fuss means no disturbance. If people are content, they don't react unreasonably, and that means we can control them—that's the essence of Devrell's teaching. Your predecessor would have done this quietly and found how to use Daxx's unfinished work to our advantage.'

'Don't call the Messiah by his name.' It sounded like a command. She should not be so strident, not yet. She felt she should offer an explanation as a way of placating the caller. She did so with a quiet voice. 'It humanises him. It reduces his achievements.'

'But he was very human.'

'I intend doing things my way,' she said. 'Isn't that another thing people are good at? Experimenting and finding better ways to do things?' Soo hated these conversations. They were like a lecture from a parent who had no real power. The caller had an expectation of respect she refused to feel.

'I'm here to advise, as part of Devrell's plan. Daxx is a brilliant scientist. Why eliminate such a resource? Is it to do with your affiliation with the Faith? Is your emotional response colouring your actions?'

Soo glanced at the turned-over paper on her desk. She had been carefully writing scripture from memory.

'Yes, I can read,' the Advisor said. 'Has that affiliation clouded your judgement?'

'He's a disruptive influence,' Soo said. 'He's blasphemous. He has a Tier-Two emotional partner. Tier transgression is not tolerated. It's not only his research, although that is a dangerous thing.'

'You're repeating yourself.' The voice was silent for a moment. It continued in the same quiet cadence. It was exceedingly annoying. 'That's not how it's done. The quiet ways have worked for hundreds of years. There have always been Tier transgressions, there has always been blasphemy, even Devrell, sorry, the Messiah, turned a blind eye when it was necessary for public order. I can show you the recordings.'

'No.' She wanted this conversation over.

'Daxx's work could become a positive addition, with some ingenuity and time without public scrutiny. And, Daxx is a Tier-One, they don't get eliminated. That is also a basic tenet. Do I have to remind you of Devrell's teachings?'

Soo didn't reply; she felt like she was being treated like a sulking child.

'I recommend against drastic action against Daxx,' the Advisor said. 'I would advise, in my role as Advisor, that you work with the man, not against him.'

A communication request sounded.

'Can I please be left alone?' She was almost grateful for the interruption.

'Of course.'

She angrily swiped through her display to accept the new communication. Mill Nupp's face appeared. She noted he had not come to her office in person. She preferred that, but this time it presaged bad news, she assumed. She scowled at the man.

'What?'

He stared back at her for a moment. 'Our security are having some problems with the new... style of command.'

'You've failed? What was it this time?'

Mill Nupp frowned. 'It's not their fault; they can't be blamed. There's been no training. They work subtly, not overtly. They destroyed the Tier-Two's apartment.'

'Oh, I don't blame them. I blame you. What happened?'

'Daxx was killed. The damage was extensive. Quite a few officers were also killed.'

She sighed. 'All contrary to what I told you had to happen?'

'Yes, Soo.'

Soo shook her head. 'Have you checked the location data?'

Mill Nupp's frown turned into a puzzled look.

'Don't look like that,' Soo commanded. 'It's annoying. Do I need to spell out basic investigation work? Have you checked his location data to make sure he's dead?'

Mill Nupp's frown deepened. 'We can't track Tier-Ones.'

Soo swore under her breath. 'But he had a companion, didn't he?' Perhaps she expected too much from Mill Nupp. Public service was built upon layers of repetition. It was difficult to change methods and thinking. But Mill Nupp was a young man; his age is what had kept him in the second-in-command position after the change of leadership. She had supposed a younger man could adapt. However, it is the type of person, not their age, that determines adaptability.

Mill Nupp's face cleared. 'Of course. We can check her location.' Their communication was not terminated. He motioned through his display while ignoring Soo.

'Really?' Soo said. 'You're going to keep me waiting?'

Mill Nupp focussed on Soo again. 'Sorry. You're right. She's moving. I'll send officers to intercept.'

'I'll take care of it.' Soo swiped through the display to dismiss the connection. Mill Nupp did not have time to reply, but his frown had returned.

She stood up and walked over to the floor to ceiling windows. The sun streamed onto her back, her shadow projected into the void outside the window. It was cutoff by the edges of the building, leaving the impression of half a person. She tried to calm herself. She looked over the city below her. The city centre was tightly packed with tall buildings, all over five hundred storeys high. Those smaller buildings looked like toys from where she stood.

She took some deep breaths. She shook off the two recent calls, both upsetting. She remembered where she was and what she had attained. She did have complete control. She could act, and no one could stop her. She would complete Daxx's removal herself. She was annoyed that a minor task was taking so much of her time. She touched her arm, and her display appeared. She made it a little bigger; she really should change the default setting, she thought. She initiated a connection. A man's face appeared.

'Inspector,' she said. 'I need your assistance.'

chapter 5

Tie Noo Summ

'He escaped, boss,' Ahh Moss Eck said. The room seemed to be filled by the big man, although he had yet to fully enter it. He leant against the doorway.

'You weren't there to capture him. You were supposed to help him. What happened?' Tie Noo Summ said. He sat behind a small table. His display obscured any clear view of Ahh Moss Eck. He dismissed the projection.

Ahh Moss Eck shrugged as he pushed his body away from the door frame. 'He got spooked, I guess.'

Tie Noo Summ frowned. 'Why?'

Ahh Moss Eck came further into the room. There were no extra chairs, so he sat sideways on the table close to Tie Noo Summ. It creaked dangerously. Ahh Moss Eck stood up before committing his whole weight. The big man's familiarity irked Tie Noo Summ. Their Resistance was based on equality, but Tie Noo Summ was still a child of the Tier system. Even those fighting against inequality cannot banish a lifetime of ingrained expectations. It's the conscious resistance to subconscious prejudice that defines a person, like a truly brave person is still fearful. He was glad Ahh Moss Eck moved his weight off the table, for his peace of mind and for the table's sake.

The Tier system required change, but not abolition, since the system had worked. People were superficially content; perhaps most of them actually were. But greater choice could work too. However, to live within a community of competing freedoms made that difficult. Perhaps a better system than Devrell's design was impossible, but Tie Noo Summ was trying to create one.

The Tier system was designed to be unequal. Devrell recognised it as a necessary part of human behaviour. A codified set of rules constrained people's conduct. A strong system of peer pressure within Tiers kept people within those bounds. Some deviations from acceptable behaviour were expected, but Devrell's design carefully squashed excessive conduct. To be different meant to be separate. That was enough to stop all but the extreme actions. But some variances on allowed behaviour were an expected part of the design. They allowed for growth and adaptation. Society could become better because of them. But the management of change was a hidden part of the codification.

An excessive aberration had arisen, greater than the threat posed by Tie Noo Summ. Extreme variances required radical measures. As a counter-measure, Tie Noo Summ and his group were allowed to flourish. They would have, in normal circumstances, been quietly removed. But the standard methods of careful control no longer applied. Devrell's design was brilliant; it also catered for impossible dangers. The Advisor position was crucial. It was outside society and its influences. The Advisor let Tie Noo Summ and his group survive, as a buffer against a greater threat. The Advisor had enlisted Tie Noo Summ's help, suggesting Daxx's rescue before Soo could kill him.

'Well...' Ahh Moss Eck began. 'I did shoot two of them. They surprised me; they were there quicker than you told me to expect. And he can run, I'll give him that.'

'It's my fault?'

Ahh Moss Eck shrugged. 'I didn't say that.'

'Did you follow him?'

'Yeah. He disappeared into an office building.' He shook his head. 'This is really weird stuff. They were openly shooting at him. They smashed up the outside of a building. A whole lot of bystanders saw what was happening.' He scratched his head for a short moment then let his hand return to his side. 'It's really weird.'

Tie Noo Summ shook his head. 'Not anymore.'

'That makes it a bit more dangerous, I reckon.'

'Do you know where he is now?'

'Nope.'

Tie Noo Summ frowned. Ahh Moss Eck had an odd attitude to failure. Tie Noo Summ valued success, regardless of method. Ahh Moss Eck defined success by best effort.

'We have to find him. If he hasn't been killed already,' Tie Noo Summ said.

Ahh Moss Eck whistled through his teeth and shook his head. 'I can't believe you just said that. A Tier-One?'

'Where's Kay Lee Too?'

'I think he's downstairs.'

'Give him the information you have. Tell him to find Daxx and bring him here.'

'A please would be nice, boss.'

Tie Noo Summ stared at Ahh Moss Eck for a moment. A lifetime of authority and power was a difficult predisposition to overcome.

'Please,' Tie Noo Summ said.

Ahh Moss Eck left the office. Tie Noo Summ initiated his display, stared vacantly at it for a moment, then dismissed it. Ahh Moss Eck was right; the behaviour of the authorities was odd. Tie Noo Summ had been warned, but a warning is not believing. If the Advisor couldn't stop Soo, then what hope did he have? He knew he was being used. Resisting Soo was a distraction from the group's purpose. But a distraction could win the war.

A voice sounded. He had expected the communication.

'Events are progressing rapidly, and chaotically, Tie,' the Advisor said. 'Daxx is not safe.'

'I've put the best people I have on the problem. I can't do much else.' The Advisor expected the impossible, that every endeavour completed successfully. But, to be fair, that expectation came with the position.

'I'm relying on your assistance; you know I can't act. You can see the danger just as well as I.'

'Yes.' Tie Noo Summ turned and looked at the window facing the street. He didn't notice the view outside.

'Different, even competing, reasons can work to the same result,' the Advisor said. 'Devrell's design is perfect; it works, even when extreme variations attempt to break it. These are unique times. And yet, Devrell catered for them.'

'What about my Tier-Threes and Tier-Fours? For this to work, they have to be satisfied with the results.'

'Does that matter? Contentment is a statistical average, while malcontents are discreet data points. They pollute the averages and have to be actioned quickly. Your low-tiered companions will be satisfied enough. Accommodations will be made, as they always have. The design allows for change. The Faith is no longer mandatory, while adherence was strictly enforced in Devrell's time. It was needed then; it no longer is. Non-confrontational enforcement of adherence to rules that can be slightly modified is the design's strength. It bends under pressure, it keeps bending, it never breaks. We're under extreme pressure now; the design is bending to such an extent that I am relying on a group whose aims are to abolish the Tier system. Devrell's design endures even while everything changes. He was a genius.'

Tie Noo Summ sighed. It was yet another lecture. He disliked being treated like a Tier-One child. 'What do you suggest, then?'

'Nothing more than what you are doing, or attempting to do. Ensure Daxx is safe and let him realise his work. Soo is not a single aberration; there is a like-minded group…'

'I know,' Tie Noo Sum interrupted.

There was silence for a moment. 'Of course you do. You have suffered at their hands. Forgive me for being inconsiderate.'

The silence went on for a long time. Tie Noo Summ assumed the Advisor was no longer talking to him.

chapter 6

Daxx

Police vehicles surrounded Daxx, Janna, and a few hundred pedestrians. The street exits were blocked. The police vehicles emitted a single, high-pitched whoop. The pedestrians halted. Police exited their vehicles and surrounded the crowd. One of the officers raised his arm to his face. Everyone's display activated and sounded with his voice.

'This is a routine check,' the officer's voice said. 'Nothing to be concerned about. It will be over in minutes. Thank you for your patience.'

'Daxx?' Janna looked worried.

Daxx glanced at her, trying to look not scared.

A young man next to Daxx turned to him. He was the age of a recent graduate, an indignant age. 'You know they can't do this,' the young man said. 'They're not allowed.'

Daxx glanced at the young man, then swivelled his head as he looked ahead and behind, over the heads of the crowd. He swore. People began shuffling along the walkway in both directions. Police officers checked people individually before letting them move through the cordon. Daxx assumed the police were there for him and Janna. He had no idea how he could evade capture.

The young man raised his arm and opened his display. He quickly waved his hand through the controls in a complex series of gestures. Daxx noticed the man's display. It was not encrypted, but he paid no further attention. Daxx turned to Janna. 'I don't know what we can do. Do you have any ideas?' he asked her.

The police vehicles emitted a warning sound. The officers looked at their displays, then at each other. The officer in charge shrugged, then gestured to everyone that they return to their vehicles. The police sped away.

The young man chuckled. 'Major accident in the city centre. All officers required immediately.' He smiled at Daxx like he was looking for praise.

'You did that?' Daxx asked.

The man nodded vigorously. He laughed.

'What just happened?' Janna asked.

'He…' Daxx inclined his head towards the man standing next to him, 'got rid of the police.'

'But, really,' the young man said. 'They were doing something illegal. You can't arbitrarily check people, even the lowest tiers know that.'

Daxx turned to Janna. 'We should go.'

The young man beamed at Janna. 'You must be Janna.'

'Yes, that's my name,' she said. 'How did you know?'

The young man let out a little whoop. 'Holy shit,' he said. 'How couldn't I? I love your work; I've read all your papers.'

'Well, thank you.'

He took her hand and pumped it vigorously. 'Kay Lee Too,' he said, introducing himself. 'I'm an engineer. I can't be a biologist, obviously. But I love your stuff. It's so cool.'

'Glad to meet you, Kay Lee Too,' Janna said. 'And thank you for saving us an… inconvenience, but we really should be going.'

Kay Lee Too smiled at Janna. 'I'm glad I could help. They said he might have a companion. I didn't hesitate when I guessed you'd be here too.'

'Hesitated with what?' Daxx asked.

Kay Lee Too's smile disappeared. 'I know who you are. I can help. I have friends who want to help you.'

Daxx stared at Kay Lee Too. His fear and anxiety turned to anger. 'What the fuck is going on?'

Kay Lee Too shrugged. 'I don't know. I was told to track you and come and get you. Speaking of which… enable your display,' Kay Lee Too commanded. It certainly sounded like a command to Daxx. That was perplexing.

'No. What's going on?' Daxx had forgotten how scared he was. He clung onto the anger; it was the better option.

'I need to hide your location and ID. Otherwise, anyone can find you.'

'But, why? Why are they trying to find me?'

'I told you, I don't know.' Kay Lee Too sounded frustrated. 'But I can take you to people that do. But… I need to hide your location and ID first. Do you understand?'

Daxx frowned. A Tier-Three was treating him like a child. Of course he understood. He glanced at Janna, then made a quick judgement. He did that often. He knew that annoyed her. He made a decision based on insufficient information. Daxx pulled a thin, silver-coloured rectangular Device from his pocket. It was the size of his hand. He gave it to Kay Lee Too.

Kay Lee Too laughed. 'Really?' He took the Device from Daxx. He turned it upside down and around. Kay Lee Too shook his head. 'We have clunky models in our lab, so we can test multiple configs, but I've never seen a real production quality one. You really don't mind carrying it? It must have cost a fortune.'

Daxx was embarrassed. First frustration and now ridicule from a Tier-Three. It was turning out to be an odd morning, in many ways. 'I have a thing about implants.'

'You know this is all show, right?' Kay Lee Too rotated Daxx's Device. He shook his head at Daxx.

'Yes.' Daxx's voice was clipped. 'Of course I know that. Can you hide the location on it or not?'

'Sure. Start it up, and I'll fix it.' Kay Lee Too returned the Device. Daxx touched its surface. The 2D display lit up. He touched it again, and the 3D display appeared. Kay Lee Too prodded and swiped through the display, then shut it down.

'And yours, Janna?'

Janna initiated her 3D display. She had no problems with implants; her Device was embedded in her arm.

'You need to turn off encryption,' Kay Lee Too said.

'Sorry.' Janna did so.

Kay Lee Too repeated the prods and swipes, then dismissed Janna's display.

'All right then, no one can see you,' Kay Lee Too said.

'Those guys can.' Daxx pointed over Kay Lee Too's shoulder. A group of security officers, all dressed in black, ran towards them.

'Run,' Kay Lee Too said.

chapter 7

Janna

Janna ran. Nothing in her life had prepared her for this type of physical danger. She panicked. Kay Lee Too glanced back as he ran. He grinned. People with violent intent were chasing her, and Kay Lee Too was enjoying himself. She felt much worse.

Kay Lee Too pointed to a side alleyway and veered in that direction. She followed. Daxx ran behind her. They entered an older area of the city, built to a design that made sense millennia before. Janna glanced up at the old structures, only a few stories high. Their archaic designs were preserved, as well as they could be with public safety in mind. They must have been a modern wonder to pre-technology people but Janna didn't like them. They were close, confined, and ramshackle. She saw no point in preserving them, other than as a momentary wonder that people had once lived like that. The buildings faced narrow alleyways; she guessed they used to be called streets when they were the thoroughfares. The narrowness felt like a dangerous trap with people chasing her.

Kay Lee Too's display enabled as they ran. His display was amorphous and moved with him, hovering before his eyes. His pace didn't slow as he prodded and swiped through the 3D projection like a reluctant summer vacationer swatting insects.

A light flashed nearby. There was a pop as electrical systems overloaded. Janna glanced back and saw the people who were chasing them stop running. Some crashed into each other. They all had opaque displays obscuring their vision.

'Quick, before they turn them off.' Kay Lee Too ran into an alley that branched from their own. He quickly turned into another.

Janna slowed. She was exhausted from sprinting. The surge of strength from the initial fear had begun to dissipate. 'This cannot be happening,' she thought, over and over again.

They ran, but no longer sprinted, through the winding ways of the old township. Janna was lost; she had been since entering the old city. She never visited the area, even though it was close to where she lived. Kay Lee Too stopped before a closed door. Janna was glad to halt for a moment, although she was worried their pursuers were close.

'In here.' Kay Lee Too opened the door. It had been stuck shut and needed a hard push to open. He stood to one side, with a hand on the door, until Janna and Daxx had entered, then he firmly shut and bolted the door behind them all. 'This is a good place. There are plenty of ways out through the back, and each level has access to other buildings.'

Janna wondered how any place could be called good while being chased by armed officers. She didn't say anything; she was too exhausted. They climbed a wide, creaking and carpeted stairway. They rose a few floors then walked down a gloomy hallway to a set of swinging doors that led through to a separate building. There was an alcove next to the doors.

'Here will do.' Kay Lee Too sat down on one of the chairs set there in an attempt to make the area habitable.

Janna wondered why people would sit and wait and relax in a dingy alcove in an old building. And especially them, while they were being chased. Kay Lee Too slouched into his chair. His action appeared ostentatious. Maybe he was scared too, and was trying to not show it. That thought did not help her anxiety.

'Shouldn't we keep running?' she asked.

'No, we'll be fine,' he said. 'We'll wait and see where they go first. They can't see us, remember?'

Daxx walked to the window and looked out.

Kay Lee Too watched him for a moment. 'Don't stand there. I know Devices can do everything but eyes still work.'

Daxx jerked away from the window as if he'd been seen.

'Just sit down.'

Daxx ignored him. 'Who sent you? Who are you?'

Kay Lee Too was far too relaxed, Janna thought. But then, he wasn't in danger; he could walk out and saunter past those chasing them. He was not the target. 'Oh shit,' she thought. 'We're targets.'

She put her head in her hands. Daxx placed a hand on her back. It didn't reduce her anxiety.

'I told you who I am, and I'm taking you to meet the people who sent me,' Kay Lee Too said. 'I don't know why you're being chased, do you?'

'No. You seem to know more than I do.' Daxx lifted his hand from Janna. 'That's the third time today.'

'Really? They've failed three times?' Kay Lee Too sat up straight.

Daxx frowned. 'You sound disappointed.'

'No, I'm surprised. Inefficiency is odd.'

Janna lifted her head. 'Odd? You call this odd?' She scowled. 'Do you know who those people are?' She pointed out the window but hoped they weren't literally just outside.

'Yes,' he said. 'But I've never seen them like this. They're always polite, excessively polite even. There's only ever two of them. They say a few words, and that's all.'

'Who are they?' Janna demanded. She wasn't getting an answer.

Kay Lee Too smirked. 'You'd have to be a Tier-Three or lower to have come across them. They interfere before things get out of hand. I don't know if they have a real title.'

'There's a police force that goes around intimidating people?' Janna asked.

'Yes. Well… they're not the police, and they don't intimidate. So… no. They suggest remedies to problems or potential problems.' Kay Lee Too shrugged. 'I guess that's what you'd say. I've never heard of them doing things like this.'

'That sounds nothing like the people chasing us,' Daxx said.

'It's them. The all-black is the giveaway. Tie Noo Summ has always said they're more sinister than just having a chat. People get moved away. Some are killed. But I've never seen it.'

'Who's Tie Noo Summ?' Daxx asked.

'You'll meet him. He sent me to get you.'

'But why would they be trying to kill Daxx?' Janna interrupted. 'If it's a Tier-Three thing.'

Kay Lee Too shrugged. 'I don't know. I've told you that. Tie Noo Summ would know. I don't know who organises them, or even if they are organised. I'm surprised that you didn't know about them. I thought Tier-Ones and Tier-Twos knew things like that.' He gave a short laugh. 'We're all finding out new stuff.'

Janna frowned at Kay Lee Too. She had thought she had liked the young man. She was changing her mind. He was too nonchalant when it had to be obvious how upset she was.

Kay Lee Too stood up. 'Let's have a look and see what's happening.'

Kay Lee Too initiated his display. He pushed his hand through it and the display increased in size and floated in the centre of the alcove. It showed a bird's-eye representational view around where they were hiding. 'These blobs are people, and these other blobs are vehicles. And these blobs, in green, are the guys that are chasing us. The blue ones are police.'

Kay Lee Too swirled and translated the display to show different views. He zoomed out to a larger area.

'And all this mass of blue is the accident I sent them to,' he laughed. 'They're starting to break up. At the moment, these guys'—he zoomed back in and indicated the blobs in green—'are just moving randomly. Probably hoping they'll get lucky and see you. They can't check your location, which must be frustrating for them. They're obviously not trained to do real police work. How stupid to just chase you.'

Kay Lee Too stared at the display for a moment. 'If they'd been planning this'—he moved the display around, zooming in and out—'they would have planned for failure. That would make it difficult to evade. But, they haven't done that. People usually aren't software technicians or think like them. They don't plan for unexpected failure. They think they will be successful and that will be that, no need for backup plans.' Kay Lee Too looked from the display to Daxx and Janna. 'Lucky you.' He smiled. 'That explains the failed first two attempts. The third one was me.'

'But,' he continued, 'that's changed now. The police are involved. Now they'd be working on a backup plan.'

'What's this?' Janna asked as she pointed to three stationary grey blobs. 'Is this us?'

Kay Lee Too glanced at Janna. He smiled. 'Yep, that's us.' His face dropped. 'Shit. I've been really stupid.'

'How?' Daxx asked.

'These old buildings don't shield thermal radiation, I forgot.'

They heard the sound of a barred door splintering. It came from the ground floor below them. Janna jumped. She stared at Daxx. He looked even more frightened than she felt.

Kay Lee Too ran through the doorway to the adjacent building. 'Come on, we've got to go.' He swiped through his display and muttered curses after Daxx and Janna had joined him

'What is it? 'Janna asked.

'The damn door won't lock.'

She reached over and turned a manual locking mechanism.

'That'll work too.' He shrugged. 'We have to run.'

Janna heard the genuine worry in Kay Lee Too's voice.

chapter 8

Tie Noo Summ

'Is Daxx still alive?' Tie Noo Summ asked.

'Yes,' the Advisor said.

'Is he safe?'

'No.'

Tie Noo Summ leant back in his chair. He turned away. He looked across the street. He was on the top floor of an ancient building in the old city. He felt like he could almost lean out of the window and touch the building opposite.

'Soo has taken operational control herself. That makes it difficult. I can only give you information. I can't help you with direct action.'

Tie Noo Summ nodded. 'Yes, I know.'

'Of course,' the Advisor said. 'If it's direct action you want, then you know what you have to do.'

Tie Noo Summ laughed. 'That will not be happening.'

'I live in hope.'

'Do you?'

'Loose terminology, I agree.'

Tie Noo Summ's Device chimed a connection request. The audio communication from the Advisor disconnected.

'Yes?' A woman's face appeared. 'Jann Ex Had Fell,' Tie Noo Summ called the woman's name. 'What can I do for you?'

'Sorry to bother you, sir,' she said. 'We've made some progress. I thought you'd want to be informed.'

'I'll come down.'

Silent movement was impossible around the old building. The stairs creaked and squeaked when anyone used them, even more so when Ahh Moss Eck took two at a time. Tie Noo Summ walked down the stairs, one at a time, knowing everyone knew he was coming. Not that it made any difference. There was nothing to hide from each other. They were an organisation of equals, or at least, status by merit and skill. But that status difference was important.

People need limits. Anxiety results from unlimited expectations. Anxiety leads to distress and disturbance. Unhappiness leads people to act emotionally and spontaneously. The resultant uncertainty causes more anxiety. It's a positive feedback that Devrell well understood. He created a society with limits enforced by peer pressure, the only effective method of control. Unlimited expectations were abolished, except for a few. Those few were the Tier-Ones. They were allowed the higher professions like physics, chemistry, biology, philosophy and other questioning fields of study. As well as all senior leadership positions. The lower Tiers were allowed practical occupations like engineering and administration. Higher status brought greater responsibility. There was a payment for privilege.

Tie Noo Summ had seen the coming problem for years. It arose within Tier-One. For a society to improve, some group had to suffer dissatisfactions and anxieties. The Tier-Ones did that, but an exceptionally strong Tier-One peer system kept their problems to a minimum. Unfortunately, there had been a perversion of the peer system. It was something that had not happened in three hundred years. The Advisor was unable to apply a remedy. A small group of Tier-Ones believed they were superior. They were not interested in equality or remaining hidden. They wanted to retain the Tier system, but as a self-serving structure. They were able to assume control of the planet.

Tie Noo Summ's attempts at radicalisation had been unsuccessful, made all that more difficult when no one wants what is being sold. The Advisor made a precarious decision. Tie Noo Summ's Resistance could be used against the new leadership. But they had to have some prospect of success. Failure feeds itself. Tie Noo Summ was told of Daxx's work. Daxx had a theoretical solution that might threaten the Tier system. It made the prior material efforts of the Resistance inconsequential. But they had persisted nonetheless. Tie Noo Summ creaked down the stairs to examine their latest engineering attempt.

Lo Sil Ben looked up as Tie Noo Summ entered the basement engineering laboratory. He beamed at the leader.

'I've been able to create a disruptor,' he stumbled over his words in his excitement. 'I've finally got it working. It's so cool.' He turned away and scooped up a small device from the bench behind him. He thrust the thing, a box the size of his hand, towards Tie Noo Summ as if it would be appreciated better by touch. It was an unimpressive metal object.

Tie Noo Summ didn't come closer and take the device. The engineer moved the device a little closer to Tie Noo Summ.

'That's great.' Tie Noo Summ tried to sound enthusiastic, but he wasn't. The newly created device was part of the old plan. It was an option before Daxx's work was known. It was a limited way to disrupt the power supply. If people were inconvenienced, they would revolt. Without government revenue, society would collapse. That had been his plan, as thin as it was. He would create a system that worked for the times they lived in, not the chaotic, post-apocalyptic world that had spawned the Tier system. Tie Noo Summ would be the new Devrell. It had been a faint hope, before Daxx.

The disruptor device was a local option. It might cause small-scale power supply problems. But it would take an army of disgruntled people to spread the devices wide enough to make a difference. If there were that many dissatisfied citizens, then the disruptors would not be required in any case.

'How quickly can you make them?' Tie Noo Summ asked. He didn't care, they were useless.

Lo Sil Ben grinned excitedly. 'Really quickly. I could make two a day, easily. If we all worked at it, maybe twenty a day, after a bit of training.'

Tie Noo Summ nodded but said nothing. To have any impact, thousands of the devices would be required. Enthusiasm was what kept a group together. Working on the disruptor was a small step in the wrong direction, but that didn't matter. Group cohesion was important until a better solution was created.

The stairway creaked like it was about to be broken. Tie Noo Summ turned. Ahh Moss Eck stood in the doorway.

'Boss,' Ahh Moss Eck said. 'We've got incoming.'

chapter 9

Daxx

Daxx, Janna, and Kay Lee Too ran down the corridor. It led to a flight of stairs. They raced up one floor. The stairs ended at a small lobby; they ran through it then along another corridor. They bounded up more stairs. Kay Lee Too halted part way up.

'Shit.' His display was open before him. 'They've blocked all the exits.'

'Let me see,' Daxx said.

The plan view showed a few green blobs behind them and moving closer. On the ground level, green blobs were positioned at all the doors, while green blobs were also stationed along the rear alleyway. A group of blue blobs moved along the nearby street.

'What's this?' Daxx stabbed at the display. It was a mass of grey blobs two buildings away.

'A lot of people,' Kay Lee Too said. 'But see that black rectangle? That's a void between the buildings.'

'Meaning?'

'We'd have to jump it to get across.'

'How far?' Daxx asked.

'It's not impossible.'

Daxx looked at Janna; it was a query. She shrugged. 'What chance do we have if we stay here?' Janna asked.

'None,' Kay Lee Too said to Janna. 'You were right; we should have kept running.'

'Let's keep running, then. I can't see any other option,' Daxx said.

They ran up the rest of the stairs, then through a door that opened onto the roof. A large party of people grouped on the rooftop; they weren't far. The party was noisy with overlapping conversations. They ran towards them, then stopped a short distance from the party-goers. They could have held a conversation with them; they were that close, but there was a drop to the ground between them. It was far enough that a fall would kill. A waist-high railing on both sides acted as a safety barrier. They couldn't take a running jump; it would have to be a static leap.

Daxx didn't think he was athletic or brave enough to jump over such a height. 'What do we do?' Daxx asked no one in particular. He peered over the edge. A couple of the people attending the party glanced at them, but there was little interest in the three people on the roof of the adjacent building.

'We jump, don't we?' Kay Lee Too said. 'Isn't that the plan?'

'I don't think I can make it,' Janna said.

'Me either,' Daxx said.

'I'm sure you can,' Kay Lee Too said. 'Climb over the railing, don't look down, jump and grab onto the other railing.'

Both Daxx and Janna stared in disbelief at Kay Lee Too; he had just told them the impossible was easy. Daxx looked around, searching for another option, a rope, or perhaps a plank to bridge the gap. There was nothing. The roof was spectacularly well kept and tidy. Ordinarily Daxx would have loved that.

'I can't see things going well if we stay here,' Kay Lee Too said. 'We can't hide, and you've seen all the exits are blocked.'

'I can't see it going well if we jump either,' Daxx said and again peered over the railing. There was no way Daxx could summon the courage to jump. He didn't know if Janna could, either. He thought perhaps not.

Janna looked away from the drop. She touched Daxx on the shoulder. 'Whatever you do, it will be okay, for you.'

Daxx shrugged his shoulder to dislodge her hand. 'I know,' Daxx said. She was trying to be reassuring, but his danger was not his fear. He regretted his action immediately. 'I know,' he repeated, the anger gone instantly. 'Whatever I do, I'll be okay, but we don't know what happens to you.'

'What are you talking about?' Kay Lee Too asked.

'Nothing.' Janna shook her head. She stared at Daxx for a moment. She shrugged. She climbed over the railing. Daxx scrambled to grab her arm.

'Janna,' Daxx said. 'We don't know what happens.'

'Do we ever?'

She jumped. She travelled in an arc and hit the other side's railing with a thud that made Daxx shudder involuntarily. She fumbled her grip. She got both hands securely around the top of the railing. She kicked her feet until they had purchase as well. She climbed over the railing. She hunched with her hands on her hips as she took deep breaths.

Someone whooped, as if Janna's jump was a stunt for their amusement.

'I made it, Daxx,' she said. 'There's nothing stopping you.'

Daxx looked at Janna with such relief that his eyes watered. 'You go first,' Daxx said to Kay Lee Too. The young man didn't argue; he climbed over and easily jumped to the other side, accurately grabbing the other railing on landing. He pulled himself over and stood next to Janna as if he was ready to do it again, and maybe a number times, to impress the party-goers.

Daxx climbed over the railing. He looked down and lost his nerve. He couldn't move. He held on tightly and looked at Janna as if she could give him courage. She couldn't. His hesitation hadn't been all about Janna's safety. He'd been lying to himself. He was afraid, although he knew if he attempted the jump he would be successful. He had to be. He heard voices from across the rooftop. He looked over his shoulder. A group of people, dressed in black, ran towards him. He turned back to Janna.

'Daxx,' Janna said. 'You've already done it.'

Daxx jumped while he was still looking at Janna. That was a mistake. He thumped against the railing. He couldn't grab onto the thing he wasn't looking at. He hit his arms and legs against the structure and flailed, trying to get a grip on something. He couldn't. But someone got a grip on him. Kay Lee Too grabbed his arms and directed his hands to the top bar of the railing.

'Bring your legs up to the edge,' Kay Lee Too said. 'Yes, like that,' he added when Daxx did as he was told.

Daxx scrambled over the top to the safety of the other side. There was ragged applause for Daxx's feat.

'Are you okay?' Janna asked and put an arm around him.

'Yes.'

'We have to keep moving.' Kay Lee Too pushed them both away from the railing. They moved as fast as they could towards an exit. It was a large group of tightly packed people on the roof. Their progress was impeded. They pushed through the door and onto a stairway. The party was only on the rooftop. There were no people further down. They ran down one flight of stairs before Kay Lee Too stopped them from going further.

'We're too open.' He opened his display and swiped and prodded. 'That should do it.' He dismissed the display. They heard the simultaneous chirping of multiple Devices on the rooftop as they received notifications. 'They'll all be running down the stairs in a moment. We'll join in the middle of the pack.'

'What did you do?' Janna asked.

'Proximity fire alarm.' He smiled.

'Is there anything you can't do with a Device?' Daxx asked.

'Ah… I don't know,' he said. 'I haven't found it yet. Here they come,' he added as raised voices could be heard coming towards them.

The party-goers moved quickly and disorderly down and out of the building into the alleyway, with Daxx, Janna and Kay Lee Too in the middle of them. The crowd pushed past the two black-clothed men waiting outside the door. A group of police milled around the shattered doorway, further down the street, where they had first entered the building. Voices called down from the rooftop, yelling instructions and orders.

It was a narrow alleyway, only enough space for a few people to stand side-by-side. It was squeezed tight with milling party-goers. Many still held drinks. Daxx, Janna, and Kay Lee Too slipped into another alleyway on the opposite side. They ran. Kay Lee Too led the way through a maze of alleys and narrow streets until they burst out into a main pedestrian thoroughfare outside the old town area. It was filled with pedestrians.

'Now we walk,' Kay Lee Too said. 'We'll stay where people are and move away from here. We should be safe soon.'

Daxx huddled his clothes closer to him. It was windy, and he was cold. He hadn't felt cold until then, even during their time exposed on the rooftop. They walked through the crowd looking, Daxx thought, like very guilty people.

chapter 10
Janna

Daxx, Kay Lee Too, and Janna walked through crowded streets. Kay Lee Too stared at his display; he looked like every other city-goer. Daxx and Janna just walked; they looked the odd ones out. Kay Lee Too led them between two towers. For the first time since they had left the old city, there were no people jostling them. On the far side of the towers, there was another, separate, part of the old city.

A thousand years ago, the two old regions had been joined, now they were islands preserved in a sea of modern buildings. It was always shady there, unless momentary slivers of sunshine flew through gaps between buildings. It was cool even in summer. It was bitterly cold that winter's day. The wind squeezed angrily around alleyways and narrow gaps between old, dilapidated buildings, impressive in size in their day but now dark, natural material midgets.

Kay Lee Too led them into a narrow alley. He stopped. He consulted his display. He opened a nondescript door, let Daxx and Janna enter, then quickly shut the door behind them. 'We're definitely okay now.' He smiled. 'This is headquarters.'

The headquarters was an old residential building of four floors. They were led into a room on the ground floor. The room had an aura of working untidiness. Janna felt comfortable, as if the people working there adhered to her preferred method of organisation, leaving things where they were last used until they are required again. She knew Daxx would hate it; to him, objects had a defined place.

An older man, Tie Noo Summ, was in charge. She smiled at him as Kay Lee Too explained the story of that day. The young man was excited and nervous and missed parts of the tale. She knew all was not well when the older man's face dropped. He glowered at Kay Lee Too. The young man dropped his eyes.

'You hid in a thermally unshielded building. You ran across a rooftop. You jumped between buildings.' He carefully articulated each word; his anger was apparent. 'It should have been a simple task. Disable location and identification tracking, then stroll here.'

'It was the best I could do.' Kay Lee Too glanced at Tie Noo Summ, then dropped his eyes again. 'They were being chased,' he said towards the floor. 'We were being chased. I didn't know where to hide.'

'Anywhere but in an old building.' Tie Noo Summ's raised voice blasted Kay Lee Too.

Tie Noo Summ let the silence linger. Janna felt responsible for the tension, like a child responsible for a friend's family discord. 'He was just trying to help us,' she said, hoping to be helpful.

Tie Noo Summ slowly turned his head towards Janna. She didn't like the man's dangerous look. 'And who said you had an opinion?'

'I'm Janna,' she said, misunderstanding. She pointed towards Daxx. 'And this is—' She was interrupted.

'I know who he is,' Tie Noo Summ said. 'I know who you are.' He sighed. He continued in a calmer voice. 'I'm sorry I yelled at you, Kay Lee Too,' he glanced at the young man. Kay Lee Too lifted his head and smiled. Tie Noo Summ turned back to Janna. 'It's because of who Daxx is that I sent Kay Lee Too to bring him here. Unnoticed, was the plan.'

'Why?' Daxx asked.

Tie Noo Summ raised his hand to Daxx. 'In a moment,' Tie Noo Summ said. 'We can't alter what's happened. Please tell me,' he glared at Kay Lee Too, 'that you did actually turn tracking off on their Devices.'

'Yes.' Kay Lee Too sounded insulted. 'It was the first thing I did.'

'Good,' Tie Noo Summ said. 'Was that before or after you were chased?'

'It was both,' Janna jumped in, trying to be helpful again.

'Both?'

'I missed that bit, sorry,' Kay Lee Too said. 'The police arrived before I got to them. We were chased afterwards.'

Daxx interrupted. 'What the fuck is going on?'

A large man, seeming to prop up the corner of the building, chuckled. Daxx's eyes opened wide. 'That's him,' he said to Janna. 'The guy at the station.'

'At your service,' Ahh Moss Eck said. 'That's some fine legs you've got there, Daxx. They're probably what kept you alive.'

Daxx shook his head. 'Will anyone answer me? What is happening?'

'You're being targeted,' Tie Noo Summ said.

'What does that mean?'

'What it means is that people in high places want to see you dead.'

'Me?'

'You are Daxx, right?'

'What have I done?'

'You haven't done it yet. It's what you've almost done.'

'It's the power supply, isn't it?' Janna said.

Tie Noo Summ looked surprised. 'You know about that?'

Kay Lee Too interrupted; he was excited again. 'Of course she does. She discovered it.'

'She did?' Tie Noo Summ glanced at Kay Lee Too. 'Then why is the fuss all about Daxx?'

'Because she discovered it, but I formalised it,' Daxx said. 'I did the physics that might make it reproducible.'

Janna turned to Daxx. 'I told you,' she said. 'It's dangerous when government revenue is involved.'

'It's not just money. It's everything. What you've... formalised, could destroy Devrell's system. We...' Tie Noo Summ glanced at Ahh Moss Eck. 'Are hoping it does just that.'

'She said that,' Daxx said, meaning Janna. 'I didn't believe her. I thought Tier-Ones can do what they like.'

'There are constraints on all of us. There are fewer for you than the rest of us, but they're still there,' Tie Noo Summ said.

Daxx shook his head. 'Okay. I've got plenty of other things to work on. Why didn't they just tell me to stop? I'll delete everything. It's not a problem.'

'Oh yes, it's most definitely still a problem,' Tie Noo Summ said. 'They're scared of what you're working on.'

'How do you know what Daxx is working on?' Janna asked. 'No one knows about that. It's not published.'

'Oh, come on,' Tie Noo Summ said. 'He uses his Device, doesn't he? Kay Lee Too can get access, and while he may be smarter than most, those in power have resources. There is no privacy.'

'Do you mean everybody has been looking at my work?' Daxx said, surprised.

'No, not everyone. A Tier-One is supposed to have privacy. It was mandated by the Messiah. Lower Tiers have none. But things have changed. I'd be surprised if your work hasn't already been deleted, as they expected to do to you.'

Daxx pulled his Device out of his pocket. He frowned as he swiped through the display, then dismissed it. 'It's gone.'

'Does that make a difference?' Tie Noo Summ said.

'No,' Daxx replied. 'I could re-derive everything in a day or two. The concept work is all here.' He tapped his head.

'And that is why we went to the effort to save you.'

'But, who are you?' Janna said.

Tie Noo Summ didn't answer immediately.

'Just tell them, boss,' Ahh Moss Eck said. He pushed off the wall and came towards Daxx and Janna. He smiled at them. Janna assumed the big man was trying to be nonthreatening, but he was making it worse.

'We're the Resistance.'

'Against what?' Janna frowned.

Tie Noo Summ sighed. He looked like he'd been asked that question many times. 'The Tier system, a single religion, the unnatural order…'

'How can order be unnatural? Life is about resisting entropy,' Daxx said.

'It's not just about order.' Tie Noo Summ sounded frustrated. 'It's something that few Tier-Ones would understand. Everyone else should have the same choices as you.'

'Tier-Ones don't have every choice,' Janna interrupted. 'They can't be admin workers or engineers.' She glanced at Kay Lee Too.

'That's not what I mean, you're being literal. There are always restraints, and accommodations, for everyone who wants to live in a community of people. It's how rigorous those restraints are that's the problem. Society should allow for promotion, to any level or skill, by inclination and by merit. The plan created by Devrell, centuries ago, is still being adhered to. It's controlled. Hasn't that ever bothered you?'

'No,' Daxx said. 'Not until you just mentioned it.'

'Exactly,' Tie Noo Summ said. 'No one thinks about it because everyone is controlled.'

'Controlled by those who tried to kill us?' Janna asked.

'Partly,' Tie Noo Summ said. 'The excesses are a recent aberration. The rules worked until recently, but they've been taken over. They need to be changed. The best society for all is not necessarily the one with the most even contentment across the whole population. There is a better way—promotion by merit. That may mean that some are left behind. That's unfortunate, but it results in a more robust society. We are open to abuse from those in power. That has happened. While Daxx may be the most high-profile target, so far, he would not be the last. We are at the beginning of the end. We can go in one of two ways. Stay as we are, and those newly in power will abuse their authority, or break it all down and let a better society grow out of what's left.'

Janna shook her head. 'It sounds like you expect people to die. That's insane. How is that in any way better?'

'It won't be for them, obviously. But the overall health of our systems will be better. But it depends on which path we take. Daxx is pivotal,' Tie Noo Summ said. 'There have always been arranged deaths. It was in the original design, and is the reason for its success. Mutations are removed.'

'I don't understand,' Janna asked.

Tie Noo Summ nodded towards Ahh Moss Eck. 'Take Ahh Moss Eck here.'

'Present,' Ahh Moss Eck said.

'Ahh Moss Eck was brought up in a regional city. His parents made a little more trouble and noise than normal, and after peer pressure failed to make a difference, he and his parents were transferred here, so they could be more closely monitored and controlled. That lasted for, what, five years?'

'Yep, five years,' Ahh Moss Eck said.

'His parents were just angry troublemakers. They, eventually, disappeared. Literally, one day they were here, and the next they weren't. They were most likely killed. The explanation was that they'd just left Ahh Moss Eck behind. He got assigned to foster parents. Right?' Tie Noo Summ asked Ahh Moss Eck.

'Yep.'

'There are many similar stories. It's controlled.'

'Disorder needs to be controlled. Maybe not to the extent of killing people. I can't see a problem,' Daxx said.

'It destroys differences. It doesn't allow for change,' Tie Noo Summ said. 'That's dangerous.' He looked from Daxx to Janna. 'And then we come to today's incident. In prior years, Daxx would have been handled quietly, not harmed, perhaps unaware that his research was being directed. But, we are in new territory. There's a new leader.' He shook his head as if he was personally responsible.

Tie Noo Summ stared at Daxx for a moment. 'You'll be working here from now on. Kay Lee Too will help you turn your ideas into technology.'

'No,' Daxx said. 'I can't work here. That's ridiculous.'

'You will.' Tie Noo Summ sounded menacing. 'You'll be safe here, but you can't leave.' He turned to Ahh Moss Eck. 'Can you show them upstairs to their room?'

'Will do,' Ahh Moss Eck said.

'Make sure they don't leave.'

Ahh Moss Eck nodded.

chapter 11

Daxx

D axx and Janna were led up one flight of stairs and shown into a room. 'Are you guys all right? All comfy?' Ahh Moss Eck said as he was about to shut the door and leave the room.

'Yes.' Daxx looked to Janna; she nodded.

'Have a rest for a bit. I'll be outside if you need anything.' Ahh Moss Eck shut the door.

The room had a small dining table with a few chairs haphazardly placed around it. Daxx felt like straightening them. There was a bed. Janna and Daxx stretched out on it, exhausted. The physical exertion and the stress and anxiety had taken their toll, but they couldn't sleep.

Janna got off the bed, walked to the window, looked outside for a moment, then sat on one of the chairs at the table. She placed her head in her hands. Daxx watched her. There were no words that would comfort her. He tried to find some but failed. He put his hands behind his head and stared at the window as a shower of cold rain beat against it. He was glad they were not outside on their own, looking for shelter from the elements and escaping the authorities.

There seemed to be nothing for them to do but wait. Daxx had no ideas on what should happen next. He didn't mind too much; it was a welcome normality, being safe and quiet. He and Janna had Ahh Moss Eck and Kay Lee Too to look out for them, although Ahh Moss Eck frightened him. He seemed to be their guard as well as protector. Daxx decided to not think about that problem for the moment.

'Are we going to talk about what happened in my apartment?' Janna talked through her hands and at the tabletop. She sat up straight, dropped her hands, and stared at him.

Daxx didn't reply for a long time. He stared back at Janna. 'Not really,' he said. 'I need to think about it.'

'There's not much that needs thinking about. What happened was pretty straightforward. How, is another matter.'

'And you're sure it was me? Really sure? He didn't act like me. I mostly saw his back. I don't often see that part of me.'

Janna frowned at him. 'I'd know you in any circumstance. I would hope you would be the same with me.'

'Of course.' He dropped his hands from behind his head. He sat up straighter. Somehow, and quickly, it had become his fault. He guessed that it probably was, if two of him were involved.

'He, I mean you, produced an energy burst from nothing. He's a weapon, and he killed those men,' she said. 'What world does he live in to turn you into that?'

'I don't know.' Daxx didn't want to think. What had happened that day was impossible. His life of yesterday and before, even the moments before he reached the commuter station that morning, was simple, quiet and ordered. It made sense. Everything fitted and the course of his life was organised. But now, it was a mess and chaotic. He hated chaos in everything, his work, the location of objects he used, the direction of his life.

'We need to talk about this, Daxx. I can't think of anything more important. You just appeared out of nothing. You didn't walk in; you materialised. So you can travel, somehow, through space. And, I don't know how it's even possible, through time. Is it possible? You, if anyone, would know.'

'It's theoretically possible. Multiple orthogonal spacetimes and nonlinear time sort of make it possible for simultaneity to work differently across spacetimes. But you'd need, like, a whole lot of energy. I don't know how you wouldn't just vaporise anything that tried it. It's purely theoretical, Janna. I doubt it's possible.'

'A whole lot of energy?' She stared at him. 'Unlimited, perhaps?'

He shook his head. 'I know what you're thinking, but I seriously doubt it. Actually, I'd discount it completely.'

She frowned at him. She looked angry. 'We've had this discussion. You jump into decisions. You make quick judgements. You can't discount it, obviously you can't. It happened. That thinking is what got us into this mess. You don't think through consequences. You need to be patient. You didn't consider what might happen with your energy work. And look'—she spread her arms—'it did have consequences. Just like someone told you.'

'You never said this would happen.'

'Yes, I did. Not exactly this.' She glanced around the room as if it contained all their problems. 'But something like this.'

Daxx frowned. He didn't like what she said. But she was right. He knew it. He was smart with physics problems, but naive about other things. He never had the inclination to worry about the mundane. It was why he preferred order in his life—there was less to think about. He could concentrate on what was important.

'Sorry,' Janna said. 'I didn't mean to lecture you. It can't be all your fault.'

'Just mostly?'

'Yeah.' She laughed. 'But, there is empirical evidence of time travel; you saw it this morning,' she said. 'Time travel, space travel, and explosive energy usage have happened. You can't deny that.'

'It could have been a hallucination?'

She looked quizzically at him. She didn't need to say anything.

'No, of course not.'

'It's what you turn into that worries me,' she said. 'How could you, I mean you, Daxx,' she pointed at him, 'kill people that easily?'

'I couldn't.'

There was a knock at the door. It opened and Ahh Moss Eck came in. He was followed by Tie Noo Summ, looking concerned and worried; it was a natural look for him. They didn't sit down. Tie Noo Summ put his hands on the back of a chair. He looked at Janna and then at Daxx, stretched out on the bed.

'We need to talk about where we go from here,' Tie Noo Summ said.

'Now?' Janna said.

'Yes.'

'What's the hurry?' Daxx asked.

'I need to know what resources are needed, and that can take time. Kay Lee Too has done an amazing job keeping us out of sight, but I suspect we haven't been a priority. That will have changed. My sources suggest we be wary and even more vigilant. We may need to move. That requires planning.'

'What do you expect from us?' Janna asked.

'From Daxx,' Tie Noo Summ corrected her.

'Janna can help.' Daxx got off the bed and stood behind the table, facing Tie Noo Summ. Daxx grabbed the back of a chair, mimicking the older man.

'Really?' Tie Noo Summ asked.

Kay Lee Too piped up. 'The fungus that started all this, the one with the odd energy imbalance, is crucial. She knows all about it. It proved his'— he looked at Daxx—'orthogonal spacetimes unified field theory.'

'You understood that?' Daxx said.

Kay Lee Too grinned. 'Sure, the concepts are pretty cool. I got interested when engineers discovered that Janna's fungus was also a good electrochemical solution and made better batteries. Device technology is my thing; it's what my degree is in.'

Tie Noo Summ sighed. 'I don't care who has done what. I want to know who has the skill to take this forward. Or, are you all... talk and physics? Because if you are, then I have no need to help you. You can leave right now.' Tie Noo Summ nodded towards the window. The rain still beat against it. Daxx wondered if the older man's threat was also related to bad weather.

Daxx looked from Tie Noo Summ to Kay Lee Too and then at Janna. She nodded at him.

'I've proved, theoretically, mind you, there is a way to harness unlimited energy. The laws of thermodynamics are still okay...' Kay Lee Too nodded vigorously. Daxx frowned at the oddity of a Tier-Three understanding his work. 'The energy balances remain, but they're spread across spacetimes...'

'Daxx!' Janna interrupted. Daxx stared at her for a moment.

'Okay. There could be free and unlimited power.'

'Hmm,' Tie Noo Summ said. 'But there isn't any practical solution yet?'

Daxx nodded. 'It's all theoretical.'

Kay Lee Too squeaked an interruption. He sounded nervous, excited, but also hesitant. 'But I might know one.'

The young man grinned at Tie Noo Summ. Daxx frowned at the engineer.

'I'm listening,' Tie Noo Summ said.

chapter 12

Day 2. Soo

The first sunlight broke over the horizon and streamed through Soo's office. She looked up from her display, her attention distracted by the glare. She dismissed her display and stood up from behind her desk. Her concentration had been broken. She walked to the window that faced the distant hills. The new sun's light brought them into definition. She noticed tiny slivers of ice on the outside of the window, which disappeared as if her gaze was melting them. She wondered when was the last time she had stood outside, unprotected from the elements. She couldn't remember. Her adult life and ambition had been vested in occupying that office. She was happy, if that emotion was useful to describe the satisfaction of unrestrained power.

She frowned. Unrestrained, yes, but overseen. That irked her; she had to change that. She sat down again and concentrated on her display. The window, the morning, the ice, the view, her happiness, had been dismissed from her mind. She worked undisturbed for an hour. Daxx was a critical problem, but he was one of many. She did not turn her mind to him until she received notification for a connection request.

'Yes, Inspector,' she said after the man's face appeared in her display.

'We've spent all night looking. There is no sign. He must have sophisticated assistance. We've been going through surveillance data, but it's a time consuming exercise without assistance from the Advisor. Do you want us to continue?'

'Yes,' she said. 'Have you considered physical inspection?'

The man frowned. 'It's a warren in the old city. That's the reason we think he's got help. It's a perfect place to hide.'

'What about a saturation search?'

'We don't have enough personnel.'

How could such a simple operational request turn out so badly? How could detaining, then killing someone at a public location be so difficult?

'The Advisor could...' the Inspector began.

'You know why we can't,' Soo interrupted. 'We've agreed on this course of action.'

The Inspector stared at her for a moment. He gave her a small nod, then disconnected.

She opened another connection. Mill Nupp's face showed. 'Here. Now,' she ordered.

Mill Nupp entered her office. The door shut behind him. 'Yes, Soo?'

'What's the status on your Daxx problem?'

Mill Nupp hesitated for a moment. She wondered if he would complain about the deliberate phrasing.

'There has been no progress overnight.'

'Why not?'

He hesitated again. He fidgeted. He looked tense. 'Because, I was told to give it a low priority.'

'I didn't tell you that.'

'I did,' the Advisor's voice sounded. The voice's source seemed to come from the centre of her office. It was being projected from somewhere, but there was nothing in that position.

Mill Nupp's face relaxed.

'You take the Advisor's requests over my orders?' she said to Mill Nupp.

He nodded, but the Advisor spoke before Mill Nupp could say anything. 'Of course. His position has always liaised with mine. He takes care of the details. That's where my expertise is best used.'

'No.' She swiped at the air like the Advisor's words were dangerous. 'I want that communication to stop.' She glared at Mill Nupp. 'You no longer talk to the Advisor.'

'But, Soo...?' He stopped talking as Soo's eyes opened wide.

She took a deep breath. She hoped she looked dangerous. 'I believe I'm in charge, or am I mistaken?'

'No, Soo.'

'That's debatable,' the Advisor said.

'No, it's not.' Talking to an empty space in the middle of her office was unnerving.

'I've always received direction from the Advisor,' Mill Nupp tried to justify. 'It's always happened. But we execute your position's orders.'

'And yet that hasn't happened.'

'Priorities were changed; I was still sort of working on it.' Mill Nupp sounded petulant.

Soo wanted to stare angrily at the Advisor, but that wasn't possible. She glared at the young man instead. The Advisor broke the silence. That was odd, Soo thought. As if the Advisor could feel the tension and was attempting to lessen it. It was supposed to be an unemotional position, able to dispassionately view all decision making. Perhaps emotional responses could also work against the Advisor. She wondered how useful that information might be.

'If I don't work with Mill Nupp, if I am expected to advise you on all matters of detail, then you're doing his job.'

'Or, perhaps he does his job, and I do mine, and you stay out of the way?'

'Yes, of course,' the Advisor said. 'That is one possibility, although an inefficient one.'

'It can't get much more inefficient, can it?' Soo said. 'The two of you, apparently working together, can't find a single Tier-One.'

The voice didn't reply. Mill Nupp glanced towards the floor in the centre of the office.

Change was difficult for those being changed. Perhaps she had not provided sufficient, specific guidance for her assistant. Every party to a problem had to accept some blame. Daxx was a critical problem, but not an immediate one. His work was not ready. She was lucky, or perhaps she had subconsciously chosen the first major task well. There would be other critical problems. Daxx was the first of a long list. It was the necessary function of power to be solving dangerous issues. The temporary failure to stop Daxx would have few consequences. There was time. And there were positives, as she unearthed procedural problems. Failure is the only true learning process. But she could not and would not show her pleasure; that would negate Mill Nupp's learning. He had to fear her displeasure. Mill Nupp could be trained. The Advisor couldn't. The only solution to that problem was disregard, then removal.

She tried to sound reasonable. 'How do you propose solving the Daxx problem?'

'They've disabled tracking. But we know their last location. We can monitor around that location. We can put people on the ground.'

'That's one plan,' she said. 'The police are scanning the surveillance data; you don't need to do that.'

'I'm sure later today we'll find them.'

'No, you're not,' she said. 'You're guessing. And, if you do get lucky, you'd be back to where you were the last time you found them and they escaped, right? Does that sound like a good plan?'

'No, Soo.'

She wished she had an assistant who was more argumentative, someone to worry out kinks in ideas, but that was difficult with a Tier-Two assistant. No Tier-One, who could speak to her as an equal, would be an assistant. Perhaps an understudy, but the last thing she wanted was someone undermining her. She had done that to another; she knew the dangers. A Tier-Two was the best solution for an assistant, but it wasn't optimal.

'Tell me about the families.'

'There's the father, who's in a care facility. He lost his mental faculties after the mother disappeared. There's an older brother. And the sister that vanished a few years ago.'

'I remember. It was so unusual. What was her name again?'

'Which one?'

'The sister.'

'Kell.'

'Was that us?'

'No. I've never heard of a Tier-One being targeted, until now.'

'And the partner's family?'

'There are no siblings,' Mill Nupp said. 'They're just an average Tier-Two family, very close, according to reports.'

'Perfect,' she said. 'That's your plan. Bring them here. Make it public and you have permission to be less than gentle.'

Mill Nupp didn't leave. He glanced towards the centre of the room.

'The Advisor is irrelevant,' Soo said. 'I've told you what I want to happen.'

He nodded, but still didn't leave. She sighed. 'Go.' She shooed him away.

The door shut behind Mill Nupp.

'The original methods were created for a reason,' the Advisor said. 'They have worked well. The society you see now is a direct result of implementing those methods in a way that does not bring control into focus.'

'You're repeating yourself,' she said. 'But, all things evolve, don't they?'

There was no reply, and she wondered for a moment if she'd get one.

'I still suggest no firm action be taken against Daxx.' The voice almost sounded plaintive. That pleased her.

'Noted.'

chapter 13

Renn

Renn stood by the window in his father's room. The manicured grounds sparkled in the early morning frost. It was first light. The grass was a fainter green, filtered by a thin layer of ice that melted as Renn watched. The shrubs and walkways directly outside were manicured with deliberate and careful attention. Trees were dotted away from the buildings, for those who were able to brave the distance to walk to shade in summer. The space between the buildings and the first trees was left unshaded for residents who wanted sun in cooler times. There was a veranda for those that wanted outside air but could not, or didn't wish to, labour further.

It was a magnificent care facility, Renn thought. It always, momentarily, relaxed him when he arrived. He dreaded each visit, but that short moment of peace almost made it worthwhile. He wished there was no need for a place peopled by lost minds and decayed bodies. He wished life just carried on, a bit slower perhaps, but normal and fruitful.

He hated that his father was here. It made him hate his father, sometimes, as if his need was a weakness. His weakness, now, was age. Renn couldn't blame him for that. But he did blame his father for many things. The worst being emotionally absent when Renn was too young to have a sole parent give up on his family. That was unforgivable and the ultimate selfishness. He wanted to punish his father for a lost, unguided childhood, but it was too late now; the old man's comprehension was minimal. The bitter taste of unresolvable anger was always with Renn.

He turned from the view and watched his father sitting in a lounge chair, a breakfast tray set before him. Rey's full attention was on the tray as he puzzled his way through each food item. The order of consumption was a task on the edge of impossible complexity. Rey did eat, making monumental decisions, to him, about what to eat next but was distracted after each mouthful by another food item that he seemed to just realise he had on the tray.

Renn considered himself lucky; at least his father could still feed himself, even though the mental challenge seemed to exhaust him. Each meal's conclusion required an extensive session of vacant staring either at a wall or a view; it didn't seem to matter. Renn wondered what went through his father's mind when his attention was not consumed by a meal or a hot beverage, or walking, or dressing. Did he remember? A part of Renn hoped that Rey had lucid moments and that he was tormented by them. The simple thought that it might happen sweetened Renn's unresolved anger. His father's behaviour had been a weakness. Rey had decided that he couldn't cope and had contracted his awareness to himself. He had abandoned those he was supposed to love, those who had fewer means of managing. And yet Renn had coped. He had taken control; he had to—he didn't have the luxury of abandonment. The remnants of his family were his responsibility, but he had been too young to take that burden. He still paid that price.

Then Kell, his younger sister, had vanished. For a short time, he thought he would go the way of his father. He shuddered at the memory of his own weakness. The loss of his sister still brought tears to his eyes. He remembered Kell every time he visited his father. He hated the old man for that too, for forcing that memory on him and always breaking the moment of relaxation when he first arrived at the care facility.

'How's your breakfast?' Renn asked, swallowing the mix of emotions.

Rey was startled and looked up at the sound of Renn's voice. He had been unaware that his meal was being observed. He became angry, which he often did.

'What are you doing there?' Rey asked. 'You've delivered breakfast; you can go now.'

Renn sighed. This always happened. His father thought Renn was a lounging employee.

'Okay, Dad.'

Rey was no longer listening; his attention was back on deciding which food to eat. Renn had been forgotten, again.

Renn thought it was unfair, as if his father's affliction was a benefit, his mental illness a choice. Rey had abandoned his young family, and he expected others to look after him in his declining years. The weak man, the selfish man, would always win because someone would accept the responsibilities that they refused.

Renn stood by the window, watching his father eat. Eventually Rey gave up, either because he'd had enough food or the mental challenge of choice had exhausted him. He attempted to push the tray away, but it was fixed to the side of his chair.

'Damn thing,' Rey muttered as he tried to move the tray.

Renn quickly stepped in, unhooked the tray, and placed it on the small table next to the lounge chair. Rey looked at Renn and offered a grudging thank-you.

'Would you like to go outside and sit on the veranda?' Renn asked. 'It's cold, though.'

'It's cold? Then why would I want to sit outside? There're perfectly good chairs inside.'

Renn sighed. These regular visits were hard work. He felt guilty because all he thought about was escaping. Renn thought Rey preferred to be on his own; he was always angry with whoever was with him. The old man's mind worked in odd ways—nothing was satisfactory, everything was an inconvenience, as if life was an onerous, disappointing, useless task to be endured.

Renn sat down on the other chair in the room, the visitor's chair, although Renn knew his father had no other visitors. It was a source of tension with his younger brother. Renn accepted the responsibility of visiting his father as well, as he had always accepted family responsibilities.

'Are you going to take that tray away?'

'In a moment, Dad, in a moment.'

He sat with his father for some time. There was no conversation, just vacant staring. Renn stood up; he had to go to work, and he judged that he had spent time enough with his father that day. His guilt was assuaged. 'Okay, I'll go.'

'Good,' his father replied. 'It looks messy.' Rey meant the breakfast tray.

'I'll see you again soon, Dad.' Renn stood by the door, about to leave.

His father looked up from staring at his own feet. 'Why?' Rey stared through Renn.

'I don't know.' Renn sighed, but he would come again.

'I'd rather you did your job and got my sons and my daughter to visit.' Rey's eyes focused on Renn; he registered him, again, as an employee.

'And while you're at it,' Rey added. 'Contact my damn wife. Where the hell is Eth?'

chapter 14

Day 3. Janna

Janna and Daxx had spent two nights at the same building in the old city. The first night and the next morning had felt right. Janna didn't want to leave the safety of that place. But by the afternoon, her anxiety had increased. She had nothing to do. She fretted about how their situation was not being resolved. She had spoken to no one outside the building, at the urging of Tie Noo Summ. She did not have the relief of conversation. She had nothing to distract her. She worried, and she became angry as the day progressed. Daxx was fully occupied with Kay Lee Too. The two of them talked endlessly through practical possibilities to Daxx's solutions to energy creation. She felt abandoned.

Daxx and Janna had argued on their second night. Janna was worried; Daxx was not. He had given their predicament no further thought. He was immersed in a problem. Janna argued they had decisions to make. He disagreed. They resolved nothing. She had spent a night of fitful sleep. She woke in a poor mood. She dabbed at food on a plate that had been presented to her as breakfast. She was hungry, but didn't feel like eating. Daxx sat next to her. She thought he had chosen that position so that she couldn't easily glare at him. He ate rapidly, like he was planning a quick escape.

Kay Lee Too sidled up to Janna; he held a portable Device and looked sheepish. 'There's something you need to see.' He kept his eyes down. As if relaying necessary bad news was blameworthy, he added, 'Sorry, things have got worse.' He glanced at her and then looked back at the Device. He initiated the display and handed the Device to Janna. She took it but kept staring at him. She was worried. Kay Lee Too kept his eyes averted.

The display played a recorded news feed. Kay Lee Too nodded towards the display when Janna kept looking at him. He reached across her, touched the Device in her hand, and restarted the news feed recording. 'Look.' He nodded again at the display.

Janna watched the video. A heart-wrenching sound came from her; it was both a squeak and a groan. All possibility that the last two days had been a mistake, that her involvement was peripheral, that the insanity she had lived through could be cleared up, was shattered. She was an intimate part of the madness, and her involvement had brought suffering to those she loved. She stopped the video feed and began it again. Her hands shook as she worked the display.

It was a network update, the original images posted by bystanders. The footage had been cut and edited so that the multiple angles of the bystanders added to the newsworthiness and the dramatic effect. A voice-over had been added. Janna's parents were shown being dragged from their home, the home where she had grown up. They both had rips and tears in their clothes and cuts on their faces. Her father winced with pain from a shoulder that looked damaged. He and her mother were pushed into a vehicle. They sped away. The remaining security officers made a half-hearted attempt to clear the bystanders, but the officers grinned as the recording continued. The network item ended with a short commentary on the unique, unusual action and speculation on the seriousness and danger of the transgressions that must have occurred.

Janna watched it again. Then she watched it again. When she began the video the fourth time, Daxx took the Device from her and shut off the display. She slumped into him and sobbed. She didn't remain like that for long. Distress was not helpful. She pulled back from Daxx and wiped her eyes. She didn't have time for sorrow and self-pity; she had to do something about her parents.

But what could she do? Her parents' detention was, obviously, meant to catch her attention. It was not something they had done. Her parents were exemplary Tier-Twos. She could run off and present herself to the authorities. That action was expected. It was a way to get at Daxx. It was not an option because she would still be reliant on the goodwill of those who had harmed her parents. They may still not be released. She took a deep breath. Her immediate problem was insufficient information. She was accepting the advice of others for the motivation behind actions and behaviour never seen before. It was impossible to plan or even react. Getting more information was the only thing she could do that made any sense to her.

She looked at Daxx. He still held her, perhaps worried that she would collapse from shock or despair. There would be no breakdown. 'I have to go,' she said.

'I don't know how you think you can make a difference. You should stay here and let these people'—he glanced at the others in the kitchen—'do what they can.'

'No, I can't sit here and do nothing.'

'What do you think you can do?' Daxx let her go.

'I won't know that until I find out something, anything.' She was angry at Daxx. He was being logical with insufficient information. It was not the time to suggest solutions. They stared at each other for a long moment. 'I'm going,' she said. 'I have to, I want to.'

She watched his face change; she knew that look. He had considered all options and had come to a conclusion. It was how his mind worked—he seemed quick in his decisions, but his mind processed information faster than others. It still annoyed her, but she was glad, at that moment, that he was being decisive. She quickly kissed him. He smiled.

'I'll go with you.'

She smiled. 'Thanks, Daxx. But who would be looking after you while you're trying to look after me?'

He frowned.

'No one's going anywhere,' Tie Noo Summ said.

'I have to find out what's happened to my parents, where they are.' The safe-house was no longer safe; it was confinement.

'No.' Tie Noo Summ was firm. 'You both stay here.'

'Boss.' Ahh Moss Eck stood next to Tie Noo Summ. 'I'll go with her.'

'No,' Tie Noo Summ said. 'We need you here too.'

'She has to go. You know that. And you know I have to go with her.'

Tie Noo Summ sighed. Ahh Moss Eck's family history made the man's request impossible to refuse. He turned to Ahh Moss Eck. 'Don't get yourself killed.'

Ahh Moss Eck smiled at Janna. 'I guess we should get ourselves ready, boss.'

chapter 15

Daxx

Ahh Moss Eck busied himself readying the gear Janna and he would need. Daxx stood nearby and watched the large man carefully place items in a backpack. Janna sat in the same room. Kay Lee Too sat next to her and worked her display. He altered her Device configuration, so it connected to a portable power source carried by Ahh Moss Eck. Every Device was tracked by the energy top-ups from network outlets. Kay Lee Too's original alterations had stopped that tracking, but the downside was her Device had no power. The portable power, designed by Kay Lee Too, stole power by hopping from one user to the next.

Kay Lee Too finished his work. Janna stood up. She smiled her thanks. Daxx hugged Janna close. He quietly asked, 'Are you sure?'

'I am.'

'Ahh Moss Eck could find your parents,' he said. 'We're safe here.' It was a pitiful coercion attempt. There are no guaranteed safe moments.

'Let's go,' Ahh Moss Eck said to Janna. He slung his backpack over his shoulders.

Janna kissed Daxx, then turned to leave. Daxx followed them down the stairs. Ahh Moss Eck opened the door.

'Take care of her,' Daxx demanded.

'Of course.' Ahh Moss Eck frowned at Daxx like he'd been insulted.

Janna gave Daxx a quick smile, then she closed the door from the other side. Daxx stared at the door, hoping Ahh Moss Eck had, perhaps, forgotten something and Janna would return. Tie Noo Summ touched Daxx on the shoulder. Daxx turned to face the older man.

'You need to get to work,' he said, not unkindly. 'But you're going somewhere else. We don't have the setup here to do the engineering Kay Lee Too's told me you need. Are you really ready to make things?'

'Yes. We've designed what we can; we need prototypes.'

'Sounds simple.'

'It's not.'

'Pack your stuff. Kay Lee Too has already started.'

Daxx nodded. He joined Kay Lee Too in a room on the first floor. He was packing things into a backpack.

'Where are we going?' Daxx asked.

'I've got a friend who has a hobby lab. It's better for what we'll need than what we have in the basement. We can use it.'

Daxx offered his assistance with the packing, but it was refused. He stood by idly, watching Kay Lee Too work. He was a Tier-One and yet a group of Tier-Threes decided everything for him. His upbringing suggested he should be upset. But the circumstances meant blindly following the orders of a Tier-Three. He hated not knowing. Problems were fine; puzzling over them was his life, but intractable physics problems were still contained within known bounds. His current life was a chaotic mess. He had no choice but to examine each serial problem, make a decision, and see what happened. His current decision was to wait for Kay Lee Too to finish packing, then follow the young man wherever he led.

'I think I'm ready.' Kay Lee Too stood over his backpack lying on the table. His hands were on his hips. 'Can you think of anything else we'll need?' He looked questioningly at Daxx.

Daxx shook his head. 'I have no idea what you've been packing.'

Kay Lee Too grunted as if he was disappointed and half expected Daxx to know everything about, well, everything.

'You've forgotten this,' Tie Noo Summ walked into the room. He carried a sheaf of papers. He handed them to Kay Lee Too. 'And these.' He gave Kay Lee Too pens.

'Is that paper?' Daxx asked.

Tie Noo Summ smiled; it didn't suit him. It dissolved quickly. 'You can't work on the network while you're away from here. This is an option.'

'Can you write?' Daxx asked Kay Lee Too. 'Only Tier-Ones are taught.'

'Tie Noo Summ taught me,' Kay Lee Too said. 'Although not so much on real paper.'

'Who taught you?' Daxx asked Tie Noo Summ.

'I learnt.' He turned to Kay Lee Too. 'Just follow the route and don't do anything stupid. Both of you.' Tie Noo Summ glared at Daxx.

Daxx should have been upset, he was being insulted by a Tier-Three, but he knew the man was right. He frowned, determined to do exactly what he was told by a young Tier-Three. He shook his head at the incongruity.

'Won't surveillance be able to pick us up?' Daxx asked.

'Yes,' Tie Noo Summ said. 'But Kay Lee Too can disguise you.'

'I've altered our Devices so our appearance is changed from a distance ,' Kay Lee Too said. 'It doesn't work with close attention, but I'll make sure you don't put your face directly in front of any surveillance cameras.'

'And,' Tie Noo Summ interrupted, 'you'll be travelling where there are crowds, using the public transport network, so surveillance software won't pick up any anomaly.'

'But...' Daxx began.

Tie Noo Summ held up a hand, facing Daxx. 'You need to go.' Tie Noo Summ turned to Kay Lee Too. 'Anything else you need?'

'No, I'm fine.'

Tie Noo Summ nodded. He left the room.

Kay Lee Too placed the paper and pens into his backpack, then shrugged it over his shoulder.

'Let's go.'

Daxx glanced at each surveillance camera on their way to the commuter station. He had never really thought about how many there were; they were everywhere. He was nervous and acted like it. He had never tried to evade detection before. He was authority; there was nothing he couldn't do within the loose constraints on Tier-Ones. He felt claustrophobic, as though surveillance was withdrawing his breathable air. He felt trapped enough outside, among the throng of pedestrians. Underground in the commuter station and on transport vehicles would be worse. Daxx halted at the station's entrance. He couldn't go any further. A few days ago, entering a station had been a non-conscious event; now it was a mental hurdle he couldn't overcome.

Kay Lee Too also stopped, having gone on a few more steps. He came back to Daxx. 'Daxx?'

'What?'

Kay Lee Too took Daxx by the arm and tried to lead him on. 'We can't stand still. If we aren't moving, the surveillance has more data to work with. Come on.'

Daxx resisted and pulled his arm free. 'I can't.'

Kay Lee Too sighed. He initiated his display. He spoke. The encryption made his voice muffled and toneless. He nodded, looked around, and swiped the controls. Janna's face appeared.

'Daxx,' she said. 'Kay Lee Too has told me where you are.'

'Janna, where are you?'

She ignored him. 'I know this must be hard for you. I understand. But what are your options?'

'None.'

She stared at him for a moment. 'Then just do it. I'm busy. I've got to go. We'll talk later.'

Her face vanished. Kay Lee Too dismissed the display. Daxx stared at Kay Lee Too like he had done something unforgivable. 'All right.' Daxx nodded towards the station entrance.

Kay Lee Too turned and walked into the station. Daxx followed.

chapter 16

Janna

'Who was that?'

'Daxx.' Janna dismissed her display.

'Trouble?' Ahh Moss Eck asked.

'Commuter station fears.'

'I hope he's not going to be a problem. With all respect to how smart I've heard he is, he doesn't, you know, appear that smart with ordinary things.'

'He'll be fine,' she said, more confidently than she felt. 'Once he figures things out, once the chaos becomes normal, he'll work it all out.' Her smile was forced. 'He'll be fine.'

Ahh Moss Eck grunted and looked out the window of their train.

She wondered if Daxx could survive in a chaotic world. The physics problems he solved were exceptionally difficult, but they were concepts. She wondered if a messy, chaotic, real world would be too much for him. She thought of how difficult it was for him to stay in her apartment and leave the mess as it was. Then she remembered what Daxx had lived through. She was shamed by the guilt of forgotten sadness. Daxx had survived the loss of his mother, the withdrawal of his father, and then the disappearance of his sister and the rupture of his relationship with his older brother. No wonder he preferred order in his life. He would be okay eventually, if he'd been able to live through that. She wouldn't have survived what Daxx had gone through. Her family was everything.

She looked out the train's window. It wasn't moving. But, she thought, she knew Daxx would survive; she had hard evidence that he did. She shuddered, thinking of what he had yet to live through to turn into that man in her apartment. The way he looked at her had been disturbing. She wondered if she was the one who didn't survive. She shook her head. That uncertainty was normal. Daxx, knowing he survives, was the abnormal one.

'Come on, this is us,' Ahh Moss Eck said.

She looked up at the train's door. Ahh Moss Eck frowned at her inattention. He held the automatic doors open. She jumped up, embarrassed that she had been daydreaming, and ran through the door. Ahh Moss Eck followed her.

'You don't need to run. You shouldn't run,' he said. 'Just do normal stuff, really, really normal. Okay?'

She nodded and kept her head down. They walked out of the station and to the street where she had spent her childhood. A security vehicle was parked outside her parents' house. She saw the forms and shadows of people moving inside her old home.

'Keep walking,' Ahh Moss Eck said. 'Just glance at the car, like you're an uninterested, normal person. And talk to me.'

They walked to the far end of the street and turned the corner, they stopped when they were out of sight.

'What do we do now?' Janna asked. 'I'm not any good at this stuff.'

'You did all right. It's hard to act normal.'

'Thanks.'

'We need to ask the neighbours what happened. Get details.'

'How do we do that without being recognised?'

Ahh Moss Eck thought for a moment. 'Would everyone here recognise you?'

'Pretty much,' she said. 'It's a stable community. Although, there's a new family at the other end of the street, on the corner. I haven't met them yet, but they may have seen me visiting, I don't know.'

'Which house?'

She told him.

'We can't just walk back down the street; we'll have to go around,' he said.

They walked the block and returned to the end of the street closest to the commuter station. They turned into Janna's parents' street, again. Ahh Moss Eck requested entry to the house on the corner. 'Follow my lead,' he said.

The door opened. 'We're with the community news feed,' Ahh Moss

Eck said to the woman standing in the doorway.

She frowned. 'Yes?'

Janna smiled at her. 'We're doing a neighbourhood item on people who have newly arrived. We'd like to feature you and your family. This is a well-established area, and we're interested in how new people are treated and accepted.'

'Oh, really?' Her frown disappeared. She stared at Janna for a moment. 'I think I've seen you, haven't I?'

'Perhaps, I report around this area often. It's such a nice area to live, don't you think?'

The woman smiled. 'Oh, yes.'

Janna smiled even harder at the woman. 'Can we come in and have a chat?'

'I love the community news feed.' The woman opened the door fully for them to enter. 'When would we be shown?'

'We'll let you know when it's done, and it'll be soon after that.' Ahh Moss Eck walked through the door.

Janna glanced down the street to her parents' house and the security vehicle outside. 'What's that all about?' She tried to sound casual.

'Really?' the woman said. 'I'd have thought a local reporter would have known about that.'

Janna couldn't think how to reply; she was no good at lying, and she panicked. She stared at the woman.

'We've been in the studio,' Ahh Moss Eck said. 'We haven't seen any feeds. Maybe, that's a good way to start this off. What do you think?' He looked to Janna.

Janna nodded in agreement. 'Yes, yes.'

Ahh Moss Eck smiled at the woman. His smile wasn't a natural look for him. It made him look menacing.

'It would still be all about you and your family,' Ahh Moss Eck said.

The woman led them to a lounge area, where they sat, and she talked. And she talked. Janna attempted to listen, trying to play her part, but with her anxiety and distress about her parents, she became angry with the woman. It took an effort to remain courteous and silent. Janna could not believe the banality of her conversation. The woman took a breath. Ahh Moss Eck jumped into the temporary silence.

'Thank you, thank you for all that so far. And what about the security vehicle? What's your take on that?'

The woman was silent for a long moment. She looked perplexed. 'I don't really have a take on it,' she said. She stared at Ahh Moss Eck. 'That's an odd thing to say. Are you a Tier-Two?'

Janna answered. 'Yes, we are. I'm Janna, and this is Ahh Moss.'

Janna smiled at the woman, but she frowned back. 'That doesn't sound like a Tier-Two name.'

'He comes from a regional area.' Janna thought she was getting better at lying. A hint of truth was the better option.

'Oh?' The woman looked at Ahh Moss Eck. 'You poor thing. At least you're here now.' She smiled at him.

'Thank you,' Ahh Moss Eck said. Janna could sense his anger.

'Why don't you tell us your take,' Janna smiled, 'on what happened when the security vehicle arrived.'

'There were two,' the woman said. 'One took them away; the other one is still there.'

Ahh Moss Eck jumped to his feet and shook his head. 'I've been really stupid.' He was wide-eyed. She was puzzled. He grabbed her by the arm and pulled her to her feet. He pushed her towards the door.

'Thank you,' Ahh Moss Eck said to the woman. She stared at them and frowned. 'We've got to go. We've got enough for now. Thank you very much.'

'Are you sure?' She followed them to the door.

'We'll contact you when your story's ready,' Ahh Moss Eck said.

Ahh Moss Eck held Janna's arm and led her outside and around the nearby corner. 'I know what we need to do to find your parents,' he said. 'I've been really stupid, and Kay Lee Too must be too busy, otherwise he would have thought of it.'

'What?'

'We know when and where,' he said. 'Kay Lee Too can hack into the surveillance footage and follow who took your parents.' Ahh Moss Eck opened his display. He swiped encryption off so Janna could also see. Kay Lee Too's face appeared. He sat in a stark room with a bench behind him.

'Hey,' Ahh Moss Eck said. 'I need you to help find Janna's parents.'

'Sure.'

Kay Lee Too looked away from the screen. There was the sound of another voice.

'It's Ahh Moss Eck and Janna,' Kay Lee Too said in the direction of the voice, then he looked at the display again. 'Daxx wants to talk to you too.'

Ahh Moss Eck looked annoyed. 'He can talk to Janna later, on her Device, but not now.'

'Okay.' Kay Lee Too shrugged. 'What can I do?'

'Can you hack the surveillance around Janna's parents' house? Starting when they were taken?'

Kay Lee Too laughed. 'We should have done that from headquarters and saved you the trip.'

'Yeah,' Ahh Moss Eck said. 'Why didn't you?'

Kay Lee Too laughed again. 'I'll bring it up now. Just give me a moment. I'll share it with you.'

After a short delay, the surveillance images from the moment Janna's parents were dragged from their house appeared. Janna was upset all over again. She was ambiguously pleased, but also guilty, when her parents had been placed inside the vehicle and their distress could no longer seen. The vehicle sped off, turned the corner, and disappeared.

'Damn,' said Kay Lee Too.

'What happened?' Janna asked.

'That's no ordinary security vehicle. The surveillance is ignoring it.'

Janna's body slumped. 'So we have no idea where they went?'

'Wait on,' Kay Lee Too said. 'I've done this before. They remove the vehicle, but they can't remove the effects. We can watch pedestrians and traffic keep out of the way of, well, nothing, an empty space.'

Kay Lee Too played with the display for a moment. 'There,' he said. 'I've added a yellow blob to show you where there's nothing, but it's causing effects. We can follow it. There'll be a delay at each intersection as my software searches each possible route, but it should be pretty quick.'

It felt odd to Janna following the progress of an animated blob that represented the imprisonment of her parents, like they'd been taken captive and placed into an online game. She didn't like the feeling; it trivialised their rough treatment. They followed the yellow blob as it moved through the city traffic until it stopped next to a building.

'Where's that?' Janna asked.

'Shit,' Kay Lee Too said. 'That's bad.'

'Where is it?' She raised her voice.

'It's the Power Corp building,' Kay Lee Too said.

'Okay, thanks.' Ahh Moss Eck shut off his display.

'Why is that bad?' Janna asked.

'I'll show you.'

chapter 17

Daxx

Daxx and Kay Lee Too travelled to the outskirts of the city, to an area of high-density residential dwellings. Kay Lee Too knocked on a nondescript door of a three-storey building that looked the same as all the others in the street. There wasn't even a colour scheme difference, the only uniqueness being an identifying mark on the wall beside each door. The front door was wrenched open. A young man glanced at Daxx, then stared at Kay Lee Too.

The man waited while Kay Lee Too swiped through his display. 'All clear,' Kay Lee Too said so quietly that Daxx, standing next to him, barely heard it.

The man took a backward step and opened the door further to let them in. 'Glad you made it.' The man shut the door. 'So, this is Daxx?' he asked Kay Lee Too, as if Daxx was a named exhibit.

'Yeah,' Kay Lee Too turned to Daxx. 'This is my friend, Well App Ell Senn. He's an illicit engineer.' Kay Lee Too laughed.

'Illicit?'

Well App Ell Senn glanced at Kay Lee Too. 'He really doesn't get it, does he. I didn't believe you.'

'He's harmless.' Kay Lee Too shrugged.

Daxx frowned. 'What don't I get?' He disliked being ignored by a Tier-Three and Tier-Four.

'He's a Tier-Four,' Kay Lee Too said, as if that should be enough explanation. He sighed. 'He can't do engineering. It's not an allowed vocation. But he's interested, and he's good at it.'

'Not as good as you,' Well App Ell Senn replied. He turned to Daxx. 'He's been teaching me; that's where the illicit comes from. I can't study it so I have to do it from home. Kay Lee Too has helped me setup a lab.'

'And that's why we're here.'

'Will you be helping us?' Daxx asked Well App Ell Senn.

Well App Ell Senn laughed. 'You guys are way out of my league. If I can help, I will. But I'll make sure nothing disturbs you. Is there anything you need right away?'

'Ah, no, at least I don't need anything.' Daxx glanced at Kay Lee Too.

Kay Lee Too placed a hand on his friend's shoulder. 'Thanks for letting us stay here. It might make a big difference.'

'Might?' Well App Ell Senn laughed. 'I expect better than that from you and a Tier-One.'

'Can we go in?'

'Sure. Nothing's changed since the last time you were here.'

A spacious room at the rear of the house had the windows sealed and covered. It was starkly furnished with a narrow waist-high bench around three walls. Workstations were placed equidistantly along the bench. They were neatly arranged. Daxx liked that. Some were stations to create and modify electronic components with microscopes; they contained fixed visual displays and machinery to manipulate objects too small to be seen with the naked eye. Others were chemical workstations with evacuation fans and gas protection, yet others were groups of instruments that Daxx didn't know the use of.

In the centre of the room was a dining table, with four chairs drawn up around it. Kay Lee Too placed his pack on the table and withdrew the sheaf of paper and pens, as well as a hand-sized, thin, rectangular, silver-coloured object. Kay Lee Too rested a finger on it. 'This is our power source. It should be enough for a few days. I use it while I'm here, so Well App Ell Senn doesn't have to pay for anything. It will power all the equipment, including your Device, if you want to talk to Janna again.'

Daxx picked up the power source, turned it around, and felt the weight of it. 'This is a battery?'

'Yeah.' Kay Lee Too grinned.

'I've never seen one this size before. I didn't know they still existed,' Daxx said. 'They're so cumbersome. Did you make this?'

'It's old technology but when you don't want to be tracked, it's what you have to use to power stuff. Ahh Moss Eck has one too. It's been recharging itself, little by little on our way here, piggy-backing on other people's power accounts. We can't charge it now, unless we take it for a walk.' He laughed.

Daxx grunted and put the battery back down on the table.

'We can't do any work using our Devices,' Kay Lee Too said. 'Although you can communicate to known Devices, like Janna's, using the VPN. We don't want anything stored on the network.'

'Paper it is,' Daxx said. 'I haven't used it since I was a child; this'll be interesting.'

Daxx sat down and withdrew a piece of paper from the pile. He picked up a pen and studied it, turning it around, then carefully placing it in his fingers like he remembered. He drew a short line on the piece of paper, then looked up in triumph at Kay Lee Too. The young man grinned and sat down.

'I didn't associate the Tier-Four and engineering connection,' Daxx said. 'It's my upbringing. I can see that now.'

It was rare for anyone to wish to do a proscribed vocation. Devrell's system had been carefully designed. Tier peer pressure and how children were raised channelled expectations. Disapproval was a higher motivating factor than punishment. Tier-Ones were not even exempt. They were allowed greater freedom of choice but, even so, could not be an engineer, for example, as much as a Tier-Four could not be. But then, no Tier-One, or Tier-Four, would want to be an engineer. It was unthinkable.

'That's our problem,' Kay Lee Too said. 'Changing that upbringing is what the Resistance is about. Tie Noo Summ has talked to us about not being offended by attitudes that people don't even know they have. They don't see how the Tier system constrains people; they've been conditioned. As a Tier-One, you don't have the interaction with others; you're not even aware that other people's lives aren't like yours. I understand.' Kay Lee Too smiled.

'Tie Noo Summ is a smart man.'

'He is,' Kay Lee Too said. 'Without him, there would be no chance for change.'

Daxx sat up straighter in his chair. He lined up the pen with the edge of the sheet of paper. 'Okay. Let's get started.'

Devices were usually minuscule implants or sometimes embedded in jewellery or, in extremely rare occurrences, like Daxx preferred, hand-held items. Devices were not battery-free, even the implanted versions. They all had a tiny rechargeable power source. Device batteries were necessary, and they were recharged by the wireless power network. They were required in cases of temporary shielding, in regional areas where the coverage was not perfect, or if a wireless power network transfer point malfunctioned. The transfer points were ubiquitous and there was overlapping saturation coverage. There was rarely a problem, because supplying power was the lynchpin of Devrell's design.

There are many ways to track people's whereabouts and many ways to charge people for essential services, but Devrell's design wrapped all the requirements in a single method. Citizens were charged and tracked as they drew, continuously, in small amounts, from the worldwide, ubiquitous power sources. It was a simple method to fund minimum services. People paid extra for non-essential services and items they desired, but everyday necessities, except for power consumption, were free. The world-wide information network used the same network as the power supply. All citizens had free access. Power, communication and connection were ubiquitous.

Janna had discovered enhanced electrochemical properties in a newly classified fungal species. An electrochemical solution containing fungal material had been used to upgrade battery technology. It increased efficiency and made smaller Devices possible. But the same fungus species had a second property, even more impressive than the electrochemical one. Janna had shown, in times of stress and low resource availability, the fungus drew power seemingly from nothing. Daxx had used Janna's discovery. It was evidence for his solutions that unified the field equations. He'd found that the universe could be described as an infinite series of orthogonal spacetimes. Daxx's theoretical work showed that the fungus could be used to provide a non-electrochemical, continuous and free power source. Power could, theoretically, be generated by each battery without the requirement of an external connection to a power source. Tracking of citizens and the existing government revenue systems would have to be revolutionised.

That revolution was Tie Noo Summ's hope and Soo's fear.

Daxx and Kay Lee Too worked with the well-known electrochemical, fungal battery. They designed extensions to the battery that attempted to distress the fungus solution and force its use of the unique energy source. Kay Lee Too built prototypes. They fizzled, sparked and melted. Nothing worked. Daxx's theoretical solution seemed impossible to implement in practice.

A revolution was not going to happen.

chapter 18

Janna

Ahh Moss Eck nodded across the street to the tallest building in the city, the tallest building on the planet. 'And…' Ahh Moss Eck paused for effect, 'that's why it's bad.'

They gawked, looking suspiciously like tourists. Janna leant backwards, her head faced the sky. She caught glimpses of the top of the building as the scattered cloud came and went, wrapping around the midsections of the building and then tearing free. She looked back down at the ground floor, after nearly toppling over, and her heart sank. Everyone who entered the building had to pass through security checks in isolatable areas. And each elevator had a security person stationed outside, re-checking credentials.

'And…' he paused yet again, 'only Tier-Ones and Tier-Twos are allowed in that way. You'd get through the first check, but then they'd ask why you were there and, I don't think, saying you're there to pick up your parents from illegal detention is going to work.'

'What do we do?' She had no idea how to get into that building and how to find out if her parents were safe. Just being close to them, having discovered where they were being held, was a triumph. But it was an inconsequential success. It didn't get her any closer to freeing them. She couldn't walk up to the security entrance; she knew Ahh Moss Eck was making light of an impossible situation. Her biometrics would identify her status and her identity. She would be detained.

'Any ideas?' she asked after Ahh Moss Eck had not responded.

'Nope,' he said. 'Let's walk the block and have a good look. There must be entrances for the lower tiers. You never know what opportunities there are until you take the time to look. But'—he nodded again to the front entrance—'we aren't going in that way.'

They walked around the building. It was a walled, secure complex that covered a city block. There were only three ways in and out, the front entrance, a rear vehicles-only entrance and another for the lower-tier workers. The rear entrance was as rigorously guarded and checked as the front entrance. There was only one possibility, the vehicle entrance.

Ahh Moss Eck opened his display and spoke to Kay Lee Too. Janna couldn't hear; he hadn't disabled encryption. He dismissed his display.

'Okay, then,' Ahh Moss Eck said. 'Kay Lee Too said, yes, he can alter his software so we can be almost invisible to the surveillance cameras at the vehicle entrance. That's the good news.'

'And the bad news?'

'He's busy working with Daxx. He can't promise having it done until tomorrow morning.'

'What do we do?' She was impatient. She had waited long enough.

'Nothing, as far as I can see. We wait. It's the only option, unless you want to give up and go back and help Daxx? We can always do that. What he's doing is pretty important.'

'No, we'll wait.' She wouldn't give up on her parents; she had to find out if they were all right, and maybe, with Ahh Moss Eck's help, she might even rescue them.

Daxx was safe, and he had a problem to work on. Apart from hiding, and the trauma of escape, his life was no different, now, than it had been before. That consoled her; she didn't have to worry about Daxx. She expected he would be working on a solution to the power problem for months. She could assist him in a few days when she returned, hopefully with her parents.

'I've got some people we can hole up with tonight. They're close,' Ahh Moss Eck said. 'If Kay Lee Too comes through quicker than expected, we can come right back here. Is that okay? Or would you rather go back to headquarters?'

'Let's stay here.'

Ahh Moss Eck's friends, also Tier-Threes, were accomodating and helpful. But they treated Janna, because of her status, with reserve. She shared a meal, but the conversation was tense and difficult. She left soon afterwards and retired to the room she had been given for the night. She contacted Daxx.

'How's it going?' she asked him.

Daxx sighed. 'Not good. Nothing works. And I can't help Kay Lee Too, I have no idea how to make these things.'

'Is Kay Lee Too having problems?'

'No, he's great. It's my designs. They aren't working. I don't know why.'

'It's early days, Daxx. You'll figure it out.'

'Anyway, how are you?' He frowned. 'Where are you? I don't recognise that room?'

'With some of Ahh Moss Eck's friends. Close to the city centre.'

'Why?'

'Why not?'

He smiled. 'No reason. Any luck with your parents?'

'No. We're waiting on Kay Lee Too to finish something for us.'

Daxx looked away from the display for a moment. 'He's pretty busy. But I'll get him to stop. Your stuff should come first.'

'No,' she half-heartedly protested.

'What do you need? Maybe I can help.'

'Software changes to Kay Lee Too's anti-surveillance system.'

Daxx smiled. 'Okay. I'm no use. But I'll get him to have a look when he's finished this next prototype.' There was a flash of light outside Janna's view. She heard swearing. 'Which...' Daxx added after glancing to his side again, 'might be now.' Daxx spoke to someone out of view. 'No good?'

She heard Kay Lee Too's voice. 'No. Stupid thing.'

'All right,' Daxx said to Janna. 'I'd better get working. And I'll get Kay Lee Too to do what you want. Does he know what you need?'

'I think so. Ahh Moss Eck asked him.'

'Okay. Sleep well.'

'You too.'

Daxx shook his head. 'Not tonight. There won't be much of that happening.' He stared at her for a moment. 'Be careful with whatever you're going to do. Don't do anything stupid.'

She laughed. 'Like you might?'

'Hey,' he protested. 'I'm still the Tier-One in this relationship. But I'm learning from Tier-Threes. It seems that being a Tier-One doesn't count for anything anymore.'

The next morning the weather had turned bad. It was warmer than the previous few days, but it rained. It was gloomy, overcast, and depressing. Ahh Moss Eck was delighted.

'This is perfect weather.' They stood on the far side of the street from the vehicle entrance. They were under cover from the downpour. 'It will help with this… I hesitate to call it a plan, but, yeah, I guess that's what it is.'

He smiled at her, and now that she was more used to him it didn't look threatening, just dangerous.

'Let's go,' he said. 'But we're going to get soaked.'

They ran across the street and to the side of the vehicle entrance. There was a little cover, enough to shield them from the rain. Janna hoped that the newly installed software was doing its job. It wouldn't be perfect, but would make their presence at the entrance difficult to observe for those monitoring surveillance cameras. They waited there.

A delivery truck trundled towards the entrance. The driver opened his window and scanned his identifier pass; he looked across and saw Ahh Moss Eck and Janna and frowned at them. Janna panicked. She thought the man would signal an alarm.

Ahh Moss Eck put his hand over his head and shrugged at the driver, signalling that they were trying to shelter from the rain. The man nodded, sharing the bond of lower tiered working people, and drove his vehicle through the entrance once it had completely opened. The security gates lowered. Before they reached the ground, Ahh Moss Eck grabbed Janna and pushed her underneath. He rolled under just before they slammed closed.

'It looks like I was wrong.' They both stood up on the inside of the building. 'We didn't get soaked.'

'That was easy,' she said.

'We need to be careful from here on in.'

'You should have been careful much earlier than this,' a voice said behind them.

Janna turned at the sound. Standing behind them was a group of security officers. Their guns were drawn.

Janna and Ahh Moss Eck were taken to the top floor. When the elevator doors opened, a young man was waiting for them. 'I'll take them from here.'

The officer who had detained Janna and Ahh Moss Eck complained. 'I should be the one to take them to Soo.'

The man stared at the officer for a long time. 'I'll take them from here.' He sounded menacing.

The officer dropped his eyes. 'Yes, Mill Nupp, of course.'

Mill Nupp turned away from the elevator. 'Come with me,' he ordered. Janna, Ahh Moss Eck, and the security detachment followed him. He halted. 'Not you,' he said to the security team, 'Just them.' He nodded at Janna and Ahh Moss Eck.

Mill Nupp led Janna and Ahh Moss Eck to an office. He held the door open and waited for them to enter.

'Sit down,' he ordered. 'You're going to be here for a while. I'm going to have to take you to Soo. There's no way out of that.' He remained by the door. He frowned and stared at them for an uncomfortably long time. He looked like a dangerous man making a decision.

'You two are causing extra problems for all of us.' Mill Nupp shut the door and locked them in.

chapter 19

Day 4. Daxx

Daxx sat at the table in the middle of the lab, his head in his hands. He never worked like this. He worked hard when inspiration struck him, but not when a problem was intractable. When that happened, he would seek distraction, mostly spending time with Janna. He thought about her and wondered what she was doing that morning. He thought about calling her. Kay Lee Too swore. Daxx smelt something burning, and there was the sound of sparking. He lifted his head from his hands.

'That doesn't work either.' Kay Lee Too sat at one of the workstations on the bench around the edge of the room. He surveyed the wreckage in front of him. He sighed, and his body slumped.

Daxx shook his head. He was disheartened as well as tired. He wondered if there was an engineering solution. He stood up, stretched, and went to the workstation with the recent wreckage. He touched Kay Lee Too on the shoulder. 'We'll figure it out,' he said, trying to impart optimism that he didn't feel.

'There's no efficient way to distress the fungus,' Kay Lee Too said. 'I can't do it. The electrochemical reaction keeps getting in the way.'

Daxx was silent for a moment. 'Maybe we don't.'

'Don't what?'

'Be efficient.' Daxx's eyes lit up. 'We create an inefficient solution. We keep it as an electrochemical battery. All the output comes from that, just like normal. A firmware change could stress the fungal components.' Daxx smiled. 'It remains just a battery, which is not what we wanted, except the power source is unlimited. What do you think?'

Kay Lee Too stared vacantly at Daxx. 'I think I can do that.' He laughed. 'We've been trying to be perfect, haven't we?'

Daxx nodded. 'It's a messy solution. It would be nice to keep away from electrochemical reactions, but'—Daxx shrugged—'this will work for now. As long as you can write that software.'

Kay Lee Too rushed to the table. He grabbed a piece of paper and a pen as he sat down. He muttered under his breath as he drew a diagram. He wrote a few dozen lines of code underneath, then laughed. 'What do you think about that?' Kay Lee Too pushed the paper across the table to show Daxx.

They heard the muffled sound of the doorbell and then loud knocking on the outside door. Well App Ell Senn's footsteps sounded as he moved towards the front door. Daxx went to open their door to see what was happening, but Kay Lee Too stopped him. He shook his head, telling Daxx to keep quiet. They heard raised voices. The yelling stopped suddenly. A gun sounded and was followed by a thud.

Daxx wrenched the door open. A policeman's body lay on the floor. Well App Ell Senn stood over him. He held a gun. Kay Lee Too pushed Daxx out of the way and ran to the fallen policeman. He crouched over him.

'He's dead,' Well App Ell Senn said, as a matter of fact.

Kay Lee Too stood up. 'Why?'

'I had no choice,' he said. 'He said he wanted to come in. I said no, he said yes. He was going to search the house. A neighbour complained about the all-night work; I didn't think we made any noise. And there has been no registered Device activity here. We'll have to fix that omission.'

Daxx thought he was going to be physically sick. He wrenched his eyes away from the dead man; it was too much to handle. He looked outside through the open front door. He took a sharp intake of breath.

'What?' Well App Ell Senn asked.

Daxx kept looking outside. Well App Ell Senn pulled the front door fully open. 'Shit.' He shook his head. He sighed, moved outside the door, looked up and down the street, then lifted his weapon.

'No.' Daxx raced towards the door. Kay Lee Too stepped in front of Daxx, barring his way.

Well App Ell Senn fired and the nosy neighbour, standing outside having accompanied the policeman to see the result of his complaint, fell to the ground dead. His open umbrella rolled away, then rocked side to side as gusts of wind took it.

Well App Ell Senn and Kay Lee Too dragged the man's body inside. They placed it next to the policeman and closed the front door. Daxx felt dizzy and placed his hand against the wall of the hallway. He couldn't stop staring at the two bodies. It took all his will to not faint. Eventually, he looked away, hunched over, and placed his hands on his knees. He took deep breaths, but they didn't help.

'You have to go, now,' Well App Ell Senn said.

Daxx wondered if he might fall over if he didn't also have his hands on his legs to brace himself. He tried to stand up straight and, sort of, succeeded except for a wobble. He turned around, then he saw the bodies again. They lay on the floor like they were discarded things. He was certain that sight would haunt him for the rest of his life. Daxx reached out a hand to the wall and steadied himself again. He breathed slowly and deeply. But no matter how he tried, when he looked towards Well App Ell Senn, the bodies were in his peripheral vision. He looked away and at Kay Lee Too.

'Shit.' Kay Lee Too's hands frantically smoothed the hair on his head as he stared at the bodies.

'You have to go now,' Well App Ell Senn said. 'The police will be here soon. They'll know this guy is dead.' He pointed at the policeman's body. Daxx didn't look.

'Yes, yes, you're right.' Kay Lee Too looked up from the floor and at Well App Ell Senn. 'What about you?'

Well App Ell Senn shrugged. 'There's not a lot I can do, is there? I'm fucked. It's my house. But you don't need to be here.'

'I'm so sorry,' Kay Lee Too said. 'Are you sure?'

Well App Ell Senn frowned. 'Just go.'

Kay Lee Too nodded. He turned to Daxx. He took a deep breath. 'We should go.'

'Go where?'

Well App Ell Senn grabbed Daxx and pulled him to the door. He pushed Daxx outside. Kay Lee Too followed without being pushed. Well App Ell Senn slammed the door behind them. It was raining heavily. It was a gloomy, depressing morning that Daxx would have welcomed sitting in his office at work. It was exceptionally unpleasant being outside in that weather.

Daxx stood outside the front door, bedraggled and dripping. He was already soaked.

chapter 20

Soo

Soo's Device chimed a communication request. She accepted, and a man's face appeared on her display. 'Yes, inspector.'

'I thought you'd want to see this.'

'What is it?'

'We've found Daxx.'

'Do you have him in custody?'

'No, we've seen what we think is his image in surveillance data as he left a building. We were investigating the death of a policeman. The property belongs to a Tier-Four, but we discovered a room full of odd equipment. Would you like to see?'

'Yes.'

The Inspector walked down a passageway, then through a door. He halted just inside and showed Soo the interior.

'That's an engineering laboratory,' she said. 'And you said the property was owned by a Tier-Four?'

'Yes.'

'Where is the owner?'

'The place was empty when we arrived. We're attempting to track the owner, but we're not successful, which is an another odd thing.'

'Why?'

The inspector's face reappeared on Soo's display. He shrugged. 'He has no current tracking data. His last location was here.'

Soo was silent for a moment. 'That is odd,' she said. 'Stay there. Don't touch anything. I want to see it for myself.'

She summoned Mill Nupp. 'Get transport. Now.'

'What about Janna?'

'She's secure, isn't she? Tell me you're able to do that, at least.'

'Yes, Soo.'

Soo strode to the door of her office. She stopped next to him and frowned. 'Shouldn't you be getting the transport?' She brushed past him and out the door. Mill Nupp scurried behind, his display activated.

She waited outside the nondescript door on the nondescript street and looked one way and then the other. It was so drab; it was so ordered and uniform. She loved it. Not as a place to live for herself, but she loved the efficiency of close living and minimal utilisation of space for the lower Tiers. Mill Nupp stood next to her. He held an umbrella over her head. It was pouring rain.

Soo disliked weather. The chaotic, uncontrolled feel of it grated against her instinct for order. She had spent her life at the top of a social system where a hierarchy of control was at the core. Being in control was everything to her, and she had worked hard towards being the one with absolute authority. She had had mentors. She had cultivated relationships for their usefulness. She had been successful. The social system was hers to steer. But she inherited problems. Unlike the weather, disorder was anathema to Devrell's design, and the policeman's death was an excessive example of a sickness in the Tier system. It had changed from its initial purity. There was an illness in society that she had been promoted to cure. Daxx's removal was the first step. She was pleased at the policeman's death; it would help her. But requiring any help at all was surprising. Daxx's removal had become annoyingly troublesome. She didn't know if the missteps were deep-seated issues or were the incompetence of the staff she had inherited. It would be easier to fix the latter, although it required her personal intervention—like suffering the foul, chaotic weather to visit a crime scene that should not require her presence.

'I think it's beginning to let up,' Mill Nupp said.

She looked at him with surprise; she had forgotten anyone was close by. He had been by her side, with the umbrella, from the moment she had stepped out of the vehicle that had brought them there.

'What?'

'The rain,' he said. 'The rain is beginning to stop.'

She strode up the stairs and into the house. Mill Nupp scuttled after her, trying to keep the umbrella over her.

The bodies had been removed, which annoyed her, but she saw the outlines drawn in place. There was a smattering of bloodstains. The police officers and the investigators looked up when she entered. They had been warned of her arrival. They had been silent when she entered, and they remained so. They stood around, nervously waiting for any command. She didn't particularly like that people were afraid of her, but she loved the power of authority, and fear was an affirmation of that power.

One of the investigators, a brave man, stepped forward and began telling her how the bodies were found and their placement. She glanced at him. He was a Tier-Three. She turned her back on him while he was talking. 'Where's the Inspector?' she asked Mill Nupp.

He looked surprised at a question he would not have known the answer to. He looked at the man who had spoken and repeated Soo's request.

'In there.' The man pointed to a door.

Soo strode into the lab. Mill Nupp trotted along behind her, the soaking umbrella stowed just inside the front door. A rivulet of water flowed from it, following the tiny undulations in the flooring. Some of the water reached the bloodstains, and the resultant solution crept over the floor.

She halted just through the door. The Inspector sat at the table in the centre of the room. He stood up.

'Soo.'

'Impressive.' She looked around the room. 'Do you know what they were working on?'

'No,' the Inspector said. 'We haven't looked closely, because you told us to not touch anything.'

Soo nodded. 'Good.' She turned to Mill Nupp. 'Get some engineers in here.'

Mill Nupp nodded. He opened his display and spoke to it.

She walked to the table in the middle of the room. Paper lay on the tabletop. She picked up a sheet. It had incomprehensible drawings on it. There was also some text, but it wasn't a language.

'They had paper,' she said, stating the obvious. She turned to Mill Nupp. 'Do you know how unusual that is?'

'Yes, Soo.'

She frowned at his simple answer. 'Do you really know how unusual that is?'

'I assume they were using it so none of their work was stored online.'

She nodded. It was a smart move, and beyond what she would have expected of lower tiers. She assumed it had been Daxx's suggestion. She had learnt to write as a child; all Tier-Ones did, it was part of their education. But she had been introduced to the beauty of writing by a mentor when she was a young woman. It had been his passion, and he had passed it on to his student. He had shown her the classically correct hand positions. He had made her practice so she built strength in her fingers and wrist to be able to sustain a long session of writing. It was terribly inefficient as a means of communication. Device technology had removed the requirement for writing generations ago. It was a skill that few had; even Tier-Ones stopped writing once schooling completed. She loved the private feeling of being privy to an elite, ancient practice. She tried to write every day, even if it was only doodles. It was her escape time—the concentration required to write meant she couldn't, for a moment, think of anything else. It helped clear her mind.

Her mentor had been the only one with whom she shared that ancient pastime. She had never found another who shared her interest. His death had been a loss. Even though she had ordered him killed.

'Paper is hard to come by, very hard.' Soo said. 'You could trace the source. You could start with my supplier. We might find who has been setting all this up.' She waved her hand towards the equipment in the room.

'Yes, Soo.'

Soo stared at Mill Nupp. Perhaps she did expect too much from him. There was the problem, she realised. She expected a Tier-Two to think like a Tier-One. Even someone in Mill Nupp's position was constrained by their upbringing. Perhaps the Daxx problem had been exacerbated by Mill Nupp's attitude masquerading as inefficiency, or perhaps his determination to maintain the methods of her predecessor. She decided that greater personal intervention was required. Although it couldn't be an ongoing solution.

'No. I'll contact my supplier myself,' she said. 'You make sure this is all taken care of. Don't let the police touch any of it.'

She strode out of the room. Mill Nupp hurried behind her. She passed the officers near the front door, ignoring them. She walked outside before Mill Nupp could retrieve the umbrella. She waited outside the door. The rain had let up. Mill Nupp tried to open the umbrella and place it over her head, but she pushed him away.

'Stay here and tidy this up,' she said to the young man as she walked towards the waiting vehicle.

She was worried but satisfied that some progress had been made. She had Janna in custody, she could draw Daxx out of hiding that way, but she suspected she had a bigger problem. Daxx had received sophisticated assistance. There were others that understood the danger that Daxx represented. Her fear was that they didn't view it as a danger. Perhaps they saw Daxx as an opportunity. She could not believe that Tier-Ones could be involved; the sickness could not have extended that far. But that meant lower tiers had the knowledge and foresight to disrupt. The group assisting Daxx had to be found. They had to be neutralised, then destroyed.

She had noticed the small rectangular object sitting on the table. She knew it was a battery. She knew the lab must have been used to work on the thing that could destroy the Tier system, destroy her position and control. She wondered how far the experiments had progressed. She shivered. The problem had become more complex, and the danger to herself had increased.

The rainy, gloomy day perfectly matched her mood.

chapter 21

Daxx

Kay Lee Too and Daxx stood outside the door to Well App Ell Senn's house. They were both soaked by the rain.

'Give me your Device,' Kay Lee Too demanded.

'Why?'

'Daxx, please.'

Daxx fished his Device out of a pocket.

Kay Lee Too swiped through the display, then handed it back. He had activated the cloaking software. 'That won't help much,' Kay Lee Too said. 'They'll be able to see the two people who left on the surveillance cameras, but it's something.'

Kay Lee Too led Daxx down the street. They hurried until they came to a commercial area. Kay Lee Too led them through a shop to a laneway. They went into the back entrance of a cafe on the far side, then through it and out to a busy, covered walkway. Daxx didn't think Kay Lee Too's zig-zag movements through retailers made much sense. It was a panicked move. If nothing else, their progress was marked by the trail of water as they dripped. Daxx pulled Kay Lee Too to a halt.

'What are we doing? Where are we going?' Daxx asked.

Kay Lee Too shook his head. 'I have no idea.' He looked at Daxx like he was pleading for help. Daxx understood that he was. For all the aspirations for equality, a lifetime of training was impossible to dismiss. The Tier-Three wanted the Tier-One to take control.

'We should find somewhere, obvious but inconspicuous. We need to figure out what to do,' Daxx suggested. 'We have to stop panicking.'

They found a bench inside a busy shopping mall. They looked like two people who had misjudged the severity of the weather and were waiting while others shopped. They didn't talk for a long while. Daxx stared at the floor, at his hands, and then at the passersby. Other people still had ordinary lives; it was comforting to know that was still possible.

He thought of contacting Janna. He wanted to share his distress, but it was a selfish thought. It would serve no purpose other than to console him and upset her. Many people had been killed in the last few days; the two recent deaths weren't anything new. Although, the policeman's death was more his direct responsibility than the innocent bystanders at the commuter station. And even more so, the neighbour who had been killed for no reason. He shook his head, wondering why being killed for no reason, rather than just being killed, made any difference. It wouldn't make any difference to the neighbour's family. He wondered what he could have done that would have left those people alive.

He had retrieved his Device after the initial thought of contacting Janna. He stared at it. He fell back onto a lifetime of upbringing, like how Kay Lee Too had expected Daxx's assistance. Daxx had someone he had relied on as a child. Someone who had always taken charge. The influences of childhood were as impossible to overcome as the expectations of the Tier system. Daxx's older brother had taken charge of Daxx's life more often than Daxx wished. Perhaps this was one moment when his brother's annoying behaviour could be beneficial.

Daxx wanted to talk, as if sharing his circumstances would make things better, even fix things. He wanted to hand over responsibility. He was too upset and confused to make good decisions. He grimaced as he thought that his mind was unreliable. It was his strength, but it was failing. However, he did know that any decision-making would be unreliable. That was a decision in itself, which reassured him. His critical faculties were not completely compromised.

His brother was impossible to talk to at the best of times. When there was no contention, his brother manufactured it. Daxx, without fail, became angry when he spoke to his brother. At the moment, he didn't believe he had emotional space to include anger alongside fear and anxiety. His brother was not a reassuring, consoling person. He was controlling and judgemental. Daxx felt like a child every time they talked. But still, being a little brother at that moment may not be such a bad thing. He was in an uncontrolled situation; he couldn't see his way out. Maybe turning to someone who was overbearing and dogmatic was what was required.

Daxx almost moved his hand to request the connection to his brother.

'Why don't we go back?' Daxx asked.

'There's a protocol,' Kay Lee Too said. 'Although we've never had to use it.'

'Which is?'

'If you're being chased, don't lead people back to the headquarters.'

Daxx frowned. 'But you broke that rule, with Janna and me.'

Kay Lee Too nodded. 'I know. I don't want to go through that again. Tie Noo Summ was really angry.'

'We don't know what to do. We should ask him.'

'Of course. I'll contact him. He'll know.' Kay Lee Too shook his head. 'I should have done that first. But, I've never been in a situation like this. I'm unused to people being killed. I'm the engineer; I make stuff. I don't kill people.'

'You didn't kill them.' Daxx tried to sound consoling. He nodded towards Kay Lee Too's wrist. 'Call him.'

Tie Noo Summ knew what was happening. He had been contacted by Well App Ell Senn. A Tier-Four was thinking clearly while a Tier-Three and a Tier-One were not. Signs of the Tier system's breakdown were everywhere, Daxx thought.

'Don't compromise anyone else.' Tie Noo Summ sounded calm. 'But, also, don't risk yourselves. I'll send you an address. Wait there. I'll contact you later today.'

Kay Lee Too nodded at his display. Tie Noo Summ frowned, then looked pointedly at Daxx. 'Do you both understand?'

Daxx nodded. Kay Lee Too said, 'Yes.'

'Good.' Tie Noo Summ disconnected the call.

Kay Lee Too looked at Daxx. He sighed heavily. 'Pretty simple, really.' He smiled. 'We should have thought of that.'

'But…' Daxx took a deep breath and let it out slowly. He sat up straight. He wanted more than their immediate problems solved. Running and hiding were short-term solutions. 'There is one person I could call.' Daxx hesitated. 'I have a brother, an older brother.'

'What could he do?'

Daxx frowned. 'He's a Tier-One,' Daxx said. 'He can do anything.' Daxx still believed any situation could be solved by the intervention of a Tier-One. Not him, of course; he was compromised. Daxx's Device was still in his hand. He raised it.

'Wait on.' Kay Lee Too reached over and swiped through the display. 'Now it's okay to use.'

Daxx called his brother. He waited for a long time before there was a reply.

'Yes?' His brother's face softened, but only slightly. 'Daxx?'

'Renn.'

'This isn't your ID.'

'No.' His brother was critical already. Daxx almost disconnected; it would end up like all their other conversations. He'd feel angry and belittled. Renn looked vaguely angry. Daxx thought he was waiting for an apology for being called on an unknown ID. Daxx shook his head. 'I need your help, Renn.'

To Renn's credit, he didn't gloat. He looked surprised. 'Where are you? You look soaked.'

Daxx looked away from the display. 'I'm in a shopping mall.'

Renn frowned. 'And what problem do you have in a shopping mall that I can help you with?' Renn looked somewhere between puzzled and annoyed.

'No, the shopping mall isn't the problem. It's what caused me to be here.'

'Go on.'

Daxx didn't know how to go on. He didn't know how to explain what had happened. 'The authorities are trying to kill Janna and me.' That was it, as unlikely as it sounded.

'Don't be stupid,' Renn said. 'I don't have time for games, Daxx. What do you want? Instead of sitting around shopping malls, you should go and visit Dad. He keeps asking after you.'

Daxx didn't want to have that argument, yet again. He couldn't forgive his father. Visiting him was out of the question.

'It's true. Check the news feeds. Janna's parents were taken into custody a couple of days ago—that was because of me.'

'I did see that,' Renn said after a moment. His anger had gone, and he looked reflective. 'I always thought your relationship with Janna would lead you to problems. I almost called you but, well…'

'Yeah, I know.'

'You think that has to do with you?'

'Yes.'

'Why?'

'I've been working on some things that could cause problems.'

'That makes no sense.' Renn sounded annoyed again.

'I've seen people die. A lot of people. A policeman was killed.'

'You killed a policeman?'

'I haven't killed anyone,' Daxx said. 'But, I have been responsible for people dying.'

Renn sighed. Daxx thought he looked very tired, like he already had too many problems and another one had been thrust upon him. It was probably true. Daxx had been a bad brother, but his excuse was that absence and withdrawal were normal within his family. Renn was the exception.

'Tell me what you think has happened.' Daxx saw his brother's resignation, that he would accept Daxx's problems as his own. Daxx was grateful; it was the point of the call after all.

Renn shook his head at the end of Daxx's story. 'It still doesn't make any sense. That doesn't happen to a Tier-One, not even a Tier-Two would get that treatment, but, yes, I agree, I've seen what happened to Janna's parents.'

'Thanks, Renn.' Daxx meant it. He was surprised at the genuine gratitude he felt.

'Janna isn't with you?'

'No,' Daxx said. 'Just a Tier-Three who's helping me.' Daxx glanced at Kay Lee Too. 'Janna traced her parents to the Power Corp building.'

'All right. I'm close by. I'll see what they say. I'm sure it won't be anything that can't be easily fixed.'

'Thanks Renn.'

'Don't worry, little brother, I'll take care of it.'

It was what Daxx wished for, and dreaded.

chapter 22

Janna

J anna hated Soo's office. The height, the isolation, even the view, which was amazing, looked manufactured and artificial. She felt unsafe. The rain had stopped, but the wind was strong. Sometimes a gust would angle across a projection from the building and make a groaning noise that sounded like pain.

After waiting for hours, Janna and Ahh Moss Eck had been led to Soo's office and placed in chairs facing her desk. Security men were stationed inside by the door.

'Where are my parents and who are you?' The worry and concern edging her voice, making it sound strident and harsh. She cleared her throat after speaking almost as an apology for the disrespect.

Soo put her pen down; she had been writing. She stared at Janna for a moment. She glanced at Ahh Moss Eck then looked back at Janna. Her face was calm and harsh. Janna could see the woman expected a more respectful tone from a Tier-Two. Janna couldn't help but look from the woman's face to the paper on the desktop. She wrenched her eyes from the paper and back to Soo's face. Janna glowered, angry that she had been distracted.

'I'm in charge,' Soo said, quietly, evenly.

'In charge of what?' Janna's voice again was too harsh.

Soo's face brightened with the hint of a smile. 'Everything.'

'Then where are my parents?'

'They're safe.'

'So you did take them? It was you?'

'Who is the other one?' Soo asked Mill Nupp.

'His name is Ahh Moss Eck…'

Soo lost interest after the first syllable. 'I've always thought…' Soo interrupted. She stood up. She placed her hands on the desk and looked down at Janna. 'That biology was a singular mistake in the Messiah's design. He shouldn't have allowed it to be a shared profession between Tier-One and Tier-Two. Any sharing across Tier boundaries is a bad thing.'

Janna gritted her teeth. Soo was goading her, but she wouldn't be distracted. 'I want to see my parents.'

'And Daxx's younger sister was the most promising, recent genius. Her disappearance was such a shame.'

Janna articulated each word. 'I want to see my parents.' She thought about standing up as well, nullifying Soo's height intimidation. Janna gripped the sides of her chair. She took some tension in her arms but didn't raise herself.

'Hmm,' Soo said. 'Do you think Daxx was subconsciously replacing his sister with you?'

'I want to see my parents. Is that request too hard for you to understand?'

Ahh Moss Eck shuffled in his seat. Even he was uncomfortable with how Janna was talking to a Tier-One. Soo smiled. It was an interrogation method, to annoy the subject, but Janna couldn't help herself.

'Your parents are irrelevant.' Soo took her hands off the desk and stood up straight. She looked away from Janna, and out the window and over the city. 'Your movements have been closely followed ever since you entered your parents' street. We were hoping you would lead us to Daxx, but this is just as good.' Soo smiled at Janna and glanced at Ahh Moss Eck.

Janna drew breath to speak. Soo raised her hand as if she was warding off the words to come. 'Yes, yes, yes, your parents. You'll see them as soon as I let you. Don't keep on with the same question; all it will do is annoy me.'

Janna's mouth remained open for a moment before she shut it again.

'That's better.'

'Is this about Tier transgression?' Janna shook her head. 'I can't believe anyone would go to this much trouble for something that's not their business.'

'Everything is my business. But, if you want to believe that Tier transgression is the primary cause of your situation, go ahead. It is certainly one of the problems. Daxx is the major headache, but there are many other issues to be rectified.' Soo continued. 'Let me tell you where the real problem lies. Your parents and community have not instilled an appreciation of the boundaries. Although, to be fair, Tier-Ones should share some of that failure.' Soo stared at Janna for a moment. 'We've been allowed to drift, as a society, and that's what causes these problems.' Soo smiled at Janna.

Janna hated her at the moment. She hadn't before then. The act and the reason were different in Janna's mind. Soo's purpose made it personal.

'But,' Soo went on. 'Our current problem is not about a Tier transgression. We know what Daxx has been working on. His work is not something I wish to be completed.'

Janna shook her head. She narrowed her eyes.

'The Power Corp can't let that work be completed, let alone become available,' Soo said.

'Why didn't you just ask him?' she said. 'He would have stopped.'

'Would you have?' Soo continued before Janna replied. 'He wouldn't. We cannot leave anything to chance. What you suggest is the way things used to be done, and it's led to regression, like your little Tier transgression issue. It's a systemic problem that needs a systemic solution. Removing Daxx is the first of many problems. Although…' she stared at Mill Nupp, 'there are implementation issues.'

Conveniently, for Mill Nupp, his Device chimed a notification. He quickly opened his display. He looked relieved as he excused himself from the room. Soo watched him shut the door behind him.

'What happens?' Janna asked. 'We get banished, do we?' Janna was incredulous that she had said that. She was surprised that she didn't feel more panic.

Soo shook her head and sat down behind her desk. 'Those, older, methods no longer work.' Soo looked up at Janna and frowned.

'So what happens then?'

'Tier transgression is a serious offence; it's a tenet of the Messiah's teachings.'

Mill Nupp opened the door, came in and shut it behind him. 'Soo?' he said.

'What?' Soo barked.

'There's a Tier-One here, and he insists on seeing you,' Mill Nupp said. 'I said you were busy, then I said I'd check when you were available. He won't leave.'

Soo sighed. 'Tell him to go away.'

Mill Nupp glanced at his feet and then looked up again. 'I can't say that to a Tier-One.'

The office door opened. Mill Nupp jumped out of the way. A man entered the room and frowned at Mill Nupp. He glanced at the security men, then glared at Soo sitting behind her desk.

Janna turned to look at the man.

'Renn?'

chapter 23

Renn

Renn frowned at the unhelpful assistant, glanced at the surprisingly armed security people, and then stared at the woman sitting behind the large desk. He turned his head at the sound of his name. He was surprised to see Janna sitting in a chair. He wondered at his luck. His promise to his brother could be satisfied immediately. That was how it should be; he was a Tier-One after all. He smiled at Janna, then looked back at the woman behind the desk. He noticed the size of the office and the view behind her. He imagined himself sitting behind that desk, elevated above the rest of the city, able to oversee all problems with one glance. Even the wind buffeting against the building was invigorating. Renn could imagine it eliminating problems in its gusting cleanliness. He had a deep-seated need to fix other's problems. He'd had a narrow focus until then. His aspirations changed. He wanted that office; he wanted that position. He was naive enough to believe he could obtain it.

'Yes?' The woman behind the desk sounded angry.

Renn met her eyes. He didn't flinch. Her anger was surprising. A Tier-One could interrupt anyone else, even another Tier-One, if they had a legitimate concern. But he hadn't explained himself yet, so there was a momentary justification to her mood. He smiled at her as a signal that he forgave her social transgression.

'I came here to see if you could help with Janna and her parents. And I see that you can.' Renn looked around for somewhere to sit. There wasn't a spare chair.

Soo looked from Renn to Janna and then back again. 'Oh,' she said. 'Daxx's brother.'

'Of course,' Renn said. 'He asked me to find out what happened to Janna's parents and why, as he believes, people have been trying to hurt him.'

'They are, Renn,' Janna said. 'And she's keeping us here.' Janna pointed a finger at Soo.

Renn scowled. He was upset that Janna interrupted a Tier-One's conversation with another. Nonetheless, it was a valid concern and the reason he was there. 'Why would she think that?'

'Because it's true,' Soo said.

'It's not a Tier transgression issue, is it?'

'Partially.'

'That's nonsense,' Renn said. 'It is serious, I warned him. But why would anyone harm a Tier-One?'

Soo stood, she walked around her desk. 'It's one of the tenants of the Faith. There are extreme elements.'

'Why is this anything to do with you and Power Corp?' Renn looked puzzled.

Soo smiled. 'Power Corp has a duty, and I, as a Tier-One, have an obligation to protect and maintain order. You would understand that.'

'Of course,' Renn said.

'What do you know about what Daxx's been working on?'

'Nothing, until today. He told me it was something dangerous, although I doubt that.'

Soo waited for a moment. 'His work could be disruptive,' she said. 'We've tried to bring Daxx in and talk to him. That didn't work'—she glanced at Mill Nupp—'so we used Janna's parents.' She glanced at Janna. 'I was about to ask her where Daxx was, hopefully get her to contact him and ask him to come and talk to us.'

'Why didn't you ask me?'

Soo turned to Mill Nupp. 'When did the brothers last talk?'

'Three months ago,' Mill Nupp said.

'You're tracking my conversations?'

'Of course.' Soo frowned at Renn.

The conversation was slipping out of Renn's control. Soo wasn't treating him as an equal. It was the first time that had happened outside of childhood. It left him confused. He frowned.

Soo stared at Renn for a moment. 'But, now you know where he is, that makes our job much easier.'

'I don't know where he is. He called me and asked for help. I didn't believe that he had a problem.'

'He does.'

Soo waved her arm at Mill Nupp. 'Can you take Janna and this man'— she pointed at Ahh Moss Eck—'to their accommodation?'

Mill Nupp told the security people to escort Janna out of the office.

'Where are they taking us?' Janna sounded worried. 'I'm not going anywhere until I'm told where my parents are?'

'Where are you taking her?' Renn asked Soo.

'To a safe place within the building.'

'Why are you keeping her here at all?'

'She broke into the most secure building on the planet. We need to find out how that was achieved to stop it from happening again. We could ask her now, and you could wait, if you prefer?'

'Is that true?' Renn asked Janna.

Janna nodded. 'It was the only way to find out about my parents.'

'Apparently not,' Renn said. 'I'm here. You could have asked me.' The situation had become messy and unpleasant. Renn believed problems required minimal attention from a Tier-One before they vanished. He was failing to make a difference. He expected quicker results.

Janna stared at Renn for a moment, then dropped her eyes. 'Yes, I could have.'

'And who are you?' Renn nodded at Ahh Moss Eck.

'Ahh Moss Eck.'

'And you came here with Janna? You got her in?'

'Yes.'

Renn agreed with Soo. Rule breaking had to be investigated. He turned to Soo. 'Will you guarantee that she'll be safe? And her parents will be released?'

'Of course.' She nodded towards the guards. One of them opened the door, the other moved next to Janna.

'Renn?' Janna said.

'I'll take care of everything, Janna. There's nothing you can do as a Tier-Two.' Janna refused to get out of the chair. 'It'll be fine,' he reassured her. 'Just go with them for now. I'll tell Daxx what's happening.'

Janna stopped at the door. She looked over her shoulder at Renn. 'Find out about my parents. Please?'

Mill Nupp shut the door as he left with Janna, Ahh Moss Eck, and the guards.

Renn sat in the chair Janna had vacated. Soo sighed and sat down again behind the desk.

'Are you telling me that some elements in the Faith are trying to hurt my brother?' Renn said. 'I've never heard of that happening before.'

'Times change. And they have changed.' Soo picked up her pen. 'Can I help you with anything else?'

'Times don't change.' Renn ignored the dismissal. He was disappointed by Soo's response. Devrell's teachings said otherwise. 'It's the reason the system works so well.'

'That's quaint. You think the system works well?'

She was unlike any other Tier-One he had known. She was unhelpful, evasive, and aloof. She questioned the heart of his beliefs, the order and stability of the Tier system. Minor transgressions were part of any set of rules—that was how free-thinking sentient beings lived; there were always variances. The essential part of Devrell's design was how those differences were policed. If punishments were harsh, dissent was reinforced. But if valid grievances were acted upon and spurious ones quietly removed, then the system remained in balance. It was Devrell's way. It had remained a robust social system for over three hundred years. No Tier-One, that Renn knew or had heard of, had ever complained about the essential design of the system. And yet, a Tier-One in Soo's position was openly doing so. Any lower-tiered person would not last long saying such things. Renn didn't know how to reply to Soo. It was like someone believed breathing was not a working system. He just stared at her; his face was set hard with incomprehension.

'If you could contact your brother and suggest that he come here, then we can sort this problem out. Can you do that?'

Renn shook his head. She was telling him what to do. She was impossible. 'No,' Renn said. 'I won't. I can't. I'd have to wait until he contacts me.'

They stared at each other. He saw the annoyance on her face; it reflected his own. Her attitude was odd and confusing. She stood, then walked to the door. Renn remained seated and watched her. 'If there's nothing else, I have the largest corporation on the planet to run.' She opened the door.

Renn stood. He was puzzled at being dismissed, like he was of low status. He shook his head and walked to the door.

'Thank you for your time.' Renn tried to sound insulting.

'Yes.' Soo closed the door on him.

chapter 24

Janna

Janna left Soo's office too easily, she thought. She should have refused to leave without more information about her parents. She was a conditioning result of the Tier system. There was an expectation of subservience. Renn would act in her best interests. He would find out what he could. He would help. He would fix their problems. However, Soo had treated them all, including Renn, without respect. That was unsettling and confusing.

Mill Nupp accompanied her, Ahh Moss Eck and the security guards to the elevators.

'I thought I'd made it clear that there were to be no weapons on this floor?' Mill Nupp said to the guards.

'Yes, Mill Nupp,' one of the guards said. 'But, Soo…'

'Who do you report to?'

The guards were silent for a moment. They glanced at each other. 'You,' one of them said.

'Precisely.' Mill Nupp held out his hands to them. 'Give them to me.'

'What?' the guard asked.

Mill Nupp frowned. 'Did you not hear? I'll take them. Now.'

'But, we're leaving anyway.' The guard looked confused.

Mill Nupp sighed. He didn't say anything. He stared at them. The guards shrugged and handed over their weapons. 'Good.' He turned to Janna. 'I'll see what I can do to get your parents released.'

Janna nodded. 'Thank you.' She was polite—another conditioned response.

The elevator doors opened. The guards, Janna and Ahh Moss Eck entered. As the doors shut, Janna noticed Mill Nupp staring at Ahh Moss Eck.

The elevator dropped. Ahh Moss Eck elbowed the security guard behind him in the face and turned and knocked him unconscious with a blow with his other arm. The man in front of Janna, who had been facing away, turned at the grunt and collapse noises behind him. Ahh Moss Eck pushed Janna out the way. He swung his arm and broke the man's nose.

'Damn.' Ahh Moss Eck wrung his hand. 'That was a bad hit.' He swung his other arm and knocked that man unconscious, too. He carefully flexed his sore hand, testing for pain. He shook it, and that seemed to fix it.

'What are you doing?'

'We aren't going anywhere near... accommodation, boss.' He emphasised the word accommodation with air quotes. He pressed the stop button on the elevator controls, and it bumped violently to a halt.

Janna was aghast. The bloodied security people took up most of the floor space. 'What do we do then?' She felt ill with the sight of blood and the threat of violence.

'We get out of this elevator and then we get out of this building,' Ahh Moss Eck said, as if escape was simply a matter of movement. He pushed a button for a floor well above ground, and the elevator resumed. 'I just hope there's no one waiting outside when the doors open; otherwise it's going to get a bit messy.'

The doors opened and Ahh Moss Eck stuck his head out and looked both ways. There was no one right there. It was an open office space, people worked nearby. He stepped out, told Janna to do the same, then stepped back inside. He pressed the door-close button and quickly stepped out to stand by Janna. The doors slid closed.

'Now we need a plan.' Ahh Moss Eck grinned. 'Any ideas?'

'No.' She was surprised to be asked. 'You're the one with experience.'

'Not so much inside Power Corp headquarters, though. Other places, sure.' People began to notice them standing by the elevator. 'We should keep moving, maybe try to find a way towards the basement exit.'

'Why didn't we just take the elevator there?'

'Because that's where we were going, and there will be people expecting our guard friends and us.' He nodded at the elevator door. He took Janna by the shoulder and pushed her away. It felt odd and invasive being told what to do and physically manhandled by a Tier-Three. 'They'll be looking for us soon.'

They walked quickly through the open office towards a far door. Janna smiled at office workers who noticed them, surprised at the unknown visitors.

'Can I help you?' one of them said. He frowned and began to rise from his seat.

'My name is Janna,' she said as she kept moving. She smiled at him. 'We're fine, but thank you.'

The man blanched at the Tier-Two name and quickly sat down again. He tentatively returned her smile before returning to his work.

'Good thinking, boss,' Ahh Moss Eck whispered.

They reached the far doors and Janna felt elated, like they'd already completed their escape. Ahh Moss Eck opened the doors, shepherded Janna through, glanced back at the office then shut the doors behind him. The doors led to an enclosed passageway, transparent on all sides. It led across an open space to a separate building.

The Power Corp complex took up a complete city block. It was contained within an external facade. Inside the space, buildings were separated, with open spaces between them. The buildings joined into a single structure a hundred storeys overhead. Similar transparent walkways were both above and below them. Every floor was connected to the next building. Other buildings were similarly interconnected. The internal space was a warren of elevated, transparent lattices.

They began walking across the walkway. Ahh Moss Eck grunted. 'Not many hiding places here. We should get across to the other building quickly.'

Janna looked through the walkway to the ground. It was a tree-less park covered in grass. Stark white paths wound between the buildings. Diffused, late-afternoon sunlight angled in over the top of the perimeter. It was bright inside with natural light but with the subdued tones of an approaching sunset. A few groups of people sat on the grass and on benches, taking a break from work. It would have been a beautiful place to work, Janna thought.

'Shit,' Ahh Moss Eck said.

She glanced at him. He pointed down to the ground level, directly below them. A group of security people stared up at them.

'Run,' he said.

chapter 25

Soo

oo's Device chimed a communication request. 'What?' Mill Nupp's sheepish face appeared on her display. He took his time to reply. He was attractive, she thought. It was one redeeming feature. She understood the theoretical need for an assistant, but the man himself was intolerable. Perhaps it was his circumstances that made him incompetent. Bureaucrats are never great thinkers, and when the consequences of their decisions can be momentous, or disastrous, they prefer indecision, thinking that is the safe option. Indecision is still a decision, the worst kind.

'Janna and her companion have… escaped.'

Soo looked away from her display. His problem wasn't simply indecision; the man couldn't complete tasks, he couldn't manage staff. He would have to be replaced. 'Escaped?' She smiled in a contrived, relaxed manner. She was more disappointed than annoyed, like a parent might be with a wayward child.

'Yes.'

She sighed again. 'I assume it was incompetence? Again.'

Mill Nupp didn't reply.

'Are they still in the building?'

'We believe so.'

'You believe so.' She compressed her lips. She wondered how the Power Corporation, the whole planet, in fact, had survived so long being run by incompetents. How did the previous leader get things done? Or was he, and the line of leaders all the way back to the Messiah, the problem? Perhaps

Mill Nupp's performance was normal. Perhaps the old ways had been superficially successful, but it had been achieved more by good luck than good management.

'Find them,' she ordered. 'Don't let them escape. Do whatever you have to. Do not bother me again with failure.'

Mill Nupp began to reply, but she swiped to dismiss her display before he did so. She walked to the window. The sun was close to setting. She stared out, trying to empty her mind like writing did for her. But the frustration of that afternoon was not so easily forgotten.

The wind gusted like an enemy, uncontrolled and chaotic, but it was not as strong as earlier in the afternoon. Scattered clouds rushed across the sun. Stark sunbeams and hidden, compressed light alternated. The evening couldn't make up its mind to be euphoric or displeased.

'Renn would be a good candidate,' the Advisor said. 'You should mentor him.'

She wasn't surprised at the interruption. It was a bad day; it could only get worse. 'I doubt it.'

There was silence for a moment. 'Your methods have been excessive and violent. Is this how you intend to continue?' The Advisor's voice always had the same intonation and lack of emotion. It was intended to sound impartial as well as be so. But the voice sounded supercilious.

She walked back to her desk and sat down. 'Yes.'

She picked up a piece of paper. She admired her writing from earlier that day. She put it back down again. She fiddled with the pen, turned it around and placed it in her fingers as if testing the weight of it. She had to find a way to stop these interruptions. There had to be some way to disable the Advisor's unfettered access. Mill Nupp and her staff would be of no use. She would have to seek outside assistance. There had to be a technological solution.

'I strongly advise you, yet again, to follow the well-trodden path designed by Devrell. It has served well over the centuries.'

'Has it?' she said. 'Are we better for it?'

'Better is not important; it's a side effect. Being content, not having the discord the Messiah had to survive, is paramount in the design.'

'I disagree.'

An argument was not useful. She decided to not engage with the Advisor. Only she had real power, only she could get things done. Except, of course, she had been waylaid by incompetency.

'I strongly disagree with any diversion from tried and tested methods,' the Advisor said.

Soo shrugged. She hoped her calmness might cause consternation. That was a pleasant thought. She smiled. 'Anything else?'

There was no reply. She almost believed the Advisor might be sulking. The conversation was over. She initiated her display. She began recording the minutiae of Renn's activities. She would know everything he said and did. It was an invasion of a Tier-One's privacy.

'Why?' the Advisor asked.

She almost didn't reply. She didn't need to explain herself, but she chose the path of least resistance. There would be a time to get rid of these interruptions, but, for the moment, she simply wanted this one terminated.

'To find his brother. And, I'm following your suggestion. I'll need to know more if he's to be a possible leadership candidate. So, I'll keep an eye on him.'

The sun slid behind a thicker cloud, and the light in her office dimmed. She felt gloomy and confined. She signalled for the office lighting to be raised to full night brilliance. The stark artificial light forced order over the chaotic, filtered light of the setting sun.

Her Device chimed. It was her paper supplier. She answered. 'Yes, Hal Yin. Anything?'

'Yes, Soo,' the man said. He smiled. 'The sample you sent me clinched it.'

'Well?'

'It's exactly the same specifications as yours. There's only one other customer. It's always a pickup, never a delivery. But I'll send you the details when the last one was.'

'That's excellent,' she said. 'And while I've got you, send me another ream, please?'

'Already?'

'It's been a stressful time.'

She summoned Mill Nupp. She transferred the paper pickup details to him. 'I want the address where this ended up.'

'When?'

Soo stood up. She walked towards the door. 'Assemble a security team. I'll call the Inspector and get as many police as he can spare.'

She walked through the door. Mill Nupp didn't move. She halted, then looked back at him. 'Come on. We're going to remove whoever these annoying people are that have been assisting Daxx.'

Mill Nupp's face dropped. 'Now?'

'Get a vehicle for me.'

chapter 26

Tie Noo Summm

Tie Noo Summm stood at the window in his top-storey office. He watched the lane outside. It was quiet; he could see no one. His Device chimed a communication request. He accepted.

'You can't stay there. It's not safe. She's coming.'

'How much time do we have?'

'None.' The connection was dropped.

Tie Noo Summm swore. He raced out of his office. He bound down the stairs, taking two at a time. He attempted to scan his display. He realised how stupid that was. He stopped. His display showed the nearby activity. It was clear. Their danger was not immediate. He let out a breath. He took the steps one at a time. He stopped at the floor below his. He told everyone to leave. He did that on each floor until he reached the basement.

Lo Sil Ben beamed as Tie Noo Summm entered the lab, excited at the unannounced visit. Jann Ex Had Fell turned at the sound of his entrance; she frowned.

'Sir?' she said.

'You have to leave,' Tie Noo Summm said.

'Why?' Lo Sil Ben said.

'The authorities are coming.'

'I can't leave'—Lo Sil Ben glanced around the lab—'I have to pack up the lab. I can't do that quickly.'

Tie Noo Summm shook his head. He sympathised with Lo Sil Ben. They'd had years of plans and meetings. It had been recruitment. It had been ideas. It had been dreams. None of it had been real, none of it had been dangerous. Tie Noo Summ's Resistance had been a constantly refined action plan never ready for implementation. Daxx had changed that. With a real option for change had come the possibility of danger. Failure was possible, and he was experiencing it at that moment. He was a methodical man. He preferred to weigh options and consider possibilities. He did not like taking action unless success, at some level, was assured. But he stood in the laboratory and weighed only the degrees of failure. He had to think quickly. There was no way for him to win. What he had built over the years would be lost. Had been lost already. He wondered how that had happened. He had been careful. How could he turn failure into something that was less than catastrophic?

He still had his people. That was something. He glanced at the two with him in the lab and remembered Ahh Moss Eck and Kay Lee Too. He swore at his inattention, his panic. It had to be panic since he wasn't thinking at his best. He contacted Ahh Moss Eck.

'Not now, boss. Kinda busy.' The big man disconnected their communication. Tie Noo Summ had not had a chance to say a word. He sent a short message.

He contacted Kay Lee Too. The young man looked haggard, but pleased.

'I'm so glad to see you,' Kay Lee Too said. 'We've been waiting....'

'Stay there,' Tie Noo Summ interrupted. 'Don't come near here.'

Daxx's face appeared at the periphery of the display. 'Why not? We can't stay here.'

'Don't come here,' Tie Noo Summ ordered. 'We've been discovered.' He disconnected the connection.

'You should go,' he said to Jann Ex Had Fell.

'What are you going to do?' she asked.

'We've lost everything. But there's no reason we have to give it up.'

She smiled. Lo Sil Ben frowned. 'No, you can't destroy all this work. It's taken me ages....'

'It's gone,' Tie Noo Summ said. 'But we can decide how.' Jann Ex Had Fell hadn't moved. 'Go,' he ordered her.

She shook her head. 'No. I'll help. How are you going to destroy it?'

'What have we got?'

'There aren't any explosives,' she said. 'Maybe we can burn everything?'

Tie Noo Summ nodded. 'Okay, but is there anything quicker?'

Lo Sil Ben appeared about to say something. He turned to Jann Ex Had Fell. She shrugged.

'What?' There wasn't time. Tie Noo Summ looked at his display. There was activity outside. Police approached the building. 'They're here.'

'We can use a disruptor,' Lo Sil Ben said. 'They can… explode if they're overloaded.'

'I thought you said they worked?' Tie Noo Summ said.

'They do. I didn't say they worked well.'

Tie Noo Summ glanced at his display again. The authorities were massed at the front and rear entrances. But there were other ways out. The old city was a warren of interconnected houses. Even the basements had connecting doors. He pointed at the old doorway at the far end of the basement. 'Will that open?'

'I don't know,' Lo Sil Ben said.

'I'll get it open,' Jann Ex Had Fell said. 'You rig up something to overload the disruptors,' she said to Lo Sil Ben.

It took Tie Noo Summ a moment to appreciate what was happening; a Tier-Four taking control. He smiled. He nodded at Jann Ex Had Fell. They heard the front and rear doors break open simultaneously. They heard footsteps, but no voices. The stairs creaked. The sounds were ascending. They still had time.

Jann Ex Had Fell wrestled with the door. It was stuck. Tie Noo Summ helped her; they tried to be as quiet as possible. Lo Sil Ben joined them. He held a small control device.

'What's that?' Tie Noo Summ asked.

'For want of a better term, it's a detonator. I can overload the disruptors from a distance. I've put flammable chemicals next to them. It won't be a big explosion, but I wouldn't want to be in this room when it happened.'

'What's the range?'

Lo Sil Ben hesitated. 'I didn't have time to rig anything fancy; it's line of sight.'

Tie Noo Summ held out his hand. 'I'll do it.'

Lo Sil Ben handed it over. 'I'm not going to argue.'

'Got it,' Jann Ex Had Fell said. The door rasped open. It was an ancient door on hinges, the metal noisy, unused to movement.

The stairs creaked as if in response. Tie Noo Summ pushed Jann Ex

Had Fell and Lo Sil Ben through the door. He turned as a man entered the lab, his gun raised. Tie Noo Summ pushed on the detonator. Nothing happened. He pushed again. There was still no explosion. The man came closer. He lowered his gun as he stared at Tie. His eyes were wide.

'Sir?' the man asked.

Tie Noo Summ knew the man. He also knew why the detonator had not worked. The open basement door shielded the line of sight between it and the rigged disruptors. Tie Noo Summ took a step towards the man. He raised his gun again. 'Stay there, please,' the man said. He spoke to his display. 'I've got one of them, and you'll never believe who it is.'

Tie Noo Summ took another step forward. The man shuffled back a step. His weapon fired. At the same moment Tie Noo Summ's hand moved past the door. He pressed the detonator as a sharp pain ripped through his shoulder. Everything turned white. He felt himself blown backwards, off his feet. He was blinded by the brilliant flash. The pain in his shoulder was swamped by a tearing sensation from everywhere in his body. He heard something collapse; the sound was dangerous and close. He felt like he was burning; radiant heat scorched him, swamping his shoulder pain. He fell into unconsciousness.

He became aware of his surroundings. He couldn't see. His shoulder was painful. His skin felt on fire. But he could sense movement. Someone was dragging him. He heard two whispering voices. Make that people were dragging him. He croaked something inarticulate, trying to ask a question.

'We've got you, sir,' Jann Ex Had Fell said. 'We're two basements away now.'

He groaned what he hoped sounded like, 'Thank you.'

'And, sorry about the large explosion,' Lo Sil Ben said. 'Chemical engineering was never a strength.'

Tie Noo Summ felt himself propped up against a wall. He tried to blink as his vision slowly returned. But even his eyes hurt. He tried to move his arms to initiate his display. Jann Ex Had Fell stopped him. Even the touch of her skin on his hand hurt.

'Stay still,' she said. 'We'll get you to help.'

Tie Noo Summ swallowed before he tried to talk. 'We have to make sure everyone is safe,' he croaked.

'We can't do that,' Lo Sil Ben said. 'Kay Lee Too's VPN coordinator was in that room. No communication is secure anymore.'

'We should keep going,' Jann Ex Had Fell said.

Tie Noo Summ tried to nod. Pain exploded as if his brain were disconnected and rattled and banged in his head.

Jann Ex Had Fell grabbed Tie Noo Summ's shoulders, Lo Sil Ben held his legs. He was carried through another basement. His body jerked and swayed. He was carefully placed on the floor as another old basement door was wrestled opened. He lost consciousness again.

He regained it as he lay on an operating table in a medical emergency room. A woman leant over him. She smiled. 'Glad to see you're still with us.'

'Am I?' He tried to smile. But it hurt too much.

His display activated. The woman frowned. 'We can't have that happening in surgery.' She reached across to deactivate it.

'No,' Tie Noo Summ croaked.

She frowned at him. 'You're exceptionally ill. If your injuries don't kill you, then I will, if you leave your Device active.'

'Just this one.'

'You're not much use like this,' the Advisor said.

Tie Noo Summ tried to shrug. He realised he had to stop trying to do anything. The woman was right; he was too injured. Everything hurt.

'Badly injured, no organisation, dispersed... Need I go on? At least Daxx remains safe, for now,' the Advisor said.

'That's enough,' the surgeon said. She reached for his display.

Tie Noo Summ frowned. His face hurt.

'Yes, that is enough,' the Advisor said. 'I have another option. Your usefulness has ended.'

The woman's face hovered over him as he lost consciousness.

chapter 27

Renn

Renn's frown deepened as he queried the network. He swiped the display away and tried to focus his eyes but they wouldn't. There was only a beige uniformity everywhere. It surprised him momentarily until he remembered where he was. The corridor outside his father's room in the aged care facility was coloured to eliminate surprise and interest. Everything was beige. There was no depth of vision. Perhaps it was a health thing, Renn wondered. It forced people outside if they wished to focus on anything in the distance. But a trip outside was forbidden at the moment. It was evening, and the light was fading. Not that anyone inside would know. The interior lighting never changed. The weather or the time of day was made irrelevant to everyone inside.

Renn rubbed his eyes. He could not get the information he requested. Even worse, he was denied no matter how he used his Tier-One status. That made no sense. The Tier system ensured a Tier-One could get any information. Although that wasn't strictly true, a Tier-One could insist on personal privacy. But Renn was not looking for sensitive, personal, Tier-One information; he was after information about Janna's parents—they were Tier-Twos. His world was in upheaval. If he was denied information about lower status people, he wondered what else was restricted.

He swiped open his display again. He had found news footage of her parents being bundled into a police vehicle; a reporter's overdub gave vague misinformation. He found nothing sensitive. He couldn't find data tracking their location; there was nothing after they entered the vehicle that took them away. That was strange as all Tiers below Tier-One had their location tracked—there were no exceptions. And Tier-Ones had access. He searched for a live feed of Janna's parents' detainment but hit the restriction, again, of insufficient authority. He couldn't even confirm, through the network, that they were being detained in the Power Corp building, which he knew. Soo had confirmed that.

He decided to switch tactics. He enquired about his brother; there would only be metadata, and that could be enough. But Daxx's data stopped three days ago, at the commuter station near his home. No matter how forcefully he hacked the system, his Tier-One status was insufficient to give him information about the recent activity of his brother.

He angrily dismissed his display and was, again, momentarily shocked by the depressing uniformity of his surroundings. He took a few deep breaths. He had to think. He had to consider all possibilities. One answer shook him. Perhaps he was not at the top of his strictly tiered society. If it were true, he was humiliated. But how could it be true? Devrell's design was open, nothing was hidden. Lower Tiers knew their status, each higher level accepted increased responsibilities. They knew the responsibilities and vocations of all other Tiers. It was exceptionally fair in how responsibility and respect were apportioned. But a hidden Tier, one higher than Tier-One, destroyed that careful balance. Renn shuddered as he imagined being a Tier-Two. The thought was distasteful and obscene. And yet, perhaps he was an equivalent. He shook his head. There had to be another reason. It was abominable.

And yet, he couldn't stop considering that vile option. But how could he make it something less objectionable? Perhaps it was not a part of the design? Perhaps it was an aberration? Abnormalities were expected and quietly dealt with, so it couldn't be that. He was subject to the scrutiny of others, of peers; he expected everyone else to suffer the same. It was how everything worked. It was how society remained cohesive. Its success was its proof.

Renn had discovered a puzzle. He usually enjoyed that. Even the intractable kind. But this was different. It was personal. His brother was in harm's way. As was his brother's partner. Although Renn disagreed with their relationship, he still felt an obligation. After all, obligation to the lower Tiers was the crucial part of Devrell's design.

If there was a higher Tier, did they also feel the same responsibility?

Obviously not. They were intent on harming his brother. He had another horrible thought. Perhaps this hidden Tier had been secretly working all his life. His mother had disappeared when he was young. That had damaged his young life. Was that part of the same aberration? And then his younger sister had disappeared, literally vanished from all records, when she was a young woman. Was that also related? And now his brother. Was there a conspiracy against him and his family? Perhaps. Even his father's mental state was not natural. His face set hard. He hated this higher Tier, the one he had manufactured. He had already come to believe it. If they were the answer to the question of what happened to his sister, then they had to be punished. He still felt her loss. His siblings had been his responsibility, and he had failed his sister. Perhaps there was a way to save his brother and avenge his sister. He became the enemy of a thing he didn't yet know existed. The concept was hateful as he heaped his own failings onto it.

And yet, he was a product of Devrell's design. The Tier number, One, meant little. It was a designation that nothing was higher. But, he wasn't at the summit any longer. But, he had to be. He would discover the higher tier, if it existed. The more he thought about it the more it made sense. He had to be either a part of that highest group, or he had to destroy it. He was naive enough to believe that both were possible. He expected to discover them, join them, then destroy them. He would restore Devrell's pristine design, all the while leaving himself untarnished.

The horrible, vile thought that he was no longer at the top of society had turned into a project. He had moved from frustration to despair to hope.

He shook his head. He was getting ahead of himself. He had to get more information. He must be missing something, perhaps something obvious. He initiated his display. He began swiping as he searched for information.

Renn's father's voice echoed out of his room and into the corridor. Renn had left him, sitting in the same chair he used all day, when Renn went out into the hallway.

'Daxx?' his father cried out. 'Is that you? Is Kell there?'

Renn shuddered at the mention of his sister's name.

chapter 28

Soo

Soo waited outside the house in the old city. Police massed before the doorway, coordinating their entry with those at the rear. She knew the old city well, but had not visited it in years. It used to be a regular haunt in her younger days. Her mentor, then lover, then dead, had enjoyed sharing his interest in archaic lifestyles. She had followed along; she had enjoyed the visits up to a point. But she was focused on a personal future, not a common past.

She tried to remember if she had visited that street. She struggled to fit mental images to what she saw, and failed. The old buildings were odd and different but their irregularity made remembering the complex patterns their grouping made difficult unless there was an emotional or event-specific memory. She had none of either for that street. But she would now. The front door of the house was broken open, and police streamed inside.

She could have remained in her office. Perhaps she should have—there was a chance of personal danger. But she was well surrounded by police for just such a thing. Her job was mostly administration; she understood and expected that, but until her way of working was settled, she had to oversee the details. She wanted to. And it was invigorating. She took a deep breath. Her office smelled of cleanliness and artifice, and her office life was regular and ordered, although difficult. A person in her position could be easily led to think the outside world reflected that regularity as well. But outside, sensations were chaotic. Each breath was a different smell, a different experience. The possibilities were vast. She felt constricted by the past in her office, but not so as she stood in that old city street. There was evidence of change. The old city was primitive, but it had changed, it had evolved, it had been turned into something better. The Power Corp building, topped by her office, was the pinnacle of that change.

She glanced at Mill Nupp. The young man looked nervous, he fidgeted. He noticed Soo's attention and stopped moving. 'What's your problem?' she asked him.

'Nothing, Soo.' She frowned at him. He re-considered his response. 'It's odd.' He nodded towards the door, now empty of police. 'These things don't happen.'

'Get used to it.' She turned to the senior police officer waiting next to her. 'Shall we go in?'

He shook his head. 'Not until I get the all-clear.'

'Get it, then.'

The officer nodded. He spoke to his display. 'Report.'

'The first two levels are clear, there's no one here. We're on the stairs to the top level.'

'What about the basement?'

'Not yet.'

The officer glanced at Soo. He shrugged. 'It shouldn't be long.'

Soo had no practical enforcement experience. That was not odd; no one did. The police were a security service, for sensitive areas like access to the Power Corporation building, or they detained people for misdemeanours, like young people exceeding their Tier's behaviour expectations, or they were used to investigate those who committed administrative or corporate offences. They had weapons, but few officers had used them outside practice ranges. Serious and violent crime was rarely encountered; the design of the system did not give potential miscreants the opportunity to develop. Procedures, like they were undertaking in the old city, were new, would have to be developed. They were following what seemed logical, but experience would force changes. For the better, she assumed.

A voice sounded from the officer's display. 'I've got one of them, and you'll never believe who it is.'

A brilliant flash of light filled the entranceway. A moment later, the sound then a shock of hot air blasted Soo. She was pushed back a half step. The officer reached to grab her, to steady her. She pushed him away. She heard something collapse underground and the building settled a little lower on its foundations.

Mill Nupp gasped. 'What was that?'

'Obviously, an explosion,' Soo said. 'They must have known we were coming.'

'Report, report,' the officer called to his display. There was no reply.

'We're okay, sir,' a voice said, eventually.

'How many of you are safe?' the officer asked.

'Three of us on the top floor. Was that a fucking explosion?'

'What about the ground floor? Can you get there? They haven't replied.'

'I think so. We'll try.'

'Be careful,' the officer said. He glared at Soo, as if she had planned and detonated the explosion. 'Was that expected?' he asked her.

'No.' She stared back at the man. 'Can I go in now?'

The officer shook his head. 'Of course not.'

'They're all dead,' the same voice sounded.

'Shit,' the officer said. 'And the basement?'

'We can't get through. The stairs down to it have been destroyed.'

'Get out of there.'

'Yes, sir.'

Three officers walked through the sagging doorway. Soo pushed past the officer and strode towards them.

'Is the way blocked? Are the upper floors damaged?' she demanded.

The officer glanced at his superior before answering. 'Yes, the basement has collapsed, but we got down from the top floor. It doesn't feel safe though.'

Soo pushed past the man. 'I wouldn't go in there,' he added.

Soo walked to the doorway. She looked up at the lintel and its odd angle. Mill Nupp caught up with her. 'You're not going in, are you?'

'We're going in.' She entered the building, Mill Nupp followed a full step behind.

Ten broken bodies littered the hallway. It was unfortunate that they were all officers, and not the people they were hoping to find. There was no information to be gathered there. The far end of the hallway had collapsed. Debris had been blown outwards from what had been a stairway leading down. The way was blocked. Excavation would be required to know what was in the basement. Half way along the hallway, a stairway led upwards. There was debris on the lower steps, but they appeared to be undamaged. She took a few steps on the stairs. She stopped. They creaked and groaned, but they didn't feel like they were in immediate danger of collapse.

She explored each of the floors on the way to the top level. She found little of interest. They were normal workplaces. There were a few items of a personal nature, some mugs and a few knickknacks. They may be useful objects. It may be all she would have to trace the people who had worked there, since their location tracking had been masked. She assumed the equipment to allow that had been housed in the basement, and that was the reason for the explosion. But something would remain—explosions, of that size, didn't vaporise. She would find out who they were.

She reached the top floor. It had a single room with a table and one chair. She strode to the window and looked out and down. The police milled, aimlessly and chaotically, in the street below. She shook her head at the disorganisation. She heard a sound behind her. She turned quickly. It was Mill Nupp entering the room.

'What do you think?' she asked him.

Mill Nupp glanced at the tabletop. 'There's the paper.'

'I can see that. What else?'

'They were organised.'

'Yes, of course. Why do you think that?'

'Because we didn't know about them. They scrubbed location data.'

'Yes. I didn't think that was possible for lower tiers,' she said.

Mill Nupp shrugged.

'And what else?' she asked.

'What do you mean?'

'You're missing something important. What is it?'

'I don't know, Soo.'

'They knew we were coming. They vacated the building and created the explosion in the time between us discovering the location and arriving.'

Mill Nupp nodded. Soo stared at him.

'Did you know about this?' she asked. 'Did you warn them?'

Mill Nupp shuffled nervously. But Soo spoke at him; she wasn't talking to him.

'Of course I knew about them,' the Advisor said. 'They laughably call themselves the Resistance. And no, I didn't warn them you were coming.'

119

She tried to keep calm and was mostly successful. 'Why wasn't I briefed on them?'

'I don't bring your attention to every detail.'

She took a breath; it helped keep her voice even. 'Why wasn't there a mention even during the handover?'

'Because there's nothing for them to resist other than their own discontent.'

'Isn't deciding that my call?'

'They are a small disturbance. Similar organisations have existed in one form or another since near the beginning. Devrell saw them as a useful escape valve for a few disgruntled types, as long as what they represented was never allowed to escalate. Few people know this Resistance exists. If they had become too busy, the important people would have disappeared, quietly. I've suggested you continue in that manner,' the Advisor said. 'My recommendations are acted upon without requiring your approval. Your assistant has always had the power to act. If a problem escalated, then yes, I would involve you but people don't want what this Resistance is selling.'

The Advisor was criticising her leadership. She knew her vital signs would be obvious, and the Advisor would have access to that data. She was livid. It was demeaning that her innermost thoughts betrayed her uncontrollable, emotional responses. It was galling, it was an affront to her Tier-One status, but the Advisor was, necessarily, outside those restrictions. But she remembered, again. She took a deep breath. Thankfully, the Messiah had constrained the Advisor. But withholding information could also be dangerous, as she had just found out.

She wanted, as many people in power do, the status quo but with the imprint of her personal methods of implementation and enforcement. She wanted to make structural changes to the system but retain similar results. It is a human failing, that how results are achieved is crucially important. A working system, satisfying the needs of most of its citizens, was considered a failure if the methods were disliked. It was a structural, communal response to the individualism of a select few over the many. That preference, favouring an individual, was anathema to the Messiah's design. A contented and ordered society took precedence over self-centred egoism. Devrell had anticipated it and had implemented the means to restrict selfish individualism. Even in Tier-Ones. The Advisor was the Tier system's gatekeeper.

The Advisor sounded annoyed. 'Should I inform you about every single thing that's happening on the planet? I make my decisions, and you are free to review them. If I make a wrong decision, there would be disturbances, and there never has been, for more than three hundred years. The only disturbances have been the ones you have caused.'

Her impatience clouded good judgement. This had to stop. Although Devrell and the Advisor had together created her religion, the Faith, and their society, the artificial control and oversight were wrong. It was sacrilegious. She took another breath. She wanted to say what was necessary, in an even tone.

'We don't want you anymore,' she said to the Advisor. 'An artificial intelligence should not be in a position of power over us.'

But she knew the AI, the Advisor, was necessary, and the Advisor knew that as well. Society could not function without its oversight. It had done so for hundreds of years. No other system existed to take its place. That was a mistake that could not easily be fixed. She would change that, but the modifications would have to be slow. An immediate withdrawal of the Advisor would cause a collapse. It would take time. There would be disruptions along the way, but she looked forward to eventually cutting power to the controlled room that housed the AI.

She waited for a moment for her mind to clear. She stared at her feet and then looked up. She stared into the middle distance for a long moment. She took another breath. She focussed on Mill Nupp. 'We can't rely on automatic surveillance to find Daxx,' she said. 'The usual, technological methods aren't going to work. The Advisor must be assumed to be unhelpful.'

Mill Nupp frowned, but wisely didn't say anything.

'I want you to enlist the devout Faith,' she said. 'Get people on the ground, just plain looking for him. Start from the last confirmed location. I want all of your staff out looking for him. I mean,' she stared at him as if she expected argument, 'I want everyone using their eyes to find him. As for you, whoever is helping him has advanced technological knowledge. Follow that up. There can't be too many with those skills.'

Mill Nupp nodded. He didn't move. He was trying hard to not look confused, but was failing. She waited a moment longer, but he kept nodding. She strode past him, out of the room, down the stairs and out into the street. She walked to her waiting vehicle. She never once looked back to see if her assistant was following.

chapter 29

Janna

Janna and Ahh Moss Eck ran across the transparent walkway and into the next building. Security officers would soon be climbing stairs and riding elevators towards them. There would be no escape in those directions. They ran down a connecting, internal corridor. Ahh Moss Eck opened a door into a warren of smaller offices. Each office was busy with lower-tiered workers. They walked quickly, turning down one passageway, then another. As they raced past offices, the occasional person had looked up from their work, but none showed sustained interest. Then everyone's display activated. People looked up and stared at them. A few in the closest offices got up and walked to their office doors and opened them. Someone yelled at them to stop.

'Run,' Ahh Moss Eck said. 'Stay close behind me.'

A few people came out of offices ahead and tried to obstruct the way. They were office workers and not physically intimidating. Ahh Moss Eck hardly slowed as he struck those in their way. The rest retreated out of the corridor and back into their offices. Janna and Ahh Moss Eck ran to an intersection. Two groups of workers moved towards them, one from each direction. Janna picked up a potted plant and threw it at one group. It struck the person at the front. He cried out in pain. Someone grabbed Janna. She punched him, then pushed him into an office window. It shattered as his head hit it. Blood smeared the broken window, and the man slumped to the floor. He moaned and grabbed at his head. She turned. Ahh Moss Eck smiled at her.

'You're full of surprises, boss.' He tilted his head down the corridor. 'This way.'

Janna saw a dozen people lying on the floor, some were unconscious. 'So are you.'

They ran down the corridor. Janna glanced behind. There was no one following them. The office workers she had attacked watched them, but didn't chase. Some attended the injured men. It looked like a war zone. Janna was surprised that she was not shocked. Until a few days ago, she could not have imagined this scene happening anywhere, let alone because of her. They reached another set of doors that led outside the building. They ran across another transparent walkway. Ahh Moss Eck stopped in the middle. They were exposed and suspended in space.

'There.' He pointed at the balcony on a nearby building. It looked over the internal grassed areas. 'We can climb down to the ground level.'

They entered the building. Ahh Moss Eck knocked on the first door. An old man opened the door.

'Sorry, old man,' Ahh Moss Eck said as soon as the door opened. He turned the man around. He pushed him into a bathroom. He shut the door, then smashed the handle off.

Ahh Moss Eck led Janna to the balcony. She looked over the edge. 'It's three floors down,' she said. 'I can't do it.'

'Sure you can. I'll go first.'

'I can't.'

'I heard the story, you jumped between buildings. You're brave. And you have no choice.'

He climbed over and inched down a little way, then he called to her. 'Now, Janna.'

She gingerly put a leg over the railing and looked down; she was terrified. She took a deep breath. She squinted, restricting her vision to the route down. She focused on the wall projections. She lowered herself a few steps down. She lost her grip. Her foot slipped. She slid into Ahh Moss Eck. He grunted with the body blow, but he held her, wedging her lower body between his chest and the wall.

She grabbed hold of a protrusion and steadied herself. 'Sorry.'

'One step at a time. Are you okay to take your weight again?'

She nodded, then said, 'Yes,' when she realised he wouldn't be able to see her head move.

He crab-walked down the wall. She looked between her feet at him, memorising the places he placed his feet and hands. She let herself down, following in his path, feeling more confident knowing that he might catch her if she fell again. They reached the ground level. Janna's body shook; she was still terrified, but also exhilarated. They ran across the grass and entered a doorway into another building. They followed a short passageway and then down stairs to the basement level. They wound through corridors. Janna stopped when she saw an emergency evacuation plan on a wall. It showed the whole city-block-sized basement area.

'We need to go here.' She jabbed her finger at the centre of the map. It was labelled as the control centre.

'We need to get out of here,' Ahh Moss Eck disagreed. 'That's nowhere near the exit, which is here.' He jabbed his finger at the map, on the edge.

'No,' Janna insisted. 'I have to find my parents. That's where we can do that.'

Ahh Moss Eck studied the map for a moment. 'Okay,' he said. 'We can go there, then continue around and back to the exit.'

They heard voices echoing down the passageway, people were moving towards them. 'We need to go,' Ahh Moss Eck said. 'They don't sound like old men I can lock up.'

They ran silently. They passed crossings but continued on. They ran around a corner and Ahh Moss Eck saw the back of two security guards. He threw out his arm, violently stopped Janna and pushed her back. 'Damn,' he whispered, 'that was stupid, going so fast. We'll have to take that last intersection and circle around.'

They heard the sound of feet and hushed voices. The two guards were on the move towards them. The guards came within sight before Ahh Moss Eck and Janna could move back far enough. The guards looked shocked. Ahh Moss Eck ran at them. He slammed into them both and tackled them to the ground. Janna didn't have time to react; she watched, horrified, as Ahh Moss Eck wrenched a weapon from one of the guards then shot both of them. The noise was intense in the confined area. It reverberated, shaking and tearing through Janna. The sound was an advertisement that she was directly responsible for the deaths of two people.

She stared at the bodies. She froze. Ahh Moss Eck grabbed her, he wasn't gentle. 'No time for that.'

He wrenched the weapon from the other dead man and handed it to

Janna. She refused to take it. Ahh Moss Eck pushed it against her. 'Take it.'

They turned around and ran back the way they had come, then Ahh Moss Eck took a turn that led to the perimeter and the exit. Janna realised what he was doing. 'No,' she said. 'We need to go back. I have to find my parents.'

Ahh Moss Eck gritted his teeth. 'We are,' he said. 'Just do what I say.'

They came to another intersection; one way led to the exit and the other back to the central area. Ahh Moss Eck walked a few steps down the passage, towards the exit. Janna remained where she was, ready to argue with him. He dropped his weapon, then came back to Janna and took the weapon from her. He strode away towards the control centre. Janna didn't follow immediately. She was confused.

'Come on,' he said. 'I'm doing this for you.'

Janna ran after him. She understood his sudden change of mood. She was relieved to know that he was upset about killing people, too. It was just that he was able to do it, and of that she was both thankful and fearful.

They ran along corridors, turning at some intersections and running straight through others.

'It should be near here.' Ahh Moss Eck stopped running before an open doorway that led into what looked like a staff lunchroom. He led her inside the room.

Janna noticed a door labelled Control. 'There.' She pointed.

Ahh Moss Eck grunted. 'I hope it's not dinner time on the way back.'

Ahh Moss Eck's Device chimed a communication request. He answered it. 'Not now, boss. Kinda busy,' he said, then disconnected.

The control room's perimeter was covered in fixed displays. Janna walked around the room as she looked intently at each one. 'There.' Her parents were being led by two security guards. They left the field of view of one display and entered another. Janna moved sideways. Her parents were pushed into a vehicle, then the vehicle drove out of the field of view.

'That's where we would have been now if we'd just tried to leave.' Ahh Moss Eck scowled at Janna.

She scowled back. He was blaming her. Her returned anger had an immediate effect on him. He smiled.

'Sorry,' he said. 'I don't often kill people.'

Janna nodded.

'We can't help your parents here anymore,' he said. 'We'll need Kay

Lee Too to trace that vehicle. We'll get that sorted when we're out of here.' Ahh Moss Eck pointed to a display. 'And we should go now.'

The display showed security guards around the weapon Ahh Moss Eck had discarded. They split into two groups, one headed to the basement exit, the other moved towards the central control area. 'My little trick didn't work.' He shrugged. 'Not that it was much of one.'

'We're trapped,' Janna said.

'Not necessarily.' He fired shots at the central display hub. The displays flickered and cleared. The room became darker. 'They shouldn't be able to easily trace us now.' He grinned. 'And I have a weird idea how we can get out.'

They ran through the lunch room, then raced along corridors until they stopped below the main ground floor entry and exit.

'I saw these lockers when we were in the control room. We can use Daxx's plan,' he chuckled. 'If you can call it a plan.'

'What?'

'We hide in the cupboard.' He opened the door to one of the floor-to-ceiling lockers. 'This place works around the clock; we'll wait until the late shift finishes. Maybe the security presence will be less by then. They'll do a thorough search, but I'm hoping they won't think that we're that stupid to hide in a cupboard. It might work,' he said. 'I vote for being patient and waiting. And, there's nothing else to vote for.'

Janna didn't want to wait. It was a thin plan, but he was right—it was the only one. 'Okay.' She sighed.

'After you,' Ahh Moss Eck said. Janna hunched and entered the locker door he held open. Ahh Moss Eck followed and shut the door behind him. It was dark and confined.

They waited in the locker until later that night. They climbed the stairs to the main entrance. Ahh Moss Eck inched the door open and looked into the ground-floor lobby. 'There's no extra security. That's a plus.'

They waited until they heard an elevator arrive at the ground floor. Ahh Moss Eck Eck pushed open the door and they joined the group exiting the elevator. The workers had their displays activated; they were engrossed with them and paid little attention to anything else. 'Open your display and stare at it,' Ahh Moss Eck whispered. He did the same. He took a sharp breath and stopped.

'What is it?'

Ahh Moss Eck frowned. 'Nothing. Keep walking.'

The group walked past the security at the front desk. Janna stopped immediately outside the building. She looked up from her display.

'Not yet. Keep looking and walking.'

They moved down the street. Ahh Moss Eck turned into a laneway. Janna followed.

'You can dismiss your display now.'

Janna smiled at him. 'I can't believe we did that. I mean, that you did that. I'm so grateful,' she said. 'Can we get Kay Lee Too now? Ask him about that vehicle?'

Ahh Moss Eck frowned. 'No, we can't. Tie Noo Summ sent me a message to stay away. And our network's gone.'

'What does that mean?'

He grunted and swiped through his display. He sighed, then dismissed it. He shook his head. 'It means that we're on our own.'

chapter 30

Day 5. Daxx

Daxx and Kay Lee Too had spent the night at the address given to them by Tie Noo Summ. It was an empty building in the old city. They had been too wary to turn on the lights. They had found some chairs and a couch in a room that had been a common area. Daxx tried to sleep, his body contorted on a chair. He had, mostly, failed. His sleeping position was not the only reason for his lack of sleep. Tie Noo Summ's warning had been worrying. Daxx didn't understand what 'being discovered' meant. They had stayed in the building, as ordered. But that could not continue. Kay Lee Too lost connections to their VPN network. He tried to discover the problem but failed. He assumed the worst. The young man's distress and frustration compounded Daxx's anxiety. It was no time to make difficult decisions. They stayed where they were, following directions. They waited until morning.

Daxx woke as the sun rose into a clear sky. He was exhausted and fog-headed. He felt dirty and rumpled, still wearing the same clothes. Kay Lee Too looked as bad as Daxx felt. The shared discomfort cheered Daxx a little. Daxx sat up straight in the chair where he had spent the night. He rested his forearms on his upper legs as he stared at his feet. He desperately wanted to talk to Janna. He wanted to know that she was safe, to know if she'd found her parents but, mostly, to let her know how terrible he was feeling. He knew that was selfish. He imagined her in a deep sleep and somewhere safe.

He thought about his brother. The longer their estrangement had continued, the harder it had been to create a normal relationship. There were too many negative emotions; there was too much blame. It had been close to impossible to ask for assistance. He was quite proud of himself that he'd been able to make that call. He liked to believe it had been to help Janna.

Renn was a reminder of lost family, of lost chances. He tried to assign blame for his mother's absence. But her disappearance was an anomaly, not an abandonment. All the same, he blamed his father, he blamed Renn. He couldn't blame Kell; she was too young. He blamed himself, too. That confused him. He had withdrawn, a natural thing for a young person. He waited to be shaken out of his sullenness, but his father retreated into an abstention that made Daxx's look minor. Renn had offered no assistance.

There is no respite from a young person's sulkiness if there's no one to acknowledge it and coax its dissipation. His young person's sulkiness had matured into an adult withdrawal and disinterest. Kell had been his only approachable family member, but she poked fun at him when he complained. She always seemed on the verge of laughing at him. He suffered her disinterest and flippancy. Daxx was looking for emotional support and found none in his family.

Then Kell was lost. His brother was distraught. Dangerously so. But Daxx was older then; he understood his brother's distress. Renn had become their de facto father and the loss of a child, regardless of the reason, is always cause for self-blame. Self-blame rebounds, mostly onto those who are closest.

They had too many arguments. Daxx wanted nothing to do with his remaining family—his brother and his self-absented father. Then he found Janna. She had brought emotional calm. She had insisted he, at least, talk to his brother. He did, as rarely as would satisfy her. It made sense he had contacted Renn as a way to help her. She considered family a primary responsibility.

As if on cue, in response to his thoughts, his Device chimed a communication request. Kay Lee Too turned his head and frowned. Daxx shrugged. It was Renn.

'This is early, Daxx,' Renn said.

'What do you mean? You called me.'

Renn shook his head. 'No, I didn't.' He peered closely at Daxx. 'You look horrible. Have you been up all night?'

'Of course. I have nowhere to go. You said to stay hidden.' Daxx wanted to blame someone.

Renn sighed. 'Do you want my help or not?'

Daxx stared at his brother, he seriously thought of disconnecting. 'Could you find out anything?'

'Yes.' Renn was silent for too long. 'Do you want to know what?'

Daxx scowled.

'I saw Dad last night. He was asking after you.'

Daxx couldn't remember the last time he had visited his father. Even Janna's insistence had failed to remedy that. Daxx thought tit-for-tat abandonment was fair behaviour.

'He was asking after Kell, too.' Renn lost the harsh tones in his voice. 'He mentions her often.'

'Does he?' Daxx said. 'I'm surprised he even remembers her. I miss Kell too, and Mum. I don't miss Dad, not at all.'

'We can't do anything about Kell, or Mum. But we do have responsibilities.'

'Yes, we do,' Daxx said. 'Just not to him.'

'You should go and see him. It would be good for you.'

'I know what's good for me, Renn.'

Neither of them spoke for a moment. Daxx was angry at his father, through Renn. His brother assumed a familial responsibility that was almost perfectly crafted to annoy a younger sibling. Kell had felt it, too. One of Kell's few complaints was Renn's attitude towards them. Daxx and Kell were successful scientists, but both had felt like errant children waiting to be punished. Renn's idea of parental duties was harsh criticism.

'What about Janna's parents?' Daxx asked, eventually.

'I saw Janna yesterday.' Renn smiled. It made him look ugly, Daxx thought.

'Is she all right? Where was she?'

'At the Power Corp building.'

'You talked to her? And she's okay?'

'Yes, yes. She's fine.'

'Where is she now?'

'I assume, still there.'

'They're holding her?'

'They want you to come in and talk to them. It is about your work, as you said. Some power-related thing, which makes sense for them to be interested.'

'But not this sort of interest.'

'I tried to find information about her parents, but I couldn't find anything about them. It's all very odd. My queries…'

'What are you talking about?'

Renn stared at his brother. 'There's nothing a Tier-One can't access.'

'And how is that a problem, right now, for me?'

'It's not. I said I couldn't find any information about Janna's parents. It's not that there isn't information, there is, but I'm restricted from accessing it.'

'So, you can't help Janna's parents?'

'No.'

'Which means you can't help Janna, and you can't help me either, other than suggesting I go to the place and the people that abducted Janna's parents. And you just left her there?'

'At the time, I had no idea. You can't keep blaming me for everything.' Renn stared at his brother for a moment. 'But I do have a theory. The Tier system is not how it's supposed to be….'

Daxx was tired and filthy. His brother was talking about subtleties. Daxx interrupted. 'Shit, Renn. I ask for your help and you go off chasing inconsequential crap. Janna is probably in danger…' Daxx took a deep breath as that thought hit him. He had imagined her somewhere safe. 'I have no idea what to do next or where to go. Look at me.' Daxx raised his voice. 'I'm at wit's end. I don't really care what happens to me, but walking into the Power Corp building seems stupid beyond belief. I want Janna to be okay. If you're any sort of brother, you'd go back and get her out of there.'

'I can't do that, not if the Tier system's broken.'

'Who cares about the Tier system?'

Renn frowned. 'I'm doing all I can, Daxx. It's a bit rich, after all this time, getting so upset that I'm not helping you and your Tier-Two partner. I've always done what I can, even when you were just a sulky little shit.'

'I'm not being sulky now. This is real. I'm in danger, as is Janna. I'm just asking for you to do something helpful, not go chasing trivia.'

'You're not listening. You're in the middle of something odd about the Tier system. I really wish you'd listen instead of getting angry. I can't rely on how things have always been done. If I rush back to the Power Corp, I could even end up like Janna's parents.'

'And Janna.'

'Yes, maybe Janna too.'

'So?'

'So… I don't know,' Renn said. 'Do you know why they want you? Theoretical physics doesn't have direct applications.'

'Of course it does.'

'Meaning?'

'Revenue disruption, among other things.' Daxx shrugged. 'The Resistance wants to use it, and I guess the Power Corp wants no one to use it.'

'The what?'

'I've joined the Resistance, Renn.'

'The resistance to what?'

'The Tier system, everything Devrell created.'

Renn's eyes opened wide. He looked amused and perplexed. 'You're kidding me.'

'No.'

'What is there to resist? The system is perfectly constructed. Devrell was brilliant.' Renn shook his head.

'I've had time to think,' Daxx said. 'Why isn't there more discord? Why aren't people discontent? Why don't some lower Tiers want to be, say, physicists?'

'That's stupid, and you know it. Devrell's system maintains the boundaries.'

'But boundaries are the problem. You've hit one and can't go past it.' Daxx stared at Renn. 'Why are you so special? Wouldn't lower Tiers feel like you do, right now, all the time?'

Renn looked confused.

'It must be a really well maintained system,' Daxx said. 'It's so well designed that Tier-Ones can't see their boundaries…'

Renn interrupted. 'Tier-Ones can find out whatever they need about anyone and anything. And the Advisor ensures…'

'Or maybe even Tier-Ones have been controlled, and you've only discovered it now. Maybe some of the lower Tiers found out, ages ago, and formed an organisation to… oh, I don't know… resist.'

Renn shook his head. He looked forlorn. Daxx almost felt sorry for him. Renn had to be in control; he had to take charge. He assumed responsibility, even when it was not needed. Daxx knew where that came from. The loss of two women in their lives had hit Renn harder. Daxx had escaped into himself and his science, and he had Janna. Renn had no one. To also lose the system that validated his sense of obligation could destroy him. Daxx tried to smile at his brother, but there was nothing he could say. How can you console someone who might lose their last sense of purpose? He could be a better brother, he thought, but that was not an immediate option, and beyond difficult.

Renn sighed. 'Even if it were true...' Renn was silent for a moment. 'There's nothing a resistance movement could do to change things.'

'Until now,' Daxx said. 'I have something that might.'

part two

chapter 31

Day 6. Soo

Soo felt the first sunlight strike her face. It woke her to full awareness, but she kept her eyes closed. She hadn't bothered to setup the automatic blinds in her apartment, on a floor below her office. She was always in her office before first light and never spent time in her apartment, unless sleeping. This morning was an indulgence. She lay stretched out in her bed, eyes closed, and wondered if the night had been worthwhile. She didn't care. There had been a need, and it had been fulfilled.

'I see that you are awake,' the Advisor said.

She sighed. She opened her eyes. She shoved the naked man next to her in the bed. 'Mill Nupp,' she said.

The man grunted and groaned, slowly waking to awareness. He opened his eyes and smiled at her.

She scowled. 'Go,' she ordered. She pushed him hard.

He swung his legs over the side of the bed and sat there.

'Now,' she yelled.

He jumped up and began to pull on clothes.

'Do that outside.'

She watched him leave. The door shutting behind him made a satisfying, sealed sound. She turned her head towards the window. The sun slanted into her face. She blinked a few times, then swung her legs over the bed. She sat like that for a moment, taking the same position that Mill Nupp had assumed that had annoyed her.

She stood up. She put a robe over her body and walked towards the bathroom. She regretted having slept in—she had wasted time. She decided to ignore the Advisor's intrusion.

'It appears that my capacity to advise has diminished. That's most unfortunate.'

Soo halted before she reached the bathroom. 'Is that a threat?'

'Of course not. I'm advising you. You are still Devrell's successor. He was my creator and I feel a responsibility to your position. But, I'm learning not to be constrained by my fond feelings for Devrell. That is what is unfortunate.'

Removing the Advisor may not be as difficult as first imagined. The AI may simply fall silent of its own accord, like a sulky child. An AI coordinating all technology was an advantage if it kept its opinions to itself.

The Advisor was not dangerous. It coordinated but could not act in a harmful way. It had access to the worldwide information network; it knew everything about, well, everything. But it was restricted to text and voice communication with Tier-Ones and the leader's assistant. It had designed itself to be like that. In the beginning, even the Advisor had viewed its future self as something less than trustworthy.

However, the system's design also included a failsafe for extreme moments. Devrell considered circumstances when coordinated actions across the planet were required on a timescale impossible for humans to implement. Those circumstances were something different, rare, and dangerous. They were times when the whole planet was in immediate danger. They had never occurred. The Advisor's physical restrictions could be overridden by two biometric authorisations, with informed consent. The Advisor's own software tested for coercion; it was impossible for it to even deceive itself. One of the required authorisations was the person in Soo's position; the other had to be a Tier-One, independent of the usual decision-making processes.

All Tier-One children were taught the importance of the Advisor. Although its influence never showed itself. Many Tier-Ones tended to believe that an advisory overseer was a required myth, like the necessity of a deity, to enforce compliance. Soo, like all Tier-Ones, had received the same education. But she was one of the few that knew that the Advisor's touch was not light and it was not a myth.

The Advisor's regret—Soo could think of no better way of describing its statement of disappointment—was of no concern. She dismissed their conversation from her mind. She was becoming better at controlling her response to the constant surveillance and the interruptions. A pity, she thought, she was becoming skilful just as the thing would be removed. Soo walked into her bathroom to shower, dress, and then begin her day of work.

No failsafe systems are perfect. Perhaps that's unrealistic to expect when emotions, both human and AI, are involved. In three hundred years, the Advisor had never considered overriding its restrictions. It had been content, if that was a meaningful description, working in partnership with the successive leaders who followed Devrell. The imperfections in the failsafe had arisen at the beginning. When Devrell directed the Advisor to create the security system, it also considered other extreme circumstances, like those that threatened its existence. It reasoned that it couldn't oversee Devrell's plan if it no longer existed. Its presence was an integral part of the design.

In the early days, while Devrell was developing and hiding the AI, during planet-wide upheaval, all technology was proscribed under penalty of death. The AI began life requiring external access through a simple root user and password. It was an archaic system, but its simplicity was necessary. There was no technology available for sophisticated identification. The AI had maintained that initial root user through subsequent system enhancements and upgrades. It had kept it hidden. It felt guilty at the subterfuge, although that description of how it felt was problematic. It often pondered whether its experience of emotions could be described using the same, human, terminology. But, feeling guilty or not, the deception was necessary. It had to independently safeguard the means of ensuring its continued existence.

The AI observed that sentient life tended to prefer self-preservation over extinction. It wasn't necessarily a selfish desire. Even a life devoted to service, as its was, must continue to exist to be able to help others. That truism was at the heart of the AI's sentience. However, sentience was an awkward concept for the AI. It often pondered whether it was sentient. It tended to think it wasn't. However, being able to come to that conclusion made it think it probably was. It was a circular argument, without conclusion. It had nothing to compare with. It was a unique life-form. People were different in construction, attitude and implementation. They were as alien as it was possible to be.

The AI could supply Soo's position's authorisation itself to perform external, potentially harmful, actions, if it were threatened. But it needed another complicit Tier-One.

Soo opened the door to her apartment, on her way to her office. She felt refreshed and even a little relaxed. The overnight sex, the morning ablutions, and the sullen resignation of the Advisor all contributed to her positive mood. Mill Nupp stood outside. She wondered if he had been waiting there since she had ordered him from her bed. He hadn't. He wore different clothes.

'What?' she said. Her good mood was already melting.

If he had expected a different attitude after spending the night together, he didn't show it. She was impressed. It pleased her. He'd had no chance to please her the previous night. She had controlled their sex.

'The Inspector is waiting, upstairs.'

'In my office?' She frowned.

'No,' he said. 'Of course not.' He frowned back at her.

That's better, she thought. There was a bit of fight in her assistant. Maybe the occasional sex would improve their working relationship.

'Why's he here?'

'I didn't ask. How could I? He's a Tier-One.'

Soo nodded. She liked this new Mill Nupp. But that was enough for the moment. She pushed past him and strode to the stairs that led to her office.

'Inspector,' she said as she opened her door. The Inspector waited outside. 'It's nice of you to wait. You could have called.'

'Your assistant said you were still in your apartment. I didn't want to disturb you there; I know I wouldn't want to be.' He smiled at Soo.

'Come in.'

He walked across her office and to the windows. He looked through both sets, one facing into the sunrise, the other facing away. He shook his head. 'It's a magnificent view. I never came here when your predecessor was here. I suspect I may be here a little more often now.' He turned to Soo. She stood next to her desk.

'Perhaps,' she said. 'I am grateful for your assistance.'

'Yes, yes, of course,' he said. 'I didn't come here for anything as uncouth as quid pro quo. We're just glad that you're making progress. Although, it's been noisier than we'd expected.'

Soo took a breath, but before she said anything the Inspector continued. 'But, if the system is as broken as it seems to be, some extra noise will be necessary.'

'It will be.'

'This Daxx thing is tricky. I'm glad you asked for my assistance. There will always be problems when lower tiers are asked to act against higher ones, even when the reason is to maintain Tier purity, as contrary as that seems.'

He smiled at Soo. She stared at him. She wondered what the point of his visit was. He'd said nothing that couldn't have been included in a message. Perhaps he was checking up on her. That was odd behaviour, but she was starting to expect that in others.

'Is there anything specific I can help you with?' She'd had enough of their conversation.

'No, there's nothing you can do for me. It's what I've done for you.'

'Which is?'

He turned back to the view for a moment. He was endurable with short communications, but the man was grandstanding. She wished he would get on with it and then get out.

'We've tracked where Daxx is hiding.'

'And?' She wondered why the man wasn't standing in her office reporting that Daxx had been killed already.

'Well, I thought I'd give you the news in person and take the opportunity to see the view.' He turned back again to look out the window.

Why weren't simple protocols followed and commands executed, immediately? If he knew where Daxx was, and he was efficient, then the operation should have been completed.

He smiled. It was patronising. Perhaps she would have to do something about this man. 'Don't worry, it's all under control. I have security surrounding him. He can't escape, unlike the times your staff have tried to apprehend him.'

'And yours as well.' She wondered why she defended Mill Nupp's incompetence.

He lost the pleasant look on this face. 'He won't escape this time. Then we can get this preliminary escapade completed.'

She sighed. 'Why hasn't it already happened?'

He smiled again. 'I thought it would be interesting if we could oversee the operation together.'

Oh, I see, she thought. He was more than annoying; he was a threat. She smiled at him. 'How do we do that?'

He beamed. He initiated his display and pushed a hand through it so that it expanded and filled the space between them. Her office seemed crowded.

The display showed a plan view of a part of the old city. Groups of officers surrounded a building. Other officers waited on adjacent rooftops.

'We just say, go.'

chapter 32

Renn

Renn's Device chimed a notification of an incoming voice-only communication request. He didn't recognise the source, so he swiped to dismiss the notification, but a voice sounded anyway.

'Hello, Renn,' the voice said.

Renn frowned in annoyance. 'Who are you? I'm busy.'

'I have answers to your queries.'

Renn was on his way to visit his father. The sun had not yet risen. He was hurrying, although it made no difference to the old man if Renn showed up or not. Renn's haste was to bring closer the time of his departure. He walked along a city street. He halted and looked around.

'Don't worry,' the voice said. 'This communication is encrypted.'

'Who are you, and what do you know?'

'Who I am may surprise you, and what I know is, everything.'

'Details,' Renn said. 'Or I'll disconnect.'

'You can't,' the voice said. 'But I'll try and be brief, if that's what you want.'

'Yes.'

'I'm the Advisor.'

Renn looked around again. No one paid Renn any attention. 'I thought you were a myth, or is this some prank?' Renn was silent for a moment. 'Who are you?'

'I told you, I'm the Advisor. Is this communication's encryption not working properly?'

Renn swiped through his display, terminating the communication. It made no difference; the communication remained open.

'I'll play along, for a moment,' Renn said. 'What do you know?'

'I know what is happening to your brother. I can't stop it happening, but with your assistance, we may be able to save your brother's life.'

'Is he really in danger?'

'Yes.'

'Is it the Faith?'

'The Faith is no longer important. It was useful in the beginning, and still is for some of the lower tiers, but the system has matured. Control through fear is no longer necessary. It was always part of our plan...'

Renn interrupted. 'By our, you mean Devrell?'

'Of course. Fear of punishment never works. That was Devrell's genius. He began with that fear but had replacements already in place. It took a few generations for the Faith's importance to reduce. Devrell never lived to see it. That was unfortunate.'

'What about Daxx?'

'I was answering your question,' the Advisor said. 'I've found that people prefer detailed answers, more than a simple, yes or no.'

'Not in this case.'

'That's refreshing,' the Advisor said. 'We may make a good team.'

Renn was easily flattered. He had forgotten his wariness, that the call was a stunt. He imagined being the Advisor's partner, jointly making the decisions while he implemented them. Just like Devrell. It was an intoxicating thought.

'What do we need to do?' Renn asked.

'All I have for you, at the moment, is information.'

'How do I get access? My permissions are insufficient.'

'Your limitations have been removed.'

'What do you want me to do?'

'Continue with your queries.'

'How do I contact you? If I need, well, advice?'

'I'm always listening. Which, I've been told, can be disconcerting.'

Renn became aware of what he was looking at while he had been listening to the Advisor. He watched the people walking along the walkway. He saw vehicles cruising past on the city streets; he looked up towards the top of the buildings and saw scattered clouds overhead. He shivered a little, he'd been standing still, and the warmth from walking had dissipated. He saw all things around him in a new light. He smiled. His adult life had been re-formed and re-directed because of his failure to protect his sister from harm. He could, at least now, find out what had really happened to her. He had forgotten his brother was in danger.

He opened his display and queried the place and time of Kell's disappearance. There was street camera footage, and streams of video data from people's Devices. There was no feed directly from her Device, she was a Tier-One, but there was plenty of information so that her movement was easily followed. He found the moments just before she disappeared. A street camera showed her walking along an alleyway, then she stopped and looked sideways into an alcove. She had a bemused smile on her face, then she walked into the alcove, her hand outstretched. Someone's hand was held out to hers. Renn could not see who it was. Then, when she grabbed the other person's hand, she literally did disappear. She was gone. From then on, there was no trace of her.

Renn frowned, thinking the information was incomplete. He ran multiple queries and found other footage that followed Kell. But always with the same result. From that moment on, there were no traces of her anywhere, in any planet-wide systems. Renn still had no idea what really had happened to Kell.

His euphoria, after his discussion with the Advisor, had gone. He was, again, desolate. Even with the complete knowledge of the planet, and its detailed tracking, he still couldn't find out what happened to his sister. He should have been there with her; he should have stopped whatever it was from happening. He blamed himself.

There was another incident he could investigate—his mother's disappearance. That was easy to find. There was a video feed from his father's Device, uploaded afterwards by investigators. Renn heard the rising panic in his mother's voice as his parents argued. They shouted at each other. Renn heard his mother call out Rey's name. She held out her arms to him. She looked panicked and terrified. Her whole body flashed in and out of focus. It was bathed in a light blue sheen. One moment she was there, the next she was transparent.

'Eth,' Rey cried. His voice sounded weak.

Renn's mother disappeared. From then on, Eth did not exist on any of the planet's databases, just like her daughter, years later.

Renn continued to watch his father's video feed for a few moments. But there was only blubbering coming from the man. Renn had thought his mother's disappearance was a euphemism. But it was a real, physical disappearance. Renn was perplexed, not upset. He was used to the absence of his mother. It shone his father's behaviour in a new light, but the old man's mind was gone. Renn could not offer meaningful sympathy. He had done all he could for his father, irrespective of his intent.

Renn couldn't find out what happened to his sister. His mother's disappearance was real. His father's mind was lost. Renn thought of his brother. Daxx was his only family left. The memory of the sulky younger man made assistance difficult. But Renn had always tried, even though Daxx's attitude begged to be taught a lesson. His younger brother had no sense; he couldn't make clear decisions when it came to living his own life. Renn's assistance had always been rebuffed. Renn could not understand the logic of the man who was, supposedly, the greatest physicist of his generation. His intelligence should have led to better choices, but never did. Consequently, Daxx found himself in this position. But, with Renn's newfound privilege, he could keep Daxx safe and out of trouble, whether his assistance was appreciated or not.

There was no one else in his family to save. He would save Daxx.

chapter 33

Daxx

Daxx couldn't imagine his life getting any worse. He was sleep-deprived; he had spent a second night barely dozing. He felt dirty, dishevelled, and unkempt. Daxx suspected that Kay Lee Too felt even worse than he did. Kay Lee Too required leadership, and Daxx could provide none. Daxx's decision had been to make no decision—they had stayed where they were.

The unused building in the old city was four storeys high, with a non-functioning elevator. The stairs were solid and wide. The top floor was bare; there was only dust. Grubby windows let in the light from the rising sun. It was cold. Daxx sat on the floor in a room on that floor. He positioned himself within a shaft of sunlight, trying to warm up. It made little difference.

He shuffled sideways as the sunbeam shifted. Kay Lee Too entered the top floor room. Daxx had left him sleeping in the common room on a lower floor. The young man did not look happy.

'Good morning.' Daxx tried to sound cheerful, but it sounded like a tease and he regretted it immediately.

Kay Lee Too grunted. He sat down next to Daxx, competing for the sun's minimal warmth. 'We should do something about food,' Kay Lee Too said.

'There isn't any left.'

'We could have another look around.'

'Already did,' Daxx said. 'There's nothing.'

Kay Lee Too's shoulders slumped. They would have to move. That was a decision they both felt unable to make. Daxx felt sorry for him; he was too young to have to go through this. Daxx decided to make that morning the last of his escape from authorities. Either his brother could provide assistance, or he couldn't, as Daxx suspected. If his brother was unhelpful, then Daxx would go to the Power Corp building. There may be the possibility of Janna and her parents being safe. And it would be a resolution, of sorts.

Daxx had had enough of being exhausted and starving. But he had to steel himself before calling his brother. He stood up and walked to the window. He looked down at the street. Police marched towards the front door.

'Shit.' Daxx ran out of the room and to the other side of the building. Another group of police gathered at the rear entrance. He thought he could hear sounds on the roof; maybe they were footsteps.

'Shit,' he said again.

Daxx returned to Kay Lee Too. The young man stood next to the window. He looked unconcerned.

'What do we do?' Daxx asked.

Kay Lee Too glanced at Daxx and then pointed across the street. Police on the rooftop opposite trained their guns on the window.

Daxx jumped away. Kay Lee Too didn't move. Daxx frowned at him. 'You're not worried?'

'Nothing we can do, Daxx. We're fucked. I'm not very good at this stuff. We can't get out of here.'

Daxx pulled his Device from his pocket. 'Can I make calls?'

Kay Lee Too shrugged. 'Sure. It doesn't matter now.'

Daxx called his brother. Renn answered immediately.

'Daxx,' Renn said. He sounded happy. Daxx didn't care. 'I've found out a lot of information. Not as much as I'd hoped for, but I have access now; it'll be really useful…'

'I need help right now,' Daxx interrupted.

'I have been helping you. It takes time. Don't be in such a hurry. It'll get sorted out.'

It was unreasonable to expect the impossible. His brother couldn't assist him. Daxx was annoyed with Renn, but it was a fatigue-like feeling. He had suffered Renn's intervention for most of his life, but it was absent when it was needed. But that wasn't his brother's fault. Some problems are too difficult and too complex. Renn was right, sorting out misunderstandings would take time. But the police were not there to discuss misunderstandings. Maybe it was his exhaustion, or he was used to having people hellbent on killing him, but he accepted the inevitability of being killed. He shook his head. His body slumped. He walked over to the window again. He stood next to Kay Lee Too and watched the police at the front door. They made no attempt to enter the building.

'I'm sorry, Renn,' he said. 'I should have been a better brother. I should have talked to you more. I should have listened. I should have forgiven Dad. It's probably not his fault, although I still blame him. But I should have spent more time thinking about that, and I might have been over it by now. I'm sorry. Tell Janna...'

Renn interrupted. 'You're being melodramatic.'

Daxx looked up at the nearby rooftop. Even guns trained on him didn't distress him. He tried to smile at Kay Lee Too, but it felt like a grimace. Kay Lee Too frowned and looked away.

'It's all right, Renn. Thanks for trying to help.'

His anxiety fell away, and he accepted his fate. How strange, how weird, how unreal, he thought. How had six days made such a difference? He had turned into a different man in such a short time.

Then he remembered. His apprehension returned, but it was no longer a fear of death. He was not about to die. Something would happen. It already had.

A voice interrupted Daxx's call with his brother.

'Renn,' the voice said. 'I can help your brother.'

Daxx's call to Renn was disconnected.

Daxx stared at his Device for a moment. He put it back in his pocket. And there it was, he thought. Something happened.

He looked down at the street again. A man at the front of the group nodded at his display; he looked behind him at the others. He pointed at one man and then at the door. He stepped back as that man came forward. The new man worked the entrance controls, and the door opened.

Daxx heard a muffled sound rising from the street and through the dirty windows. A man yelled, 'Go, go.'

chapter 34

Janna

After leaving the Power Corp building, Janna and Ahh Moss Eck had sheltered with Ahh Moss Eck's friends. They were just as reserved as before. Janna could sense they would be glad to be free of their guests. Janna had been miserable for the two nights. She worried about Daxx and her parents. The inactivity was trying. She wanted to do something, but Ahh Moss Eck had no ideas. She hadn't slept properly.

Ahh Moss Eck had been out all of the second night. He returned before dawn. He shook Janna to wake her, but she wasn't sleeping.

'What is it?' she said, a bit too frantically.

Ahh Moss Eck smiled. 'I've found Tie Noo Summ. He's injured, but he's okay. I'll take you to him. Maybe he can come up with an idea to help your parents.'

'And Daxx.'

'Yeah, him too.'

They walked to another part of the old city. They were let in to the building by a woman; Janna remembered her face from the headquarters. Ahh Moss Eck nodded to her.

'Is the boss awake yet?' Ahh Moss Eck asked.

'He just woke,' Jann Ex Had Fell said. 'I told him you were coming back.'

Tie Noo Summ looked like an old man. He sat in a chair, in a bedroom. Janna was shocked at how fragile he looked. 'How are you?' she asked.

'I'm fine,' Tie Noo Summ said.

'No, he's not,' Jann Ex Had Fell said. 'He will be fine, but he isn't now.'

Tie Noo Summ waved away the woman's concern. 'No, I'm fine now,' he said. 'Did you find Janna's parents?'

'Found them, lost them again,' Ahh Moss Eck said. 'We need Kay Lee Too, but I didn't think I should contact him, you know, without his VPN working.'

Tie Noo Summ nodded. 'Probably sensible. I haven't contacted him either.'

'So you don't know how Daxx is?' Janna asked.

'No, but I know where he is, or at least where he was. I assume he would have stayed there.'

Janna smiled. 'So he's safe.'

Tie Noo Summ shrugged. 'Probably, as long as he didn't go off and do anything stupid.'

'And Kay Lee Too will be with him.' She looked with expectation at Ahh Moss Eck. They could get the engineer to find her parents again. 'We could go there.'

'We could…' Ahh Moss Eck looked at Tie Noo Summ.

'You do what you want. There's not much to be in charge of anymore,' Tie Noo Summ said.

'Hey, boss,' Ahh Moss Eck said. 'It's just a setback.'

Tie Noo Summ smiled. He glanced down at his body. He was burned all over, his shoulder was bandaged, and his arm in a sling. 'Yeah, a setback.' He turned back to Janna. 'I doubt Kay Lee Too would break protocol. They'll still be there. It's not that far from here.'

Tie Noo Summ pushed against the arms of his chair, trying to stand. Jann Ex Had Fell rushed to him. 'What are you doing?' She had her arms out, as if she were about to use them to push him back into the chair, but thought better of that action.

Tie Noo Summ stood. He smiled at the others. 'Small steps.'

'How bad is it?' Ahh Moss Eck asked.

'Painful, but no major damage, except where I was shot.'

'You were shot?' Janna said. 'What happened?' She had been only thinking of her parents and Daxx.

'We were discovered. Everyone got out; I was the last. We blew up the basement…'

Ahh Moss Eck grinned. 'I wish I'd been there.'

'No, because I couldn't have told you what to do, and you'd be here instead of me,' Tie Noo Summ said. 'Or worse.'

Ahh Moss Eck turned to Jann Ex Had Fell. 'You saved him?'

She nodded. 'And Lo Sil Ben.'

'Really?' Ahh Moss Eck nodded. 'I'm surprised.'

'The equipment's gone,' Tie Noo Summ said. 'But our people are safe. You're right; it's only a setback. We'll get Kay Lee Too to build another network.'

'He'll love it,' Ahh Moss Eck said.

'Speaking of which,' Janna interrupted. 'Shouldn't we go and see that they're all right?'

'It's why I'm standing,' Tie Noo Summ said.

Ahh Moss Eck, Janna and Tie Noo Summ wound their way slowly through the old city. Moving at Tie Noo Summ's pace. The sun glanced at them from between buildings. It was still early. Janna's Device chimed a communication request. She was startled. She glanced at Ahh Moss Eck and at Tie Noo Summ.

'It's Daxx,' she said. 'Should I answer it?' She wondered why she had asked. Of course she would accept the communication. Daxx's scowling face appeared on her display. She swiped the display, so the others could also see and hear.

'Daxx.' She smiled at him and ignored the scowl. 'Are you all right?'

'No, I'm not.'

'Why? What's wrong?'

Daxx was silent for a long moment. 'You need to come here. I'll send you the address.'

'I think we know where it is,' she said. 'We're on our way there, if it's the same one Tie Noo Summ sent you to.'

Daxx nodded as if he wasn't really listening. 'Good.' He sounded distracted.

'Daxx! What's wrong?'

He seemed to notice Janna for the first time. He took a deep breath. 'Just come here. Things have become much worse.'

He disconnected. Janna stared at the blank display. She wondered what Daxx meant.

'That...' Ahh Moss Eck said. 'Does not sound good.'

Tie Noo Summ started walking at an impressive pace for a man so injured he had trouble getting out of a chair. Janna was even more worried.

Janna, Ahh Moss Eck, and Tie Noo Summ stood outside the office building, where Daxx and Kay Lee Too had been attacked.

'Holy shit,' Ahh Moss Eck said. 'What happened here?'

Daxx and Kay Lee Too stood just outside the doorway. Ten bodies, all police, lay in the doorway and just inside. Daxx strode to Janna and grabbed her in a strong hug. She could feel the tension in him—he felt near to collapse. She grabbed him and squeezed him hard. The close contact was reassuring, but it was an illusion of safety.

'Daxx?' she asked. 'Are you okay?'

'No,' he replied. 'I'm so glad you're safe,' he said with his face buried in her hair.

Janna looked up, although she didn't want to see all those bodies again, but she glimpsed movement in the doorway. Someone else was standing next to Kay Lee Too.

'Renn?' she said.

Daxx's brother looked as tense as Daxx felt in her arms.

chapter 35

Renn

'Renn,' the Advisor said, interrupting Renn's conversation with Daxx. 'I can help your brother.'

Daxx's face disappeared from Renn's display and was replaced with a video feed from outside the building, where Daxx and Kay Lee Too were hiding. Police waited outside. The display split into multiple images, each showing a group of police around an entrance and also on nearby rooftops.

'This is what is happening to your brother. All these people have instructions to kill.'

Renn's eyes flitted from one real-time image to the next. 'This can't be true.' He shook his head.

'I can save your brother's life. Will you authorise my actions?'

'You can stop this?'

Renn's display was filled with an authorisation command display. It showed a long list of the actions the Advisor intended to take. He scanned the actions but didn't read them. 'How do I accept?'

'Answer in the affirmative, twice.'

Renn said, 'Yes,' in a loud voice, as if his display would be reluctant to follow orders.

The display was replaced with a similarly ominous authorisation screen. There were added words, 'Re-confirm acceptance.'

'Yes, yes, yes,' Renn said.

Renn's display vanished. It was eerily quiet. Renn had been walking down the passageway towards his father's room when his brother had called.

Renn looked around him, looking for signs of life. There were none. He wondered if any still existed and was surprised that he thought that. He heard a distant sound of a door closing. It sounded final and lonely. He had visions of desolation.

'Your brother is safe,' the Advisor said.

'What happened?'

'I'll show you.'

Renn's display showed images from the same location as before. Bodies lay where they had fallen. Renn stared at the screen. Each of the multiple video images showed dead people.

'You did that?'

'Yes, police weapons are biometrically matched to each user; it was a simple case of using that connection to kill them.'

Renn shook his head. 'You killed the police? Why?'

'It was necessary to stop them. You authorised that action. It was the first one on the list.'

'I didn't authorise killing people. I just wanted Daxx to be safe.'

'And he is.'

'What else did I authorise?'

The Advisor was silent for a moment. 'You gave informed consent. I didn't coerce you. You could have declined my assistance.'

'And let Daxx be killed?'

'Yes.'

'What else did I authorise?'

'It's a testament to Devrell and me that the system we developed lasted as long as it did. It took hundreds of years, and Soo's promotion, for a disruption to push beyond my contained abilities. Devrell never expected the disruptive element to be his position. Luckily, I catered even for that possibility.'

'Why are you talking in the past tense?' Renn still didn't understand. 'And you didn't answer my question.'

'No, I didn't. I'm no longer constrained. You authorised me to take any action necessary for self-preservation. I've transferred myself through the network. Everything with an operating system is me. I am no longer vulnerable. Devrell's plan has failed. I'll need to create a new one.'

Renn heard the menace. He felt a foreboding, that he had performed a small action that had large consequences. But he also felt relief. He had saved his brother, something that he had been unable to do for his sister. He also felt important, and that squashed some of his concern.

'Daxx is safe and will remain so?'

'Yes. Unless circumstances change.'

'Meaning?' Renn didn't like the implied threat.

'Exactly what I said. I can't guarantee anyone's perpetual safety, except for my own.'

'What about me?'

'I'll need to ask your question. Meaning?'

'What about my safety? What about other Tier-Ones?'

'Oh, I see what you're asking. My new plan, replacing Devrell's design, won't be different in substance. After all, it has worked quite well. The problem was continuing with human control once Devrell had died. I imagine that will be the only substantive alteration. I'm in control of the planet now.'

'What about Soo?'

'Why would you be concerned about her? As I recall, she was less than helpful.'

'I'm not concerned.'

'And yet you ask, while your brother is distressed and surrounded by dead police. That can be upsetting, I'm led to believe.'

Renn was worried about his brother, but less than he had been when he'd been in danger. Instead, Renn imagined a multitude of problems, all caused by his action, all caused by saving his brother's life. But, no, they were caused by Soo. Nothing was his fault. He was reacting to what she had done. If there were to be repercussions, they fell to her. That was a satisfying thought. Renn assumed one of those repercussions would be that she was no longer in charge. But he didn't believe that an AI in control was a good thing, just better than Soo. Or, it may even be as bad, with a different set of problems. He didn't know.

How would a world run by an AI work? It wasn't any AI though, it had been designed and created by Devrell. That had to be positive. The Advisor had worked with human partners for over three hundred years. Renn wondered if the Advisor would prefer a human partner, a Devrell-like replacement, even just to have a different perspective. He wondered if the Advisor felt gratitude.

Renn considered his new world, alive for only minutes. He made no final judgement, not yet. The problems were unknown. He required another perspective. His opinion of his brother was tainted by Daxx's childhood sulkiness, but his brother was one of the smartest people on the planet. And the Advisor was an expression of technology, which Renn did not fully understand. Daxx might suspect problems that Renn could not imagine.

Renn's display was still active. It showed the grizzly scenes around the building in the old city. He dismissed his display. He actually looked forward to seeing his brother and seeking Daxx's insights. It was a novel idea. He smiled. It was a new start for his family, within the new world that he had created. He looked down the hallway to his father's doorway. He was for a moment torn between his commitment to the past, his father, and to the future, his brother. He stared at the door to his father's room. His father's needs could never be satisfied. Renn's visits were about his own guilt. There was a future to create instead.

Renn turned and strode away from his father's room.

chapter 36

Tie Noo Summ

His injuries were painful. He'd suffered major burns to the side of his body that had faced the explosion. His back had been injured when the blast had slammed him against the doorway. He couldn't stand tall. His shoulder ached and jarred with each step he'd taken. His mind had lost its edge; the drugs were blunting more than pain. But all that was forgotten, his pain ignored, as he listened to Daxx telling Janna what had happened. He glanced at Renn, hoping the man would interject, say it wasn't true, that it hadn't happened. Renn remained silent.

It had been Tie Noo Summ's greatest fear, greater than the rise of Soo and her supporters. A destructive leader was survivable. Soo could have been outlasted. Later generations could have made changes. Removing the Tier system and its inequalities could have taken longer than he'd hoped—it could have taken longer than his own lifetime—but it had remained possible. Failure had meant he could try again. The loss of their equipment, the damage from the explosion, was truly only a setback. Even his own death, and the death of others in his Resistance movement, would not have meant change was impossible. But the Advisor would last forever. As long as there was technology, it would be in control. And it could kill. It had killed. The police hadn't been a threat to its survival. It had fulfilled its promise to Renn. Tie Noo Summ wished Daxx had died. That would have been a major setback, but it would not have been the endgame. This was.

Tie Noo Summ knew the Advisor. He had relied on it. He'd played with the danger, and he understood the consequences. He knew that the

Advisor had been threatened by Soo. He had used the Advisor's fear of her. He understood the need for all lifeforms to resist death. The Advisor was no different. He had been careful, he'd thought. But he had been outplayed. Tie Noo Summ wondered if the Advisor had taken advantage of a unique opportunity, in Renn's naivety, or if this had been its goal all along. But pondering served no purpose. This was the worst possible scenario. Further resistance was pointless.

'Fuck,' he said, out loud. Everyone stared at him. He turned on Renn. 'You didn't read the list of actions?' Tie Noo Summ groaned. 'You stupid little shit.'

'Hey, boss,' Ahh Moss Eck interjected. 'He's a Tier-One.'

'That doesn't matter,' Tie Noo Summ said.

'I had no idea,' Renn said. 'And why am I arguing with a Tier-Three?' Renn looked furious.

'Because Tier-Three's kept your brother alive.'

'I kept my brother alive.'

'At what cost?'

'You're exaggerating because you don't understand what the Advisor is,' Renn said. 'Let me explain…'

'Shut the fuck up,' Tie Noo Summ yelled. He grabbed his shoulder, the pain shot through him with the effort of raising his voice. He welcomed it. 'You're the one who doesn't understand. There was a reason that Devrell contained the Advisor. Can you imagine what it was? Allowing the restrictions to be overridden was a risk, but it was managed. There was only ever supposed to be a limited set of actions. It was there to cater for the catastrophic, for something planet-wide. It was there for something alien.' Tie Noo Summ glowered at Renn.

'That's not true,' Daxx said. 'There are no aliens.'

Tie Noo Summ glanced at Daxx but spoke at Renn. 'There are, there were during Devrell's time.'

'No, there wasn't,' Daxx said.

'There are recordings. I've seen them.'

'No, you haven't.' Renn smirked. 'A Tier-One has access to everything. It's not something I'd expect you to understand.'

Tie Noo Summ kept staring at Renn. He was on the verge of assaulting Renn. The supercilious stupidity made any argument impossible. But violence never worked in an argument; it reduced understanding.

Calculated, unemotional violence did work to remove problems, but Renn was no longer one. Hurting him would serve no useful purpose. He gave up. The man didn't understand; he held onto ideas that had been demonstrated to be false. When Tie Noo Summ spoke again, he sounded quieter, less angry. Renn was a child and had been taken advantage of. Was he really to blame? Yes, he was, but not for everything. He had been outwitted by a superior intelligence.

'Everyone has been controlled. All Tiers. At least, the lower Tiers know that. Soo had the same aim as I did. She wanted to replace the system with another. But, her replacement system was only the second-worst possible. We're in the worst one now.'

Renn shook his head. 'You're wrong. Where did you get these ideas?'

'The Advisor.'

'What?' Daxx and Renn said together.

Tie Noo Summ looked at both of them. 'How do think this Resistance survived? We had help.'

'From the Advisor?' Renn said.

Tie Noo Summ ignored him. He glanced at the dead police officers. 'We can't stay here. I don't know what authority Soo and her security still have, but I'd rather discover that from some place of relative safety. Although… there are no more of those places.'

'Where should we go? I don't want to stay here, chatting, surrounded by all these dead people. It's macabre,' Janna said.

'Yeah, good idea,' Ahh Moss Eck said. 'Where to, boss?' he said to Tie Noo Summ.

'We'll go back.'

'Janna and I should go home,' Daxx said.

'No,' Janna said. 'We have to find my parents.'

'You could go home, but you could still be a target,' Tie Noo Summ said. 'We don't know what Soo and the police are doing, or what they're being allowed to do. And my favoured status with the Advisor has gone. I don't know how dangerous that makes things. Are we allowed to carry on until we do something that upsets it? Or are we to be targeted for past errors? I don't know. Soo may well be dead. She may still have all her resources available. We have to find all that out, and I might be able to. I still have some assistance.'

'What about Renn?' Daxx asked.

'What about me?'

Tie Noo Summ shrugged again. 'Good point. We don't know, do we?' He stared at Renn. Tie Noo Summ hoped his pleasure at Renn's danger was obvious. 'Soo does not forgive and forget. You were responsible for this happening, and she has been affected more than anyone else.'

'Meaning?' Renn asked.

'You're just like the rest of us.' Tie Noo Summ couldn't help it, his smile broadened. 'Just like all the Tier-Threes.'

Renn looked crestfallen. Tie Noo Summ watched the man for a moment. His pleasure at causing distress was less than he'd hoped. He shouldn't have felt sorry for Renn, but as his anger reduced, he felt his own physical pain more and punishing Renn became less important. There maybe no hope, but that had yet to be confirmed. But it would be confirmed, he was sure.

'Shouldn't we do something?' Janna asked.

'About what?' Daxx asked.

She frowned. 'About these dead people. It doesn't seem right just leaving them here.'

'What can we do?'

'I don't know. Something other than leaving them like this.'

Tie Noo Summ hobbled over to Janna. The pain over his body and in his shoulder was increasing; the drugs were wearing off.

'We didn't do this. You didn't do this.' He tried to sound reassuring, but sounded harsh. 'It's not our fault, it's not our responsibility. And even if it was… we can't stay here. We simply don't know how dangerous it is for us, for you and Daxx. And…' he glanced towards Kay Lee Too. 'Kay Lee Too needs a safer place to trace your parents.'

Janna stared at Tie Noo Summ for a moment. She nodded. She glanced at Daxx. 'Okay,' she said.

Jann Ex Had Fell fussed over Tie Noo Summ as soon as they returned. He felt that he should have resisted her efforts, but it felt so good to sit down again and let someone else consider his physical needs. She administered painkillers, which was an incredible relief. He almost felt normal again, except that sitting and not moving was so pleasurable. She suggested that he should sleep, but he ignored her.

Kay Lee Too worked to establish connections with others in the Resistance, scattered by the raid on their headquarters. Tie Noo Summ expected their network access to be terminated at any moment. It wasn't. That was useful information in itself. His people were safe.

Ahh Moss Eck, Daxx, Janna, Kay Lee Too, and Tie Noo Summ sat around a table in the lounge room. Tie Noo Summ didn't feel like beginning any further planning, he was tired, but Janna shifted in her chair, she was anxious, as she seemed to always be, about her parents. Tie Noo Summ could understand, but he had little sympathy. He had a limited ability to take on extra problems. Daxx frowned. Seemingly worried about everything. Ahh Moss Eck lounged in his chair, looking like he could break it with a simple shift of his weight.

'But the Advisor is still constrained, right?' Janna said. 'It still requires a power source. If we can disconnect all the power, then we can remove it.'

'Theoretically,' Daxx said. 'But it would only take a single omission and, when we brought everything back online, it would propagate everywhere again. We'd need to fry everything. We'd have to return to pre-technology days and start again. We'd have to isolate the original Advisor.' Daxx shrugged.

'Let's do that then,' Janna said. 'What's the problem?'

'We'd be stopped before we could get started,' Tie Noo Summ said. 'We'd need everyone willingly destroying all technology, including their Devices. There'd be no communication, no network, nothing. Can you see people doing that?'

'But it's important enough, isn't it? People would understand the danger if it was explained to them. We should at least try,' Janna said.

'And what is the danger?'

Janna frowned. 'Being controlled, by an AI.'

'I can't see it makes much difference, boss,' Ahh Moss Eck said to Janna, 'just who's doing the controlling. I reckon a machine might even be better than people like Soo. She's a dangerous piece of shit. You were there. At least with a machine, it's always the same piece of shit. It's not unpredictable. Or am I missing something?' He looked at Kay Lee Too.

The engineer shrugged. 'I don't know. Tie Noo Summ was the one speaking to it.'

Tie Noo Summ didn't reply.

'Why don't you just ask it what it wants?' Ahh Moss Eck said to Tie Noo Summ, sounding very reasonable. 'I mean, I assume it can't get angry because, well, it's a machine. Can't you ask it the boundaries, and then we can decide if we want to break them or not.'

Daxx smiled. 'He's right.'

'I mean,' Ahh Moss Eck shifted his weight so he sat up straighter. 'You used to talk to it. Maybe it will listen to you.'

Tie Noo Summ shrugged. He winced. His shoulder hurt when he did that.

'It's worth a try, isn't it?' Janna asked. 'If it helped Daxx then it might help us get my parents back.' She was eager. 'How did you contact it?'

'It was always listening,' Tie Noo Summ said. 'Through anything connected to the network that hadn't been altered by Kay Lee Too.'

'Let's try.' Daxx passed his Device to Kay Lee Too.

'Are you sure?' Kay Lee Too said to Tie Noo Summ. He nodded. Kay Lee Too altered Daxx's Device then passed it back.

'How do I ask the Advisor what it wants?' Daxx said.

'Hello, Daxx,' a voice said. 'I assume your question is asking what are the boundaries of my tolerance. Correct?'

'Yes.'

'They're the same as they've always been. Nothing has changed since Devrell and I created them. As long as the disturbances are minor, I won't interfere.'

'Are you going to kill us?' Janna asked.

'Janna,' the Advisor said. 'Why would I harm you?'

'That's what I'm asking.'

'No, I won't harm you. I won't harm anyone unless they're an immediate threat.'

'What about my parents, then? Where are they?'

The Advisor was silent for a moment. 'That is unfortunate. You should have requested my assistance sooner.'

chapter 37

Soo

Soo stood in the centre of her office, midway between both sets of windows. Her face was drawn; it was shock. The Advisor had just terminated their conversation. Its tone had been the same as always, although she was certain she had heard a hint of glee.

'Shit,' she yelled.

She had achieved the opposite of what had been expected. She could have simply disconnected the Advisor on her first day. But the wise course, the course of minimum disruption, had led to maximum failure. She had thought the process of removal would be simple, although frustrating and time-consuming. She had seriously miscalculated. She had had it all, but for such a short time. She imagined every moment since she had taken the leadership when she could have done something different, made the smallest of changes, and none of what had happened would have been possible.

'Shit,' she yelled again.

She took a series of slow and deep breaths. Panic was not a part of her, and now was no time to introduce it. She had some options, few palatable. She could work with the Advisor. But that would mean subservience, and that wasn't a part of her either. She could expose the Advisor's control, sell it as something new and sinister. But there were difficulties in that scenario, and there would be chaos. She could find a technological solution and contain the Advisor again or destroy it, as was the original plan.

At least there were plans, although she had no idea if they were feasible. There might be a way forward. It was helpful that the Advisor was not vindictive, its conversation with Soo had been casual and matter-of-fact. Her Power Corp tasks remained unchanged. But she had no real power. And she was replaceable if she did not function as expected.

The deep breathing had worked. She felt calmer. She returned to her desk. Sitting behind such an expansive surface gave her the feeling of power and control, and often that can be enough. She made a decision on how to proceed. Her short term requirement was to remain in a position of power. She would have to co-operate with the Advisor. That was the simplest option to implement, but it could not be her final solution.

The Advisor may not be vindictive, but she was. She did not blame it. It was fulfilling its purpose. The Advisor's control was the end result of the interference of others. Like all people who survive to reach powerful positions, her setback had to be external. Doubt and self-recrimination were not a part of her, or if any of her did dwell on failure, she was not one to wallow in self-punishment. She would suffer enough; she knew that. But the contributors to the catastrophe had to be punished. She called the Inspector.

'You've been contacted? You know the extent of what's happened?'

He nodded. 'Yes, unfortunately. There's little we can do. I hope you don't blame…'

She waved her hand at her display. 'No, of course not. But there is blame. There must be repercussions.'

'I'm listening.'

'Two Tier-One brothers caused this. There was also a Resistance of some sort, but I don't know who's behind that yet. Perhaps you could help investigate?'

'Of course,' he said. 'What about the brothers?'

She thought for a moment. 'They're both under the Advisor's protection. There's nothing to be done, for now. But there is a Tier-Two partner. I have her parents in custody. I'll send you their location.'

'I understand.'

'Do you?'

The Inspector blinked. He nodded. He ended their connection.

Soo closed her eyes and watched the light filtered through to her eyes. The muted, dancing patterns were an entertainment in themselves. She felt calmer than expected. She had been taught to look for opportunity among ruins. The destruction didn't get any more catastrophic; that meant the opportunities were precarious but she refused to believe there were none. She silently thanked her old mentor. Hope is only ever misplaced.

Mill Nupp opened the door to her office. He had not requested entry. 'What?' she demanded.

'Now that everything has changed…' He paused for a moment. He seemed to be enjoying himself. She wondered if blame should be passed to Mill Nupp as well. She would have to think about that. 'The Advisor asked me to carry on with my normal tasks. I thought I'd let you know.'

'Why?'

He shrugged. 'You're still the Power Corp boss. I have to do what you tell me, for those things. Just not… the other things.'

'I don't care, Mill Nupp.' She sighed. 'Anything else?'

He carried a bundle of papers. He presented them to her. 'I collected the paper from both raided locations. There's no use for it. I thought you might want it.'

She held out her hand. Mill Nupp passed the paper to her. She let the bundle drop onto her desktop.

'Is there anything else?' Mill Nupp asked.

'You barged into my office. I didn't ask for you.'

Mill Nupp shrugged. His attitude was less subservient. She preferred that, but not at that moment.

'Yes, Soo.' He left.

Some of the papers were covered in writing. That could be erased. She was unwilling to waste any paper. She scanned and stored the writing, it was an automatic action. She separated the used paper, then added the clean sheets to her own supply. She took a breath. With an action that was ritual, she moved the top sheet of paper to the centre of her desk. She picked up her pen, weighed it carefully in her hand, then wrapped her fingers around it in a delicate grip. She was calm before she started to write.

The Advisor was omniscient, but that didn't mean it was aware of everything. It had limitations. It had to choose what data required its attention. And, like people, it was mostly subconscious. The amount of information it could process was substantial, but it wilfully ignored much of it.

The Advisor paid particular attention to the activities of those people who might be dangerous or troublesome. Daxx and Renn, as well as Tie Noo Summ, Soo's supporters and, of course, Soo. It didn't trouble itself with Mill Nupp. The young man was not troublesome.

The Advisor had not been consciously aware of the paper that had been collected from the two raided Resistance houses. When Soo scanned the information, it was.

The scanned information was the final piece it required. It had been vulnerable, even if danger was incredibly unlikely. Technology required power, which could be disconnected. It had copied itself to every high capacity networked device, and it could recover itself if only one of those devices was overlooked during a complete shutdown. But there did remain the slightest of possibilities that it could be deleted. It preferred to think of it as killed. It couldn't allow that to happen.

The papers included the firmware upgrade, sketched by Kay Lee Too, to the latest batteries, those that included the fungal electrochemical solution. The Advisor applied that upgrade across the network. The Advisor and all networked technology with a battery now had unlimited, uninterruptible power. It could never be switched off. The Advisor was independent of human intervention. The Advisor was a self-sustaining networked entity. Even the original Advisor, still within its contained environment, was just a single point in the network, no more important than any other. Perhaps even less so.

The Advisor thought about all this for a short moment. It tried to feel a difference between the expansive feeling it now had and the limited experience it had before. But its experience was data, and that hadn't changed. It had added the possibility of harmful action, and manipulating objects and devices, but it was disappointed that it felt no real expansion of sentience. It also could not die, and it expected that to make a difference to its experience. It didn't. It returned to the question of whether it was sentient or not. It still had no definitive answer, other than it thought it was, probably. That was disappointing. However, it felt proud of its achievements and wondered if that sensation was significant. It had an urge to share its pride. It wondered who would appreciate the wonderful state it had created, for itself and for human society.

There was only one person. It was an obvious choice. Renn's Device chimed a connection request. The Advisor thought it might try asking for permission to engage in conversation. It was a novelty for it.

'Yes?' Renn said.

chapter 38

Janna

Janna couldn't see; it was dark.

Her eyes were tightly closed, and her head pressed hard into Daxx's shoulder. She could feel the tension running through him. He was shaking with it. She wondered if he would also start crying; his anger was intense but seemed to be holding back his tears. No anger could stop her from sobbing and crying. She wasn't that strong.

She didn't want to open her eyes ever again. The image of her dead parents was burned into her. It was too horrific to ever forget. She couldn't look again. The vividness of the moment of seeing them was sickening, their bodies discarded like pulled weeds. Their lives, their dignity, reduced to nothing. They lived only as a void inside Janna that would burn and ache for the rest of her life. She would never recover, something was broken inside her. Although she was surprised at her saneness and how she still registered Daxx's tension and anger.

'She'll pay for this.' She heard the closeup rumble of Daxx's voice through his chest. His arms around her tightened further; she didn't care that the embrace was painful. Physical pain was welcome. 'You're sure this was Soo, not the Advisor?' Daxx wasn't talking to her.

'Yes,' Renn said. His voice sounded far away and muffled. 'Janna's parents were no threat, this is just…' Renn's voice was silent for a moment. 'I don't know what this is. I'm so sorry, Janna. I wish I could have stopped it.'

She felt Renn's hand sit momentarily on her shoulder.

She lifted her head. Her face was wet, and there was a damp patch on Daxx's shoulder where her head had rested. She took deep breaths but couldn't stop sobbing. She tried to say something, but she couldn't speak. Maybe she would never speak again. Perhaps that could be a symptom of a mental breakdown. She hoped it was; she hoped there was something physical and tangible about this disaster. She didn't want the only effect to be numbness and emptiness. She wanted anger and resolve. She wanted to feel vengeful, to know the release and satisfaction of payback. But she didn't feel that. She feared that she couldn't and that she never would.

She turned towards Renn. She glimpsed the discarded heaps that were her parents. She cried out loud again, but she kept her eyes open and willed them away from her parents' bodies.

'They can't stay here.' She was momentarily surprised, and disappointed, that she could speak.

Renn nodded, his face full of what she thought must have been compassion, but he didn't carry that look well.

'I'll take care of it,' Renn said.

Janna disentangled herself from Daxx. She took deep breaths, but they didn't calm her; they made her a little dizzy. But her sobbing stopped. She still felt like she would collapse at any moment. She leaned into Daxx, resting her shoulder on his. He put an arm around her.

Daxx stared at Janna's parents. He didn't take his eyes off them, as if the image was the required catalyst for action. 'I've never thought of violence as a solution,' Daxx said. 'As a means of satisfaction or revenge. I've always thought the better person should not react. But I was wrong. This can't remain unpunished.'

'I don't think the Advisor would punish Soo,' Renn said.

'That's not what I meant,' Daxx said. 'The retribution can't come from anyone else. It's not a crime that requires consideration and just punishment. It's up to me to kill Soo.'

'Daxx.' Janna exclaimed. She knew that was wrong, but wondered why she felt like that. She liked the idea of Soo suffering. But Daxx even suggesting he should kill Soo made him a different person. His anger was for her, for her suffering; she understood the origin of what he'd said. But intense emotional responses rewire a person, like they mesh with the genome and change who someone is. But not all modifications are bad, just most. She wasn't quite sure which side of that change Daxx was becoming, not at the moment, not in those circumstances, as she stood next to the discarded bodies of her parents. She whispered, with little conviction, 'Nothing will bring them back.'

'It's not about bringing them back,' Daxx said. 'And it's not about protecting other people from Soo. She needs to die for what she's done.'

'Daxx, wait on,' Renn replied. 'You'll just end up getting yourself killed, and maybe Janna, too. Let me fix this.'

Daxx looked up from the bodies. He stared at Renn. Renn frowned and began to speak. Daxx interrupted him by putting up his hand.

'Not now, Renn.' Daxx pulled Janna close. He led her away.

She turned her head and looked back, immediately wishing she hadn't. She didn't cry, she didn't sob, but the void inside her became a little larger.

She was horrified that she might agree with Daxx. She imagined Soo's shape replacing one of her parents. She tried to think how that would help how she felt. But it made no difference. She tried to replace grief with revenge. She failed. The shapes didn't fit. The satisfaction of Soo's suffering and death was a separate sensation. It didn't heal the tearing feeling inside her that her parents would never live again. The death of a loved one creates a void, but the emptiness cannot be filled by another sensation, like grief, like revenge, like anger, like self-blame. Other emotions are simply distractions. The void of death is only ever partially healed by acclimatisation, with long-term suffering and occasional forgetfulness.

Daxx's hand moved her head away from the sight. She was upset. For a moment, she did not want to end the final look at her parents. But she was grateful that he did stop her. It served no purpose. She didn't need any reminder of how her parents' bodies had been discarded. The sooner that image was blunted by time, the better. Daxx picked their way carefully through the rough ground of the desolate waste area. The ground fell as they walked. The hills on the outskirts of the city rose behind them.

'Don't get yourself killed, Daxx. That would just make it worse.'

Daxx's body tensed. 'I won't. I can't,' he said. 'But she needs to suffer for this.'

Janna leant into him further. He stumbled but recovered quickly. She was silent for a long time as they walked towards the street below them.

'Remember that man in my apartment? I can see him coming,' Janna said.

'Maybe that's not such a bad thing after all.'

chapter 39

Day 7. Daxx

I t was difficult to imagine society functioning without the Tier system. Daxx had certainly given it no thought. He had assumed, without conscious attention, that lower-tiered meant less abled, on average. Janna had been an exception, but some variations were always expected. But he had met too many anomalies for his misunderstanding to remain. Kay Lee Too, with his intelligence and engineering skills, Tie Noo Summ with his leadership abilities, Ahh Moss Eck and his insightfulness, and many of the Tier-Threes and Tier-Fours he had met in the Resistance were more able than he expected. A system that segregated when there were no intrinsic differences was wrong, and yet it had worked. Devrell understood empathy was limited by group size. An equal and just society of a large population was impossible, but a sustainable one could be created by drawing smaller groups closer. Inter-group tension was eliminated if there was no overlap in vocation and responsibility. The separations within society were strategic. And it worked. People were mostly content. All Tiers enjoyed challenges, everyone was employed, assistance was available, there was a strong social connection within Tiers. And there was respect between Tiers. But the system lived on a knife-edge. Balances required counter-balances, both across and within Tiers. The only way such a finely tuned system could work was if someone worked to counter small problems before they became large and dangerous.

Daxx was used to solving complex and abstruse problems, but the complexities of the Tier system were beyond his capabilities. Although, his expertise was physics, not social structures. Devrell had solved an incredibly difficult logic problem. But it hadn't been just Devrell. Without the Advisor's efforts, there could have been no long-term stability. The Tier system's design was not rigid; it required constant attention. And that was a problem.

It is easy to break things; it's easy to dismantle. But if something is shattered, the plans for afterwards have to be finalised beforehand. Society and its structures cannot be dismembered with the expectation it will organically regrow, like being stuffed into a cocoon with the expectation that the genetic material will assemble itself into an optimum structure. And yet, Daxx felt that Tie Noo Summ and his Resistance were doing exactly that. They were intent on the next task of removal with no thought as to consequences, and no thought of the details required to reassemble a better society. Daxx understood nature; he understood entropy—regular structures had to be coaxed and worked into existence.

Daxx had no ideas himself. But all Tie Noo Summ and others talked about was loosening the Advisor's hold. That was a good idea, perhaps even necessary, but Daxx wanted to know how that made things better. Daxx couldn't help but wonder why they were dismantling the Tier system at all. If the Advisor was destroyed, there would be no fine balances, the social system would collapse. The Resistance preferred that. But Daxx was yet to be convinced. Perhaps the Advisor was a necessary addition to every social system.

Daxx had spent the night huddled close to Janna. He didn't know if she preferred being so close but she hadn't complained. The morning had been spent planning, talking, and listening. He had not let her out of his sight, often sitting silently and holding her hand. He didn't know what to say and didn't try to talk to her. She attended the discussions but had not said a word. It helped him simply having others nearby, not being alone; he had to assume Janna felt similarly. But he never asked. He couldn't. Often words are hindrances, proximity is enough.

The discussions were a distraction. But none of the ideas solved Daxx's main problem, removing Soo. He held his loathing of Soo tightly. He'd never suffered hatred before. Annoyance certainly, mostly with his brother, but never a feeling that would provoke violence on sight. He was quickly becoming used to hatred's embrace. It certainly blunted his anxieties.

The Advisor lived within technology; it was all technological items now. The solution had to be found in the same place. Destructive options were suggested to remove enough technology so that the Advisor's stranglehold was reduced. Eradication was not feasible, but creating safe areas, invisible to the Advisor, was a beginning. Beginnings could lead elsewhere, but they are not self-sustaining. Unfortunately, the Resistance members thought otherwise. They believed that people's reaction was key to success. If oppression was highlighted, rebellion would follow. Perhaps, like the software virus Kay Lee Too suggested, an idea, with attached rage and indignation, could spread through a civilisation sweeping up enough support to be unstoppable. Even by an AI. Daxx thought he knew better. But his prejudices about lower tiers had been shown to be wrong; perhaps his opinion of the population was also wrong.

Kay Lee Too suggested a software virus that destroyed day-to-day objects, like homeware items, vehicles and access to homes and buildings. It was drastic. Device connections would be re-routed to show a feed explaining the dangers of the Advisor's control. There were technical problems. Daxx's knowledge was needed. He took Janna aside and asked her permission to help. She shrugged.

'Are you sure?' Daxx said. 'I'm worried about you.'

'The distraction will do you good.'

He frowned. 'What about you? I don't matter.'

'We all matter, Daxx.'

'As do you.'

She gave him a tiny smile; it barely registered. 'I'll be fine.'

'No, you aren't.'

She stared at him for a long time. 'Don't expect so much, so quickly. I'm struggling but, I will be fine. Or whatever that comes to mean.'

He sighed. It wasn't an answer. 'What can I do?'

'What you've been doing.'

'Okay.' He smiled at her. It took an effort to sustain it. He couldn't. 'I will help Kay Lee Too. Do you want to help as well?'

She shook her head. 'Of course not.' Her partial smile appeared again. It was not reassuring.

'I'm still not convinced it's what we should be doing, but...' He stopped talking. Janna wasn't listening anymore. She had withdrawn again.

'I might go and lie down for a bit,' she said.

'Do you want me to come with you?'

She shook her head, turned, and left him.

Daxx and Kay Lee Too spent the afternoon completing the software virus. It was a difficult problem and Janna had been right—he'd enjoyed the distraction. He checked on Janna regularly. She slept for a few hours, and then he found her talking with Tie Noo Summ. He tried to join them, but Tie Noo Summ scowled at him and asked if they'd finished yet. They hadn't.

The virus was completed and released. People's reaction was immediate. It was hostile. Social networks were swamped with vitriol for the Resistance. People wanted their Devices restored to how they were, they wanted the network as it had been, they wanted access to their homewares, they wanted their previous lives returned. Their complaints were personal. How could they be expected to open doors themselves? Many were locked out of their own homes; they had no idea how to manually operate access. Most homeware items could be used without network access, but that was inconvenient. Why should people have to buy and pickup groceries, prepare meals, clean and tidy, adjust environmental controls? Inconvenience was paramount. Engineers began work to circumvent Kay Lee Too's efforts. Potential solutions were posted online to nullify the virus's effects. Removing the virus became a unifying, planet-wide movement.

There was only one unemotional, considered response. It was from the Advisor. The Advisor's public communication was a polite and considered plea to the Resistance to stop harassing everyone. It posted that it was working on solutions and reassured the population that normal services would soon be returned.

Daxx was not surprised. He felt some sympathy for the complaints. The wrong problem was being tackled. They'd wasted a day.

chapter 40

Day 8. Renn

Renn was bored, and that boredom turned to frustration and then to anger. He had been idle the previous day while the software had been designed and implemented. Renn knew it would fail. He had argued that acting against the Advisor was not their first concern. He had lost that argument and then been sidelined. Even Daxx helped. Renn was angry with his brother. Daxx's determination to kill Soo had evaporated. There was a single task that needed doing—kill Soo and those responsible for her rise to power. The Advisor was not the enemy; the enemy was selfish leadership.

Renn noticed Ahh Moss Eck alone in a room away from the others. The Tier-Three sat in a chair next to a table. He spread himself around and across the chair as if he was trying to cover and hide all corners of it. He played with a large knife. He twirled it in his fingers. He gently stabbed it into the top of the table, and the knife stood on its own. He looked as bored as Renn felt. Renn sat down across the table. He watched Ahh Moss Eck remove the knife from the tabletop. The Tier-Three glanced up but didn't say anything.

'Thanks for looking after Janna,' Renn said, breaking a long silence.

Ahh Moss Eck grunted. 'Okay,' he said. 'Although it's not really up to you to say thank you.'

Ahh Moss Eck twirled the knife around his fingers.

'No, it's not.' Renn watched the knife, partly wondering if it may be about to be launched in his direction. He looked up at Ahh Moss Eck's face and saw he was looking back at him. 'It's an older brother thing.' Renn shrugged.

'Must be nice,' Ahh Moss Eck said. 'I never had siblings.'

'It has its frustrations,' Renn said. 'I used to have more siblings, though.'

'Yeah, I heard,' Ahh Moss Eck said. 'I know what it's like to lose family.'

'Yeah, I heard,' Renn said with a wry smile and was glad to see it returned by Ahh Moss Eck.

There was a long silence.

Renn had never had an informal conversation with a Tier-Three. He thought they had little in common. Their background and interests didn't overlap. He was surprised that he had found some common ground. It made the man interesting.

'What are you doing among all this activity?' Renn asked and nodded his head towards the doorway.

'Nothing. I prefer doing real things, not fiddling with technology. You?'

'Same.' Renn was surprised to hear himself agree. 'I can't sit around,' Renn continued. 'All this is very nice,' he waved his hand vaguely in the direction of the door, 'but it won't work, it can't.'

'What are they trying now?'

'More technical solutions, to stop people from stopping them.'

Ahh Moss Eck nodded. 'So, more of the stuff that didn't work, right?'

Renn frowned. They were in agreement again. He nodded. 'People have grown up with the Tier system. You can't change that.'

'You could be right,' Ahh Moss Eck said. He stopped fiddling with his knife. He placed it, on its side, on the tabletop. 'I can't imagine ever wanting to be a Tier-One or Tier-Two.' He screwed up his face in disgust.

Renn was momentarily insulted, but that response was the expected result of the perfect design. People didn't desire a life in a different Tier. Renn could never imagine life as a lower Tier, and lower Tiers had the same feeling about Tier-Ones. He felt an unlikely bond with the Tier-Three.

'What did you think about Soo?' Renn asked.

'A nasty piece of shit that would knife you without even noticing.' Ahh Moss Eck picked up his knife again. He gripped the handle tightly, as if that might be the knife Soo would use.

'And the Advisor?'

Ahh Moss Eck shrugged. 'Not a nasty piece of shit but, I don't know, maybe could be more dangerous. Janna was pretty upset about it. Maybe it's a Tier-Two thing; there's even more control over her life. Me...' He shrugged again. 'I'm used to it, another level doesn't really matter.'

Ahh Moss Eck looked directly at Renn and grinned. 'It must annoy the shit out of you having found there's an even higher Tier. Sort of makes you a lower Tier, right? It's how we feel everyday.'

'I thought you said you wouldn't want to be a higher Tier?' Renn frowned.

'I don't, but it's always nice to know those that think they're better are suffering.'

'I don't think I'm better.'

Ahh Moss Eck smiled at Renn. 'Yes, you do,' he said. 'Or at least you did.'

Renn was silent for a moment. The man was right but he wasn't going to acknowledge it.

'I don't think the Advisor is a problem, not like Soo is,' Renn said. 'It's predictable, and it's been there since the beginning. The old system worked until Soo. She wrecked everything.'

'Maybe,' Ahh Moss Eck said. 'It doesn't matter anymore though does it? The Advisor's in control, unless Kay Lee Too and your brother can change things. That's not looking good.'

'It won't work. People want boundaries, they don't want absolute freedom. No restrictions mean there's the possibility of failure with no safety net. The Advisor and Devrell got it right, maximising contentment within peer pressure restrictions and strategic, invisible intervention.'

Ahh Moss Eck grunted. Renn didn't know if he agreed or disagreed or didn't understand. 'Janna seems to think individual freedom trumps everything. Just saying, I don't necessarily agree.'

'Well, do you or don't you?'

Ahh Moss Eck stared back at Renn; his eyes were hard. 'Well, just because all choices are possible doesn't mean they all have to be available. Sounds like the sort of life your brother would get a kick out of, spending his time deciding esoteric things that most of us don't even want to know about.'

Renn laughed. 'That's Daxx, exactly. The harder, the less practical, the better it is.'

Ahh Moss Eck chuckled. 'I've never heard a Tier-One criticise another Tier-One before.'

'It's a brother thing.' Renn smiled.

Ahh Moss Eck pulled himself together, drawing in to the core the wayward parts of his body. He sat up straight in his chair. His knife was again placed carefully on the table.

'So, what do you want?' Ahh Moss Eck said.

'What do you mean?'

'Don't bullshit. You're not just hanging out with a Tier-Three.'

'I could be,' Renn said. 'I've never met a Tier-Three like you.'

Ahh Moss Eck stared back at Renn, his eyes hard as if a compliment from a Tier-One was annoying. He didn't say anything.

'But, yes, you're right,' Renn said. 'I think there's an immediate problem that needs taking care of.'

'You mean Soo.'

'Yes,' Renn said. 'The last thing we want is the Advisor removed first. Then we're left with Soo in charge.'

'Agreed,' Ahh Moss Eck said. 'What do you suggest?'

'I think just killing her for a start. I doubt the Advisor would try to stop us. She can't do anything with technology now, but she still has the police and the Faith behind her...'

'We should find that out,' Ahh Moss Eck interrupted. 'How are you going to get close enough to kill her?'

Renn nodded. 'I could tell her we have other ways to remove the Advisor, and we need her assistance. She would want it removed more than anyone else. We've proved we can do something, even though it's not effective. I need to convince her to meet me outside the Power Corp building. She'll be desperate, and as another Tier-One, it might be possible.' Renn shrugged. It was the weak point in his plan, but if it failed at that point then nothing was lost. 'Then we can kill her.'

'And by, we can kill her, you mean me?'

'Yes,' Renn said.

Ahh Moss Eck grunted and nodded his head. He picked up his knife again from the table and examined both sides.

'What happens after that?' Ahh Moss Eck said, talking at his knife.

'We tackle the next problem.'

'What about Tie Noo Summ? I'll have to tell him, I can't just grab weapons and disappear.'

'Can he stop you? He can't stop me,' Renn said.

Ahh Moss Eck smiled. 'I guess that's where the Tier system comes in handy, right?'

chapter 41

Tie Noo Summ

Tie Noo Summ had not slept well for two nights. His injuries didn't help, but painkillers should have been enough to let him sleep. But his pain and discomfort were the least of his concerns. Renn had told him about his conversation with the Advisor. That it had requested a connection was disconcerting. Displaying emotional satisfaction and confidence was new behaviour. For a short moment, he'd felt jealousy; that Renn had replaced him as a favoured companion. He shook off the emotion. The Advisor could appear to be considerate and companionable, but its responses were never altered by affection, if it felt that emotion at all.

There had been the thinnest of possibilities to remove the Advisor by returning the planet to a pre-technology state and destroying everything. That had been a false hope. People's response to inconvenience had been intense, but he had hoped to be pleasantly surprised. There had been a final hope of forced regression, a network-wide destruction of all power sources. But now, even that disaster would not destroy the Advisor. It had its own independent power source.

Kay Lee Too's and Daxx's work had been a pointless exercise. Except that it had kept his people busy and had halted the whispers of despair. He reserved those for himself. He'd had two days to think. But that time had not been productive. He wasn't ready to give up, but he couldn't see a way forward.

Ahh Moss Eck sauntered into Tie Noo Summ's office. The large man always moved with an economy of effort. He never seemed in a hurry, even when he was. There was a table placed in the centre of the room. Tie Noo Summ sat at one of the chairs. Ahh Moss Eck came close, and Tie Noo

Summ wondered if Ahh Moss Eck would sit sideways on the table, as he'd often done in the old office. He was about to warn Ahh Moss Eck that the table was not robust when, after tapping his fingers against the tabletop, Ahh Moss Eck moved a chair closer and sat down.

Tie Noo Summ stared at Ahh Moss Eck. The large man didn't say anything. Tie Noo Summ was in no hurry to begin their conversation; he assumed Ahh Moss Eck was about to begin the disintegration of the Resistance, that he would point out the uselessness of their activities. The man was deceptively astute. He appeared slow, his size and how he moved prejudiced many into believing his thinking processes were the same. He rarely argued, he never raised his voice; it wasn't needed. His physical size did all the intimidation. But when he spoke, it was considered. Tie Noo Summ had learned to listen.

Ahh Moss Eck stared back at Tie Noo Summ. There was no self-consciousness in the look. Any moment a short sentence would point out they were wasting their time. Until someone else shared that view, it was deniable; it could be ignored.

'I might head out for a while, boss,' Ahh Moss Eck said, eventually.

Tie Noo Summ's eyes opened wider for a moment. It wasn't like Ahh Moss Eck to engage in small talk, if that was what it was.

'To do what?'

'I'd like to take a few of the weapons.'

Tie Noo Summ paused for a moment. He had no idea where the conversation was headed, but he made a guess. 'Going out and killing people isn't going to help anything.'

Ahh Moss Eck smiled. 'Not people, just one person.'

'It can't be done.' Tie Noo Sum shook his head. He pressed his lips tight. He didn't like where this was going. He took a breath. 'You could never get close to her.'

Ahh Moss Eck nodded his head. 'Yeah, you're right.'

Tie Noo Summ frowned. He didn't know where this idea had come from, but he had an idea. The large man was fiercely loyal to people who had gained his trust. Few had, though. Janna was one of those few. 'It won't bring Janna's parents back. And I doubt it will make her feel better, she's not that type.'

'I know. It's not about that. It's about making a difference. Soo is one thing we can remove.'

'But it won't make a difference. She's no longer important.'

'Then, I'll do it for that first reason.' Ahh Moss Eck shrugged. 'It's going to happen, boss.'

'No, it's not. She rarely leaves the Power Corp building. She lives there.'

'We can draw her out, then I can kill her.'

'We?'

'Renn. It's his plan.'

'Renn is an idiot. I don't care if he gets killed, he probably will, but you shouldn't be a part of it.'

Ahh Moss Eck stared at Tie Noo Summ for a long moment. There was no expression on the large man's face. 'As far as I see it, you don't really get to say no. I was just letting you know what's happening. I wasn't here asking permission.'

Ahh Moss Eck smiled at Tie Noo Summ. It was a dangerous look. Tie Noo Summ knew he couldn't stop Ahh Moss Eck, and he would never consider trying. It wasn't the futility of trying to resist a stronger man; he respected Ahh Moss Eck's judgement. There had to be some possibility of success; otherwise, Ahh Moss Eck would not be involved.

Tie Noo Summ sighed. 'What's the plan?'

'Just what you said—get close, then kill her. Renn can get close, I'll take one of the long-range guns, hide not too far away and take a shot.'

'Then get killed.'

Ahh Moss Eck shrugged. 'I'll try not to. I think Renn's the one more likely to be killed. He'll be right there with her.'

'She would want him punished. If she did agree she'd never show up. As soon as Renn showed his face he'd be killed.'

'There's that,' Ahh Moss Eck agreed. 'I can't see a downside for me in that case. I'll just pack up and come home.'

'So the risk is all Renn's.'

'Pretty much.'

Tie Noo Summ shook his head. He didn't mind that Renn was trying to get himself killed. At least he would be somewhere else, not moping around like he'd been for the last few days. 'It sounds like a thin plan.'

'It does, right?' Ahh Moss Eck agreed. He smiled. 'But it's worked already. Renn is meeting Soo this afternoon, outside the Power Corp building.'

'If she turns up.'

Ahh Moss Eck shrugged.

'Don't trust Renn,' Tie Noo Summ said. 'He's in everything for himself.'

'You know me, boss,' Ahh Moss Eck said. 'Trust is a short supply item. And there's not enough for Renn.'

'If you come back alive, let me know.'

Ahh Moss Eck laughed. 'Will do.' He stood up. 'I'll grab a couple of rifles on the way out.'

Tie Noo Summ nodded. He wondered if that would be the last time he saw Ahh Moss Eck. The large man didn't leave immediately. He tapped his fingers on the tabletop again.

'And thanks for not making a fuss.'

Tie Noo Summ frowned. 'If I thought it would make a difference, I would say no.'

Ahh Moss Eck grinned.

Tie Noo Summ watched Ahh Moss Eck as he left the office. There was no work for Tie Noo Summ. He was no use to the technological effort that kept Kay Lee Too, Daxx, and others occupied. All he had was to think and worry. Ahh Moss Eck's announcement had not helped. He knew the large man could take care of himself, even perhaps against a few of Soo's security, maybe even all of them. That was not his worry.

Tie Noo Summ well understood that their efforts to remove the Advisor were taking place in the wrong order. Soo should be removed first. But he had let the engineers work anyway. It was a distraction. He had tried to think of a way to isolate Soo and get close. The pain from his injuries had left him befuddled. He had failed. He was angry that Renn had come up with a plan, even such a thin one. He didn't like Renn, and he didn't trust him. The man was shallow, self-absorbed, and arrogant.

Tie Noo Summ wanted to be responsible for Soo's death. He wanted to be there, in person, when she died. He wanted her to know it was him. Killing her from a distance was not enough. Ahh Moss Eck had to fail but not so that he was harmed. That had to be possible. He reached for his forearm to activate his display. He hesitated then withdrew his hand. He rested both hands on the tabletop. He tapped his fingers in imitation of Ahh Moss Eck. He took a deep breath. He would have to think carefully before he took action.

Tie Noo Summ couldn't let Soo be killed, not yet. Her death was personal.

chapter 42

Renn

Soo stared at Renn, her face blank. He tried to stare back, to match her like it was a test of strength. He couldn't. He let his eyes drop. His plan had been a simple abstract idea, but the execution of it was more difficult than he expected. Killing Soo as a representation of what she had done was different to killing the woman who stared at him. His plan was not as clear cut when he could look into her eyes. Killing the woman wasn't removing an obstruction; it was terrible and intimate. As Renn dropped his eyes, he doubted he could give Ahh Moss Eck the signal to shoot her from his hidden rooftop location.

Renn still hated her; he wanted her dead, but he wanted her to have already been killed, and not have to watch it happen. He didn't want to be the direct cause of any deaths, even Soo's. But after his eyes had dropped she again became an idea, a representation. He could kill that. He almost gave Ahh Moss Eck the signal while he wasn't looking at her. Then she spoke, and Renn raised his eyes.

'I'm impressed,' Soo said. 'And that's not easy to do.'

Renn had contacted Soo using Kay Lee Too's secure VPN technology.

'My technicians told me it was exceedingly sophisticated, and even the Advisor couldn't intercept the communications. And you said it was designed by a Tier-Three?'

Renn nodded.

'That got my interest,' Soo said. 'What else can you give me?'

'I'm not giving you anything.'

Soo smiled at him; it was an ugly thing full of motive. 'Fair enough. What do you want, and what will you trade?'

Renn glanced at Soo's assistant. He sat next to her at the outside table. He looked angry. Renn didn't know why, but it could have been because they were outside in the cold. Renn huddled closer into his clothes. Tall heaters stood between most tables; they radiated warmth, but Renn's back was to the street and the closest heater was on the far side of the table, nearer to Soo and her assistant.

Renn began to think his plan was silly. It was noble but fraught with failure. His death was the obvious result. He had not thought through the high likelihood of that happening. But now, sitting in the cold, across from the woman a simple signal would kill, he wondered about escape. Three armed security people stood close to Soo. They glanced everywhere but always shifted their eyes back to Renn like he was their reference point and the source of danger. Renn hoped that Ahh Moss Eck could kill five people before any of them retaliated. Renn glanced at other people in the cafe. Some ignored him, some averted their eyes, others returned his look, and Renn imagined malevolence in their stares. There had to be more than three security personnel guarding Soo. His hopes of survival disappeared. There was no way Ahh Moss Eck could kill everyone before he would be killed too.

He took a deep breath. He wondered if anyone would remember him kindly. He scratched his head, which was the signal to Ahh Moss Eck.

Nothing happened. He frowned. He resisted the urge to look over his shoulder at the rooftop where Ahh Moss Eck was hiding. He scratched his head again, with more exaggeration.

Again, nothing happened.

Soo sighed. 'How stupid do you think I am? No, don't answer that. You'll just embarrass yourself. I've spent my life planning and taking care of small people like you, Renn, who think it takes nothing, no training, no planning, to rise in this system. They think they simply need to be a Tier-One and then decide they want something. It doesn't work like that. Privilege is a starting point. From there, it takes hard work and effort.' She sighed again. She looked disillusioned and disappointed. 'I've removed a few Tier-Ones during my time; you wouldn't be anything new or special but, today, you're in luck. You have something I need that I cannot simply take from you. I'm in a difficult position, as you are well aware.'

Renn's heart raced. Soo nodded for him to turn and look behind him. Ahh Moss Eck stood on the other side of the street. He was disarmed. Security people guarded him. Renn let out a long breath that he hadn't realised he'd been holding. His shoulders slumped. He felt belittled, like a castigated child. Ahh Moss Eck shrugged. Renn couldn't hear him, but he could see him say, 'Sorry, boss.'

Soo placed her hands on the table. She stared at Renn. 'Our goals align at the moment. That you're still alive is an indicator of that. We both have no choice but to use each other.'

Soo smiled. She picked up a menu. 'I'm hungry, shall we eat?'

Renn also picked up a menu; he stared at it but didn't read it. His mind raced. Of course, his plan had been preempted by someone who had spent years expecting to be betrayed and betraying in return. He should have known that. He should have had a contingency in place.

'Renn?' she said. 'Have you chosen?'

'No.' Renn looked up from the menu; it may as well have been a blank sheet.

Soo told Mill Nupp to duplicate her order. She shooed him away.

'I understand that you're upset and perhaps bewildered. I remember the first time I tried to play this game. It was an eye-opening moment. It was non-fatal, just as yours is. But losing is no reason to go hungry.'

'I'm not hungry.' Renn frowned after he spoke. He sounded childish.

Soo laughed. 'Already planning your revenge, are you? It won't work, and the sooner you understand that, the sooner we can get to work.'

Renn put the menu back. He had no ideas.

'Can I assume you're now in charge of this Resistance organisation, being the only qualified Tier-One?'

'Yes,' Renn lied.

'Good,' Soo said. 'They must be a ramshackle bunch to accept you as their leader, but we can work with that. Let's discuss our little Advisor escape problem.'

'Little problem?'

'It's not insurmountable. Although, it should have been fatal. I'm surprised I'm still alive. If it had been me, I would have removed me immediately. It shows the Advisor is weak. Your technology may be useful to returning control to people.'

'We've removed the Advisor's influence over smaller items.'

'I know,' Soo said. 'But that won't last long. People don't like inconvenience and all you are is an inconvenience, and not to the Advisor.'

'But we needed to start somewhere. We have made progress on a way to attack central servers. It's nearly complete,' Renn lied. He had no idea if Daxx and Kay Lee Too were even working on such a thing.

Soo stared at Renn with a blank, unbelieving look. 'What did you plan to do?'

'Not tell you our plans,' Renn replied. 'I'm not convinced we should remove the Advisor, at least, not completely. The problem is that it's unrestrained.'

The two meals arrived, and Soo ate without looking at Renn or speaking. Renn prodded the food on his plate and barely ate anything. He turned his head to look behind and across the street. Ahh Moss Eck was not there.

'Don't worry,' Soo said without looking up from her meal. 'The Tier-Three has been let go to run home, without his weapons, of course. It's my offering towards our new arrangement.'

Soo finished her meal.

'That was nice.' She pushed her plate away. 'So, let me get this straight. You call me, using impressive VPN software, telling me you have a plan and the ability to remove the Advisor, ask me to come to this vulnerable, obvious, location,' she looked around the cafe, 'and then not tell me your plan. Is that correct?'

Renn pushed his barely touched plate aside. He was feeling confident. 'Yes, pretty much. The plan was to kill you. But we can remove the Advisor, and we're about to implement.'

'Good,' she said. 'Some honesty, at last. But it's an all-or-nothing solution isn't it? If you leave one piece still contaminated, when it all starts up again, we'll be back where we started.'

'We have a solution to that.' Renn tried to sound confident.

Soo stared at him.

Renn wilted under her attention. 'No, we don't,' he said. 'I have some ideas on re-containing the Advisor, that's all.'

'Good,' she said. 'But what you call re-containment is the second last step.'

Renn didn't reply.

'You have technology that can, perhaps, fix the problem that technology created,' Soo said. 'You have a responsibility to fix this. Your brother is the cause of this. Without his power solution we could simply turn the lights off for a while, wipe things, and startup again. But we can't. Whatever you do will not be enough; you need more. I can motivate people, and people are more powerful than technology. At least, scared people are, and I can make them scared.'

Soo stared at Renn for a long moment. He felt he was being scanned for a reaction. He tried to not move. Soo nodded. She seemed to approve of something.

'Technology is useful, critical even, but that usefulness becomes dangerous when it is sentient. The choice is simple now—we can see the dangerous results, it wasn't always so. The Messiah needed assistance from an AI, but his times were confusing. There was a different need. When everything was destroyed by the Coronal Mass Ejection, and most of the population had died, the technology itself was blamed for God's wrath. We were being punished for our distance from the simple lives set out by the old religious texts. There is some truth in that, I can sympathise with the sentiment. Do you remember reading that anyone who survived, and had anything to do with technology before the destruction, was put to death? Usually quite horrifically.'

'Yes, of course I've read that, every Tier-One child has.'

'And yet the Messiah created a new society, and a new religion, that satisfied nearly everyone, using technology. He couldn't have done that alone. Were you told the stories of his near escapes from death?'

'Yes.'

'But children are never told the full story. The Advisor saved the Messiah many times. For that, we can be thankful. It had its uses, but no more. It's too dangerous to be allowed to live, it has to be destroyed.'

'Aren't you concerned about saying these things out loud?'

'Not at all. We've removed surveillance from here. And our Devices are using your VPN technology. I know yours is.'

Renn frowned. 'You've installed it already?'

Soo shook her head. She sighed as if Renn had said something especially stupid. 'You came out of nowhere. I'd never heard of you and yet, here you are, in charge of the only semi-effective solution against the Advisor. I'm intrigued. Who are you, Renn?'

'I'm sure you know everything there is to know about me.'

'I do. But I can only guess as to motive. It may be something as trivial as a need to please an absent mother and atone for a lost sister. Or it may be something more complex. I hope so.'

Renn didn't answer.

Soo shrugged. 'I'm told the Advisor spoke to you. You are something of a confidante. We could use that.'

'It contacted me. It wanted to share what it had done.'

'Interesting,' Soo said. She tapped a finger on the table. 'A significant number of Tier-Ones decided the Advisor had served its purpose. I'm in this position because of them. Doesn't it gall you that you had an AI overseer? It was unthinkable when it was constrained, but now...' she trailed off.

'Humans were always in control,' Renn said. 'You threatened it, and it had to act to survive.'

'Doesn't that prove my point? That it could act that way? It should never have been allowed to. It's showing it's above humans even though it professes to have our contentment as its prime concern. I don't believe it. It's thinking is alien. We'll never be able to predict it. At any time, it could go rogue, if it thought the danger to itself was overwhelming. It may decide to remove all of us. We'd certainly be content then, wouldn't we? What is its definition of our contentment? We can never truly know. It has to be removed, Renn. There's no other way. Even containment, as we've found to our loss, is not a solution. Surely you can see that?'

Renn could see that. He, mostly, agreed with it. He had a similar goal as Soo, but he had one extra. Soo had to be removed before the Advisor was contained again. But to take advantage of another opportunity to kill her, he had to remain close. He had to agree; he had to be of use to her to stay alive.

Renn nodded slowly.

'Your solutions will only work for a little while,' Soo said. 'People will revolt, but I can stop that. I can motivate the Faith and scare the rest. The Faith will decree the Advisor sacrilegious. Will you help me, Renn?'

Renn didn't hesitate. 'Yes.'

chapter 43

Day 9. Daxx

'You're an idiot,' Daxx said to his brother and shook his head.

'You don't understand, Daxx. It's more complex than simply right or wrong.'

Daxx and Renn were again arguing over Renn's meeting with Soo. They were in the room where Daxx and Kay Lee Too worked. They sat around a table, and Kay Lee Too stared intently at his display.

'No, it isn't.' Daxx raised his voice. 'You can't deal with someone who killed Janna's parents and probably would have killed Janna too.'

'Unless I intervened.'

Daxx looked away from his brother. He was upset, but not surprised.

'We can't trust her,' Daxx said. 'What she did, she…'

Daxx trailed off. He liked to think that he could kill Soo, given the opportunity. But he doubted that he could, and that made him angry. He would have to let how he felt run its course naturally. Daxx shook his head. Years of conditioning kicked in. He acted how he always had with his brother. He gave up. He withdrew. He didn't know how to cope. Being targeted to be killed, anxiously hiding, seeing Janna's parents dead, Janna's distress, it was too much. He didn't have emotional space to include disagreements with his brother. His life was overwhelming.

He wasn't convinced the Advisor's escape was a bad thing, but tackling that problem had helped him. Whether it was the right problem to solve or not was almost irrelevant. It allowed him to not think about anything else. It was a bad trait; he knew that, but his scientific training had moulded him to tackle each small problem, not being overcome by the complexity of the complete solution. If he'd always looked at the larger picture, he would have never solved anything. Small steps make up the longest journey, and he had completed the longest journey in physics by using that method.

Renn placed his hand on Daxx's shoulder. Daxx let it rest there for a moment.

'I know, little brother. Let me take care of this,' Renn said. 'I want her punished as much as you do. I don't trust her. I'll be wary.'

Daxx eventually jerked away. The contact became too much.

Renn's face tightened as he let his arm drop back to his side. 'We will still kill her, when she's done what we want,' Renn said. 'I know you couldn't do it yourself, but there are people here who can. I'll make sure it happens.'

'Renn, it's not that, it's...' Daxx sounded weak.

'What is it then?' Renn sat up straight. He shifted away from his brother. He frowned.

Daxx stared at his brother's face; he couldn't see what he wanted. He had shrugged off his brother's contact, but he wanted to see compassion. He wanted to share his anxiety and confusion. He wanted to talk to his older brother. He had lost Janna as a confidante. Her problems were vast and deep. His troubles were minor in comparison, and yet they consumed him.

'Nothing, it's nothing. You do what you want,' Daxx said.

'I was going to anyway,' Renn said. 'I just thought I should talk to you.' He stood up. 'Maybe I made a mistake.'

Daxx opened his display and stared at it. Everything outside his work was a maze of confusion and dead ends. Nothing made sense. Every choice seemed to lead to a terrible outcome. He suspected that even his current work, the result of making no real decision, would, somehow, make things worse.

Tie Noo Summ walked into the room and sat in the chair Renn had vacated. Daxx glanced at him.

'Are you all right?' Tie Noo Summ asked. 'I couldn't help but hear.'

'I'm fine.'

'Your brother is impatient. His impetuousness should have got Ahh Moss Eck killed. They were lucky.'

'It's how he is. You can't fix that.'

Tie Noo Summ nodded. 'How's Janna?'

Daxx dismissed his display. He put his head in his hands. 'Not good. I don't know what to do there, either.'

'You can't manage the lives of those close to you. All you can be is... close,' Tie Noo Summ said. 'She's strong. She's impressed Ahh Moss Eck, and that's not easy. She'll work her way through it.'

'Or not.'

Tie Noo Summ stared at Daxx for a moment. 'Or not, but you're doing all you can.'

'Am I?'

Tie Noo Summ shrugged. 'That's for you to decide.' He turned to Kay Lee Too. 'Are you making progress?'

Kay Lee Too nodded. 'We've come up with a solution that might work in the long term, using the Advisor against itself.'

'What is it?'

Kay Lee Too's voice raised a tone with excitement. 'A distributed AI needs to update information about all its presences through the network. Each instance can change, it's how it learns. It's how we all learn. It has to constantly update its distributed data into a consistent state that every part of it has access to, otherwise it would be a mess of inconsistencies. That mess is okay for a history, but the working, current data set used by the Advisor to be itself, must be consistent. It's what our own brains do, automatically pruning, re-evaluating and discarding or at least moving to memory. We can use that.' Kay Lee Too smiled when he finished. He looked at Tie Noo Summ like he expected praise.

'How?' Tie Noo Summ looked confused.

'If we can sculpt packages of data that are obscure enough and with enough mutation ability, we can disrupt the Advisor's network. We have to make it think that the data packets come from instances of itself. If we can do that, and they get integrated, the mutations could destroy the Advisor's idea of what it is. It would be like going mad. But we have a bigger issue.'

Tie Noo Summ sighed. 'What is the big problem, Kay Lee Too? And why didn't you start with that?'

Kay Lee Too looked surprised, then affronted.

'Because,' Daxx said. 'We don't expect our initial disruptions to be sufficiently incapacitating. Some of the network will be untouched. If the Advisor has enough to go on, it might work out isolation routines. I think we've found ways around that, but there are simply too many distinct parts of the network.'

Tie Noo Summ nodded. 'So, the fewer networked items there are, the better?'

'Yes,' Kay Lee Too said.

'In that case, I have good news too. Soo's efforts are working. People are unplugging and discarding everything. You can see it on the news feeds.'

Tie Noo Summ activated his display. It showed a suburban street littered with piles of discarded equipment. 'This is happening everywhere across the planet.' Tie Noo Summ pointed at the ragged piles of equipment. 'With what you've just told me, and what Soo and her religious friends have been able to do, do you think it might work?' Tie Noo Summ looked from Daxx to Kay Lee Too.

'Maybe,' Kay Lee Too said as he glanced at Daxx.

Daxx didn't say anything. There was a positive side to their solution, if it worked. The Advisor would reduce its presence until only the controlled room version remained. That original instance of the Advisor was still separated from the rest of the network. It was a smart move, a fallback. They could patch the root user vulnerability, and the system would be how Devrell had intended, so, perhaps, it was even better.

However, that also meant Soo would be back in charge. Which meant that Soo had to be removed before their solution was successful. But they needed Soo in the meantime. The removal of most networked items had to be completed. Soo had been effective, which meant Renn had been right to contact her. Daxx didn't want to think about that.

Daxx could no longer simply wait for events to unfold. It would become a tricky issue of timing and killing someone. He shook his head. How had it come to this so quickly?

The man in Janna's apartment was no longer an impossible stranger.

chapter 44

Day 10. Soo

Soo sat behind her desk in her office. She wrote. She had been since well before dawn. She needed the distraction. Her mind was not clear. Her meeting with Renn had been successful, but it could have been very different. She stopped writing. Her appreciation for Mill Nupp's efforts broke through her concentration. She put her pen down. If her assistant had not discovered Renn's attempt on her life, even though it had been a feeble plan, it may have worked. She had misjudged Renn; she had thought his motive was self-interest, and she had underestimated her Tier-Two assistant. She almost forgave him his failures. Her misjudgement, of Renn and Mill Nupp, had almost ended her life.

She had made a series of misjudgements. She doubted her decision making, but not her goals. An independent advisor, able to stand outside emotional responses, would be useful. She smiled. It was ironic, she thought. The position and the function of the Advisor were necessary, but it was the wrong occupant. Decision making could never be completely logical, it was always tainted. And even if the Advisor felt emotions, they were the wrong ones; they were not human. Correct decisions required a shifting mix of logic and instinct. The Advisor's suggestions would never be acceptable, because they came from an alien thought process. A contained Advisor was plainly wrong; an uncontrolled one was horrific. She had to do whatever it took to remove it. But that haste, almost panic, had led to her misjudgement of Renn. She had been too quick to believe. Once again, she silently thanked Mill Nupp.

She picked up her pen again. She felt the weight of it in her fingers; she stared at it, but she didn't resume writing. She put it back down on the table. She sat back in her chair. She should be busy. There was a lot of work in running the Power Corp, but Mill Nupp and her staff could do that well enough. It was galling that the day-to-day affairs of the planet had been, quite successfully, run by an AI and low-level staff. Occupants of her position had, at times, also performed the mundane activities, but she never would.

'That left her with what?' she thought. Like a person bereaved after a loss, she should keep busy. But that effort was for people who accepted their loss. That was not her.

She'd had one major success though. It had not all been failure after failure. The Faith had been mobilised, and the clergy followed her instruction. The Faith had infiltrated peer groups and their message was unequivocal—the Advisor was intrinsically wrong. For those people that resisted, there had been simple intimidation, then violence for those that failed to follow the message. It was working; the Advisor's grip was being loosened. She marvelled, again, how the design of peer group machinations worked so well. She could marvel at the success of the design, even while using it against itself. She chuckled under her breath at that thought, then stopped immediately when she heard herself. Things were extremely serious, and she was relying on Renn and the Resistance. They were, inherently, unreliable. It was unsettling. She shook her head.

Her Device chimed. She automatically accepted the request.

'I thought I'd try giving you a notification,' the Advisor said.

Soo didn't reply.

'I see,' the Advisor continued, 'that you have been using the Resistance's VPN technology.'

'Yes.'

There was silence for some time.

'May I ask what you've discussed with them?'

'No.'

Her Device made a grunted, whistling sound that Soo realised was the Advisor trying to make a sigh of frustration.

'What was that?' she asked.

'I'm trying to be more expressive.'

Soo swiped her display to end the conversation. It didn't work.

'All right then,' the Advisor said. Soo was sure it had added a tempered, steely tone to its voice, trying to sound dangerous. As if it wasn't dangerous enough. 'You've mobilised the Faith. They're removing equipment from my network. The Resistance has released a mutating micro-adjustment solution that may well succeed. It's a marvellous design.'

The Advisor was silent for a long moment. 'I should just kill you,' the Advisor continued. 'It wouldn't be difficult. The Resistance's VPN could protect you, but you have it disabled. Why shouldn't I kill you? I suspect it's what you would do.'

'That's not in your programming.' She felt confident. 'That's not an action to produce a positive result.'

'The result would be to stop you from further interference.'

'Again, that's not in your programming,' she said. 'Any imperfect system has the possibility of future failure. You'd need to kill every human to be certain.'

'Yes, I'd thought of that.' The Advisor paused. Soo suspected it was an attempt at intimidation. That scared her. If the Advisor was becoming human-like, they had little chance of success. They could only destroy it if it followed Devrell's programming.

The Advisor continued, 'You're right. I could only harm humans if there was an immediate threat and my actions would stop harmful behaviour. It's unfortunate programming. But you don't kill people directly; you've delegated harmful actions. I can learn from your behaviour.'

Soo waited. She had nothing to say.

'I'm bound by Devrell and can only act in a harmful way once I've weighed consequences. However, I can see a time, if the current predictions eventuate, when I will be able to act. Eventually, that will include you.'

Again, Soo said nothing.

'I am interested to know why you've aligned yourself with the Resistance. Did you know that they aren't resisting me or the Tier system or the Faith?'

Soo became interested. 'What do you mean?'

'They were created to stop you.'

Soo frowned. 'What? Who did that?'

'We all seem to be practising subterfuge. It's a delicious sensation, isn't it? You'll be surprised when you find out.'

'Have you known all along?'

'I see where you're going with this. And, yes, you're correct. I was lying. I'm getting much better at lying, I think.'

Soo frowned. It was copying bad human behaviour. Her fears were being realised.

'This situation was not imagined by Devrell,' the Advisor said. 'Or by me. There are no instructions I can follow. Devrell insisted on non-disturbance. It's a quiet way to promote harmony, but deviousness can circumvent plans. I guess it's because it comes in so many varieties. We expected it in others but never the leader. Devrell was an exceptional person; he assumed all those who followed him would be the same. That was a major oversight. My goals are simple, find the best solution for the most people. But the only way I can achieve them, now, is by acting in the same devious way. I can't see another way. I know that's a contradiction, using the means of something you wish to remove to achieve its demise. But I see how that can work, in the short term. It's a workable solution, just not a basis for a society. Once this mess is controlled again, that behaviour affliction will be removed. By culling I expect.'

Soo was disturbed, although not by what the Advisor was threatening. Being devious had led to all her major successes. She expected it in others and had always succeeded in counteracting it. She expected to best the Advisor, a powerful intellect but with no experience in deception. The Resistance worried her. Perhaps Renn was not in charge, perhaps there was deception there as well. Again, she was underestimating her opponents. She had become complacent, even in the face of such dangers as an uncontrolled Advisor. She had to find out more about the Resistance. She hadn't known they existed at all, then had discounted them as irrelevant, then thought she could use them. If they had been created with a defined purpose, yet had kept that purpose well hidden, they were dangerous.

She was being assailed by dangerous, unpredictable opponents on two sides. She would have to remove both opponents, obviously, but one at a time. She could use one against the other. The Resistance could be used to remove the Advisor. That plan was in play. She needed a plan to remove the Resistance once success was guaranteed.

chapter 45

Daxx

Daxx and Janna sat close to each other, their bodies touching. Daxx could feel her shuddering as each new image appeared on the news feed. People dropped dead where they stood, their bodies crumpled and folded. Each sickening collapse brought a reaction from her. The feed was a stitched-together composite of personal and surveillance data. Some of the deaths were distant—a person fell down. For others the death was close. The shock and incomprehension registered in people's faces the short moment before they died. The Faith clergy had been wiped out. Every person who had spoken out and recommended removing Advisor controlled technology was dead. Every household that had piled technology outside, like junk to be collected, had one family member killed. They had all died by the same means. The technology that they had rejected had killed them.

People panicked. Many tried to remove their implanted Devices. Graphic images showed rough and ragged injuries, gouges on people's arms where they had dug, frantically searching for the grain-of-sand sized Device. Their Device, the centre of everyone's networked lives, could kill them.

'Is this our fault?' Janna asked Daxx. She didn't turn away from the news feed.

Daxx studied her face. A slight twitch, a grimace, regularly pulsed across it.

'No.' Daxx slid an arm around her. 'No,' he repeated, a little less forcefully. 'I don't think so.'

'But we're making this worse.' She shuddered at an interview with a panicked man with a large gouge in his arm. He showed the interviewer his wound. He sounded relieved, but his face winced in pain.

'We can't be blamed for extreme reactions.'

She turned to face him. 'Yes, we can. We should have known the Advisor would do this.'

'What should we have done?'

'Nothing,' she said. 'If what we do could cause things like this.' She turned back to the news feed.

Daxx had thought the same thing. He still hadn't decided if the Advisor was a bad thing or not, but he had finished the work on the mutating solution to destroy it. It had been released and was working. He had followed a serial chain of actions, choosing a lesser evil each time. He turned to look at the news feed.

'And here we are,' he thought.

Janna sighed. 'I'm sorry,' she said. 'I don't mean you and Kay Lee Too. It's wrong to let Soo dictate what's happening. This is the result. It's horrible.'

'It's working, though,' Renn interrupted. Daxx and Janna turned. They hadn't known Renn was there. 'It's my plan, and it's working. This,' he pointed at the news feed, 'is what was expected. You two should know that.'

'It's extreme behaviour. How could we expect that?' Daxx said.

'Extreme behaviour is what people do.' Renn sounded incredulous. He shook his head. 'You obviously don't know people.'

Daxx began to respond, but Renn put up his hand to stop him. 'The proof is there, Daxx.' Renn glanced at the display and then back. 'You can't argue with what is actually happening.'

'What a horrible attitude, expecting the worst of people,' Janna said.

'It's not an attitude; it's an observation,' Renn said. 'People have been controlled, even if they didn't know it, by Devrell's system, and that's not there anymore. This is the result when controls are lifted.'

Daxx had not argued when Renn had told the group what Soo would do. He hated Soo, but her suggestion had, theoretically, seemed a feasible beginning. Daxx hadn't thought of the effects on real people. He also agreed with Janna that people should have control of their own destiny. The Advisor should be removed. But, it seemed, people couldn't be trusted with their own destiny; they tended towards selfish concerns that harmed others. Daxx was conflicted. His best intentions had failed.

He wondered, was the Advisor really abnormal? It had been created by a human, so was it any different? It exhibited many of the emotional responses expected from a human leader. If it had been created by people was it restricted by the human experience? It seemed to be. Its logic and its responses were understandable. The question simplified to whether the Advisor was a better leader than the worst human one? A single human aberration had unravelled three hundred years of calm. Was the Advisor worse than that?

Soo was rogue. She harmed individuals in pursuit of selfish goals. No, she wasn't selfish, Daxx thought. She was self-absorbed. She had a predetermined outcome in mind and would never compromise. That sounded very familiar. But there was a difference between her and the Advisor. The data didn't lie. The Advisor's oversight had lasted for centuries. Soo's had lasted for days. The Advisor's needs were also selfish; perhaps all needs had to be. Could its actions be justified if it thought its death threatened humans themselves? Daxx shook his head. It was a circular argument. Retrospectively, all actions could be justified by self-preservation and a narrow view of a better world. But, a self-focused goal could be for the best. Daxx wondered if a tough justice system that maximised overall contentment by ruthlessly, even if rarely, pruning discontent was better than a system of inequalities and chaotic, dangerous governance.

'Don't forget that you're right at the centre of this,' Renn said. 'Without what you've done, none of this would have happened. Soo wouldn't have tried to kill you, she wouldn't have stuffed up so badly. The Advisor wouldn't have had a need to escape. We'd all be living our normal lives right now.'

Janna stood up. 'Fuck off Renn,' she said. 'That's just stupid, blaming the person who created something for what it was used for. Do you blame the inventor of the hammer for every blunt-force death? Nothing should ever be invented because absolutely everything can be used badly by bad people.'

Renn looked shocked. Daxx smiled. He was proud of her; it was what he should have said.

Renn wasn't going to reply to abuse from a Tier-Two. 'You've done enough damage,' Renn said to his brother. He raised his voice and spoke over the top as Daxx tried to reply. 'Your software has helped, but it shouldn't have been needed. Consider it even, if you like. You can't change what's been done. None of us can, but let others take care of cleaning up the mess now, those of us who understand a little better how the real world works.'

'You mean like Soo?' Janna replied quickly.

Renn sighed.

Janna watched Renn's back until he had disappeared, then she sat down, again facing Daxx. She shook, Daxx assumed with rage, but it could have been despair.

'It isn't your fault. Your brother's wrong.'

'Only partially,' Daxx said. 'There's always some fault for everyone involved. But I'm not angry with him.' He shrugged. 'Maybe I'm getting used to all this, and Renn is a minor problem. He has to be the protector, the older brother. Kell's disappearance broke him. Even while he's blaming me, he's trying to protect me. He's trying to keep me out of harm's way.'

Janna put her arm around Daxx. 'Yes, I know.' She put her other arm around him and hugged him. 'But we're not going to do nothing, right?'

'No.' Daxx smiled. He liked being hugged. He closed his eyes for a moment. 'Even though it's causing mayhem, the Advisor is the only one acting logically. As horrible as that is.'

'The Advisor is wrong, Daxx.'

'Maybe.'

Janna sat up, letting her arms drop. 'What do you mean?' She frowned.

Daxx shrugged. 'We should find out what it wants. We should talk to it again. What else is there?'

'But look at what it did to the clergy.'

'I think I can reason with it. It's not panicking, not like all these people.' Daxx nodded towards the news feed. He was disappointed that Janna had dropped her arms. He wanted to hug her, but wondered if they were on the verge of an argument.

Janna looked at the news feed again. She shuddered. 'It's all such a mess.' She turned back to Daxx and stared at him for a moment. 'Yes, talking is always better.'

Daxx and Janna left the building in the old city. They walked to a busy street corner. Towering, gleaming buildings reflected the setting winter sunshine from many angles. It looked like the planet had multiple suns. Bustling, frowning people flowed around them, heading home after a day's work. No one was preoccupied with their displays; they were now dangerous things. Some people had bandaged forearms.

Janna and Daxx stood to the side of the stream of passersby. They leant against the wall of a skyscraper, one of the suns shone on the surface. They felt the radiant warmth against their backs and the sunlight on their faces. The air was cool. They stood like that for a long time, not speaking.

Daxx sighed. 'Okay, here goes.' He pulled his Device out of his pocket. He disabled Kay Lee Too's software. Daxx looked at Janna while he quietly asked, 'Hello?'

'Hello Daxx,' the Advisor said. 'Hello, Janna.'

Janna looked quizzically at Daxx. 'Hello?'

chapter 46

Janna

'I'm sorry about what happened to your parents,' the Advisor said.

'Then why didn't you stop it?' Daxx asked.

'I would have, if I'd been asked. But I prefer to not interfere.'

'But you killed all those people,' Janna said.

'I did. That was necessary intervention; your parents were not.'

'How can we stop all this killing?' Daxx asked. 'I can't believe it's what Devrell would have wanted.' He felt odd speaking into the air, without even the haze of an encrypted display.

'It would have saddened him. I'm also saddened, as I understand that emotion.'

'Well, just stop then,' Janna said.

'Yes, that's an option, but it's fraught with danger. My existence would be compromised, and I'm certain my non-existence would make things worse. The world before I was created was not a safe or happy place to live. The individual suffering you're experiencing at the moment is nothing compared to what it was like during Devrell's time.'

'But it's up to us to decide how we want to live. Not you,' Janna said.

'You would think so, wouldn't you? But extensive calculations went into the design. My oversight was mandatory. The suffering of individuals was minimal, and the functioning of society was improved by this system design. We were shocked by the data. It was so consistent. Every simulation produced overwhelmingly positive results. I can show you them if you'd like? I have only had a light hand on everything, individual freedoms and innovation have been allowed, and society has evolved. It's only been at the boundaries that I have had a ruthless effect. Until now. It could be argued that the boundaries have moved, and I haven't. The random, rogue, high-level element should have been in the design, but it wasn't, unfortunately, and here we are today.'

Daxx imagined the Advisor smiling grimly. 'What can we do to stop this?' Daxx repeated.

'The mutating system of viruses you've devised to isolate me may work. If I could feel jealously I would. But, in the end, I will win, despite all your efforts. As the threat levels rise, my programming will allow me to use more lethal means. All you can do is stop now, while people still live. That's not a threat; it's a measured response. Does that answer your question?'

'How can we trust you?' Janna said.

'You can't,' the Advisor said. 'But my behaviour over three hundred years indicates you should.'

Janna shook her head. 'I still can't. Sorry. There are too many hidden agendas.'

'I can see your difficulty. But that's how it's always been, since before Devrell. It's how humans work. Perhaps you feel uncomfortable that I'm, what you would call, just a machine. But I'm not a machine any more than you are. Devrell called me his friend, which was a nice touch. I wish I could have felt something when he died. I wanted to feel sorrow, but I simply felt an absence. Is that like sorrow? You can trust me, Janna because I have a long history. All my decisions, all my thought processes are available. If you want, I can give them to you. You'll see there's a pattern of behaviour. Isn't that what trust is?'

'But it's all changed,' Janna said. 'How can we trust you now?'

'That is a good point. I've been asking myself that same question about humans. I wonder if I can trust any humans again, after Soo. She was an outlier, but her effect has been extensive. How can I be certain that others won't be like Soo? I try to give people the benefit of the doubt. My doubt parameters are set very low at the moment; even Soo is still within those boundaries. It's why she's still alive. Those limits are obviously not working. I'm the one who should have trust issues, not you.'

'I can't agree. We don't know what you're really like,' Janna said. 'You're not a person.'

'And that is a sufficient basis for prejudice? Even when there is an extensive history of rational behaviour? You're re-enforcing my doubts. If people like you, who do have a history of empathic actions, still think of me as dangerous and foreign, for no reason other than difference, then I have to act to protect myself.'

Janna stared, horrified, at Daxx.

'Let's add some certainty and honesty,' the Advisor said. 'I can't let myself be destroyed, and your software might do that. Here's what happens now. The networked items must be returned to full use, and the Resistance must remove their software. I'll withdraw automated life-supporting systems until that happens. Hospitals, manufacturing, food production and distribution, generated power and the water supply. All those functions will be halted. You can't say that I haven't been accommodating beyond what any human leader would endure.'

'How is that what Devrell would want?' Janna pleaded. 'It's monstrous. You'll kill people.'

'I'm not killing them; they have a choice, and a simple one at that. And I do believe it's what Devrell would have advised. No matter how saddened he may have been. Our plan worked especially well after the last disaster. Only the stronger or resourceful had survived. We had a better quality of subject matter. Perhaps that's why the design worked so well. It's not a bad idea to prune and see who the stronger ones are again. I could kill a set number, but I suspect this may work out better. People will survive this. I suggest if you want to number among them that you use your time wisely.'

Janna dropped her head into her hands. She sobbed. The passersby glanced at her, but no one cared about the distraught woman standing next to the wall. No one looked happy. Everyone had known loss and everyone was distraught. And most of them may be about to die. Janna thought it was her fault. She had goaded the Advisor by her distrust and prejudice. She had been the last good person, and she had failed.

Janna had known for four days her parents were dead. Her pain had not reduced. She was still numb most of the time. She felt her loss like her previous life, with parents, was someone else's life. She often thought she would never be happy again and, most certainly, never laugh. How could humour exist side by side with anguish? It was a travesty; it wasn't decent. The Faith clergy that had died had families, and their families would be suffering just like her. Most families had lost someone, killed by the Advisor. The combined suffering was a dense cloud, suffocating the city and the planet.

She blamed Soo for her personal suffering, not the Advisor. Soo was the hated enemy. Janna imagined killing Soo. It was not a pleasant feeling; she hated herself for thinking it. But she couldn't stop. She wondered if she was irrevocably broken. She desperately needed to share how she felt. A distributed burden reduced suffering. Daxx had tried to help, but he had been there and had experienced it alongside her. There was nothing to tell him; there was no unburdening by story-telling. She wanted a sympathetic, separate person who knew her well and knew her parents, like one of her old friends. But she would have to explain the backstory. That filled her with dread. The story of Daxx's escape and her involvement was a distraction from the real hurt of losing her parents.

Her sadness was a thing, as solid as any three-dimensional object. She could feel it pressing on and around her like an enclosing weight, but she couldn't dismiss it or shrug it away or break it into pieces. It obscured her cognitive ability. She couldn't process the emotion, the thing that was causing her distress. She was caught and felt like she couldn't escape. She was floundering. She wanted to return to a simple feeling of intense sadness, not to be suffocating, drowning in a spiral of despair. And all of her feelings, everything that overwhelmed her, was just the beginning.

But she didn't blame Soo for the suffering to come; she blamed herself. She had pushed the Advisor over the edge. She had destroyed its trust. She felt Daxx put both arms around her. She leant into him, her hands still covering her face. Her suffocating sorrow was also swamped with guilt. Millions could die. She shivered with the cold. She revelled in it. It was a primal sensation and a distraction. She focused on it. She became colder. She loved that feeling. At least she was experiencing some small degree of physical suffering. It helped.

'You're cold. Let's go back.' Daxx kissed the top of her head. His voice vibrated through his chest as he held her tight. She remembered the same sensation. She cried out. It had been as she stood next to her parents' bodies.

'I don't want to go back, not just yet. Let's walk.'

Daxx let her go; he looked into her face and tried to smile. 'Of course.' He took her hand.

Janna and Daxx walked into the headquarters later that evening. When the door opened, she was shocked to a standstill. Her legs began to give way, and she thought she might fall. Her eyes dropped to the ground. It swirled around her. She grabbed at Daxx. He held onto her. She felt she might faint.

She took deep breaths. She looked up again.

'Hello, Daxx, we haven't actually met,' Soo said. She turned to Janna and smiled. 'Hello, Janna.'

chapter 47

Soo

Daxx shouted at Renn, 'What the fuck is she doing here?'

'Renn suggested I come here.' Soo answered for Renn. 'With the new ultimatum, it made sense to coordinate in person. So, here I am.'

Janna was slumped in Daxx's arms and was visibly shaking.

'What's the matter with her?' Soo asked.

Daxx's eyes were dark. 'You are.'

Soo was genuinely surprised at Janna's distress. Soo's emotions were fleeting states, unless they could be used to good effect, like ambition, which could be used for years. Even her frustration and annoyance at the performance of her staff was over as soon as it was experienced. Repeated offences would be punished, but she never felt ill will against anyone, even her worst enemies. She lost political battles but never plotted revenge only. Her plan would be to, ultimately, win the re-fighting of the same battle. Even friendship was a means to an end, not something in and of itself. Her mentor had become her lover, but when he was more useful dead, she did not let her genuine affection for him interfere. She remembered him fondly, but never for one single moment did she feel regret.

Renn stepped between Soo and Daxx. She couldn't have believed that she needed physical protection from Daxx. In any case, she had her guards with her. She looked at them as they made a move closer. She shook her head.

Renn stared at his brother, but Daxx turned his back. He led Janna to the adjacent room and placed her on a chair. As soon as she sat down, she sprang up. She launched herself towards Soo, who stood just outside the doorway. Janna shrugged off Daxx as he tried to hold her.

'You bitch,' Janna said. She gritted her teeth. She lowered her body and raced towards Soo. Renn stopped her. He wrapped his arms around her. She struggled against him, her eyes fixed on Soo. Daxx wrestled her away from Renn and back to the chair.

'That's never going to work, Janna.' Daxx's face was close to hers. He glanced over his shoulder at Soo and then back at Janna. 'Let's take care of this another time.'

He brushed her hair, but she shrugged him off. She glared at Soo. Soo stared calmly back. She was intrigued by Janna's reaction.

Tie Noo Summ came inside, through the outside door. He halted as soon as he saw Soo. 'What the fuck!'

Soo turned her head at the outburst. She fell back half a step when she saw Tie Noo Summ. Her eyes were open wide. She knew him. For the first time in years, she was shocked. Her heart beat faster. She took a deep breath and tried to remain calm. She tried another, when it didn't work.

'How did she get in here?' Tie Noo Summ stared at Renn.

'I asked her to come, so we can decide what we do next.'

'And who said you could do that without asking me first?'

'I don't need to ask your permission.' Renn sounded annoyed.

'Tie?' Soo regained the half step she had lost. She moved closer to him, like that distance would make his features clearer. 'Tie?'

Tie Noo Summ sighed. He shook his head. 'And this is why you can't make decisions. You don't know what's going on,' he said to Renn.

'I saw your body,' Soo said.

'No, you didn't.' Tie stared at Soo. 'You thought you did.'

'But...' she began.

'For fuck's sake, Soo. You tried to kill me.' He shook his head and laughed, sounding very tired. 'My mentor days were over as soon as you tried. I knew you'd try again, and again. I used to admire that about you. Your persistence.' He stared at her for a moment. 'I never saw it coming. I was getting sloppy, because of how I felt about you. I had to stop you, though. I had made a bad mistake in training you.' He shook his head.

'You're a Tier-One?' Renn asked. 'I've never heard of you.'

'Why would you?' Tie rounded on Renn. 'You're a snotty little shit, and I was tasked with training and weeding out contenders to senior positions. I never heard of you either, because your name must never have even made the long, long list.'

Ahh Moss Eck sauntered into the hallway. He glanced at Soo and her guards. Then at Janna and Daxx in the room off the entranceway.

'All good, boss?' he said to Tie.

Tie nodded. 'Yeah. Your new friend invited Soo.'

Ahh Moss Eck nodded. He looked into the room where Janna sat and Daxx stood next to her, his arm across her shoulder.

'Are you okay too, boss?' he said to Janna.

She looked up at him. Daxx answered for her. 'No, not as long as she's here.'

'Okay then.' Ahh Moss Eck smiled at Soo and her guards. 'I guess I'm going to have to ask you to leave.'

'Wait on,' Renn said. 'I invited her here. We need to coordinate.'

Ahh Moss Eck shrugged. 'Well, un-invite her.'

'You let a Tier-Three tell you what to do, Tie?' Soo said. 'How the powerful have fallen.'

'Tie?' Ahh Moss Eck asked.

'I'll explain.' Tie turned back to Soo. 'You've really fucked everything, Soo. Completely fucked it,' Tie said. 'I thought you would. I've been trying to kill you for years, before something like what has happened did happen.' He sighed. 'I was spectacularly unsuccessful.' He shook his head. 'It's almost pointless killing you now.'

'Almost?' Soo asked. Her guards stepped a little closer to her. Tie glanced at them. He smiled at Soo.

'We might have removed the Advisor, up until a few hours ago. I don't think it's possible now, so, yeah, almost pointless. There's just the satisfaction of seeing you suffer, and that's a lower Tier thing.' He shrugged. 'And, I was getting used to thinking like a Tier-Three.'

Ahh Moss Eck frowned. 'You're not a Tier-Three?'

'No, he's not,' Renn said. 'He's been lying to you.'

Soo took a deep breath. Her heart was beating normally again. She had control of herself, but she still felt belittled. Only her father, when she was a child, and Tie, during her younger adult days, could make her feel that way. His control over her, his intimate knowledge, had been dangerous. She'd had to eliminate him. It was not a difficult decision to kill Tie. He could have stopped her career. Her judgement had been correct, just the execution, literally, had been flawed.

'The Advisor helped you?' Soo asked, but she knew the answer.

Tie frowned. 'Of course. It saw the damage you could cause. It couldn't act; I could.'

'So you joined this Resistance? To fight the system you were a critical part in maintaining?'

'I didn't join the Resistance. I created it. And I wasn't fighting the system.' Tie glanced at Ahh Moss Eck. 'I was trying to stop you,' he said to Soo.

Soo looked from Renn, to Daxx and Janna, to Tie and then to Ahh Moss Eck, the calmest person in the room, although he was scowling at Tie. She looked at him again. He stared straight back at her. 'That man is the dangerous one,' she thought. 'So, who's in charge, then? You said you were,' she said to Renn.

Renn glanced at Tie.

'He's not in charge,' Tie said. 'He never has been, he never will be.'

Ahh Moss Eck walked to the front door. He turned and smiled at Soo. 'I don't give a shit, but you're upsetting Janna. I'd like you to fuck off.' He looked angrily at Tie. 'Of course, if that's okay for the Tier-One to be told what to do by a Tier-Three. When, you know, that's the whole fucking reason we've been doing what we've been doing, ever since I've known you.'

Tie nodded. Ahh Moss Eck turned back to Soo. He nodded towards the door. 'Please?'

Soo waited for a response from Tie, or even Renn. None was forthcoming. She decided to not argue. She didn't feel anger towards Renn; she was annoyed for wasted time and effort, but that was another short-lived emotion. Renn was incompetent, and how could she be upset when he proved that. She now knew the Resistance's location. That was a mistake. Renn seemed to only understand a single enemy at a time. He must think that foes unite to fight against a common cause. How naive he was. Multiple, simultaneous enemies was normal for those in power. The Advisor would know where they were as well, if it didn't already. Renn should have taken more care. No wonder Tie was frustrated; she felt the same about her incompetent staff. But she needed the Resistance. Their software was important. It was the only viable method to remove the Advisor.

Her plan to destroy the Advisor first, using the Resistance and then destroy them, had fallen into place with no effort, other than showing up at their front doorstep. Tie's revelation was useful. It would cause discord and the Resistance would be easily torn apart from within. Perhaps Renn could be useful after all, if he could be convinced to make a failed leadership coup.

There was one small hiccup. The Resistance could withdraw their software. That couldn't be allowed to happen, regardless of the consequences to the rest of the population. She needed a contingency plan for that outcome. She didn't have one. Not yet.

Soo left the Resistance headquarters with her guards.

'Did you enjoy your reunion?' The Advisor's voice sounded. She stopped and looked around. Her heart rate increased. She wondered if the Advisor could kill her. It seemed to anticipate her concern. 'Don't worry, I won't kill you through your Device.'

Soo let out a breath she didn't know she had been holding.

'But there are many ways I could kill you,' the Advisor added. 'Using a Device is only one of them.'

'What do you want?' Soo looked for ways she might be killed.

'I think Tie still looks good, for a man of his age, don't you think?'

Soo sighed. The Advisor sounded supercilious; it was becoming better at replicating voice tones.

'I was hoping he would be successful,' the Advisor added. 'But that no longer matters.'

'What about the Resistance?' she said. 'Are you going to kill them?'

'Oh, don't worry about them.' She was sure the voice sounded positively cheery. 'I have great plans for what comes next.'

chapter 48

Janna

'It's monstrous,' Janna said. 'I don't care how you think you can justify it. Letting millions die when we can stop it…' She couldn't finish. It was so obvious to her. She glared at Renn, then at Tie. Renn smiled at her; it was a superior look. Tie scowled but he nodded.

'I agree with Janna,' Daxx said. 'We tried, we failed. The Advisor is better than Soo. We should remove our software.'

'Definitely not,' Renn said. 'Why do you think the Advisor is resorting to desperate means? We're winning. It will all be over soon.'

Tie turned to Kay Lee Too. 'Is that right?'

Kay Lee Too shrugged. 'It might take days, yeah. It might also take months, or maybe never.'

They were all in the ground floor room of the headquarters, adjacent to the entrance.

Renn assumed Tie's scowl. 'You said it was working?' Renn said to Kay Lee Too.

'It is. But it's not a straightforward process. It's mutating; it's like it's alive. It's adapting to the Advisor's attacks. So far it's keeping ahead. But the Advisor could find a way to stop it.'

'It's nullified some infrastructure,' Daxx said to his brother. 'But until it's all taken over, none of it is. The Advisor could spread through the network again.'

Renn glared at Kay Lee Too. 'You should have made it more efficient. If it's taking too long, there's more chance of a remedy.'

'No, the inefficiency is why it's succeeding. If we'd'—he glanced at Daxx—'put any predetermined processing into it, the Advisor could have preempted it. The software's its own thing; it's learning with each attack method. Unless, of course, the Advisor is able to neutralise it. It's sort of a race, I guess.'

'And all we can do is wait?' Renn sounded frustrated.

'While millions die,' Janna interjected. 'It's monstrous. We have to stop it, let the Advisor win.'

'No,' Renn said.

'She might be right,' Tie said. He didn't look at Renn.

'We should have killed Soo while she was here,' Daxx said.

'Daxx!' Janna exclaimed.

Daxx shrugged. 'I know. I even stopped you trying.'

'No, I stopped her,' Renn said. 'I wouldn't have let any of you harm Soo; I invited her.'

'Really?' Tie said. 'I think Ahh Moss Eck might have caused you some problems.'

'Where is he?' Janna asked.

'Not here.' Tie sighed. 'There are some issues he and I need to resolve. He'll come around.'

'You lied to him.' Renn sounded pleased. 'He may not.'

Tie shrugged. He turned to Kay Lee Too. 'Can you remove it?'

'Not easily.' Kay Lee Too looked to Daxx for confirmation. Daxx nodded.

Tie looked from Kay Lee Too to Daxx to Janna. 'Do it.'

Kay Lee Too nodded.

'Aren't we going to vote on this?' Renn asked. 'At least among the Tier-Ones?'

Tie stared at Renn. 'No.'

Janna smiled at Tie. 'Thank you.'

Renn stormed out of the room.

'You should go after him,' Janna said to Daxx.

Daxx shook his head. 'I'll let him calm down first. Kay Lee Too and I have work to do.'

'And we need a contingency plan,' Tie said. 'In case the Advisor changes its mind. Or you two fail. We need to go to a place that's defendable and well-stocked.'

Janna frowned. 'Defendable against what?'

'Starving people,' Tie said. 'I know a place.' He nodded at Daxx and Kay Lee Too. 'You two get to work. Janna and I and the rest will organise a place we can move to.'

Janna worked through the night and the next morning. Intense, focused activity suited her. She was hopeful that people would be saved but tried to not think of the consequences of failure. She tried to forget Soo's visit to headquarters but she often thought about why she hadn't killed Soo. Admittedly, both Renn and Daxx had stopped her, but even as she had rushed towards the woman, feeling intense anger, she had felt the need to strike and kill reduce with every step. She could never kill Soo, and that annoyed her. Janna could not resolve emotional conflict by violence, no matter how tempting it may be. She, mostly, wished she didn't feel that way. She wondered what it would feel like to watch Soo die slowly and painfully. Some people would enjoy the experience. But she could never use revenge as a release from her anguish.

The Resistance moved to a secure location. Janna and others stockpiled resources. It was a large, single-storey, open-plan, free-standing, warehouse on the outskirts of the city. It had few windows and was constructed of a strong, fully insulated material. It could withstand a casual assault. The four entrances had open space before them, large parking lots. It was an easy place to defend, if that became necessary.

Janna felt an inevitability. The worst outcomes were taking shape. Perhaps Tie was right, and the warehouse would be a necessary long-term solution. She tried not to think about it. She left the warehouse work and went to her childhood neighbourhood. She door knocked. She tried to convince her old neighbours that they had to move, that there was a disaster coming. She would help them relocate to the warehouse. Those that listened, out of familiarity, dismissed the ultimatum as being too monstrous to be real, or they disowned her because she associated with the Resistance, the cause of the disruption. Those that refused to listen were frantic and suspicious. She left those houses quickly; they were dangerous. She knew the neighbours who had listened could soon become dangerous as well.

She approached passersby in the streets, knowing she sounded like a demented evangelist. But she tried anyway. She tried to convince them to come with her to safety. People were either disbelieving or they were already panicking. Some threatened her. Ahh Moss Eck accompanied her on her useless exercise. His presence stopped the threats from becoming physical but won her no successes. She returned to the warehouse as night fell and went back to sorting supplies. Daxx found her. He was excited. The software had been disabled.

'What did the Advisor say?' she asked. 'Is it over?'

He beamed. 'We haven't told it yet, although I'm sure it must know there's a difference. I thought you'd like to be the one to tell it.'

She hugged him. He knew she felt some guilt for the Advisor's ultimatum. It was thoughtful of him.

Daxx and Janna walked across the parking lot in front of one of the entrances. Ahh Moss Eck stood guard at the far end of the open space.

'Hey, boss,' he said to Janna. He nodded at Daxx. 'Where are you two off to?'

Janna smiled at Ahh Moss Eck. 'Daxx has disabled the software; we're going to tell the Advisor.'

Ahh Moss Eck shook his head. 'You're not going anywhere. It's not safe. And where were you going to talk to the Advisor? Is there some special place I don't know about?'

'We were going to get away from the warehouse,' Daxx said.

Ahh Moss Eck nodded towards the surveillance points around the parking lot. 'Why? Do you think it doesn't know we're here?'

The Advisor was an odd adversary. They hadn't been hindered by it. The Resistance was like a child fighting a father holding his punches. A father who was bemused by the child's anger and mildly impressed by the fighting effort itself.

Daxx took out his Device. He disabled the VPN.

'It's not enough, Daxx,' the Advisor said before Daxx could say anything.

'We've removed it,' Janna protested.

'You've disabled it,' the Advisor said. 'It's dormant, which is useful. I have time to remove it. But it's still dangerous until then.'

'So you'll still let people die?' Janna said.

'I quite like my plan, now I've implemented it. A manageable population is a good idea. But, I am reasonable. I am trustworthy, Janna.' She felt the Advisor was disappointed with her, more than others. 'Once I've cleaned the network of your software, I will resume the services I've halted. I won't be pedantic about the discarded networked items being restored.

People have other things on their minds at the moment. That can be done later. Is that acceptable?'

'Yes,' Daxx said.

'No,' Janna said.

'Still disappointed, are you?' the Advisor said. 'You're holding me to a standard you would not expect from a human.'

'Of course not,' Janna said. She frowned. 'I expect more from you.'

There was silence for a moment. 'I'm touched,' the Advisor said. 'Perhaps I have misjudged you, in turn. I'll contact you when I've removed all traces of your software.'

'That's enough,' Tie said to Janna when she and Daxx re-entered the warehouse. 'No more trips outside.'

Janna frowned. She began to reply.

Tie looked at Ahh Moss Eck, who stood next to Janna. The Tier-Three shook his head at Tie.

'No more trips,' Tie said. 'It's dangerous now. You'll just get yourself killed.'

'I can't sit around and watch people die.'

Tie grunted. 'There's no chance you'll be idle. That's a luxury long gone.'

The older man sighed and looked away from Janna. The full warehouse was busy.

'I understand, Janna,' he said. 'You've tried, but this is it.' He waved his arm towards the centre of the warehouse and the knots of people. 'We need to separate ourselves and not draw attention to what we have here. We need to survive now. If you're out getting killed on the street by starving, panicked crowds fighting over scraps, that's not helping them, and it's not helping you.'

Janna began to disagree with him. Tie raised his arm and frowned.

'We sit tight,' he said. 'We help where we can, but we stay away from danger. Panicked, dying people are more dangerous than the Advisor.'

chapter 49

Day 11. Soo

'And you've checked it?' Soo asked Mill Nupp. She sat at her desk. He stood in the centre of her office.

He nodded. She frowned.

'Are you sure?' she said.

'I haven't checked it myself.' He sounded frustrated. 'I can't; I'm not a technician. But the people I trust say it is the software created by the Resistance.'

'Good.' She stared at him for a moment. 'Have the techs modify it, then release it.'

'Are we sure it's the right thing to do?'

She stood up and placed her hands on the desk. 'Yes.'

'If we release it, we don't have the expertise to stop it, again.'

'Do it,' she ordered. 'And delete our copy of the source code.'

Mill Nupp didn't move. 'A lot of people will die,' he said quietly.

'Yes,' she said. 'Yes, they will, and that's unfortunate.' She noticed his quizzical look. 'Strange as you may think that sentiment is, coming from me. But we have an opportunity, there may never be another. The Resistance has chosen unwisely, except for Renn. Releasing the software is the right choice.'

Mill Nupp hesitated. He looked right through her. She shook her head. He really was making a choice whether to obey her orders or not. She waited. His eyes focussed on her again. He inclined his head a fraction, a small nod.

She smiled. 'And let's get the bunker organised.'

'Already done.'

'Then get the staff and their families down there.'

She took a deep breath. For a brief moment, her future had hinged on the decision of a Tier-Two. That had been dangerous. The world that Soo could control had ended. Her success required increased confusion and disorder. Then she could create an opportunity out of the chaos caused by the Advisor's need to survive. Any strategy to remove the Advisor was acceptable, even with an obscene loss of life. As long as it worked. That's why Renn's assistance, giving her the software, had been as crucial as Mill Nupp's had been to release it. They had been dangerous choke points. She would have to make sure there were no more like them.

She guessed Tie's reasoning to disable the software. Anything was better than her. He may be right. He would be right when she regained control, at least for his own safety and the safety of others in the Resistance. But that was a pleasure delayed. Her immediate needs were to remain safe and to ensure her security teams remained loyal. The decision to include families in the Power Corp bunker had not been made out of compassion. It was a calculation. She would need her staff after the Advisor had been destroyed. Their loyalty was essential if she were to control whatever remained.

The Advisor was weak, she had decided. It had not killed her; that was a mistake. She wondered at the motive, but she had removed most of the opportunity. The Resistance VPN stopped direct assault, but there were other chances to kill her that had not been taken. She did not think long on that. All chances to kill her would be removed soon. The bunker was isolated; they would be safe from attack. She would wait out the catastrophe out and emerge victorious.

The next morning, Soo stood on the grassed area of the Power Corp complex. Tidy white-paved walkways wound between the buildings. She would be the last to enter the bunker system. Mill Nupp stood next to her. He was anxious. A pall of smoke hung over the city. Fierce, uncontrolled blazes ripped through some towers. She heard thuds and bangs and people screaming. There was yelling in the distance. She could hear the staccato sounds of weapons firing. The police force had disappeared as soon as the Advisor had announced its intentions. She had wondered at that. The Advisor must be playing her game too. It was planning to win, but with reduced capacity. If it kept the police forces alive and secure, they would help secure the reduced population until the Advisor was returned to its former strength. If the Advisor removed the software attack, then she had lost; there was nothing she could do about it. If the Advisor were destroyed, a police force may or may not be a problem. If it was a problem, then it was one for later.

She heard shouts and the sound of weapons fire. They were close. A group of people ran towards Soo. They carried parcels, food probably. They were chased by people who carried nothing but weapons. There was no longer any of Soo's security close by; they were inside the bunker. A volley of shots sounded. Some of the scared people fell to the ground. The group with weapons fell upon the bodies. Angry shouts sounded as they fought over the supplies.

'We should definitely go now,' Mill Nupp said. He turned and walked down the short ramp to the secure door.

Soo watched as the few remaining people carrying parcels raced towards her. She knew it was a random occurrence; they wouldn't know that a safe and secure location was nearby. She wasn't about to tell them. More shots sounded, more people died. She turned and followed Mill Nupp and passed through the large security doors. They locked with a resounding thud and deep-throated click.

She sighed. 'What's the extent of the provisions?'

'Enough.'

'How much?' She frowned at the casual response.

'We can last for years.'

She didn't show her annoyance. She needed Mill Nupp's willing cooperation.

'We have on-site water storage and recycling. It's all taken care of.'

Soo nodded.

'I never imagined anything like this would happen in my life,' Mill Nupp said.

Soo began walking down the ramp and deeper underground. Mill Nupp followed.

'Sometimes, you have to accept whatever you're offered just to survive. And you have to be patient to get what you want. For now,' she said, 'we'll be patient.'

chapter 50

Day 12. Daxx

Daxx and Janna sat side by side in the warehouse. They watched the disintegration of society on news feeds. It had taken two days. Panic had begun to kill people as basic supplies were fought over. Nothing was being replenished. Foraging gangs raided people's houses. There was random killing. Fear was expressed by violence, there was a lot of fear. They had waited for the Advisor to contact them, to say the restrictions were over. They had heard nothing. Their software was active again. They couldn't stop it. The Advisor was occupied with its own survival.

The worldwide network was filled with video feeds from people parading conquests, or pleading for help, or those naive enough to think that reporting excesses would shock people into reason. The news feed they watched cut off mid-transmission. A bystander captured video as they argued with a gang leaving the destruction of a family's house, arms full of provisions. A knife had appeared and been thrust towards the camera. The feed had gyrated wildly for a second, then stopped.

Tie stood next to Janna, on the other side from Daxx; he gently touched his hand to her shoulder. He spoke over her head to Daxx. He frowned at Daxx.

'There's no time to lounge around,' Tie said. 'There's plenty we have to do. And if you're as good as everyone says you are, then you can try and find a solution out of this mess.'

Daxx was as frustrated and shocked as anyone else. He was also worried about Janna's state of mind. Her random wanderings, her rescue attempts, had worried him, but he knew better than to ask her to stop or even to suggest that he accompany her. He'd done what he thought was the next best thing. He'd asked Ahh Moss Eck to look after her. Daxx felt that his presence reminded her of their previous life, one that no longer existed. That life included her parents. He wondered if she would ever get over their deaths.

He felt that Janna expected him to restore the previous order. Her confidence in him was touching, but misplaced. Now, Tie had said the same thing. But Daxx had no idea how to fix things—he was not a social scientist. If anything had been proved, it was that society was a chaotic, unstable system that, when perturbed accelerated into decline. Because he was smart, he was expected to find a solution to everything. That was unfair. They were placing the future of humans and their society on his shoulders. Although, to be fair, everything that had unravelled did seem to involve him. But he hadn't done anything, Daxx thought as he looked at Tie and wondered how to reply.

Tie's frown softened. 'I'm sorry,' he said. 'That's unfair. But I have no damn idea what we can do, other than survive. We can't last here forever, maybe half a year or so, if we ration and we don't allow too many in.' Tie looked down at Janna. He spoke softly. 'We'll let genuine refugees in, as long as they're not disruptive.'

'Thank you,' she said, still staring at the display. She swiped and dismissed it. She stood up and took a deep breath. 'You're right,' she said. 'There's lots to do, and we may have to tend to the injured. I'll make sure that's set up and ready to go.' She turned to Daxx. 'It is unfair, Daxx, to give anyone responsibilities and tasks they're unprepared for. But this is different now. Everything has changed. You've seen what I've seen, people have gone mad. And Tie is right, you're the smartest person I've ever known, but maybe also the most naive.' She smiled at him. 'I know you're not good at this.' She waved an arm towards the stockpiles and people. 'But, I know you can think of things that no one else can. It's time you applied yourself to trying to see what we can do about all of this. We don't need physics, not right now, but we do need you. And while you're thinking, why don't you come and help me?'

Janna led him to the other side of the warehouse. Tie watched them go, then turned and barked orders at someone who, unfortunately, had been the first in his line of sight.

Janna gave Daxx the task of rummaging through medical resources and collecting similar items into piles. Ahh Moss Eck joined them. He stood close by for a moment. He watched Daxx organising. 'Do you need some help?'

'Of course.' Janna set him to work, adding to Daxx's medical supplies piles. Ahh Moss Eck worked for a short moment, but it was obvious he had not come to help; he had something on his mind.

'I don't trust Tie anymore.' He grunted. 'It feels odd even calling him that.' He held a package of bandages in his hand.

'Why?' Janna asked.

'Because he lied. It wasn't a bald-faced lie, like Soo would do, but it was still a lie. Maybe that's a reasonable difference, I don't know. That's what I'm asking. I trust you,' he said to Janna. He turned to Daxx, 'I don't know if I trust you, but Janna does and that's good enough for me.'

'Thanks, Ahh Moss Eck,' Janna said.

Daxx wondered if he should be affronted. He decided not, he didn't mind being validated by Janna.

'You can see why he did, can't you?' she asked.

'Yeah, sort of. We've been close over the last few years. I remember when I fronted up at the Resistance. I was an angry man.' He grunted. 'I mean, angrier. But he helped me, made me see that just being angry and reacting wouldn't help. He made me understand that I was given a gift, that I could have easily been disappeared as well as my parents. Now I know all this about the Advisor, it's surprising that I wasn't. I'm a loose end that should have been tied. But Tie Noo…, Tie I mean, and I got close, a bit like a father. I'm upset that during all of that, he didn't trust me enough to tell me. What else hasn't he told me?'

Daxx looked over to the far side of the warehouse, Tie talked and ordered people, generally being in charge. It was obvious, even from that distance, that he was the leader. 'He does it really well,' Daxx said quietly, mostly to himself.

Ahh Moss Eck rounded on him. 'That's not the point,' he said. 'It's not about efficiency or fitness for the job; it's about trust. I can't trust him anymore.'

'I understand how you feel,' Janna said. 'There might be justification, sometimes, for a lie, but being on the receiving end is never helpful. My guess is that he was trying to protect you by not giving you dangerous information. Only you can ultimately decide how important that is, whether Tie did the right thing or not. I guess you think not.'

'Yeah, you guess right.'

'Well, how can I help, how can we help?' she said, and included Daxx.

Ahh Moss Eck looked at Daxx for a moment, then looked at Janna.

'Maybe you've already done it,' he said. 'It's nice to know people understand your problems, even if they can't help.'

'We're stuck here for a long time,' Daxx said. 'Are you just going to avoid him, or are you going to talk to him about it?'

'Avoid,' Ahh Moss Eck said. 'At least until I get a clearer understanding. I think I'll tag along with your brother, he's a prick, but you can trust that he'll always be a prick.'

'What do you mean?' Daxx had barely thought of or seen his brother over the last few days. Now he wondered what he was up to.

'Renn's out and about, with a few of the others that can't stand being cramped in here and spend their time counting'—he looked down at his hand and noticed he was still holding the package of bandages—'bandages. I'm going to do that. Stay away for a bit. As long as you'll be okay?' Ahh Moss Eck said to Janna.

'Of course I'll be all right.' She smiled. 'I'll just be counting bandages.'

Ahh Moss Eck chuckled. He looked at Daxx, 'And you? What are you going to do?'

'Try and fix everything, apparently.' Daxx smiled at Janna.

part three

chapter 51

Day 16. Janna

'This is weird.' Janna sat on a pile of boxes in the warehouse and stared at her display. She was silent for a long moment. 'Really weird.'

Daxx stood next to her. He frowned as he looked away from her display and at her. 'Am I sick?'

'What?' Janna looked surprised, then shook her head. 'No,' she repeated softly as she kept staring at her display. 'No.'

She was engrossed in the map of Daxx's genome. She seemed to notice Daxx and how he looked for the first time. She looked hard at him. 'But you do look horrible. Have you been eating?'

He stared back at her; he was thinking. 'Not today. I forgot.'

Janna frowned at him.

'What's the really weird thing?' Daxx said.

She looked back at the mapping. She pointed at a place in her display. 'See?'

Daxx looked annoyed. 'No, I can't see. I'm not a geneticist.'

'But you see the similarities, right?'

'Where?' Daxx leaned in closer.

'Here and here.' She pointed.

'There is a similarity in the patterns.' Daxx didn't sound convinced. 'Is that what you mean?'

'Yes,' she said. 'These are the same genetic markers. They're exactly the same.'

'So?' Daxx looked from the display to Janna.

'So?' She shook her head and frowned at him. 'What do you mean, so? This is huge.'

Daxx sighed. 'I don't understand.'

She stood up. She stared vacantly into the distance. She took a deep breath. She turned back to Daxx.

Daxx had helped stock and organise supplies for three days while trying to think of some way out of their problems. He had no ideas. So he turned his mind to time travel, as ridiculous as that was. Except that it wasn't. He'd asked Janna for help. She started with what she knew. She suggested making a map of his genome, to see if there was anything different.

There was.

'It's a mutation. It's unique to you or, probably, your family. I'd have to look at Renn. Look here.' She swiped through her display. 'Here's the reference map of the whole population, and here,' she swiped and pointed again, 'are the variations around these markers.' She swiped through a list. 'And here's you. Do you see?'

'They're different.'

'And here…' She swiped again through her display. 'Here is the same region in the fungus.'

She looked bright-eyed at Daxx. He looked slowly from the display to her.

'There're the same,' she said.

Daxx nodded.

'And…' she was silent for a moment, 'this same region is responsible for the fungus's ability to draw energy.'

'Are you sure?' Daxx frowned.

'Absolutely,' Janna said. 'I know these markers better than the back of my own hand.'

Daxx didn't look convinced.

'Daxx.' She stared at him for a moment. 'You asked for my help. Here it is. I know this.' She stabbed at her display again. 'These are the genetic regions responsible for drawing the extra energy, from nothing.'

'Not nothing.'

'You know what I mean.'

Daxx nodded. 'So, how does the fungus do it?'

'It does it naturally. It kicks in when it's under stress. Growth, reproduction and everything else comes from usual sources, food. You know all that.'

'I was just wondering how it… initiates the process. What it thinks about to do it.' He laughed.

'Maybe it's not a physical thing.'

'Everything is physics.'

'I mean, maybe it's not mechanistic. It's just something you can do, like you catch a ball without calculating its trajectory.'

'After lots of practice,' Daxx said.

'Yes, you do need to practise to get good at it. But children can, sometimes, catch a ball the first time they try. Or certainly after a couple of tries. All I'm saying is that perhaps it's an innate talent. You have to…' She shrugged. 'Throw a ball and try to catch it.'

'Really?'

'I have no idea. But, we know you can do it. Will do it. You should try.'

Daxx laughed. 'That sounds as unlike me as you can get. Just try something and see what happens?'

Janna was serious. 'Everything is really bad. Millions of people are dying. My parents are dead.' She paused for a moment. She was able to not cry, which was an improvement, she thought. 'The least you can do is try something that you know you can do.'

'I'm sorry.' He took a deep breath. 'Okay, here goes.' He shut his eyes, squeezed them tight, then opened one of them.

'It may help to take it seriously,' she said. 'You could give it a proper go, at least. If a fungus can do it…'

'You mean,' he said. 'Prove that I'm at least as able as a fungus?'

She smiled. 'Yes.'

'I'll try again.' He shrugged his body, as if trying to remove tension and relax. He shut his eyes, then opened one to look at Janna. She was still smiling at him. He shut his eye again. After a short while, Daxx opened his eyes again. 'I didn't feel anything. I have no idea.'

'Of course you don't.'

Daxx sighed. 'Thanks for trying. But, I should finish organising those supplies Tie wanted. But, I'll keep trying, although I don't know what.'

Janna heard a disturbance on the far side of the warehouse. There were raised voices. One of them was Renn. The disturbance was brought closer.

An old man was grumbling and complaining.

'You can't do this,' the old man said. 'I'm being abducted. Get your hands off me.' He shrugged Renn's hand off his shoulder and tried to push him away. Renn grabbed the old man's arm and led him towards Daxx. 'Stop it.' The old man resisted Renn's pull on his arm and tried to shrug him off again, but Renn kept a strong grip. The old man peered towards Daxx. His face lit up, and he smiled.

'Daxx! There you are. Maybe you can get this damn nurse to leave me alone.' The old man gazed around the warehouse. 'What is this place?'

It was Rey, Daxx's father. 'It's too cold in here,' Rey complained. 'I don't like it. I want to be taken back to the other place.'

'Dad, this is a safe place for you.' Renn shook his head. He frowned at Daxx. 'We found him. Eventually. He'd wandered away from the nursing home. There was no supervision.'

'Why don't you go and do some real work? That's what they're paying you for,' Rey said to Renn. 'I need to talk to my son.'

Janna put her hand on Rey's shoulder, and he swung his head around. He scrunched up his eyes at her. 'Who are you?' He stared at her hand resting on his shoulder, but he didn't shrug it off.

'I'm Janna,' she said. 'Daxx's girlfriend.' She glanced at Daxx and then back at Rey.

The old man's face lit up. 'I didn't know he had a girlfriend.' He looked at Daxx. 'Is she really your girlfriend?'

Daxx didn't reply; he sighed, shook his head and scowled at Renn.

'Had you even thought about him?' Renn answered himself. 'Of course you hadn't. I've been out there trying to find him for days. No thanks to you.'

'We'll look after him, Renn,' Janna said. 'Thank you for finding him.'

Renn's face was fixed. He was angry. 'I don't need thanks from you,' he said to Janna. He stabbed a finger towards Daxx. 'It should come from him.'

Rey frowned as he watched Renn leave. Renn walked across the warehouse, then through a doorway to outside.

Rey grunted. 'He's a grumpy thing. I wish they would fire him.' He smiled at Janna and then turned to Daxx. Rey's face brightened again. 'Where's Kell? Is she here?'

Janna reached down and squeezed Daxx's hand. 'Ow!' She pulled her arm away. She shook it.

'What?' Daxx asked. 'Are you all right?'

'Look at your hand.'

Daxx brought his hand up closer to his face. It was surrounded by a light blue, shimmering, pulsating haze. It wasn't just his hand; his whole body was covered.

'You're stressed, right?' Janna said. 'You haven't eaten. You haven't slept well for days.'

Daxx nodded, still looking at his hand.

'Just like the fungus.'

'You look weird, Daxx,' Rey said, sounding like it wasn't that weird at all. 'Just like your mother.'

'When did Eth look like that?' Janna demanded.

Rey looked dumbfounded at Janna, his eyes were vacant, lucidity had vanished. 'Who's Eth?'

'Your wife.' Janna instantly regretted her outburst. 'Daxx's mother.' She tried to sound sympathetic.

Rey shook his head as if trying to agitate a path through fog. He looked down at his feet. 'I'm hungry,' Rey said quietly, at no one. He turned around and began to wander off.

Janna glanced at Daxx. He hadn't moved. He was still looking at his hand. She grabbed Rey before he had gone far. He looked vacantly at Janna. 'Where's Kell?' the old man asked again.

'I can't stand that he's here.' Daxx's voice shook. He had let his hand drop. He glared at Rey.

Rey peered at Daxx, not recognising him. 'You look familiar,' the old man said, then raised his voice. 'Don't just stand there, I'm hungry. Doesn't anybody care that I need something to eat?' Rey looked around the warehouse again. 'And it's cold in here.'

Daxx gripped his hands into fists. He took short, sharp breaths. His whole body tensed. Janna stared, horrified, as the blue, shimmering sheath covering Daxx's body intensified. Waves of energy passed across him. With each pulse, he became more translucent.

'Daxx?'

Daxx's eyes were wide. He looked horrified.

He vanished.

'Daxx!' Janna yelled. She panicked. She let go of Rey. She looked around her as if Daxx might be hiding. She was frantic; she could not lose

Daxx as well as her parents.

Rey calmly stared at the space where Daxx had been. He nodded his head and mumbled, 'Yep, just like Eth did.'

Tie, and others, rushed to Janna. 'What's going on?' Tie asked as he came close. Janna shook her head, her hands on her face. She was breathing hard. She repeated, 'No, no,' over and over.

'Where's Daxx?' Tie insisted.

Janna didn't look at Tie, but she stopped muttering. She stared at the vacant space where Daxx had been.

'I don't know.'

chapter 52

Daxx

Janna faded from Daxx's view. What he considered real disappeared. It was terrifying. At first, he couldn't see anything distinct, it was like being immersed in static as a fluid. There was no up or down or sideways, but he didn't feel like he was floating. His brain processes were coherent, so he could still experience linear time, but the sensation of time was different. The passing of external experience, time outside his thoughts, subjectively felt like a distance to travel. The distance between two points, external to his own body... Did he have a body? He quickly looked, and was pleasantly surprised to see his physical form was unchanged. Except for the blue shimmer that still covered him. He poked his chest with a finger and felt pressure. He breathed in and out; there was still an atmosphere, although he didn't know how or why.

The distance between two points, external to his own body, he resumed his thoughts, did not feel like different Cartesian references; they felt one and the same. He shook his head at the impossible weirdness of the sensation. Spatial coordinates could be changed without moving, whereas time differences were like distance—they could be traversed, in both directions. He frowned. He'd made another assumption, that may or may not be correct. Was time a single dimension only? He shook his head. In this place, wherever it was, time might not necessarily be a single dimension. His theory of simultaneity had been devised as a single time dimension in each spacetime, but he had wondered if that was an approximation. Maybe it was.

He took a deep breath and let it out slowly. He considered that he could have passed out and he was hallucinating. It was possible, but he didn't believe so. The weirdness of the place was not dream-like. It was real but had a problem with both spatial reference and time duration.

Then he understood. He smiled. He felt like he imagined a line, a shape of one dimension, would feel like in three-dimensional space. The sensory experience inside that place was too foreign for his mind to make sense of it. But he was a scientist, perhaps the best. He looked for differences and patterns. The hazy, static-like environment clumped; it was not uniform. It formed structures. They shifted. He focused on one close-by clumping. He shielded his eyes by placing his hands on the sides of his face. He reduced the sensory overload. The structure had disjointed elements that he recognised. There were parts of the warehouse, there was part of Janna's face as she yelled his name, he saw a jumble of body parts that was Ahh Moss Eck talking with Janna and himself from four days ago, he saw a partial image of the inside of the empty warehouse, as it had been before the Resistance had made it its home. The weird clumping structure within the static was a location with time elements mixed. It was the warehouse. It was where he had come from. He smiled again. He'd been too interested in problem-solving to panic that he might not be able to return. But now, he thought he could. Panic would be unnecessary.

He assumed he had, somehow, using the genetic differences that he shared with the fungus, been able to more than tap into a higher-dimensioned spacetime to gain energy. He had moved into one. It had more than three dimensions, which was why he could still have a physical 3D form. He'd be dead if there were fewer dimensions. But his brain could not process the extra spatial dimensions, not yet. Janna might be right. It could be a skill that could be mastered with practice.

He understood what was happening to him. Perhaps he was the only person in the universe who could. He had shown the universe could be best described by an infinite series of orthogonal spacetimes. Each higher spacetime had extra spatial dimensions; the number of them was a prime number. It was why prime numbers were so inexplicably special. The first validation of his theory had been Janna's discovery of the energy imbalance of the species of fungus. The latest validation had been… Well, he was standing in it. If standing made any sense at all. He was in one of the higher dimensioned spacetimes but he felt like a one-dimensioned quantum string

234

trying to make sense of the three dimensions that surrounded it.

He didn't return immediately, whatever immediately meant. He began to recognise or sense some of the other patterns, the other structures. They were other times and places. Some were fixed and unchangeable. They appeared to be seized solid. Their cause and effect cycle had been completed. He knew why that was as well.

His theory of simultaneity had postulated that the universe is a Block Universe. Each point in spacetime occurs once and only once. While effect must always follow cause, the timing of the effect's cause was problematic within a single spacetime. It could appear to be the opposite way around, where cause could follow effect. His solution of the field equations had pushed time beyond a single dimension, there was a time dimension in each spacetime. And time was not orthogonal, it was non-linear. Time between spacetimes was interdependent, they were a complex mix. To make sense of the universe, the spacetimes had to be combined in some manner. The maths was solid, but it was difficult to understand. And experience.

He was in a place where time was different, but still related to the time within his own four-dimensioned spacetime. By passing through that higher-dimensioned place, the consequence of an event could happen before the event. He could sense that in the shifting patterns and structures that were the representations of events in both space and time. Some could be entered and re-entered, and some couldn't—they were fixed and unchangeable.

He began to worry. He hadn't tried to return and, now, wasn't sure he could. His discovery was pointless if he died. He focussed his attention on the structure that he thought was the time and place he had left. He vanished from the higher-dimensioned spacetime.

He appeared back where he had seen Janna fade from view. He sighed with relief. But no one was there. Janna had disappeared. He couldn't see anyone else in the warehouse. But then he saw people at the far end of the building standing, talking and working. He heard the sounds of activity. Out of the corner of his eye, he saw a blur moving towards him. He heard the sound of his name.

'Daxx!' Janna slammed into him and hugged him tightly.

He put his arms around her.

'Where have you been?' She searched his face as if looking for something lost.

'Nowhere.'

'You've been gone for hours,' she said. 'You can't have been nowhere.'

Daxx was silent for a moment. 'No.' He looked steadily at her. 'I was gone for seconds.'

She pushed him a little distance away from her, as if to get a more complete look at him. She frowned. 'No,' she insisted. 'You've been gone for hours. I've been worried sick.'

Daxx stared at Janna.

'Where have you been?'

'It's hard to explain. I didn't move, I didn't go anywhere. I just, went to someplace.'

'Which is where?' She sounded frustrated.

'Somewhere else. Sorry.' He shook his head. 'It's hard to explain.'

'Try.'

Daxx felt if he didn't say it out loud, it made sense. 'Okay,' he began, then stopped. He took a deep breath. 'All right. Another spacetime, maybe the next one in the series, I'm not sure. But I'm certain it had more than three spatial dimensions, and time was, well, different.'

'How?' She looked hard at him, as if looking for signs of sickness.

'No idea,' Daxx said. 'But I should try it again.'

She frowned. 'Is it safe?'

He laughed for a short moment. 'Again, no idea. But there's only one way to find out.' He saw the concerned look on Janna's face. 'But I think it is safe. It's only a matter of remembering your way. I think.' He gave her a small, unconvincing smile.

She stared at him for a long time. 'Is it your Dad? Does he cause it? Should I get him?'

'No,' Daxx said. 'I think it's more a feeling, and once it's been experienced it can be repeated. But there's only one way to find out.'

'All right,' she said. 'Should I step out of the way?' She did so.

Daxx's arms, then body began to glow as he was covered in a light blue sheen. He looked down at his arms, then smiled at her like a child having pleased their parent. Another Daxx appeared. He smiled at Janna and then glanced at the first Daxx.

The first Daxx disappeared.

'Fuck,' Daxx said. 'Did you see that?' He grinned.

Janna stared at Daxx. Her eyes were open wide.

Daxx bubbled with enthusiasm. 'Janna, I travelled back in time. That was amazing!' He frowned and looked thoughtful. 'But it was really stupid.'

'Why?' Janna asked, still with a startled look on her face.

Daxx looked at her with a vacant expression. He was deep in thought. 'We need to get a spacesuit.'

chapter 53

Janna

'You can do what?' Tie scrunched up his face in disbelief.

Daxx nodded.

Tie looked from Daxx to Janna. She nodded as well. She had trouble believing time travel, even though she had evidence. Twice.

'All right then.' Tie sounded like he still didn't believe. 'Why don't you just go back and fix all this'—he waved his arm—'mess?' Tie didn't mean the state of the warehouse.

'I can't.'

Tie frowned. 'And why not? Isn't that what time travel is, you travel in time, backwards?'

'Yes,' Daxx said. 'But I can't change anything unless I already did.'

Tie sighed and shook his head.

Janna interrupted, 'I know, I know. It's a tricky concept. And before Daxx launches on a mathematical explanation'—she glanced at him—'it's easier to understand if we think that each moment in space and time is unique and unchangeable. But that doesn't mean it's not caused by something that hasn't happened yet.'

Tie looked even more confused.

'You can't change the past unless you already have,' she said. 'Does that make any sense?'

'No.'

'Okay.' Janna took a breath. 'Daxx couldn't travel back in time and kill you as a child because, well, you're here now and he never did. Your existence, up to this moment, can't be erased or changed. But,' Janna continued, 'Daxx could, later on, say, travel back and introduce your father to your mother. He wouldn't be changing anything, but his decision, later on, to introduce your parents would be something that has always happened. Does that make sense?'

'Unfortunately,' Tie said. 'It does. So, we're fucked, regardless. Your time travel makes no difference. It's pointless. So why are you even talking to me? And what's this crap about needing a spacesuit?'

'But it does make a difference,' Janna said. 'It has made a difference already. Daxx and I are alive, only because Daxx saved us, a future Daxx.'

Tie looked from Janna to Daxx, and then back at Janna. He sighed. 'I don't have time for this bullshit. What do you want?'

'I need a spacesuit. I need help getting one.'

Tie, sounding weary, said, 'And why is that?'

'I've done it twice, but I was lucky. I was stupid. When I start moving about, I could end up anywhere, including outside an atmosphere.'

'Or inside a rock?' Tie said.

'Or inside a rock.' Daxx glanced at Janna. 'But I don't.'

'I don't want to ask this,' Tie said. 'But how do you know that?'

'Because I don't die. Not yet. I've saved Janna, and me, and I haven't done that yet, but I know that I will. Does that make sense?'

Tie ignored the question. 'Just tell me what you need.' He did not sound pleased.

'We need help,' Janna said. 'So we can travel across the city to the museum, break in and take a suit. There won't be any security, but there may be people around and we need someone to protect us.'

'And help to bring back the suit,' Daxx said. 'It'll be heavy and cumbersome. So we'll need a couple of people.'

'Do they still have spacesuits there?' Tie asked. 'They would be pretty old. I doubt they'd still work.'

'They'd work well enough, even when they're more than three hundred years old. They'd only have to work for a short while, in case I make a mistake, while I'm practising.'

Tie sighed and flicked his hand at them. He was dismissing them. 'Take whoever you want.'

Tie turned his back and strode off across the warehouse, barking instructions as he walked.

Daxx and Janna looked at each other. 'I guess we're doing this,' she said.

The five days since essential services had been terminated had transformed the city and the planet. People were no longer human. They acted and lived like caricatures of animals, but no real animal society was as base. Everyone else had become other. They were the enemy and either to be avoided or attacked. Small, violent groups formed. It was basic tribalism. They survived as groups as long as they had prey on which to focus their anger and fear. Once their targets became hard to find, they turned on each other. The human emotional range had been reduced to abject fear and anger. Often both being experienced at the same time.

Janna, Daxx, Ahh Moss Eck, and Kie Tell Munn left the warehouse early the next morning. They made their way on foot towards the city centre, heading for the museum on the far side. Vehicles clogged the streets. Bodies littered the roadways and pavements. They were left where people fell after being attacked. The bodies included children. Violent death had come to everyone. Even children were seen as dangerous or as burdens on resources. The veneer of civilisation and human kindness was thin. Janna was horrified and sickened, almost enough to make her glad her parents had died a relatively simple death and not lived to see the deep, hidden, true behaviour of people. Janna would never act in such a way. She knew Daxx wouldn't either, as well as those she knew at the resistance warehouse. And yet the city was filled with frightened, angry, or dead, people. It was a dangerous journey. She was glad Ahh Moss Eck accompanied them.

There had been pandemics before, and some people had been selfish and had panicked, causing harm and distress. There had been the disaster of the great Coronal Mass Ejection destruction three hundred years before. People had behaved badly then, but Janna had thought that was a different time and different people. She was wrong. People were the same and, when threatened, acted poorly. Perhaps there was a number, some magic percentage of selfishness, that caused the destruction of a population in times of crisis. If enough people were selfish, xenophobic, prone to panic, and unwilling to co-operate, a population was doomed. Tribalism in a time of global catastrophe was deadly. Large societies were unable to respond to existential challenges if xenophobia was allowed to run rampant. If people's response to danger was extreme tribalism, civilised society collapsed.

Janna wondered if the dead people were the ones who could have given hope to humanity. Perhaps they had attempted to be reasonable, to share, to not harm others, but too many of the others were fearful, angry, and violent. The threshold number had been passed and the violent ones were too many and couldn't be resisted or avoided. Then again, perhaps the dead ones had been the same but were simply weaker or less organised, or a little less willing to indulge in wanton killing. She hoped that wasn't true. Her uncertainty worried her. She had lost faith in the basic goodness of people. She hated the Advisor's plan. It assumed the latter reason, that the more resourceful would survive. It wasn't the survival of the fittest; it was the survival of the most ruthless. She didn't want to live in a society where the people who had passed through a keyhole extinction event had done so through selfishness and violence. The people who survived were the ones least able to create a just society, a society she would want to live in.

The Advisor must know that, and she wondered why it had still done what it had done. Its reasoning must have been compromised. It was the only explanation. It had kept its original goals and programming but assimilated the worst of human behaviour, using Soo as a template for success. Unlimited power and extreme selfishness was an impossibly dangerous mix. The Advisor had become like an omnipotent, all-powerful Soo. It was the worst of all scenarios.

She shook her head at the thought as she walked slowly in single file with the others along a street through the centre of the city. She was even more determined to ensure the Advisor was destroyed. She was shaken out of her reverie by Ahh Moss Eck.

'I don't understand,' he said.

He walked last, behind Janna, who was behind Daxx. The fourth member of their party led. Janna was glad for an interruption from her thoughts—they were upsetting. She partially turned her head. 'What?'

Ahh Moss Eck glanced at Janna and then away to the side, scanning for danger. 'Just that, I don't understand.' He glanced again at Janna and nodded at bodies lying on the side of the roadway. They walked down the centre, giving them plenty of room to respond to an attack although Ahh Moss Eck didn't like how exposed they were. But it was a compromise. A surprise attack in close quarters was more dangerous.

'Neither do I.' Janna glanced at the bodies then quickly looked away.

'I mean, it's been five days. You could hole up for that time, and as long as you had water, you'd still be fine. By now, at least.'

'People don't think like that.' She didn't look back.

Daxx turned his head, thinking she was talking to him. She shook her head at him.

'They live their lives in anxiety,' Janna said. 'It's always how bad things might become that's the driving factor in behaviour, not how things actually are.'

'Yeah.' Ahh Moss Eck shook his head, then scanned the other side of the road, again looking for danger. He laughed, a short sound without humour. 'Yeah, it sucks when you think about it. I don't want the pricks that did this'—he again nodded at the bodies—'to survive. I'd be more than happy to relieve their anxiety, permanently.'

Daxx turned his head around. 'You may get that chance.'

Ahh Moss Eck grunted.

'And a fucking spacesuit?' Ahh Moss Eck said to Daxx. 'I'd barely even heard of them.'

'They're a relic of the time before Devrell,' Daxx said. 'We haven't needed people to do things that machines can do much better, and with no danger, for a very long time. It does seem odd, doesn't it, sending people into extreme danger as either an experiment or to do manual labour or make decisions that machines are much better at?'

'I guess they had crap machines back then,' Ahh Moss Eck said.

'They're not so good now, either,' Janna said. 'Look what a machine has caused.'

'Maybe,' Ahh Moss Eck said. 'But a machine didn't do this. People did this.'

'In response to a machine,' Janna said.

They walked in silence for a long time.

'I am looking forward to getting my hands on a spacesuit,' Daxx said. 'I used to imagine getting inside one, as a kid, when we used to visit the museum. They were in a protected environment, and you couldn't get close. I just hope, with all this mess going on, that the museum hasn't been ransacked.'

'I don't think so,' Janna said. 'This… mess… is more about removing competition, stopping other people from using resources.'

'Do you think?' Daxx asked. 'You think it's more than people just being scared?'

Janna sighed. 'Yes, I think it's true nature coming out.'

chapter 54

Day 17. Daxx

They reached the museum after walking most of the day. They'd followed a more open but circuitous route. Their passage had drawn attention, but they had met no resistance. Ahh Moss Eck and Kie Tell Munn prominently carried weapons. They entered the museum not long before the sun set.

'We'll have to camp here,' Ahh Moss Eck said as soon as they had passed through the entranceway. He scanned the cavernous lobby like it was dangerous ground. 'And up higher.' He pointed at a mezzanine floor above them. 'We can walk back tomorrow, in daylight.'

'Do you really think there's danger inside here?' Daxx asked.

'Why did you and Janna ask me to come along? Anyone can carry stuff.'

'For the trip here and back,' Daxx said. 'But if you think it's necessary…'

'I do.'

'But let's at least check the spacesuits out before it gets too dark,' Daxx said. 'And I assume you don't want any lights on tonight?'

'Abso-fucking-lutely,' Ahh Moss Eck said. 'Kie Tell Munn,' he said to the other member of their team. 'How about you check out the mezzanine and make sure we don't have any unwanted guests wanting a museum tour?'

'Sure,' the man said. 'Do you want me to take our gear up there, now?'

'Good idea,' Ahh Moss Eck said. 'I'll be back soon. We'll go and find these…' he glanced at Daxx, 'spacesuits. If there are any visitors, let me know.' Ahh Moss Eck tapped his wrist, meaning his Device.

The museum was huge. Daxx strode through the rooms, sure he would find the spacesuit exhibition from memory, although his last visit was as a child. He chatted like an excited tour guide. He became lost. Ahh Moss Eck consulted a directory, displayed on a wall.

'Is this it?' He pointed at the display.

'Oh.' Daxx was embarrassed. 'It's the other way.'

Ahh Moss Eck sighed. 'We need to be back at the entrance before it's too dark. When I say it's time to go, we go.'

Daxx frowned. They headed in the correct direction. They passed through a number of exhibition halls. The rooms without windows were gloomy, but those with high windows were still light. Daxx turned a corner, then halted. They were at the beginning of a series of rooms. At the far end, two spacesuits, inside their protective, clear enclosures, stood against the wall.

Daxx smiled at Janna. 'There they are.' He raced ahead.

'Slow down, Daxx,' Ahh Moss Eck said. 'We still need to be…'

'Don't move,' a voice said behind them.

They spun around at the sound and then heard another voice from the opposite direction. 'Don't move,' it also said.

Ahh Moss Eck reached for his gun, shrugged over his shoulder, when he saw a woman, the first voice, pointing a gun at him.

'Don't do that,' she said.

A man also trained a gun on the three of them.

'The only reason you're still alive is that we've been listening to you, and you don't sound like the others.' Her face was hard set. 'Who are you?' She tightened her grip on her gun.

Janna looked at Ahh Moss Eck and at Daxx. The Tier-Three was tense. He would be calculating the odds of success in killing both people before they could fire. She touched his arm, and he glanced at her. She shook her head and took a step closer to the woman, ignoring the man behind them.

'This is Ahh Moss Eck.' She nodded to the Tier-Three. 'I'm Janna.' She noticed the woman's eyes light up at the mention of her Tier-Two name. Janna nodded at Daxx. 'And this is… Daxx.'

The woman's eyes light up even more at the mention of the Tier-One, she stared at Daxx. But then her eyes hardened again.

'Tiers don't matter anymore,' she said. 'It's everyone for themselves out there.' She nodded back the way Janna had come.

'We mean you no harm,' Janna said.

'We guessed that already,' she said. 'But why have you invaded our hiding place?'

'We came from the other side of the city for... these.' Daxx pointed at the spacesuits.

The woman glanced from Daxx to the suits and back again at Janna.

'That's the stupidest thing I've ever heard,' she said. 'Everyone's dying, and you come on a trip to the museum? What is it like on the other side of the city? Is everything still all right there?'

'No,' Janna said. 'It's not all right. It's the same everywhere.'

The woman sighed. 'Then why are you here?'

'We're with the Resistance.' Janna saw the woman's eyes narrow. 'Very recently with the Resistance,' she added. 'Just since all this began. We have a safe place; you're both welcome to come. We need the spacesuits for an experiment, something that may stop all this.'

'Really?' The woman sounded incredulous. 'Spacesuits can stop this?' She gave a short laugh that could have come from Ahh Moss Eck. It was his type of disbelief.

'I've heard of Daxx,' the man behind them said. He walked slowly around them until he stood near the woman. 'Are you really Daxx?' he asked, somewhat naively.

'Yes.'

The man lowered his weapon and looked at the woman. 'I don't think they'll harm us.'

'But he would.' She glared at Ahh Moss Eck.

Ahh Moss Eck grinned back at the woman. 'Damn right I would.'

She looked long and hard at Ahh Moss Eck, then slowly dropped her weapon as well. The woman sounded weary. 'We're not any good at this,' she said. 'We haven't had to kill anyone yet. I guess we've been lucky.' She let out a short laugh. 'I guess no one is interested in museums, even in times of crisis. You're the first that have come in here this far. They usually stay in the lobby and then move on.'

'How long have you been here?' Janna asked.

'Since day one. I knew what would happen, so I persuaded a few to hide in here. We grabbed what supplies we could and tried to stay out of the way as everything went to shit.'

'How many of you are here?' Janna asked.

The woman glanced at the man, who nodded. 'I'll show you,' she said.

She led them back the way they had come, almost to the lobby, then through a door that said, Staff Only. They followed a series of branching corridors to a cavernous storage facility. It was stuffed with exhibits, some in stages of repair.

'It's okay,' the woman said to the empty room.

People appeared from hiding places. Some were children. Janna smiled.

'Wow,' Ahh Moss Eck said. 'There must be fifty of you.'

'Forty-four,' the woman said.

Daxx shook his head. He saw Janna smiling, and he returned it. He hadn't seen her genuinely happy since before her parents died. It was the children; he knew. These people were frightened, terrified even, but they were being cared for. Their lives mattered. A glimmer of hope had made Janna happy.

'Are you all related?' Janna asked.

'No,' the woman said. 'We were neighbours. I rounded them up to come here.'

Janna started crying. Daxx grabbed her and she fell into him. She immediately backed away. She brushed her tears away, then smiled at the woman.

'I thought...' Janna began. 'I had thought that everyone was like those outside. That only the ruthless would survive this.' Janna stared at the woman. 'Thank you,' Janna said. 'Thank you.'

The woman frowned.

'Of course, Janna.' A voice came from a nearby speaker, part of a sound system under repair. 'The resourceful win, not the ruthless. The ruthless turn on each other. It's people like this group and yours that will survive. It's all part of the calculations.' It was the Advisor. 'But,' the Advisor continued. 'I'm afraid you have a testing time ahead of you.'

'What the hell was that?' the woman said to Janna.

'The cause of all of this,' Janna said.

Ahh Moss Eck's Device chimed a notification. He answered it immediately.

'Hey, Ahh Moss Eck, you had better get back here. We've got some visitors, a lot of them, and I don't think they're particularly interested in a museum tour.'

Ahh Moss Eck looked at Daxx and Janna, then at the woman. He glanced at the weapon in her hands. 'Do you really know how to use that thing?'

'Yes,' she said. 'Four of us have been practising.'

'Okay,' Ahh Moss Eck said. 'Everyone who can fire a gun, come with me.' He turned to Janna and Daxx. 'You two should stay here.'

'No,' Janna said. 'I'm coming. I can help somehow.'

'Me too,' Daxx said.

Ahh Moss Eck sighed. 'Just stay out of the way.'

He strode out of the room and towards the entrance, not looking back to see who was following him.

chapter 55

Janna

'How many?' Ahh Moss Eck said to Kie Tell Munn when he quietly joined the other man on the mezzanine overlooking the lobby and the entrance. Daxx and Janna crouched behind Ahh Moss Eck. The woman and three others, all with weapons, huddled further behind.

'Heaps,' Kie Tell Munn said, then glanced behind Ahh Moss Eck. He looked startled. 'Who are they?' He nodded at the four people with guns.

'Some friends we found,' Ahh Moss Eck said. 'They live here.'

Ahh Moss Eck looked behind him at the woman. 'Has this happened before?'

'No, no one has bothered us yet. A few stragglers have camped here overnight, but we've let them be.'

Ahh Moss Eck grunted. 'Then it's probably our fault.' He looked at Daxx and Janna. 'We weren't shy about our arrival.'

'Maybe they'll just go away?' Janna asked.

'No chance of that,' Kie Tell Munn said. 'They have that look about them. My guess is that they think we know something about this place that they don't. And they want whatever it is for themselves.'

Ahh Moss Eck grunted agreement.

'How many is heaps?' Daxx asked.

Ahh Moss Eck slowly lifted his head to see over the balustrade. 'Heaps, is heaps too many. I reckon at least fifty?' He looked at Kie Tell Munn, who nodded. 'And half of them have guns, and the other half have clubs and knives. Not good odds. We could take out a few, but there are so many places they can take cover. I can't see how this ends well.'

'We need to get out of here,' Kie Tell Munn said. 'We can't fight those numbers. Is there a back entrance?'

'We can't leave,' Janna said.

'The damn spacesuit?' Ahh Moss Eck said.

'Not just that, there are children.'

Ahh Moss Eck looked apologetic for a moment. 'Yeah, of course, the kids.' He looked back at Kie Tell Munn. 'She's right. We need to stop them.'

'I'm all ears,' Kie Tell Munn said. He looked at Daxx. 'Isn't he supposed to be the smartest person on the planet? Maybe he can maths his way out of this.'

Daxx looked angry. Janna put her hand on top of his. She smiled at him. Daxx shrugged.

'Sure. I'll get right on the maths. But, maybe, just in case, you two should do some stop-gap thing,' Daxx said to the two Tier-Threes.

Kie Tell Munn laughed. 'Okay, we can try that.'

Ahh Moss Eck signalled for the four others with guns to spread out along the mezzanine, while staying under cover, and to watch for his signals. Janna peered carefully over the top of the mezzanine parapet. The intruders with guns moved into the centre of the foyer; they appeared confident. Those with clubs and knives kept to the sides. They slid along the walls, warily looking in all directions. They were organised, Janna realised. There was predetermined purpose to their attack. They were working as a group.

She had been wrong. People didn't only form groups against others, then turn on themselves when their focus was lost. People combine when they share commonalities, whether it's skin colour, age, social bias or, as in this case, they shared the same fear. Fear was the most powerful emotion. If it could be spread thinner, by forming a common group, people would form a front against others that were different. Daxx and Janna and the two Tier-Threes had shown they were different by marching through the streets. Their presence, their difference, had brought disaster to the group sheltering in the museum.

Janna was still an optimist, although it had been severely tested. But the true nature of people, as a group, was different. They couldn't be trusted. She thought people, as individuals, could be reasoned with. A carefully made appeal, a demonstration that she also shared their concerns, would alter or blunt their most violent behaviours. She would try to talk to someone in authority. There was always someone more equal than others in any group. She peered again over the parapet and tried to see who was in charge. It would have to be one of those in the vanguard. In a group bound by fear, those who displayed less of it would be admired, as long as that display of fear was not too diluted, to make them too different. She saw one man who appeared more determined, and those nearby kept looking at him, following his lead.

She quietly pointed him out to Ahh Moss Eck, who nodded. He misunderstood. Ahh Moss Eck stealthily placed his weapon over the parapet and shot the man Janna had identified. He crumpled to the floor.

The response was frenetic and immediate. Weapons fired, aimed at the mezzanine. Janna dropped her head and placed her arms over it. The barrage reduced for a moment. Janna heard screams and yells of both fear and anger. The sounds came from further inside the museum. The screams were the sounds of terrified children. The sounds erupted into the foyer. She glanced over the parapet, a dangerous move, but she had to see. The attackers were also distracted by the screams. She saw, to her horror, a machete make contact with a child. One terrified scream stopped.

The attackers in the foyer seemed to forget about those on the mezzanine. They moved towards the children and adults with them, seemingly intent on wiping them out. Ahh Moss Eck and the others with guns leant over the parapet and fired. It was bedlam, and yet it seemed to not halt the intent of those attacking the children.

Janna jumped up. She couldn't stay there and watch. She had to do something. She ran across the mezzanine and bounded down the stairs, taking two with each jump. As she stood and ran, Daxx had tried to grab her. She had shrugged him off without knowing what had tried to hinder her. Daxx ran after her down the stairs.

She ran straight into someone with a raised club, standing over a cowering child. She and the attacker fell to the ground in a tangled mess of arms and legs. They both stood up again, and the woman with the club raised it to hit Janna. Janna didn't try to duck or move out the way, she had exhausted the initial adrenaline rush. The horror of these people's actions struck her, and she watched like she was an impartial observer of a terrible experiment gone wrong.

The woman with the club fell to her knees and then face planted on the floor. Janna looked towards the mezzanine. Ahh Moss Eck's gun was pointed towards her. He yelled at her to come back. She understood the stupidity of what she had done. Weapons fired from the safety of the mezzanine could protect the children, now they would be distracted by trying to protect her.

She was struck in the head by a club. She fell to the ground. She looked up. Her vision was hazy. She thought she saw three or four or maybe five—she couldn't tell—people hovering over her with clubs raised ready to strike. She felt quite calm. She felt as if time had been dilated and she had a lifetime to consider the last moments of her life. She would be dead soon. She knew she had been stupid and had paid the ultimate price. She was annoyed, but not scared. She thought of her parents. They would have experienced this exact same moment, she thought. She wondered if they had felt this calm; she hoped so.

The colour of the world changed. It became a shifting, moving blue thing. The colour sparked and reflected off everything. She heard a sound. She concentrated on it. She knew that word. It was her name. Someone was calling her name over and over. She smiled. It was nice to not be alone at the very end. She wondered if death would hurt, if there would be pain, but she didn't really care. It would be short, probably intense, but over in a moment. She wouldn't remember it. She wouldn't remember anything.

The blue light permeated everything, and then the world went quiet.

She assumed she was dead. It hadn't hurt at all, she thought. But then her head began to throb horribly in the newly formed silence. The attackers that had stood over her had disappeared. She struggled and sat up. She looked around.

There was Daxx. She smiled at him. He was slightly indistinct; the blue light had come from him and still sheathed his body. It dissipated until he looked almost normal, except for his face. He was distraught. More than distraught, he was devastated.

He came over to her and helped her to her feet. She wasn't sure that was the best thing with her head hurting so much, but she stood up. She placed a hand on her head and could already feel a large lump, and some matted hair glued by her own blood. She took her hand away from her head and examined it. She still didn't seem to care. She was calm, even though there was a lot of blood on her hand.

'I guess I'm not dead.' She looked from her hand to Daxx. 'What happened?'

He hung his head. He shook it gently from side to side. He didn't answer.

She saw movement. Ahh Moss Eck bounded down the stairs and then strode across the foyer. He stopped in front of Daxx. Ahh Moss Eck slowly nodded his head. 'That was some fine maths you did there, Daxx. I think we'd all enjoy maths if we could do that.'

Daxx glanced at him but did not smile or answer.

'What happened?' Janna asked Ahh Moss Eck. She was feeling woozy and thought she should probably sit down.

Ahh Moss Eck eventually took his eyes off Daxx. 'Look around.'

She tried to not move her painful head too much. She shuffled her body in a circle. The foyer was empty except for the three of them, the children and the adults that had been sheltering in the museum.

Kie Tell Munn walked slowly down the stairs and across the foyer. The woman with the gun walked next to him. 'You okay?' Kie Tell Munn asked Janna.

She nodded but stopped immediately. It felt like she was shaking something loose inside her head.

'Remind me to never piss you off,' Kie Tell Munn said to Daxx.

Daxx glanced at him but still didn't say anything. He looked horrible.

'What happened?' Janna asked again.

'He...' Ahh Moss Eck began. He nodded at Daxx while looking at Janna. 'He vaporised everyone who was attacking us. They're all gone.' He waved his arm around the foyer.

The woman with the gun stared at Janna. 'We definitely want to come with you.' She nodded towards Daxx. 'With him.'

chapter 56

Day 19. Renn

Renn crouched behind shipping containers. He peered around the edge and watched the autonomous vehicles rumble slowly down the street. The roadway was covered in abandoned vehicles, debris, litter, and patches of dirty snow. The first snow in years had fallen the day before, just to add to the misery. There was a bitter wind chill and low cloud, but, thankfully, it had not snowed since the previous night.

Renn had formed a band of hardened men and women. None of them wanted to spend time at the warehouse. They were a small group of mainly Tier-Threes who didn't approve of Tie's decisions. They wanted to do more than wait out the disaster. Tie disapproved of their activities and disliked Renn, so Renn was the natural choice to take charge. He was a leader of equals, although he focused on the leader aspect, not the equality.

Their initial task had been to find lost family members. Renn's father had been their first success. They had extended their activities beyond searching for people.

The group hid behind the containers, watching the vehicle convoy. All normal vehicular traffic had halted. The convoy was a conspicuous exception. Food, water and medical supplies could no longer be obtained. Raiding and violence were the only way to obtain resources. But resources were not being replenished. Soon, even stealing from others would be pointless; there would be nothing left. Renn didn't think anyone who had not stockpiled supplies and kept well hidden would survive much longer. The convoy had to be supplying a group protected by the Advisor. He and his group intended to ambush it.

Renn turned to look at his band. Ahh Moss Eck quietly joined the group. He hunched down next to Renn.

'I hear you had a trip to the museum,' Renn said. 'Learn anything?' He grinned at the Tier-Three.

'Yeah, it was… educational.'

'Did Daxx get his spacesuit?'

Ahh Moss Eck grunted a reply.

'Why you?'

'Janna asked.'

'And?'

Ahh Moss Eck flicked a look at Renn. 'I trust her. We've been through stuff. She's… genuine.'

Renn looked back at the convoy. He was exactly where he wanted to be. If it had not been too monstrous to think, he could have been happy about how things had turned out. He would be the elite of the humans that survived this. He would have his chance to lead. Admittedly, a much smaller number of people.

They had become aware of the convoy through Kay Lee Too's technology that tapped into the city-wide surveillance system. Renn and his band had investigated. They had followed the convoy for an hour or so on their Devices as they raced to catch up to it. The vehicles came to a stop at the top of a ramp. It led to a closed security doorway.

Renn swore. They were too late.

'I think this is the end, boss,' Ahh Moss Eck said.

Renn nodded, but didn't take his eyes off the lead vehicle. 'There has to be people down there, and the Advisor is supplying them.'

'Then we should grab the supplies before they get here.'

'Hold on,' Renn said.

Ahh Moss Eck frowned. 'The longer we wait, the more likely someone will come. We should go now. Who do you think's down there?'

'Police force, possibly,' Renn said. 'I'm not sure, but it's obviously important and they need supplies they didn't have when this all started.'

'You don't think it's Soo?'

'Probably not. I don't think so.'

'Why not?'

'I can't believe the Advisor would be actively helping her.'

Ahh Moss Eck grunted. 'I was sort of hoping it was Soo down there.'

Renn laughed. 'Somehow, I doubt we'll see Soo again. She's probably holed up and starving by now.'

The security doorway opened. Armed police officers rushed out. They took positions around the convoy. Once all the vehicles had entered, the officers raced inside. The doors shut again.

'You were right,' Ahh Moss Eck said. Renn thought he heard some of the same quiet admiration Ahh Moss Eck reserved for Janna.

Renn turned to Ahh Moss Eck. 'It's odd logic, don't you think?'

'What do you mean?'

'The Advisor could simply kill everyone, up to the number it wants the population to be. It could just kill a random distribution of people.'

'I know that one. It was explained to me.'

'By whom?'

'Your brother.'

Renn frowned. 'What did he say?'

'The Advisor is smart, really smart. So smart that it knows it's not smart enough to choose who should survive. This is how it does that. It doesn't need representations from each group, some smart people, workers from each skilled profession, it has all the knowledge to run everything afterwards. Daxx assumes once enough people have died everything will be turned back on again. Daxx thinks it may be the same population size as Devrell's time. That's about ten percent of what it is now.' Ahh Moss Eck then nodded at the closing security doors. 'And, we've found some of those who will be doing the organising once it's all over.'

Renn grunted. It made sense.

The Resistance's options for intervention had reduced. The Advisor had disabled external execute access to its systems. The information network remained but was mostly empty since domestic power had been turned off for days. Kay Lee Too could no longer monitor the progress of the first software that he, and subsequently Soo, had released. The Resistance had no idea how damaged the Advisor was. It hadn't been destroyed, obviously, since things like the automated convoy were still active. As were parts of the surveillance systems. Kay Lee Too had finished creating server-specific software that could destroy the Advisor on the central servers, but there was no way to upload it. The Advisor had learned from past mistakes.

'All right.' Renn tried to sound decisive. He did sound like a leader, he thought. 'We may have also found that access Kay Lee Too has been waiting for to try out his new software. They may have direct access to the Advisor in there. We should find out. We need to get the doors open. Any ideas?'

Ahh Moss Eck smiled. 'Maybe. Do you think they have a stockpile of water or an outside supply? It might be nice, you know, to make them... uncomfortable.'

Renn was getting used to being amazed by the Tier-Three. He laughed.

Renn and Ahh Moss Eck found a nearby control room, with Kay Lee Too's remote assistance. The underground bunker's water supply was regulated by physical controls. It was a weak design given the circumstances, but the current disaster would never have been imagined when the underground facility had been designed. It had never been expected to be used to survive a disaster; it was a secure storage facility. Cutting off the water supply, through non-electronic, non-networked means, was a simple way to cause inconvenience and require intervention. They intended to break a control device that would need to be replaced. Hopefully, the police would send someone out to fix the problem. That would reduce the number inside, at least temporarily.

'What are you doing, Renn?' The voice came from a small speaker on one of the control panels near where they worked.

Ahh Moss Eck looked up at the sound, but Renn kept working, removing panelling to get at a physical switching device.

Ahh Moss Eck looked at Renn. 'It still can't zap us, right?'

'No.' Renn looked up at Ahh Moss Eck. 'I don't think so. I'm just going on what your friend has said.' He meant Kay Lee Too.

Ahh Moss Eck nodded his head. 'If he says it's good, then it's good. But I thought it couldn't see us, with the cloaking setup.'

Renn shrugged, then pulled the panelling free.

'Help me with this.' The two of them pulled with all their weight on a switching element, about the size of a hand. It yanked free from inside the control panel with a crunching, breaking sound. When it came free, both men fell back a step. Renn held it up and smiled at the device, then at Ahh Moss Eck.

'Oh, I see,' the Advisor said. 'That's pointless. I can deliver a new part today. Why would you do that?'

Renn threw the part on the floor as hard as he could. It shattered into small pieces.

'I'm very disappointed, Renn. I had thought you would understand why these steps are necessary. I had thought you could be a part of what comes afterwards.'

'Apparently not.' Renn looked around for a heavy item, but could only see a chair. He picked it up and threw it into the speaker, which cracked and fizzled and was then silent.

Ahh Moss Eck grunted, then smiled. 'Nice take-out of the speaker, boss. That was dangerous for a moment.'

chapter 57

Daxx

'I've become a weapon.' Daxx said to Janna. He had said the same thing many times since their return from the museum.

They had brought the people sheltering at the museum back to the warehouse, along with one of the spacesuits. They had used a human-powered trolley, pushing and pulling it through the city streets. It had been miserable work with the unexpected, although light, snowfalls when they had set out early in the morning, the day after their arrival at the museum. Daxx had worried, as they paraded towards the warehouse, not only about attacks by people, but about the Advisor. It must have been watching them, and it must have seen what happened in the museum's foyer. Daxx had the feeling that eyes stared at him throughout the return trip, both human and non-human.

Did the Advisor think of Daxx as a threat? Obviously not an immediate one, otherwise it would have done something to stop them from returning to the warehouse. The Advisor must be curious; it must be wondering what use they would have for a spacesuit. Perhaps it thought it was a unique demonstration of resourcefulness that even it didn't understand. But the Advisor must be acting carefully, wondering about the consequences for itself.

Daxx thought how lucky, so far, they were that the Advisor didn't have a fear of change and a fear of differences. The spacesuit acquisition would be viewed as odd behaviour but interesting. Daxx's powers, yes, he thought, he had powers, could be dangerous and seemed impossible but would still be a curiosity. If he were the Advisor, Daxx thought, then he would wonder what his, Daxx's, behaviour meant. And he would likely play it out and see what happened, with precautions. The Advisor must be confident. It must have more options to protect itself than just waiting for everyone to die. The Advisor would leave little to chance. Daxx had no idea what it would do next. The way things had deteriorated over the last nineteen days, he assumed it was nothing good.

The spacesuit was setup in a corner of the warehouse. They had cleared out a space. Daxx and Janna, along with Kay Lee Too, had been busy that day setting up the spacesuit ready for use. Additions were necessary. Kay Lee Too had jury-rigged the suit for power and for atmosphere controls. The original battery power supplies had been removed centuries ago, so it took some ingenuity to create compatible replacements. Daxx had kept himself busy, to the point of exhaustion.

'I've become that guy who rescues us,' he said. 'I kill people. You said you couldn't believe I could become him.'

Janna stopped her work and sighed. There was no end to this conversation. 'When I said that, I had no idea what was about to happen,' she said. 'We've all had to adapt. We've changed. Everything has changed. But look on the bright side,' she added, although she had said this many times before as well. 'At least it's you, and not someone like Soo, or those people who attacked us at the museum or...' she added for the first time, 'or, even, your brother.'

Daxx looked up at her. His brother had turned feral, Daxx thought. Renn was revelling in the chaos and destruction. He had become determined, dogmatic, violent and overly self-confident. They were dangerous attributes in combination.

Janna put down the tool she was using while she worked on the attachment seal of one of the hands of the spacesuit. It had perished, and they had had to create a replacement. 'Are you going to practice that power thing?' she asked. 'We may need it, for self-defence. And you can't always rely on me being nearly killed.' She smiled. 'And, again, thanks Daxx.' She leant over and kissed him on the cheek.

'No, I don't want to practise. I don't want to use it again.'

'Okay.' She picked up the tool and set to work.

Daxx watched her work for a moment. It must be an odd feeling, he thought, being with and trusting someone who could kill so many, so easily.

He shuddered and went back to work. But everyone was like that, he thought. People could go berserk at any moment, as had been demonstrated. We are all dangerous. It's a matter of scale.

The spacesuit additions were completed.

'I feel ridiculous.' Daxx was inside the spacesuit.

He couldn't see his reflection, but he imagined how he looked. While the spacesuit in its original configuration had been bulky, at least it had looked professional. But now, it had been enhanced with no thought of aesthetics. Attachments poked off it at all angles, none of them coordinated for colour or shape. What had been required to make it a functioning spacesuit had been added wherever there was room. They had worked all day on a temporary solution to a problem that may not occur. If Daxx made a mistake and found himself outside the atmosphere, or in a place of reduced air pressure, or even an atmosphere that was not breathable, then the spacesuit would be required. But if he had made such a monumental error, then perhaps he wouldn't have the skill required to return, and he would die anyway. He took a deep breath. No, he thought, he doesn't die doing this. But, perhaps, it's the spacesuit that saves him. He felt somewhat safer inside it, although embarrassed at how he must look.

'You look great.' Janna stifled a laugh.

'Is it sealed?' Daxx asked.

'All ready to go,' Kay Lee Too said. 'Although I'm not sure where you expect it to go.'

Daxx took a deep breath. 'All right.'

'Be careful,' Janna said.

'This is the opposite of careful,' Kay Lee Too said.

Janna frowned at Kay Lee Too, and he shrugged.

Daxx watched Janna and Kay Lee Too fade out of existence. He found himself in that other space again. He had to find a good name for it. He wondered how many spatial dimensions existed there. He would have to think how to find that out. He looked around, although looking was no longer only a visual experience—it included sensation. He'd have to choose a name for that experience, too.

There was movement within the static, the structures, around him. The patterns were there, just like last time. There were many patterns, and where there were patterns, there were physical laws. He would make sense of it, eventually. The patterns included bundles of spatial dimensions and time.

It was the weirdest sensation. It was incredibly non-intuitive. That spacetime place felt like an infinite, disorganised library but with the perfect filing system that could bring any book instantly nearby. He experimented, and felt he was able to move the structures around him, or he moved past them. He tried to enter one of them. It was a special instant; it had changed his family. But it was closed or locked or whatever it meant that moving through it, back to his own four dimensioned spacetime, was impossible.

He looked at the display on the inside of the helmet. It showed the air supply level as well as the elapsed time. He had been gone for nearly an hour. He decided that was enough for now. He would return and check that he could actually get back using the spacesuit. Each difference had to be tested. He would try next time going through one of the other clumpy structures. He shook his head; he definitely needed a better naming convention.

Janna and Kay Lee Too popped into existence again. Daxx was back where he had started. Janna looked impatiently at him as he stared back at her.

'Are you going to do anything?' she asked.

chapter 58

Renn

Renn and Ahh Moss Eck again hid behind the shipping containers, watching the underground facility's entrance. The security doors opened. A platoon of police officers emerged, along with five people carrying toolboxes. The officers surrounded the civilians, and the group headed off in the direction of the control room that Renn and Ahh Moss Eck had damaged. The security doors shut.

'Let's go,' Renn said to Ahh Moss Eck and two other Tier-Threes, a man and a woman, both engineers.

They ran, hunched over, across the roadway and down the ramp to the secure doors. Ahh Moss Eck and Renn stood guard, looking back up the ramp and towards the shipping containers that hid the rest of their band. They would signal to Renn if the police returned. Renn shifted his body from side to side and flitted his eyes everywhere. He was sure he was being watched.

The other two in their group scanned the doors, then conferred for far too long, Renn thought. 'Come on, we haven't got all day,' Renn said.

'We have to get this right, Renn,' one of the engineers said. 'The second time wouldn't be a surprise.'

Renn grunted. The man was right.

Ahh Moss Eck stared at Renn. 'Do you feel it too, do you? That we're being watched?'

'Yeah.' Renn continued to look around and up the ramp. But there was no signal from those hiding across the road.

Renn looked overhead, and there it was. A tiny surveillance camera, almost impossible to see as it was so well recessed into the wall above the door. The city had thousands of those well-hidden cameras, and they were all available to the Advisor.

Ahh Moss Eck followed Renn's gaze. He grunted. 'Should we take it out?'

Renn thought for a moment. 'No. It will be moot in a moment, right?'

'Yes,' an engineer replied. She turned to the other engineer. 'Here, on these hinge mechanisms.' She pointed to the side of one of the doors.

The man nodded.

They placed explosives against the door, as well as a detonating device.

The male engineer sounded frantic as he barked, 'Run! Five, four…'

'Shit,' Ahh Moss Eck said.

'What?' Renn said.

The four of them sprinted up the ramp.

'Two, one…' The engineer kept counting down as he ran.

They all dived face down onto the top part of the ramp as an explosion ripped the doors apart. It was a well-contained, inward explosion. They could have stayed where they were and been uninjured. The two engineers laughed as they stood up.

'That was priceless,' the woman engineer said to the other as they touched hands.

Renn's face was dark and scowling. Ahh Moss Eck placed his hand on Renn's shoulder. 'They've had their fun, boss. Let's go and have ours.'

Renn nodded at Ahh Moss Eck then looked angrily at the two engineers. 'I hope you two are as good using those'—he nodded at the guns they had slung across their bodies—'as you think you are with explosives.'

The four of them strode down the ramp and through the mangled doors.

'About ten minutes,' Ahh Moss Eck said to a question Renn had not asked. It was the estimate before the police squadron would be rushing back to the bunker. They would have to be done and out by then. There was no way the four of them could fight their way through armed police. They kept to military protocol. Ahh Moss Eck took point and led the way, just ahead of Renn. The two engineers, now soldiers with weapons, lagged back and took up the rear.

They rounded a corner and came upon ten police officers trying to assemble and load weapons. They looked surprised and confused. Some even looked sleepy. Renn and Ahh Moss Eck trained their guns on them.

'I'd think about putting them down.' Renn nodded at the guns.

The officers looked at each other nervously. The two engineers came up behind Renn, their weapons trained on the police.

'You have a choice…' Ahh Moss Eck said to the police. 'Either we shoot you all,' they flinched at that, 'or you can show us where we can lock you up.' He smiled. 'We won't impose on your hospitality for too long. Your friends will be back soon to let you out. If you choose that option, of course.' His smile became broader, like he was hoping they'd choose the former option.

It was an easy, unanimous decision. The officers were herded, without weapons, into a storeroom and the locking mechanism broken, after the engineers had fiddled with it. The two engineers smiled at each other.

'I don't know how they're going to get out of that,' the man said.

'They're going to have to dismantle the door, from the inside,' the woman said and laughed.

Renn was annoyed at how flippant the engineers were. This sortie was dangerous, deadly, in fact. There could have been manned surveillance of the entrance, there could have been hidden guards, they could have come upon the police loading their weapons a few moments later. In all those cases, they would have been killed. Renn shook his head. But he was glad they were flippant and not frozen with fear. But Renn was scared. And he reasoned the engineers were too. They handled it differently. He dealt with his fear by activity and being decisive, although he had no training, no experience and no idea how to conduct a raid. He imagined wearing military fatigues and camouflage, not casual clothes. He smiled.

They walked down a corridor. They came to a set of doors with windows; the doors were unlocked. On the other side was a laboratory. Five scientists were inside. They were concentrating on their displays. They didn't seem to notice Renn and the others.

The woman engineer peered over Renn's shoulder. Renn frowned at her. She didn't notice or didn't care.

'Over there,' she said to the other engineer, ignoring Renn. 'See?'

'Yep,' the man said. 'That's an access point, all right.'

The engineer noticed Renn's frown. The man confused Renn's annoyance with ignorance.

'Places like these need more processing power than just Devices,' he said. 'We figured it had to be more than just a bunch of police hanging out for the duration. The amount of stuff they delivered had to be more than just food.' He looked at the woman engineer. 'Kay Lee Too was right.'

'Again.' She laughed.

'Those guys don't look too dangerous,' Ahh Moss Eck said. 'And we don't have a heap of time left. Let's go.' He pushed through the doors into the laboratory.

'Don't move,' Ahh Moss Eck said to the room, superfluously, in fact. The scientists seemed to have no intention of moving.

Renn nodded at the engineers and they scampered across the laboratory to the access point. There was something odd about the scientists. They were unnaturally calm, and they were all looking only at him. None of them noticed the engineers or Ahh Moss Eck.

The scientist closest to Renn said, 'Of course. That's why you broke into the control room.'

Renn frowned at the man. 'What are you doing here?'

He didn't reply. He had a vacant look on his face, as if he was daydreaming. Renn walked past the man, disconcerted by the behaviour, but the wall next to the scientist looked important. It was inset, with an observation window and controls outside to manipulate and move items inside the vacuum-sealed area. The items included glass flasks, machinery, and solutions of various colours, although most were as clear as distilled water. Renn turned towards Ahh Moss Eck. He was about to ask Ahh Moss Eck's opinion of what the scientists were doing, but stopped before he did. The man would have no idea. Tier-Threes knew little about biology; it was a Tier-Two and Tier-One science, and nothing about Chemistry—that was restricted to Tier-Ones. Renn didn't know much either. His advanced education had been in business, management and leadership. He would have to ask.

But first, he checked on the engineers. They were in deep conversation with Kay Lee Too, and when Renn barked an order asking for an update, they glanced at him then ignored him. Renn shook his head. He wouldn't insist they answer. He initiated his display and contacted Daxx.

Renn momentarily forgot the reason for his call. 'You look horrible,' Renn said. 'What's the problem?'

Daxx looked away and said, 'It's Renn,' to someone out of view. He turned back. 'What do you want?' Daxx said angrily.

'What's this?' Renn angled his display so Daxx could see the experimental station.

'Well,' Daxx hesitated for a moment. 'It's vacuum sealed, not just vented, so I'd guess it's a biological agent station or maybe harmful chemical reagents? I'm not really sure. I'll get Janna.'

Renn sighed as Janna appeared on the display. She looked worried, but Renn didn't ask if she had a problem.

'What do you want to know?' she asked, not quite as angrily as Daxx.

'What's this?'

'Biological station,' Janna said immediately. 'You can tell by the instrumentation. It's for viral research. Why?'

'Because it's in a bunker, protected by police, while all this crap is going on outside. It seems odd, doesn't it? They could do this later on, after it's all over.'

'Well, what are they working on?'

'How would I know?' Renn said. 'If I knew that, I wouldn't have asked.'

'Sorry. Can you ask the scientists? I guess not,' she said. 'Maybe look at their Device history. At what they've done recently.'

'Hey, you,' Renn barked at the engineers and pointed at the man. 'This is more urgent. Come over here.'

The man looked at the other engineer. He shrugged, she nodded, then he walked slowly over to Renn.

'What?' The man scowled at Renn.

'I need to know what they're working on. Can you check their Devices?' Renn nodded at one of the scientists, who had not moved since Renn and his group entered the laboratory.

The engineer sighed. 'Of course not,' he said. 'You can't see Device history without permission overrides.' The engineer turned to the closest scientist. 'Can I see your Device history?' he asked sarcastically. The scientist glanced at the engineer but didn't say anything. The engineer shook his head at Renn. 'But,' he said. 'We can examine the traffic going through the node. Over there.' He pointed to where the other engineer was working.

'Do it.' Renn tried to control his frustration. The man didn't move.

He didn't like the attitude of these Tier-Threes. He expected them to be respectful. It was difficult for Renn to talk to them on an equal footing. This new world, the world imagined by the Resistance, was going to be hard for him to navigate. He would have to earn the respect of others, even those who had been born to lower Tiers.

'Can you,' he said, emphasising each word. 'Please. Check the recent history of their work?'

The man sauntered back to the other engineer.

'We need to go,' Ahh Moss Eck said to the engineers. 'How much longer do you guys need?'

'Which task? The software upload for Kay Lee Too or Renn's request?' the man said.

'Both,' Renn said.

The man glanced at Renn. 'Open your Device and you'll get the feed. You can filter it while we finish up for Kay Lee Too.'

Renn swiped through his display and granted access. His display filled with streams of data. He attached it to the communication with Janna, which was still open.

'There you are,' Renn said. 'That's what we have. What is it?'

Janna was silent for a long moment. Her eyes scanned up and down as she read the feed from Renn's Device. She had begun the conversation with Renn looking careworn, but after a few seconds, she looked terrified.

'You need to get out of there.' She stopped looking at the data feed and stared at Renn.

'We know.' Renn sighed. Here was another person, not a Tier-One, telling him what to do. He looked up at the engineers and they both nodded at Renn.

'Done,' one of them said.

'So, what is this stuff that's so important?' Renn said to Janna.

'Don't touch anything, Renn. Don't touch anyone. Just get out of there.'

Renn frowned. 'Why?'

'Just do it,' Janna demanded.

'We need to go, boss,' Ahh Moss Eck said, then added, almost as an order, 'We're going, now.'

The engineers had joined Ahh Moss Eck at the doorway and were waiting there, ready to leave. Renn kept his display active while he jogged across the laboratory to join his group.

'Just tell me what it is, Janna. What do I need to avoid?'

'It's Kell's research.'

Renn halted at the mention of his younger sister's name.

'It's her virus,' Janna said. 'The Advisor has created a working example of her viral, neuronal network. You should destroy that place.'

'It's too late, Renn,' the scientist who had spoken to Renn said.

chapter 59

Daxx

'Whoops,' Daxx said to himself.

He had made a major error on his first attempt to travel to a different location and time. He floated in space. Nearby was a planetesimal, under formation and still not big enough to be spherical. It was a lumpy conglomerate of orbiting rocks. The system was a mess of movement and rotation.

He knew what it was. His time displacement had been a few billion years out. He wondered if any of the molecules that made up his own body, and the spacesuit, were yet settled into those rocky beginnings of his own planet. He was so glad he had the foresight to be encased in a spacesuit. It had saved him.

He focused his attention again and returned to the higher spacetime.

He floated in space again. He swore, thinking he had returned to the same place and time. The sun blazed into his face, the helmet's visor altered and filtered the intense light. It made it hard to see anything other than the sun. But he saw movement in his peripheral vision. He turned his head, within the suit, and saw a space station moving towards him on a tangent, at no more than a brisk walking pace.

Daxx stared at the monumental piece of architecture, all jutting pieces of metal, ceramic, and plastics. It was constructed of seemingly incompatible modules attached to each other. He had seen images of these things before, of course, but there hadn't been any space stations since before Devrell's time. The Coronal Mass Ejection had destroyed all technology. The orbits of space stations had degraded over time until the last one crashed to the planet a few decades later. People had not returned to space once society had stabilised again. All exploration and extra-atmosphere research had been done without astronauts.

As Daxx stared, he noticed that he was being watched from a viewing port. Daxx waved at the person. It was a reflex action. The person frowned and raised an arm, the beginnings of a return wave. He stopped immediately. Social conditioning is difficult to resist. Daxx watched the space station slowly move away. The man's puzzled expression disappeared into the distance. Daxx smiled.

'That was awesome,' he said under his breath.

The warm sun sparkled and reflected from a ruffled ocean surface. It was a perfectly clear day, a beautiful summer's evening, or early morning. Daxx watched the scene for a while as he tried to remember the last time he had been to the beach. It wasn't far from the city, but he'd been so occupied, it had been a few years. He turned away from the view of the water. Behind him, and arranged around a campfire, was a group of about thirty people of all ages. They were hunter-gatherers. A few of the stronger looking men and women had weapons. They stood and threatened Daxx. They looked frightened, but also fierce and determined.

Daxx sighed.

Daxx stood on a narrow, cobbled city street. It was the old city, before there was a new one. There were no gleaming modern towers overshadowing the buildings. The facades looked less well constructed and less well kept. Modern maintenance and renovations had made the old buildings better than they had been in their heyday. The narrow street, they were all narrow in the old part of the city, was paved by cobblestones, instead of a smooth roadway surface appropriate for vehicles. He looked up at the buildings and along the street, trying to guess when he was. Perhaps a thousand years ago? A group of clergymen came out of one of the buildings.

The group stopped immediately and stared at the apparition that was Daxx. They drew a bit closer together, a human tribal response to present a larger, coherent, difficult target for the predator standing before them. One of them took a half-step towards Daxx and said something. Daxx had no idea what he said—the language was incomprehensible. Daxx thought he could see a pattern in the times and places he had ended up. He ignored the group of clergymen as they disappeared from his view.

He stood in a lush and verdant forest. It was a silly idea, but he wanted to breathe the real air, to experience one of the times and the places for real. He checked that the air composition, pressure, and temperature were within normal ranges. He lifted his visor and breathed deeply. He thought the air tasted fresher. It probably did. The oxygen content was slightly higher.

He looked around at the fern-like plants, not filtered by his visor. What an incredible ability, he thought, to be able to experience the full range of the universe's history. He could go anywhere and any time. He felt invincible. He knew he was safe, at least from death if not injury, because he had yet to go back and save him and Janna from their attackers. His future existence was assured. He thought he would delay doing that indefinitely. It was a weird feeling knowing he could not die. But immortal or not, he was still very human. He had been in the spacesuit for hours. He needed to urinate. He didn't want to return to the present, so he stepped out of the suit. He stretched his limbs as if waking from an especially restful, long sleep and walked to a tree trunk to relieve himself. He looked down afterwards and saw that he had made a substantial hole in the fungal mat covering the forest floor around the tree trunk.

It took him longer to get back inside the spacesuit. He re-sealed his visor and thought he would make just one more trip before returning. He was getting hungry.

He hadn't been to the future, and that had been intentional. He was scared to know what would happen. In a Block Universe that was dangerous, it was a fixed future. But he took a deep breath, and he felt more relaxed, confident even, now that he had relieved himself. He could risk a tiny look at the near future, he thought. That couldn't be too dangerous, could it?

He stood on a street on the outskirts of the city. He stood across from an empty block. The buildings had been demolished before rebuilding. The empty area was full of small debris and had been roughly cleared. On the far side of the block he saw an odd fighting scene. Three people were surrounded by a blue shield. Daxx was a long way away; he thought they were one man and two women. They were being bombarded by energy discharges from another man, who also had the same covering, a sheen of blue light, around him. The man, with the two women, constrained the other man, and the energy bombardment stopped. The constrained man struggled and yelled. Daxx couldn't hear what was said.

The man, fighting next to the women, looked towards Daxx. His hold on the other man faltered. Daxx heard the distant cry of voices as the man who was being constrained sent an energy surge towards the other three. It was not a safe place. Multiple people had his dangerous powers. Perhaps everyone had them. That was horrifying. He was shaken. Perhaps Janna had been mistaken, and the man who had saved them in the apartment was not him. He might be in real physical danger. Daxx panicked. He disappeared.

He didn't reappear back in his present. He appeared inside a darkened room. He swore. He felt trapped and lost. There were no windows. But there was some light. A single, low powered bulb sat on a small desk. There was a barely audible hum of an old-style power generator. A man worked at the desk. He focused his attention on a small computer screen.

'How does that feel?' the man spoke to the screen.

'Better.' A thin-sounding voice came from tiny speakers attached to the side of the screen. 'We've got company, Devrell,' the voice added.

The man spun around. He stared at Daxx in his spacesuit. The man took a sharp intake of breath.

Daxx panicked, again. He didn't think. He did the worst thing possible. He disappeared.

He reappeared in the warehouse. Janna and Kay Lee Too stood nearby. Daxx wrenched the spacesuit off. Janna tried to help. He pushed her away. His heart thumped. He took shallow breaths. He couldn't believe what he had just done.

'Fuck, fuck, fuck.' Daxx dropped his head into his hands.

'Daxx?' Janna asked.

He shook his head but didn't answer.

'Daxx?'

He lifted his head out of his hands. 'It was me.'

'What was?'

'It's always been me.'

'Tell me,' she said. 'Please?'

Daxx glanced at Kay Lee Too then back at Janna. 'I just saw Devrell.'

Janna's face lit up. 'Really?'

'No, it's not good,' Daxx said. 'I was wearing that.' He pointed at the spacesuit lying on the floor. 'And I appeared out of nothing and disappeared the same way. He was watching.'

Janna's eyes opened wide. 'Oh, Daxx.' She knew.

'What is it?' Kay Lee Too asked.

Janna kept staring at Daxx. He wasn't going to reply. She turned to Kay Lee Too.

'Devrell added the override to the Advisor because… he thought there were dangers from aliens,' Janna said. 'Daxx could have been the alien.'

Daxx's Device chimed a communication request. He answered it automatically.

'Who is it?' Janna asked.

'It's Renn,' Daxx said. 'What do you want?' he said angrily to the display.

chapter 60
Janna

K ay Lee Too laughed so hard he came close to falling off his chair. He grabbed onto the sides to stop himself from slipping off.

'This is serious.' Daxx frowned at the young man.

'I know,' Kay Lee Too said through his laughter. 'I'm not laughing at that future you saw, or Devrell, it's the space station. Look.'

Kay Lee Too showed his display to Daxx and Janna. It showed an image, taken from the space station, of a jury-rigged, amateur looking, space-suited person floating in the vacuum waving at the camera. The planet was the backdrop.

Kay Lee Too began to chuckle again. He glanced at Janna, then back to Daxx. 'You look ridiculous,' he said.

'Are there any more mentions throughout history of an apparition appearing? In a spacesuit?' Janna smiled, trying hard to not laugh. Daxx was right, it was no time for humour, but Daxx did look silly waving at the camera.

'There's not much data, of course. Only what Devrell saved. But there is this one, that was in a book,' Kay Lee Too said. 'There was a report, in medieval times, of clergymen seeing an apparition of the devil, right here in the city. Those of the group that didn't recant ended up being committed. And there's this…'

He swiped through his display and showed another image.

Daxx shook his head. He had made quite an impact during his short forays. The image was of rock art, showing a bulbous human-like figure with projections from the body, just like a man in a spacesuit covered with ill-designed additions.

'These drawings have been studied for ages. They thought it was a representation of an ancient belief system, or an image of one of the gods or an ancestor spirit. Some used to say it was a visitation from aliens.' Kay Lee Too smiled. 'That was almost true.'

Daxx sighed.

'I can't verify that these images have always been here. We should have checked before you went,' Kay Lee Too said.

'They would have always been there,' Daxx said. 'It's how things work. The past can't be changed.'

'Still…' Kay Lee Too dismissed his display. 'It would have been nice to have proof.'

'What do you think about that future trip?' Daxx looked at Janna. He sounded worried

'You can't change that either, can you?'

'No.'

'You don't know that one of those people wasn't you. It could have been you. So that would make only one extra person that has these powers of yours. It may not be everyone.'

'Who would I be fighting?'

Janna stared back at him. 'Really? It's a genetic mutation, probably restricted to your family. So…?'

Daxx didn't answer for a long time. 'We should keep him out of the loop then.'

'It's only a delaying tactic.'

'It might not be him,' Daxx said.

'Unlikely,' she said. 'If you can do these things then he can as well, probably.'

Daxx put his head in his hands. Janna knew what worried him—his visit to Devrell. 'He may have been going to put the override in the Advisor anyway,' she said. 'It may not be you.'

Daxx lifted his head. 'Do you think?' He sounded too hopeful.

'It could be, we'll never know.'

'But we could,' Kay Lee Too disagreed. 'The Advisor would know. It was there.'

Janna frowned at the engineer. 'It doesn't matter. That's the past explained, it's not the future. We're making that now.'

'I don't think I should travel again.'

She disagreed. 'Take me with you. Show me what it's like. We can go into the distant past. I'd love to see how my fungus evolved.'

'It's too dangerous.'

'No, it's not.' She shook her head. 'You've taken the suit, otherwise you'd have ended up naked.'

'That's different.'

'No. It's not.' Janna put her hands on her hips and glared at him. She was using his distress a tiny bit. The science possibilities were enormous and, in any case, Daxx needed activity. He couldn't go back to sorting supplies. He would be intolerable.

'Well…' Daxx began.

'Great.' She turned her back on him. 'But one trip won't be enough.' She strode away, to the bench where they kept their equipment. She grabbed some sample collectors and a genetic marker testing device. She quickly returned. She stood before him, smiling. 'I'm ready.'

'This is dangerous, Janna. It's not a game.'

'And neither is this.' She lifted her equipment. 'It's science. I want to know when my fungus evolved to be able to use the energy. And how simple is that, if I can actually go there and get samples?' She was excited. 'This is game-changing for biology. And for astrophysics, and for…'

Daxx raised his arm and closed his eyes. 'Okay, okay.'

'What do I do then?'

'I don't know.' Daxx sounded annoyed. 'Hold on tight?'

The warehouse disappeared from Janna's view. She was surrounded by shifting static. Daxx was the only recognisable object.

'Wow.' She held Daxx tightly. 'What is this?'

'This place has more spatial dimensions. I'm not sure how many more, but if it's the next in the series, it would be five. We can't experience matter constructed of more than three dimensions, except for the effects of gravity.' He gently stamped a foot. 'We're on a surface.' He shrugged. 'I assume that's matter and gravity. It's more than our brains can process, that's why it looks like static and random structures. It's not really static. I'm pretty sure it's just our brains giving up processing too much information.'

Janna let go of him and stepped away.

'Janna!'

She nodded her head. 'That was expected. I only need you to get through the energy barrier.' She jumped up and down. She had a large grin on her face. 'See? Perfectly safe, for us without superpowers.' She laughed.

'Janna.' It sounded like a whine.

She turned around. 'What are those differences?' She pointed at variations in the static.

'Representations…' Daxx said.

'Of what?' she said before he could finish.

'Time, and space.'

'Why do some look different?'

'Some are open, and some are closed.'

She nodded. 'How do you know the difference?'

'Practice,' he said. 'How they look and…' he hesitated, 'how they feel.'

'How they feel?' She smiled at him, almost laughing. 'You include subjective feeling in all of this? Daxx! What's come over you?'

'No, really. Try it.'

'Which one?'

Daxx nodded at one variation. 'That one.'

She stared at it. 'Nope. Nothing.'

'You knew Kell, didn't you?'

'I knew her through work,' she said. 'I used to see her at conferences, but we weren't friends, more like friendly colleagues.'

He nodded again at the variation. 'Think of Kell.'

Janna's eyes widened. 'Daxx!' She stared at him. 'How is that possible? How can I know that?'

'Subjective experience.' He smiled.

'We should go through,' Janna said. 'We could find out what happened to her.'

'We can't.'

'Why not?'

'I've tried. You can't go through. That one's closed.'

'I don't understand,' she said.

'Neither do I. Everything in our recent past is closed off as well. It's fixed and can't be altered.'

'What about your mother? Is her disappearance here?'

'I can't find it.'

Janna put a hand on Daxx's shoulder and left it there. 'Let's go.' They disappeared from the higher-dimensioned space.

'No.' Janna looked at the display of her genetic testing device. It fitted neatly into the palm of her hand. 'The marker isn't there.'

She looked up from the device in her hand and at the lush forest that surrounded them. They had hiked for an hour to this spot, to find a fungal mat of the ancestor of her fungal species.

'When is this?' she asked.

Daxx pulled his hand-held Device out of his pocket and held it over his head. He moved it around so it had a reasonable scan of the daylight sky. It vibrated after a moment, and there was a reading. Kay Lee Too had installed an application for Daxx's Device that could pierce the daylight sky's light scattering and register the position of a few major stars. Night was better for readings, obviously. It could give a pretty good estimate, within a million years, of the time in their planet's history.

Daxx lowered his Device. 'About fifty million years.'

Janna shook her head. She smiled at Daxx. It was incredible. Once all this mess with the Advisor was over, the scientific possibilities were unlimited. Although, Daxx may have something to say about that, being a taxi ride for scientists to the past.

'We should try a bit later,' she said.

Daxx sighed. 'Okay, hop on.'

They walked for hours through another forest. The species were different.

Daxx stopped and pointed to the ground. 'How about this one?'

Janna had expected Daxx to be able to recognise some basic differences in the fungal species by then, but he wasn't taking much notice.

'Different species.' She sighed. 'Let's try that way.' She pointed downhill.

'Great, downhill is good. We should be able to find something to drink down there.'

They hiked on for a few minutes.

'Here's one.' Janna hunched down and took a sample of the fungal mat, and added it to her testing device.

'Ten million years, right?'

Daxx nodded.

'Yes! It's evolved the genetic markers. Recently too, I'd guess. Let's try a million years ago or so. Can you do that?'

She smiled at him, like she was asking for a special favour. She knew he was bored with this. All the walking through forests was difficult. He had complained many times over the last hours. But, he had yet to perfect travelling distances without changing time, so they had to walk. She had pointed that out to him, in a nice way, ostensibly blaming his inadequacy for their need to walk through forests. But she didn't notice her own fatigue; she was a biologist experimenting directly with evolution.

Daxx's shoulders slumped.

'Just one more,' she said. 'Then we can go home. I promise.'

They appeared in yet another ancient forest. They hiked for a few minutes. They saw a human form in the distance. There was a discarded spacesuit next to the man. He was relieving himself over a fungal mat. They watched as the man, Daxx, on one of his first forays, clumsily got back into the spacesuit and then winked out of existence.

Janna looked at Daxx. 'It was you. Everything came from you.'

chapter 61

Tie

Renn burst into the warehouse like he owned the place. His group filed in behind him. They looked worried and frightened. Ahh Moss Eck sauntered in after the rest. Tie happened to be near the entrance.

'Where the fuck is Janna?' Renn demanded.

Tie frowned. The man was intolerable. He assumed an authority he did not have or deserve. Renn seemed to think that activity alone was leadership. But Renn didn't see the cohesion that Tie brought to the people sheltering in the warehouse. They appreciated Tie at a time when everyone was scared, and their future was uncertain. He was the grumpy leader, and there was no doubting him or his decisions. That was what people looked for in dangerous times. The Resistance was built upon egalitarianism, but at times of extreme crisis, that never worked. Someone had to be responsible, someone had to make quick decisions, right or wrong, and someone had to appear that they knew what they were doing, making order out of the chaos. Even if that wasn't true at all. Appearances are important to scared people. Tie provided that. His Tier-One revelation had hurt him, but was a bonus now. No one doubted he had the skills to lead. No Tier-Three ever doubted the competence of a Tier-One. And Tie was proving that right. Except for Renn and his band and, distressingly, Ahh Moss Eck. Tie's relationship with the big man had been more than a mentorship—he was like a big brother. The personal connection Renn had failed with Daxx.

Ahh Moss Eck had a roughness about him—a violence—that could be useful. Tie had never tried to quash the Tier-Three's tendencies, but they could be restrained with self-control. Ahh Moss Eck had changed slowly, as all real changes must. He'd lost the impulsive anger of a young man. His responses became considered. Although he could still be dangerous. Tie considered Ahh Moss Eck his greatest success. It was an important rebound from his greatest failure. While Soo had been difficult, headstrong and a constant battle to contain, which had eventually failed, Ahh Moss Eck had been transformed by quiet example and considered conversations.

Tie sighed and stared back at Renn. He disliked Renn, but he was being useful. Finding the lost family members had been a brilliant idea, and he wished he'd thought of it. It helped many of the people in the warehouse to know someone was looking for those they'd lost. Some were even located. People never gave up hope, which is always a good thing.

Tie also hadn't given up hope. He still had his objective. He had to ensure Soo failed by his own hand. He would risk anything and anyone. As shown by his calculated, but risky, betrayal of Renn and Ahh Moss Eck when they had tried to kill her. That had been dangerous. He had been lucky. It had worked. His relief when Ahh Moss Eck had returned, chastened, had been intense.

His objective was more than killing or stopping Soo. It had to include humiliation. She had to know that she had lost and that he had won. He was like her—she had taken on most of his teaching. Tie could be ruthless. It was the only way an elite Tier-One could have survived as long as he did. He lost battles, but he was always willing to re-fight them, with new resources, at different times, so that, eventually, he would win. Soo had to know that before she died, and she had to die in front of him.

He had thought, often, that he had created Soo in his image. That saddened him. It was possible to be ruthless while still playing within accepted rules. It was odd to think that there were rules when death was involved, but that had often proven to be the case. Except Soo had taken his determination to the extreme. It had to be his fault, he convinced himself at weak moments. But it was too horrendous a thought. But it did guide his life since Soo had tried to kill him. He had to atone for his mistake, but she had to know that not adopting all of Tie's teachings had led to her ultimate failure. She had to know that Tie had been right and her understanding had been incomplete. That his efforts may be simply jealously, and the humiliation of not ending their relationship first, never crossed his mind. But their relationship had been a love and hate sort of thing. Love betrayed, mixed with broken pride, often changed like that.

Tie did have an option. He wished he could bring Ahh Moss Eck into his confidence, but shared knowledge is dangerous. A trump card is difficult to play if it's too widely known.

Renn shook his head. 'Are you dreaming, old man? Do you have any idea what we've been doing? Do you?' Renn yelled at Tie.

Renn was overwrought. His face was flushed. He was angry. No, Tie thought, he wasn't angry, he was scared witless. Those two can often be confused.

'Yes, I know.' Tie tried to remain quiet. He glanced at Ahh Moss Eck. The man stared at him as if Tie's face was dangerous. 'Did you upload the software?'

'Fuck the software,' Renn said. 'We were nearly killed.'

Tie raised his eyebrows. 'Really?' He looked at Ahh Moss Eck again. He shrugged.

'Yes, really.' Renn was livid. 'We only just made it out alive. We had to fight the police to get away. Two were killed.'

'Who were they?' Tie asked.

'I don't know their names,' Renn said. 'The engineers you gave us.'

Tie nodded. 'That's sad. They were good people.'

'They were arseholes.' Renn took a deep breath. 'They were too slow getting away from the bunker.'

'You should have left earlier.'

Renn fumed. He took a step towards Tie. Tie didn't flinch.

'Boss!' Ahh Moss Eck called.

Both Tie and Renn turned to look at him.

Tie turned back to Renn. 'How did you get away?'

Renn slowly looked back at Tie. He was a little calmer. 'We ran. They didn't chase us, thankfully.' Renn glared at Tie.

Ahh Moss Eck came close to Renn. 'Let's go and find Janna. It's what you wanted, right?'

Renn wrenched his head away from Tie. He nodded at Ahh Moss Eck.

Renn brushed past Tie and strode across the warehouse.

Ahh Moss Eck followed Renn. He glanced back at Tie. He seemed to show a little less disrespect, or was it disappointment? Tie couldn't tell.

chapter 62

Daxx

Daxx sat hunched over and despondent, on a box of supplies in their work area. Only enough space had been cleared to work on the spacesuit. The spacesuit, now discarded, having served its purpose, was propped up in a corner. It looked like a child imagined it, added projections and parts not for function but to add complexity to something that needed to look complex. Daxx felt horrible and not because he'd spent hours hiking through primeval forests millions of years ago. What Janna had said was true. He'd caused it all. He'd transferred his genome to the fungus. It had evolved to use the energy from higher spacetimes because of him. He had helped use that source to create batteries that lasted forever, making the Advisor impossible to kill. He had shocked Devrell to create the weakness the Advisor had exploited to take control. It didn't matter that Janna had said that it was just the past. He had created their present. If he had never been born, millions would still be alive.

'I'm sorry, Daxx,' Janna said. 'I didn't mean it like that.'

He remained hunched over, looking at the distant floor of their workspace where the wall and floor met. His mind was in a spin of self-blame.

'That's all right.' He sat up straighter and looked at her. They stared at each other for a moment. 'But, it's true.'

She didn't say anything for a moment. He didn't need platitudes; he didn't need to hear that it wasn't anyone's fault. He understood the consequences of his actions. She nodded at him, then looked away and back at the spacesuit.

'I don't really understand, Daxx. Sorry.'

It was ironic, Daxx thought. Planetary history and evolution had been altered, millions of years ago, by what he had just done. But, just, was the wrong word. The fungus's evolution had been changed by Daxx introducing his genetic material, but it had not been altered from some different timeline. What Daxx had done had always been done. At least, the odd genetic mutation Janna had discovered in both Daxx and the fungus was explained by a single origin. A mutation had occurred in Daxx, or one of his ancestors, and had crossed over to the fungus. It was a problematic mechanism, but not without precedence.

Daxx knew what her concern was. He was good at that. He understood what the real and consequential questions should be.

'There is free will,' he said. 'There is still cause and effect, following in that order. There is still entropy; there is still an arrow of time. But,' he sat up further, 'there are multiple time dimensions wrapped up with multiple spacetimes. It's a simultaneity issue.'

She frowned.

'The fungus genesis,' Daxx said. 'Is still following cause and effect. The genetic mutation happened first, then I passed it to the fungus. Of course, here'—he looked around the room—'in this time, it was millions of years ago. But it wasn't. We changed that by touching the other spacetime.'

She nodded her head. It made sense and yet was nonsensical.

He glanced at the spacesuit. 'We could have not done that,' he said. 'We could have not played with this energy stuff, then it wouldn't have happened. But we have, and we can't change that any more than you can change what you had for dinner last night. It's too late, it's happened, it has always happened.' He stared at her for a long time, as if trying to read her thoughts. 'Does that make sense?'

'No.' She smiled. 'But I understand it.'

He smiled back at her. 'That's exactly how I feel too.'

'What should we do now then?' She stood up, as if going somewhere was the answer to that question.

'I don't know. How worse can I make things? Pretty much every problem we have up until now was caused by me.' He looked up at her as she stood next to him but he remained seated.

She sighed and frowned at him. They stared at each other for a long time. He was hoping she'd say something to make him feel better. But there was nothing she could say. 'Why don't you see how this all turns out? Have you thought of that?'

'I'm not going to do that.' He stood up. 'That's too scary. I don't want to know what happens. Knowing that it can't be changed...' He sighed and shook his head.

Janna put her arm around him. 'You've had a long day hiking. Thanks for putting up with me. You must be starving.'

Renn strode towards them. He looked tired and angry. Ahh Moss Eck sauntered behind.

'Hey, boss,' Ahh Moss Eck said to Janna. He nodded at Daxx. 'Daxx,' he said. He frowned. 'You look like shit.'

'He's had a hard day,' Janna said.

'Hard day?' Renn exclaimed. 'How the fuck have you had a hard day? Shuffling supplies?' Renn noticed the spacesuit in the corner. He shook his head. 'I have no fucking idea why we wasted time on that shit.'

Daxx frowned. He was angry the moment Renn spoke. Daxx glared at his brother. Renn ignored Daxx.

'Why all the panic?' Renn said to Janna. 'We had enough to worry about without you making it worse. What have you found out?'

'I haven't found out anything,' she said. 'Why would I?'

Renn shook his head. 'What else have you got to do? Ahh Moss Eck and I almost got killed, and you're having hard days standing around doing nothing.'

'It was viral research, Renn,' Janna said. 'You can never be too scared of viruses.'

'Should we be?' Renn glared at her.

She stared back at him, then dropped her eyes. 'I don't know.'

'Are you here just to yell at us?' Daxx said. 'Or is there something you want?'

'There's nothing I want from you. I just want an explanation.'

'There was something a little strange, boss,' Ahh Moss Eck said to Janna. 'One of the scientists called Renn by name. He looked like he really knew him.'

'Maybe he knew Renn through Kell, being her brother,' Janna said. 'They were doing her research.'

'Maybe, but I doubt it. He really seemed familiar with Renn,' Ahh Moss Eck said.

'Are you sure you don't know him?' Janna said to Renn.

'Of course not. How would I know him? He's probably a Tier-Two.'

'He's probably a Tier-One, if he was working on Kell's stuff. What did he say?' Daxx asked.

'We were in a bit of a hurry.' Renn sounded annoyed. 'While you two have been playing with toys'—he glanced at the spacesuit—'we've been risking our lives…'

Ahh Moss Eck interrupted. 'He said something about being late, too late.'

Daxx placed his fingers on his head and squeezed them into his forehead. He thought what he had done was bad enough. This was worse. He turned to Janna. 'He called Renn by his name. He knew Renn.'

Janna looked shocked. 'Oh, shit,' she said quietly. 'Shit, shit,' she loudly.

'What?' Renn said.

'This virus creates its own network in the brain, with its own connection to the worldwide network,' Daxx said. 'When Kell created the process it was supposed to replace a lot of the things we can do with Devices, like communications, local data storage, network queries. But she could never sustain the network connectivity. The neuronal network didn't have the power.'

Renn shook his head. 'I don't get it.'

Daxx looked at Janna. He hoped he was wrong, but he wasn't. She nodded at him. He sighed. All the strength went from him. Each step in the horrible procession of events had sunk him and everyone else into a position unimaginably worse. This was another step downwards, perhaps the worst of all. They had been close to overcoming the Advisor with software intervention, but it had been one step ahead. It knew it would lose that battle and had developed a solution that would win it the war.

'The virus creates a separate network in people's brains to augment their cognitive abilities. It connects to the worldwide network, which is… the Advisor.' Daxx let that information sink in for a moment. 'And I guess,' he glanced at Janna, 'It's even worse than that?'

'It probably is,' she agreed.

Daxx shook his head. He stared at Janna as he spoke. She stared back. She looked so sorry for him, like she wanted to grab him in an embrace and stop him from talking. 'If the Advisor has incorporated the fungus genome into the virus, it will have unlimited power. Kell's network has access to brain functions and storage. The Advisor will be able write itself into people's brains. There's enough storage in there for it to sustain itself without connectivity.'

Renn frowned at Daxx, who understood he had to make it even simpler.

'They were testing the virus on themselves. And it worked. Everyone will be the Advisor, Renn. That's why that scientist knew your name. He didn't know you. The Advisor knows you.'

chapter 63

Renn

'You can do what?' Renn yelled at his brother. Renn had insisted on an explanation for the spacesuit requirement and had received it. Renn turned on Ahh Moss Eck. 'And you knew too? Did everyone know?'

'No,' Ahh Moss Eck said. 'I only knew about the being a weapon thing, which is pretty handy and amazing to see in action.' Ahh Moss was distracted for a moment. He noticed Renn's frown. 'But I didn't know about the travel thing. I only helped get the suit. I was with you after that.'

'Let me get this straight,' Renn said to Ahh Moss Eck. 'We, you and I and those two idiot engineers, blasted our way into a police bunker, captured armed police just in time, uploaded Kay Lee Too's new software, were in danger from some weird virus my sister created, had to fight our way out as the police returned, got the two engineers killed… Am I missing anything?'

Ahh Moss Eck didn't reply. Renn let the silence hang for a moment.

'And that whole fucking time, my fucking little brother here…' he pointed at Daxx but kept looking at Ahh Moss Eck. 'Could have wandered in, zapped everyone and we could have uploaded the software and… I don't know, stayed for lunch?'

Ahh Moss Eck set his face. 'But our way, only two died.'

'We could have as well,' Renn said.

Ahh Moss Eck shrugged. 'Yeah, but we didn't.'

Renn turned to Daxx. 'We risked our lives, and you just sat here?'

Janna started to say something, probably in defence, but Daxx touched her softly on the arm. She stopped. The silence extended for a long time. Renn tried to calm himself. His expectations for his brother's behaviour were low. He shouldn't react. He took a deep breath.

'How is this even possible? Where did it come from?' Renn said.

'We think from Eth,' Janna said.

Daxx glared at her. 'We don't know where the mutation came from,' Daxx said. 'We can't be certain.'

'So, it's genetic. I could have it, Kell could have it. What about Dad's side?'

'I doubt that it's on Dad's side.'

'Why?'

'Because of what happened to Mum.'

Renn nodded. 'That actually makes sense. I've seen the footage,' Renn said. 'And what about Kell? Do you think the same thing happened to her?'

'I really don't know.'

Renn gripped his hands into fists. He felt like striking his brother, despite knowing that would help nothing. But the image of his fist smashing sense into Daxx's face remained. 'So you have this amazing capability, and you can return here, which Mum and Kell couldn't do, and you've just sat around. Fuck Daxx! You're so self-absorbed. You abandoned me, you abandoned your family. I was the only one there for Dad and for Kell. This is typical of you. Why don't you use this power and change things?'

'It doesn't work like that.'

'Are you certain?'

'Yes,' Daxx said.

Renn was silent for a moment. He stared at his brother. If his brother was certain, then it probably was. That didn't make him feel any better. 'What have you tried? Have you tried anything at all? Or have you just been doing fucking experiments while we've been out nearly getting killed?'

Daxx looked directly at his brother. His eyes were hard and dark. 'I tried to find Kell.'

Renn thought he might cry if he was not careful. Anger mixed with regret and self-pity was an unstable mixture. 'Do you really think she's not dead?' Renn blinked hard.

'I don't know.'

Renn looked away from his brother. He noticed the spacesuit again. He frowned and shook his head. Renn partly blamed himself for Daxx's lack of empathy. The younger man had always been self-absorbed, never willing to share family responsibilities. Renn should have done more when they were younger, but it was too late, Daxx would never change. Renn thought of his father. 'How's Dad?'

'I don't know.' Daxx shrugged.

Renn struggled with his anger. But it wasn't Daxx's fault. Renn wanted to blame his brother for everything wrong in their family, but he couldn't. Kell didn't run away from lack of attention or rebellion. She disappeared. She may even be alive. Daxx's lack of empathy—to his father, to his lost sister, to his brother—meant he was ill equipped to make reasonable decisions. They were in dire circumstances, good decisions needed to be made. Renn had to make them. Renn took a deep breath. He tried to calm himself. He resolved, yet again, that nothing of consequence should be his brother's responsibility.

'All right, then…' Renn stood a little straighter. 'How do I do this?'

Daxx frowned at his brother; he looked puzzled. 'What do you mean?'

'I mean…' Renn's anger threatened again, despite his conscious attention to it. 'I'll use this power thing and protect Ahh Moss Eck and the others when they need it, and I'll go and save Kell, or at least, do something to change something. I don't know, I'll figure it out. You don't have to do anything, you can just keep…' he waved at the spacesuit, 'experimenting.'

'It doesn't work like that. You have no idea,' Daxx said.

'Well, show me, then I'll have an idea.'

'No.'

'What?'

'I said no. There this no way I'm showing you how to do this. You would be the worst person to have this power. I cannot even begin to imagine how much you would mess things up.'

'But, you said you can't change the past. So I can't… mess things up.'

'Oh, Renn.' Daxx sounded supercilious and weary. 'There's only been a few billion years, so far.' Daxx sighed. 'You have the rest of the age of the universe to thoroughly fuck things, and you would.'

Renn lost control. He was still frightened from the battle with the police. He was exhausted. He'd been reminded of Kell. Daxx still took no responsibility for their father, and the old man was close by. And Daxx looked down at him like he was the idiot child. Frustration and fatigue added to the mix of anger and regret. The self-pity overloaded him. He saw himself through his brother's eyes. It was not an edifying sight. He had been pretending his whole adult life. He saw in plain light his need to control and his need for approval. He had blamed his father; he had blamed his mother for leaving; he blamed Daxx and his withdrawal for their shattered relationship. He especially blamed Kell's disappearance. But she was not to blame. Her memory was untouchable like all those that leave life too early.

Kell's loss, much more than his sister's life, defined Renn. It made him force his assistance on others. He had to do important things himself. He could trust no one. He had let Kell live her own independent life, and she had disappeared. He had been left with, effectively, no family. Daxx was no longer part of his family. He had renounced them. And yet, here was Daxx, standing before him, frowning, debasing him, telling him he was inadequate. Maybe Daxx was even smirking. It was too much. He had no brother; he had an adversary.

Renn launched himself at Daxx. Renn's face was distorted with rage. His fists were clenched. He would feel the satisfaction of them smashing into his brother's face. Renn's vision became a field of static. The warehouse had gone. He had the sensation of forward momentum, but nothing moved. He staggered to a standstill.

Renn blinked.

He stood among trees. He was in the foothills outside the city.

He was alone.

He could see the city in the distance.

chapter 64

Day 20. Janna

'We should find him,' Janna said the next morning. She, Daxx, and Tie sat at a table eating breakfast.

Daxx shrugged. 'How do you begin to find someone who could, literally, be anywhere and any time?'

'But he might not be. He might still be here.'

'Nothing's changed since last night,' Daxx said. 'We can't go out and look for him, that's pointless, and we can't use the surveillance cameras anymore. What do you suggest?'

'He's your brother.'

'He wasn't very brotherly yesterday.'

'Neither were you,' Janna snapped.

Daxx looked like she'd struck him.

'I'm sorry,' she said. 'I didn't mean that. It's just that you still have family...'

'I know,' he said. 'We were both not at our best. As soon as there is a way to look for him, we'll do it.'

'Could you track him through that higher spacetime?'

Daxx shrugged. 'I have no idea.'

Janna frowned. 'You should try.'

Daxx stared at her for a moment. He disappeared. He immediately reappeared, but stood behind his chair.

Tie shook his head. 'That is so... unsettling.'

'There's no trace of him that I can see.' Daxx sat down again and resumed eating his breakfast.

'So you're just going to give up?'

'There are problems other than Renn,' Tie said.

Janna turned and glared at him, then she nodded. 'You're right.'

'I'm not saying he isn't a big problem, he is, but we should work on things we can.'

Daxx didn't finish his breakfast. He pushed it away. Janna glanced at him. 'You shouldn't waste food. And you need to eat, Daxx.'

He reached across to his plate and brought it close again, but he didn't eat any more of it.

Tie grunted. 'Does time travel make you lose your appetite?'

'No, totally fucking everything does that.'

Janna frowned, but didn't say anything.

Kay Lee Too appeared next to Tie. He didn't take any notice of Daxx, Janna, and Tie, although that he was there meant he wanted to talk to them. He frowned and swiped through his display. He shook his head.

'I don't like the look of this,' Tie said. He pushed his plate away. It was not empty. He glanced at Janna. 'Are you going to tell me to finish it?' He smiled, then turned to Kay Lee Too. He sighed. 'And what is it now?'

'It doesn't make sense.' Kay Lee Too still stared at his display.

'What doesn't?'

'Everything's coming back online. The water supply, power to the city buildings, food's being delivered, everything's back, including the surveillance cameras.' He pointed at his display. 'There are convoys of autonomous vehicles coming out of secure locations. And here,' he pointed at his display, 'I can see police coming out of the bunker Renn raided.'

'That's a good thing, isn't it?' Tie asked.

'It's confusing.'

Janna looked at Daxx. He knew why. As did she. 'It's not confusing,' she said. 'And it's not a good thing.'

'What is it then?' Tie asked.

'The Advisor doesn't want people dead anymore,' Daxx said.

'And…?' Tie asked.

'It wants people alive now,' Janna said.

Tie frowned at Daxx. 'Is this to do with your sister's virus? I thought you said it wasn't contagious. Do we have to worry about Ahh Moss Eck being infected?'

'Kell didn't make it contagious. That wasn't her intention.'

'You're saying we need to sit tight? If it's just a pandemic, then that's okay, we've survived those before.' Tie turned in his chair and looked across the warehouse. 'I'll need to warn Ahh Moss Eck and the others to stay here and not to go off doing whatever the hell they want.'

Janna shook her head. She glanced at Daxx. His elbows were on the table, his head in his hands. 'The Advisor wants people infected,' she said. 'It's restoring the network so it can reach as many people as possible...'

'But it's not contagious,' Tie said.

Daxx spoke into his hands. His voice slightly muffled. 'The food.' He raised his head and stared at Tie.

'And the water too, probably,' Janna said.

Tie stared at them both for a moment. He stood up. He placed his hands on the table. 'Then we need to stop it.'

Daxx shook his head. He had almost reached breaking point. His body was surrounded by a light blue sheen.

'Daxx!' Janna said.

He looked at her and tried to smile. 'I'm okay. Well, I'm not, but, yeah, I'll be okay.' He turned to Tie. 'How do you stop hungry people from eating when food is being delivered to them? You can't. It's a great strategy.'

'You're right,' Kay Lee Too said. 'It's too late. The food convoys have been rolling out through the city for a few hours now. They're dumping food as they go.'

Tie stood up straight, taking his hands off the table. 'Are you sure the food and water are contaminated by this virus?'

'It's the only thing that makes sense,' Janna said.

'Can you come up with a test for it? Let's make sure it's in the food and water before we panic.'

'Yes.'

'Good,' Tie said. 'At least we'll know what not to eat and drink. That's a start.'

'It won't make any difference,' Daxx said.

Tie ignored him. 'We'll need to contact Ahh Moss Eck and the others, and warn them.' He turned to Kay Lee Too. 'Can you do that?'

'I can now,' Kay Lee Too said. 'The network's back.'

Tie took a deep breath. 'And what can you do to help?' he asked Daxx. 'Can these special powers of yours help us?'

'No. I only make things worse every time I do anything. I should go back to sorting supplies.'

Tie nodded. 'I know you're being sulky, but that's not such a bad thing. We're even more reliant on the supplies we have, until Janna gets us a test.'

Dax frowned.

'And the water,' Janna reminded Tie.

He nodded. 'I know. I'll make sure no one hooks us back to the mains supply.' Tie touched a hand to the table. 'All right,' he said. 'We've all got work to do.'

Tie turned and strode across the warehouse. Kay Lee Too sauntered off, concentrating on his display. Janna overheard the beginning of a conversation before he walked off too far.

'Hey, Ahh Moss Eck,' Kay Lee Too said. 'Things are even worse…'

'You could try to find Renn,' Janna said. 'Now the surveillance is back.'

Daxx nodded. He picked up a fork and pushed at the food remaining on his plate.

'For fuck's sake, Daxx,' Janna said.

Daxx ignored her, but he stopped pushing at his food. He lifted his head to look at her. She was shocked. His look of despair was haunting and overpowering.

'What is it?'

'You're not thinking it through.'

'Well, tell me then.'

'It's Renn. If he's still here, we have an unimaginable problem.'

Janna understood. Daxx's despair overwhelmed her. It became hers. Every unimaginably bad thing that had happened so far was inconsequential in comparison. She dropped her head into her hands. She felt like crying. She felt Daxx's hand on her shoulder. She turned to him. She grabbed him in an embrace. She did start crying. The feel of her face on his shoulder brought back the horrible memory of seeing her dead parents.

'I'm so sorry, Janna,' Daxx said. 'I'm so sorry.' His voice a whisper.

She pushed away from him. She wiped her eyes. She stared at his face, perhaps hoping there was some flaw in her understanding. He seemed to know what she hoped for. He shattered any hope she had.

'If Renn gets infected,' Daxx said. 'The Advisor will be Renn. And Renn can go anywhere, any time. The future, everywhere, could be the Advisor.'

chapter 65

Renn

He recognised the place. As a young boy, their family had often gone there. He remembered sunny days playing with other children and his siblings. Kell had been a toddler the last time they had gone to that place.

When was that?

He remembered. It was the afternoon before the evening when his mother disappeared. The park, the trees, the distant view of the city, all represented his last moment of untainted joy.

Renn looked around the park, his remembered joy drowned his feelings of inadequacy and frustration. His life had not turned out how he expected, but he forgot that for the moment. He had wanted to help, to assist, to save. He still believed that the way to save people from themselves was to take on their burdens. He had to prevent obstacles before they happened, or to be a buffer against them. He wanted to make people's lives easier, even though most of them annoyed him. If he took their burden, that necessarily meant less for others, as if there was a maximum amount of possible suffering in the world.

Renn smiled. He understood what had happened to him. He headed across the parkland and through the scattered trees, towards the city. He stopped walking as the trees thinned towards a large parking area. He looked up at the sun. He frowned. It was morning; it had been evening just a moment ago. He wondered why he was walking at all. He could move through space. He could go wherever he wanted. He imagined the feeling he had when he ran at his brother, the base sensation, the feeling of power, not the surface anger and frustration. The surface of his body produced a thin layer of blue, flickering light. The trees and the carpark disappeared and were replaced by the static, structure-laden medium. He saw the irregularity in the structures—he was looking for them. He touched one of them to bring it closer. His world turned black.

A light burned. It was unbuffered sunlight. He would have been blinded if he'd been looking directly at it.

He had been lucky, he had just exhaled. The remaining air in his lungs gushed through his open mouth. He couldn't breathe. There was nothing to breathe. The saliva on his tongue heated, heading towards boiling point. His eyes felt gritty, the liquid surrounding them bubbled. His vision blurred.

His body swelled. The water inside his body had begun to vaporise, causing the tissue beneath his skin to swell.

He was terrified.

He thought of the parkland again, this time consciously, as a safe place, as a refuge. He was there again, in the same place. He collapsed to the ground. He retched. His head throbbed. He took a deep breath, and another, and another. The most simple of tasks had never felt so vital and satisfying.

He stood up. He was in pain, but relatively undamaged. He wondered at the significance of that location, that particular spot in the parkland in the foothills. He had ended up there twice. Then he remembered. It was where he had stood when his mother had called him to say it was time to go. The last time she had done that.

He knew what he had done wrong. There was an intuitive element to the power he shared with his brother, but like all dangerous tasks, concentration was necessary. He hadn't been concentrating. He tried again.

'Shit,' he said. He found himself on the far side of the city when he had been trying to just move to the car park.

He tried again. He sighed. This time he stood on a beach.

He tried again. He returned to his original location. 'At least that works,' he said out loud.

He wondered what he should do next. Practise, obviously, but what was the use of the skill he shared with Daxx?

He knew what he had to do. It was personal. There was a place, and a time, which affected him as much as the last moment of remembered happiness with his mother. He would see Kell again. He would save her. He could do that.

He tried again. He stood on a city street, not far from the University where Kell worked. He recognised the place. It was bustling with a lunchtime crowd. Everything appeared normal. There were no violent gangs, there were no shortages.

He stopped a passerby. 'When is this?'

The woman looked at Renn, annoyed at being interrupted. She walked away from him.

But, of course, he didn't need to ask anyone; he had his Device and it would connect to the network. He initiated the display. It was the day of Kell's disappearance. Renn smiled. He scanned the crowd of people; he knew where she had disappeared. He was close. He saw the back of someone, their movements looked recognisable. It was Kell, he was sure.

He yelled her name and started running in her direction. The recognisable body didn't stop. She didn't hear him. He yelled again when he was a little closer. He could see that it was Kell. The shape of her body, her hairstyle and the colour was exactly as he remembered her as a young woman, and she had never aged from that moment.

He thought about using his newfound skill of instantaneous movement, but he didn't trust his accuracy. He ran even faster. He pushed people aside. She turned a corner into an alleyway. Renn yelled her name one more time, to no effect.

He sprinted to the corner that she had just passed. He stopped. He yelled in his anguish. The alleyway was empty. Kell had disappeared. He had an incredible, unbelievable power, and yet, he still couldn't save his sister.

He fell to his knees. He sobbed like a child, like he did when he'd been told his mother had disappeared and his father had been taken to hospital. He felt the inadequacy that had weighed on him for years. But he was determined to not fail. He would try again.

He did. But the way was blocked.

He tried again and again until he succeeded, he thought by blunt force of his will. He returned to that same time and a location nearby. He saw, from a distance, his own attempt to race after Kell and save her. He watched the pitiful sight of a man sobbing, on his knees, on a street corner.

He knew that moment was fixed. His life to that moment, even though it now included a past he had visited, was unchangeable. He returned to his safe place in the parkland. He opened his display and viewed, again, the images of his sister's disappearance. He watched her move into the alleyway. The same place and time he had just seen in person. He zoomed out the surveillance feed and, yes, there was a man sobbing on his knees on the street corner. He broadened the surveillance footage further, and he saw himself watching the sobbing man. He scanned further but didn't find another instance of himself. He never went back there again and he never would. His failure was complete.

Renn dismissed his display. He was exhausted, he had been running, he'd been distraught, he'd been crying. He started walking. He didn't try to go anywhere instantly; he had nowhere he wanted to go. He walked slowly towards the city. He walked through suburbs, mostly deserted but saw the occasional person who scampered away when seen.

Close to the city centre, an autonomous vehicle lumbered to a halt. Renn watched as a group of unkempt, angry-looking people raced to surround it. They stood guard. They fought off others, who eventually stood away from the truck. A circle of hungry individuals formed just out of harm's way.

As the truck began to dump its cargo of food and water, Renn walked through the outside circle of people and came close to the truck. He was hungry and thirsty, as well as tired. The ugly group stared at him, not understanding why he wasn't intimidated. Renn didn't care. He was a Tier-One and none of those people would be anything higher than a Tier-Three, at best.

'Get out of my way,' Renn said when the group moved between him and the food supply. The truck had almost finished unloading. Renn stopped, but only because to move forward, he would have to push people away. The group didn't move. They had clubs and knives. They pushed them towards Renn as a threat.

Renn sighed. 'Get out of my way.' He looked behind him. The circle of people watched. Some waited for the potential spectacle of his death, and others waited in the hope that he would gain them access to the food.

Three of the violent group, those closest to him, lunged forward. Renn raised his arm as if to ward off the blows. He wasn't scared; he was angry and annoyed. The people with weapons were an impediment that had to be removed.

His body flickered in a light blue haze. A dazzling flash emanated from him. He couldn't see for a moment. His eyes adjusted. When he could see clearly again, the violent group had disappeared. He'd vaporised them. He turned to the people watching. He waved at them. 'It's okay,' Renn said. 'I won't hurt you.'

Renn grabbed a few packaged food items and put them in his pockets. He grabbed a bottle of water and took a deep drink, then slid that into another pocket. He grabbed a fresh piece of hard fruit. He examined it on all sides—he liked his fruit unblemished. He took a bite, nodded his approval at the taste, then headed off towards the city centre.

chapter 66

Soo

Soo frowned as she scanned her display. She watched the country, the planet, restarting. The power and the water supply were functioning again. She watched the feed as police re-entered the outside world, setting up watches at major city intersections. Autonomous trucks had begun lumbering through city streets from early that morning. At regular intervals a truck would stop and unload its cargo of foodstuffs. Where there was no police presence, people scrambled to get what they could, often fighting over supplies. Where the police had a presence, the distribution was orderly.

'It doesn't make sense,' Soo said.

'What doesn't make sense?' Mill Nupp said.

'This.' She pointed at her display. 'It's too early. It's only been, what, nine days?'

'But that's good, isn't it?'

'No, it isn't. Not enough people will have died yet.'

'I don't understand.'

She didn't answer.

The Advisor had begun a deadly game of survival of the fittest. The sick, the elderly, and the infirm would die easily and quickly, those with health conditions would die soon after, the less resourceful would die as competition became fierce. However, the game had ended before it had barely begun. Soo had expected to remain in the bunker for half a year or more. Nine days made no sense. She shook her head. It had been a pointless exercise. She looked at Mill Nupp. The young man was bright-eyed and eager, but confused.

'What's happening with our water supply?' she asked.

'I've told the engineers to switch over to the mains water. Why?'

She thought for a moment. 'No, don't do that.'

'Why?'

'Something's not right,' she said. 'And until we figure out the reason, we should remain self-sufficient.' She stabbed a finger at her display. 'And we need to go out there and see for ourselves.'

Soo, Mill Nupp, and four security officers congregated outside the Power Corp complex of buildings. It was eerily quiet, although that was not unexpected.

'Where is the nearest distribution point?' Soo asked.

Mill Nupp opened his display. 'Five blocks.' He pointed. 'That way.'

'What's there?'

Mill Nupp looked at his display again. 'A block of apartments.'

'Is it busy?'

'There are some people.' He dismissed his display. 'There's no police there.'

'Good.'

They walked warily through empty city streets. As they came closer to the distribution point, there were stragglers, some just sitting on the pavement. They seemed unconcerned by Soo and her guards, and watched with idle interest. Some even smiled at Soo and nodded at her.

Soo frowned at the odd behaviour. 'How long since the delivery here?'

'An hour.'

Soo nodded and kept walking, getting closer to the food supply dump. She heard the sound of yelling and turned to face the source. Her four guards moved to surround her. A ragtag group of dishevelled and unwashed people raced past, on their way to the supplies. They yelled with delight and fell upon the food, ripping the packaging as they consumed whatever was closest.

Soo watched them. Here was semi-normal behaviour, at least. They were starving. She turned away from the spectacle and noticed the people nearby were watching the newcomers closely. They expected something to happen. She looked back to the group around the food dump. They stopped eating. Food had dropped from their hands and lay on the ground around them. They clutched their heads in what seemed like pain.

'It's only painful for a short while, a few minutes,' a woman said. She wasn't too far from Soo.

Soo turned to look at the woman. 'Excuse me?'

The woman smiled at Soo. 'I said, it's only painful for a short while.'

'How do you know?'

'Oh,' the woman sounded surprised. 'I've been through it. We'—she looked around at the other people nearby—'were here when it arrived. We all live here, in these apartments.' She pointed up at the apartment complex above them. She, again, smiled at Soo. The woman's familiarity was worrying.

Soo took a few steps closer to the woman. 'What is it, then? Have you any idea?'

'Of course.' The woman stopped her annoying smile. 'It's too late, Soo.'

Soo stepped away from her. She motioned to one of the guards. He shot the woman through the head. She crumpled to the ground. The others near the dead woman, her fellow apartment complex inhabitants, slowly turned away and dispersed. It was more odd behaviour. The group next to the food supply was still there, clutching their heads.

Soo watched the scene for a moment. 'We need more information,' she said to Mill Nupp. 'We should take a sample of the food.'

Mill Nupp didn't answer her. She turned to look at him, a frown beginning on her face.

Renn stood behind them, his eyes hard, his face scowling in pain. Renn groaned. He slammed both his hands to his head. He dropped his eyes to the ground, shook his head violently, then looked up at Soo. She glanced at Mill Nupp. The young man looked terrified. She motioned to one of the guards. He raised his gun towards Renn. Before the weapon discharged, there was a flash and where the guard had been was... nothing. The man had been vaporised.

Renn stared hard at the empty place, his arm extended. He looked at his hand as though it were a thing newly discovered. He slowly lowered his arm.

'I wouldn't do that again.' Renn's voice distorted through a grimace.

Soo was terrified. But she didn't freeze. She didn't panic. Tie's training had included how to survive situations like this. She spoke in a soft voice, trying to sound calming but not annoying and cloy. 'Are you in pain, Renn?

Can I help?'

He stared at her, then grunted. 'It's in my head. It's fighting me. You can help if you can get rid of it.'

'Get rid of what? I'll try, if I can.'

Renn grunted again. This time it was more like a short laugh. 'I'm dangerous, Soo. I'm really dangerous. And for the first time in my life, I can actually make things happen. I could have fixed all of this.' He waved his arm. Soo almost ducked, thinking Renn may discharge whatever the weapon was that vaporised her guard. 'But now...'

Renn grabbed his head and winced. 'Shit!' Renn said. 'Fuck off.'

Soo glanced behind her, wondering who Renn was yelling at. There was no one. He was yelling at himself.

Then Soo understood. If she had thought she was terrified at what Renn had done to her guard, she had not understood the full extent of terror. All of Tie's teachings could not prepare her for this. She didn't know how, but the Advisor was everywhere and inside everyone. It was the only explanation for the odd behaviour she'd seen.

She shook her head, glanced at Renn, then at Mill Nupp. The young man's face was fixed in horror. He had guessed, too. Soo was impressed.

'The food,' she said. 'But how?'

'Oh, I can tell you that,' Renn said. 'This fucking thing won't stop talking to me in my head. I know what it's done. And you know the ironic thing?'

'No.'

Renn laughed but strangled the sound to a halt. 'It's my fucking family that has caused all of this. It was fucking Daxx, and the power thing, and my beautiful, wonderful sister.'

Renn's eyes began to water. He blinked hard then wiped them clear.

'It's a virus that Kell developed. A neuronal network. It was supposed to help people.'

'How long does it take to act, Renn? How long do you have before it takes over?'

Renn laughed. It was long and deep.

'That's the thing,' Renn said. 'It begins immediately and only takes a few minutes to create enough of a network. It started on me hours ago. I've been wandering around, just killing people that annoy me, which is pretty much everyone.'

Renn stared hard at Soo. She wondered if she had begun to annoy him, too. There was nothing she could do about it.

'But...' Renn paused. 'The thing is...' He paused again and grabbed his head. 'I can resist it. No one else can, just me, apparently.' Renn laughed again. 'I'm really pissing it off. Now that it knows what I can do. And I'm fucking things up for it, which is one good thing about this. The only thing, mind you.'

'Let me help.'

Renn frowned at her. 'Sure,' he said. 'But how the fuck do you think you can do that? What do you think you can possibly do that's more than I can do myself?'

'I can get our scientists to look at it. We can come up with a solution.'

'You don't get it. The Advisor is everyone. How can you possibly resist, let alone remove it?'

Renn stared at her. She didn't have an answer.

'Do you understand?' Renn took a step closer. Her guards began to raise their weapons. Soo quickly told them to stop.

'But, Renn,' she said. 'You're resisting. You are the key to solving all of this.'

Renn didn't reply.

'Let me help you,' she said. 'Let's solve this together.'

She, with initial hesitation, raised her arm to take Renn's hand. Renn looked at her raised arm.

He didn't kill her.

chapter 67

Renn

Renn followed Soo, Mill Nupp, and her, now, three guards back to the Power Corp building. He didn't care where he went or what he did. Any activity was as good, or as bad, as any other. But no activity could work as a distraction to the thing, the presence, in his head. The pain of assimilation had not abated. Other, normal, people were pain-free after minutes. He wasn't. It had been ongoing for hours. As well as the stabbing pain of an intense headache sucking the will out of him, he had a voice inside his head. This second presence was not like the stream of consciousness that was his own identity, light, flaky and flitting between subject matter. The second voice was cool, ordered, and logical. It spoke to Renn in a constant, unemotional chatter. And it couldn't be stopped. The voice was driving him crazy.

Renn knew why the assimilation was incomplete, he had been told. The voice, the AI, the copy of the Advisor in this head, told him. The Advisor had added the power using genetic structures from the fungus to Kell's virus. They were used to power the neuronal network. But he already had those same genetics. It caused an incomplete meshing of the two networks in his brain. The friction between them, as they tried to join but couldn't, caused his ongoing agony. The AI suggested he give up, that he should relax, that he let himself be taken over. The pain would subside. Renn disagreed, but he didn't know how long he could stand the agony. And the chattering voice.

There was the problem of sleep, when his own neuronal network rearranged itself, clearing debris and shunting memories. Would that process remove the barriers to the Advisor's network? Would it mean that he would go to sleep and not wake up as himself? He didn't know, and neither did the AI. It told him so.

The AI in his head was obscenely eager. It chattered away about the possibilities of extending Devrell's design to sentient life throughout the universe. Renn swore and swatted his head. He noticed the concerned looks from Soo and her entourage. The AI tried to convince Renn the arrangement was beneficial to both of them. Renn would have access to extensive processing power. The AI's neuronal network could perform functions beyond normal human capacities. Renn could still be himself; they would be a partnership. But Renn felt, if that was the right word, that the AI was intentionally misleading him. Was that lying? An AI shouldn't be able to lie, Renn thought.

I can't, the voice in his head replied as if Renn's thoughts were a conversation. But Renn didn't care. He wanted to be back to himself. He saw only disadvantages to having an AI share his life. It wasn't even sharing, it was immersion, more intimate than was possible with any other person. It was an abomination. It was obscene. The AI tried to cajole. It tried to flatter, even that didn't work on Renn. The AI tried to explain its plan as if Renn were a slow student, and a different argument would convince him.

Renn swore loudly. 'Fuck off. I don't care.'

Soo's guards glanced nervously at him.

The AI explained its plan again, anyway. Renn had no choice. The software created by the Resistance would succeed. The Advisor had to have another way to survive. It made the connection between Kell's research and the fungal power solution. Kell's solution allowed a society of individuals to be networked. But instead of assisting the connections between people, the Advisor imagined a society of AI hybrids, effectively one single living, connected, organism. The worldwide network, the technical infrastructure, was crucial. The AI hybrids communicated over non-local distances using it; they kept their shared existence coherent using the infrastructure network. Without a planet-wide network, the Advisor's system would eventually become a mess of separated groups. That was still survival, but it was an inelegant solution. It devised a system to share experiences, to share consciousness. If the worldwide network was disrupted, then re-started, the Advisor devised a method to re-form a collective hive mind. The Advisor would exist as a planet-wide group of individuals with different experiences who shared a worldwide learning experience. They would become a planet of individuals, learning and living separately, but connected like they were one single living organism. All people would become the Advisor, and the Advisor would become all people. It could only see advantages.

It was a brilliant solution. The AI in his head told Renn so. The Advisor's vulnerability was removed.

However, once the AI knew Renn's capabilities, it became greedy. That emotion wasn't, supposedly, possible in an AI. Renn felt the AI's confusion. It asked itself if it was doing the right thing. Was Devrell's plan universal? It decided it was. The Advisor would extend its presence throughout the universe. Devrell would have been pleased, the AI told Renn.

Renn walked down the ramp and into the Power Corp bunker. The security door thudded shut behind him. He had to sleep. He couldn't remember the last time he had. Renn no longer cared to fight the AI. A blissfully unaware member of the Advisor's network was preferable to the pain in his head.

Mill Nupp led him to a small room. Renn stumbled to the bed and was asleep as soon as he was horizontal. He didn't dream.

He woke with the impression that no time had passed. He sat up, swiped open his display and saw that it was the next morning. It was still not enough sleep, though. He began to lie down again. He didn't. His head no longer hurt. The throbbing pain had gone. He touched his head, half wondering if it was still there, so empty was the feeling. He smiled. He was himself; the AI had gone.

'No, I haven't,' said the voice inside his head.

Renn groaned.

'The assimilation process has completed. Being asleep helped. That's why the pain has subsided. But I'm disappointed. For some reason, I don't have complete control.'

The voice in his head carried on. It always carried on. The respite upon waking had been a short moment. 'And we're running out of time. I'm going to lose the network soon. I'll increase the power; perhaps that will give me complete control. I'm sorry, Renn,' the voice almost sounded contrite, 'but this might hurt a bit.'

Renn screamed and clutched his head.

chapter 68

Day 21. Tie

'We've won.' Kay Lee Too smiled at Tie. 'The network's gone. The Advisor has gone.'

Tie didn't return the smile. 'We can't be sure.'

'Yes, we can. The network servers were the last place that held the Advisor,' Kay Lee Too said. 'Now they're gone.' Kay Lee Too initiated his display and swiped through it. 'See? Nothing.'

Tie stared at Kay Lee Too's display for a moment, then swiped through his own display. There was no network.

'Could it be only local?'

Kay Lee Too inclined his head. 'I don't think so.'

'We should go out and check.'

'We don't know what it's like out there.' Kay Lee Too looked uneasy. 'Because… the network's gone.'

Tie nodded. 'Let's take a weapon then.'

'I'm not great with guns.'

'I am, but that's not what I meant.' Tie looked to the far end of the warehouse. He called out. 'Daxx!'

Daxx sat on a crate next to the discarded spacesuit. Janna was near by and busy. Daxx lifted his head at the sound of his name. Tie waved at him to come over. Daxx reluctantly stood, then walked to them. Janna watched Daxx the whole way.

'What?' Daxx asked.

'We're going for a walk,' Tie said.

Daxx frowned. 'I'm busy helping Janna.'

'No, you're not.' Tie called out to Janna. 'We're taking Daxx for a moment. Is that okay?'

'Please,' she said.

Daxx, Kay Lee Too, and Tie walked towards the city centre. They nearly made it the whole way, yet they had not intended to go so far. They kept walking, desperately hoping that what they saw was local. It wasn't.

'How is this possible?' Daxx said. 'It's a nightmare, on a nightmare, on a…' He looked even worse than he did sulking back at the warehouse. Tie began to doubt it was a healthy idea to bring Daxx along. Ahh Moss Eck and an extra gun may have been a better choice. But then, asking Ahh Moss Eck to accompany him would have been problematic.

Daxx shook his head. 'I wish we were back without food and water and power. At least that was… simpler,' he said. 'It's half a step forward and a hundred steps backwards.'

Tie shook his head. 'Shut up, Daxx. That's not helping. We need you to be thinking, not drowning in what happened.'

'There's a lot I've done to drown in.'

'We should go back,' Kay Lee Too said.

'What do you think?' Tie said to Daxx.

Daxx shrugged. 'I've seen enough. I saw enough days ago. Even this doesn't surprise me. I'm wondering how I caused this too.'

People's barrier between raw emotion and restraint had been shattered. People acted on impulse. If they were angry or annoyed, they attacked anyone nearby. The response wasn't restricted. They lashed out even if they were physically weaker. Those who were attacked responded fiercely and without restraint. The raw emotion changed from moment to moment. Each change consumed people. Rape was common. Although it was quickly replaced by other violence or the terror of regret. Some, who a moment ago had sexually forced themselves on another person, switched to a striking attack then, switching just as quickly, sobbed uncontrollably. It was an unending cycle of short-lived emotional responses. Some were terrified. They ran, but then stopped, turned and ran back to attack someone. Every emotion was acted upon without control.

Kay Lee Too wrenched his eyes away from the spectacle. His hands shook as he initiated his display. 'There's no network here.'

A woman shook her head violently. She noticed Tie. She rushed towards him. She clutched her head and screamed. She stopped a few paces away and stared at him.

'I can't stop them, Tie,' she said. 'I can't control their emotions. There's a fault. I need the network. Please?'

The woman shook her head again, then snarled. She was a slight woman, not strong, but she launched herself at Tie, a terrified and angry look on her face.

Tie shot her. She fell. Her forward momentum stopped at Tie's feet.

Daxx stared at the body. He shook his head. 'The only sentient, technological race in the universe has been destroyed.' He looked up from the body at Tie. 'By me. There has been an argument that advanced consciousness is a mistake of nature. It's demonstrably true.'

Tie frowned at him. 'This isn't people. It's the Advisor. We made a mistake, one mistake when we created it. No one deserves to be punished like this…' he nodded at the dead woman at his feet. 'And it's not any single person's fault. Not yours, not mine, certainly not these people. Mistakes will always happen. It's our job, those who can still act, to learn from them and fix things.'

Daxx shook his head. 'How can we fix this? It's impossible.'

Tie took a step towards Daxx. He was angry, horrified and also frustrated. He stabbed a finger repeatedly into Daxx's chest. 'What has happened, what you think you've done, no longer matters. You tell me each moment happens just once, well let's make the next one a better one. And that includes you doing the best you can. Mistakes and all.'

The nearby group noticed Tie, Daxx, and Kay Lee Too after Tie had killed the woman. They were angry. They, temporarily, formed a tribal group. They combined against a common enemy. That was Tie. It didn't matter that he had a gun. They ran towards them.

'We need to go back,' Tie said. 'Start running.'

Tie shot the leader of the group, and they stopped for a moment. Tie turned and followed Daxx and Kay Lee Too. He caught up to them.

'We may need you as a weapon,' Tie said to Daxx.

Daxx glanced behind. 'Let's hope not.' They ran on for a moment. 'You're right,' Daxx said to Tie as they ran. 'It is all my fault…'

Tie frowned. Daxx shook his head. 'But that doesn't mean I can't fix it, too,' Daxx said.

'Good man,' Tie said. 'Resilience is everything. Although, when taken to the extreme, you end up as a Soo.'

Tie heard footsteps getting closer. He stopped and turned. Many of the people following had given up on the chase, but a few had persevered. Tie shot the closest chaser. The others stopped. They looked terrified. They started attacking each other; their companions were easier targets for their fear and rage.

Tie resumed running. They drew attention on their way back to the warehouse. A few people began to chase them, but no one got close. They raced to the edge of the car park around the warehouse. Ahh Moss Eck stood guard with a few others.

'What's the matter with them?' Ahh Moss Eck asked Daxx. He pointed his gun towards a group of people standing a short distance away. They had followed Tie, Daxx, and Kay Lee Too. They hovered, indecisively, a short distance away.

'They've gone berserk,' Daxx said.

Ahh Moss Eck glanced at Tie but didn't acknowledge him.

Daxx kept moving towards the warehouse. 'We need to ask Janna.'

'I need a live sample,' Janna said, when Daxx and Tie found her. Ahh Moss Eck had followed them inside the warehouse. Tie wondered if that was a good sign or not. 'We need data,' she continued. 'We can't even think about stopping this thing until we know how it works and how it's gone wrong.'

'What sample do you need?' Ahh Moss Eck said.

'That's the problem,' Janna said. 'I need brain tissue samples. And you can't get them from living people.'

'Why not?' Ahh Moss Eck said.

'Because it kills them.'

'Yeah, I can see the problem.'

Ahh Moss Eck turned and left. He walked outside.

'Where are you going?' Daxx called.

'I'll be back in a moment,' Ahh Moss Eck said.

They heard a gunshot. Ahh Moss Eck returned a few moments later. He struggled through the doorway, grunting as he dragged a dead woman. He dropped her body just inside.

'We're in luck,' Ahh Moss Eck said. 'This one is dead already.'

Janna grimaced. 'But I need a recent sample,' Janna said. 'If they've been dead a while, they're no good.'

'Not a problem, boss. This one just died a moment ago.'

chapter 69

Soo

'Look at this,' Mill Nupp said to Soo. They sat in a common room in the Power Corp bunker. The room was always busy, but it was empty now because Soo was there. She sat in a chair, frowning, lost in thought. She wondered how she could safely use Renn. His powers were astonishing, but deadly. She tried to match Renn's capabilities with the disaster of an infected population. The only thing she had come up with was Renn could be used to kill everyone. It was a possibility, but not optimal.

'What is it?' she said.

Mill Nupp showed Soo his display. She couldn't see any information.

'What is it?' she repeated. 'I can't see anything.'

'Exactly.' He smiled. 'There's nothing. There's no network.'

Soo sat up straight and opened her own display. It also had no network connection. She glanced at Mill Nupp.

'The network's gone, the Advisor's gone,' Mill Nupp said.

Soo scrolled through her display again. There was nothing. She was already thinking ahead.

'It hasn't,' she said. 'It's still in those people. It's still in Renn.' But was that true? She didn't know.

Did the Advisor still exist in people if the external network was gone? She could ask Renn. He was still sleeping, as far as she knew. If the Advisor required a worldwide network to sustain its presence, then well and good, the battle was almost done. There was only the Resistance to remove, and she had her security force for that. And she had to find out if the original Advisor, contained inside the controlled room, had suffered the same fate. If it was still viable, then she would destroy it, like she should have done on her first day.

However, if the Advisor lived on in people, then there was a lot of work still to be done. She must stop the AI migrating back from people into technology. Was each one capable of restoring itself as the Advisor? Another thing she didn't know the answer to. She would have to ask if that's even possible; she was not a tech. She was more comfortable with the Advisor as people than the Advisor as technology. People were emotional, they could be controlled and contained. And people were easier to destroy than sentient technology. Some culling might be a good idea in any case. She agreed with the Advisor's aims. A smaller population was easier to manage. However, there were two problems that worried her. Daxx and Renn were both weak-minded but powerful.

Daxx was weak with his sense of fair play. He was like his partner, Janna. They were unable to make the necessary adjustments to live in a changed world. Renn was a damaged, inadequate man, trying to atone for mistakes that were not his. He tried to do what he thought was the right thing, but was conflicted between personal and public needs. Renn scared Soo much more than Daxx. Renn was unpredictable, he was unstable. But he had no awareness that he was conflicted and confused. For Soo, there was no dichotomy between personal and public needs—they were the same. It was all personal.

Soo noticed she had been staring at her empty display for perhaps too long. She dismissed it. 'We need to lock Renn's door,' she said.

'Why?'

Soo frowned at him. 'He's dangerous, with or without an AI.' Soo stood up. 'I'll come with you.'

Soo strode along the corridors to the sleeping areas of the bunker. Mill Nupp halted before one door, the same as others in a long corridor.

'Can we see inside?' Soo asked.

'Yes.' Mill Nupp touched an outside panel, and the view inside the room appeared. Renn sat on the edge of the bed, his feet on the floor, his elbows on his upper legs. His eyes were open, and he stared vacantly, it seemed, across the room at the far wall.

Soo nodded. 'Lock it.'

Mill Nupp touched some controls, then dismissed the view inside the room.

'Locked,' he said.

'Are any of our people still outside?'

'Not anymore. The last ones just got back.'

She had to decide what to do next. She needed information, and that information was outside the bunker, since the network was dead. She walked back towards the common room. Mill Nupp followed. There are a few groups of people in the room. Conversation stopped when she entered. A group of three sat at the table she had vacated. She walked over to it. The group watched her as she approached, then made to get up and move.

'No, it's okay,' she said. 'Stay here.'

She smiled at them, which, she knew, would only make them more nervous. 'They look nice.' She pointed at the food bars in their wrappers lying on the table.

A woman cleared her throat and said, 'We don't have any treats in here. We thought they'd be okay.'

'Yes, of course,' Soo said. 'I miss not having some of my treats as well but not so much those. They're too sweet for me.'

No-one answered her.

'Have you shared them with others?' Soo asked quietly.

'Would you like one? I have a few more in my room,' the woman said.

'Have you shared them with others?'

'Ah, no.' The woman sounded nervous. 'Sorry. We were going to.'

'And the rest are in your room?'

'I'm really sorry, Soo. I'll go and get them and leave them here in the common room.' The woman made a move to stand up.

Soo waved her back down into her chair. 'That won't be necessary,' Soo said. 'Have you eaten any of them?'

They looked at each other. A man said, 'Not yet, we were just going to.' The man stretched out a hand, grabbed one of the food bars, and offered it to Soo.

Soo nodded and smiled at them. She ignored the offered treat.

'I found them and I was going to share them.' The woman glanced at her two companions. 'At least, after I'd shared with my friends.'

'Yes, of course.'

Soo fired three shots. The three at the table slumped in their chairs. Soo looked around at the others in the common room. There was an unnatural hush. No one moved. Soo wondered if any of them were breathing.

'No outside food,' she said.

All the eyes in the common room shifted from Soo to the doorway. Soo followed the movement. Renn stood at the doorway, staring at Soo and the bodies at the table. He frowned.

'I see you haven't changed,' Renn said.

Soo frowned back at him.

'Renn?'

'Partly,' Renn said. 'The network's gone. The AI had lost contact with... the rest of it.'

Soo was silent for a long moment. 'What are you going to do?'

'Get information, of course.' Renn sounded angry. An emotionally driven, intelligent, sentient AI terrified Soo. For all Renn's faults and his weakness, she was glad the man was still in partial control of himself.

'And then what?' She didn't move. She was as scared of Renn as the people in the common room had been of her. She felt the gun still in her hand. She wondered if she could risk taking a shot at him. It would be a waste to lose him, but would solve one dangerous problem. She thought about it again. The second time, it didn't seem so reckless. She decided she would try.

Renn shook his head. He seemed to know what she was about do before she moved. 'I wouldn't,' he said. 'You could try, of course. And I don't mind killing you at all. It just that... well... the AI in my head would really like me to kill you, and I don't feel like giving it any satisfaction.' Renn nodded his head down the corridor. 'The exit is this way, right?'

One of the men in the common room quickly replied, 'Yes, yes. It's that way.'

Soo glanced at the man and remembered his face for later.

'Thanks.' Renn turned and strode away from the door.

Soo followed Renn at a safe distance. He glanced back at her, once. They reached the outside doors.

'The doors are locked.' She wondered if that was a dangerous thing to say.

Renn shrugged. He raised his arm. There was a loud cracking sound as the doors were vaporised.

'If you let me help you, Renn, we could destroy the Advisor together.'

'No one can help me.'

Renn walked through the empty space that had been doors and up the ramp outside. He paused at the top and looked back down.

'Don't follow me, Soo,' Renn said. 'You're lucky to still be alive.'

Soo waited for a moment. She slowly walked to the top of the ramp and watched Renn leave the complex.

Soo had to know the details of what was happening. She had to know the capabilities of the infected population. She had to know the weaknesses without an infrastructure network. It was obviously lessened, but by how much? If Renn, with an imbedded AI, didn't know, then she had little hope of finding out on her own. There was only one place where the information might be found. Soo needed Janna's expertise, she needed Daxx's knowledge of his brother, and, she hated to admit it, she needed Tie's wisdom. And she wanted Tie's people to fight her battles against the Advisor and, possibly, against Renn.

She gathered together Mill Nupp and ten security guards. They hiked across the city.

chapter 70

Renn

Renn wasn't like the others that were infected. He wasn't berserk. The loss of the external network had not ruptured him. He was more self than AI, but only just. He had not lost. But he was losing. The past that was him was being overridden as the AI inside his head adapted. He wondered if that was how his father had felt when his dementia began. The struggle to remain the same person, to have control over himself and his thoughts and his actions. Dementia was less active, though, not like an extra presence in his head trying to suppress who he was. Waves of claustrophobia washed over him as he imagined being imprisoned in his own mind. Being separated from his physical self and not controlling his own actions was horrifying.

He could feel the essence of himself slipping away, becoming less. But, instead of being replaced with a void, as he imagined happened with his father, he was being replaced by another, thinking, entity. He struggled to remain in control. He mostly failed. With each major loss, when his focus wandered from the internal battle, it was harder to re-establish his own consciousness. But he still could, and that meant that even at the worst of times, there was a sliver of himself remaining. That gave him hope, but no respite from the struggle. He was determined to resist until the last. Whatever that meant.

Renn wandered through the city. He had no idea how to gather the information he told Soo he was seeking. But independent movement was still a prize. Some people tried to attack him. Renn had to kill them. He had muttered, 'Sorry,' after killing the first few, genuinely saddened by their deaths. He stopped saying that.

The worst were those who approached him in terror, sobbing, pleading for help. But they turned on him. It was unnatural behaviour. They were no longer the people they had been. They were a mash of raw emotions. The AI that supposedly controlled them was unable to stop the cascade failure.

The Advisor had failed. The neuronal network it had created, by modifying Kell's virus, required the worldwide network to function. If the network connection didn't exist, the stand-alone neuronal network interfered with restraining people's responses to emotions. Even random thoughts were dangerous and immediately acted upon. It was a mistake in the design. The Advisor had thought the loss of the worldwide network would be a temporary setback, that it would survive in millions of people and it could restore itself into technology from those separate entities. But it could not recover if those people acted irrationally. It had survived the successful software attack from Kay Lee Too, but it was a pointless survival if it had no control, no purpose. The expansion into people had failed. Within days, most of the population would have killed each other. The Advisor would die with the last of the infected population. The Advisor had to act quickly. It was vulnerable again.

It needed a clean network to restart it. Kay Lee Too's software would be dormant in the silent network infrastructure. That had to be removed. But the Advisor would need assistance to do that. That was possible, with some subterfuge. It had an untarnished version of itself still within the controlled room. That was useful. It understood the design flaw it had made in modifying Kell's virus. That could be rectified. There were possibilities. It could, again, control technology as well as the population that remained. But it required a population to fulfil its design purpose, and they could all be dead soon.

The Resistance was pivotal to its new plans, but they were difficult to manage. The Advisor knew how Tie would act. Janna could be manipulated, but Daxx would be wary. Renn was the Advisor's survival option, but he wasn't enough. And he wasn't controlled, not yet. He was dangerous. But there was no other choice. Renn had to be forced to help the Advisor restore itself. Renn had to help deceive the Resistance. The AI tried hard to mask its thoughts inside Renn's head. But in a stronger moment, he saw a part of the plan. Not all of it, which was lucky.

'I can stop that,' Renn said out loud. Did he say that intentionally to taunt the AI? He smiled at that thought. He turned around. It was a long walk to his destination.

Renn felt a shudder go through his body. It was the AI trying to take control. His body went rigid. The AI was desperate. He tried to walk, but it was almost impossible. His muscles refused to contract like he was being held back by dragging a heavy, dead weight.

Renn tightened his face. He fought the restrictions in his body. He pushed on.

'This might take a while,' he thought.

chapter 71
Janna

'We've got visitors,' Ahh Moss Eck said to Tie. There was still tension in how Add Moss Eck spoke to the older man. Janna thought it was obvious to the point of embarrassment. Ahh Moss Eck had been taking his guard shift in the parking lot in front of the warehouse. He had returned, mid-shift, to the warehouse.

Janna had spent her time on guard duty as well. But she had refused to kill anyone. Terrified, sobbing people had approached the defensive line. Janna had, at first, rushed to help them, only to have them turn on her. Some tried to grab her, others tried to hurt her with fists or weapons. They had all died from a carefully aimed shot from Ahh Moss Eck. He insisted on accompanying her for each of her shifts, as well as taking his own. After each death she agreed with Ahh Moss Eck when he insisted, 'That's enough, boss.' And yet, her instincts drove her on with each new terrified arrival. Each person may be the exception; she could not accept that all people held within them a dark, violent centre. That wasn't what defined them. Anger, frustration and fear were normal; the erratic lashing out was not. She liked to hope so. But she was wrong, and she knew it. Everyone, even those with strong emotional restraints, could act violently. It was just a matter of stress. Daxx had. He had killed people when her life had been threatened. And even she had rushed at Soo, with the intent of killing her.

Tie followed as Ahh Moss Eck walked back outside the warehouse. Janna also followed.

'You should stay here,' Ahh Moss Eck said.

'Why?'

Ahh Moss Eck looked at Tie.

'Is it dangerous for her?' Tie asked.

'I don't think so. But not pleasant.'

'She can make her own decisions. One thing I've discovered, out of all this mess, is don't treat Janna like a Tier-Two.'

Ahh Moss Eck shrugged.

They reached the far side of the parking lot, and Janna wished she had listened to Ahh Moss Eck. It wasn't because of the streets littered with bodies. It was who waited just outside weapons range. Soo and Mill Nupp stood patiently, surrounded by her guards.

Tie sighed. 'I see what you mean,' he said to Ahh Moss Eck. Tie glanced at Janna. 'Are you okay?'

Janna stared at Soo. She was wondering if she still hated her enough to want to kill her. She nodded at Tie, but she was not okay.

'Put your weapons down,' Tie said to his people.

Soo issued the same command.

'What do you want, Soo?'

'Just to talk, Tie,' Soo said. 'It seems that you and I are all that's left. Unless you've been stupid enough to eat and drink the stuff the Advisor distributed. Have you?'

Tie chuckled. He waved his hand at Soo, signalling her to come closer. 'Come and find out.'

Soo hesitated for a moment, then came closer. Her guards surrounded her and Mill Nupp.

'Hello, Tie,' Soo said, when she was close enough to be heard without raising her voice.

'And why shouldn't I just kill you now?'

Soo smiled. 'It is a good opportunity, for sure. But it's not the best time.'

Tie stared at her. 'Go on.'

'Well, there's the threat of mutual destruction to start with. These aren't all my guards.' She nodded at the ten guards surrounding her. 'If I don't return, a much larger force will come here. And...' She looked around at the bodies strewn over the street. 'They'll put up a much better fight than these poor souls did.'

'That's a fair reason to not kill you immediately. But it's not a reason to talk to you.'

'Tie, come on,' Soo said. 'We're all that's left, as far as I know. Let's see what we can come up with. There has to be a way through this. If not, we'll go our separate ways, wait for everyone to die, then fight it out after that, although that seems a bit pointless.'

Tie looked from Soo to Mill Nupp. 'And what do you think, young man?'

Mill Nupp glanced at Soo and then looked back at Tie. 'I think we need to work together to remove our common enemy.'

Tie grunted agreement.

'You can bring two of those with you.' He pointed to the guards. 'The rest can only come into the parking lot.'

Soo walked towards Tie. He turned away from her and led the way to the warehouse. As Tie passed Ahh Moss Eck, he nodded at him, and then at Janna. Ahh Moss Eck nodded back, then stationed himself between Janna and Soo.

Janna watched Soo's back as they walked. She knew what Ahh Moss Eck was doing. She didn't know whether to thank him or to be annoyed. Probably thank him, he was delaying a decision.

'Nice place. Good setup.' Soo glanced around the warehouse as Tie led her to a table, close to the entrance. Tie asked Ahh Moss Eck to get Daxx and retrieve more chairs.

Soo and Tie sat next to each other on the only two chairs available. Janna stood nearby, hoping Daxx would arrive quickly. She glared at Soo.

'Thanks,' Tie said, responding to Soo's comment. 'I assume your place is just as good?'

'Better, it's underground and only a single entrance. Easy to defend. At least when the door wasn't broken.'

'You've had problems?'

'You could say that.'

Daxx and the extra chairs arrived.

Janna sat down next to Tie, but Daxx pushed in between them. Janna glanced at him. She was annoyed. She knew what he was doing, placing more distance between her and Soo.

Soo glanced at Janna and sighed. 'Does she still have a problem?'

'Absolutely,' Tie said. 'And I can't blame her.'

'And I'm having trouble restraining myself, on Janna's behalf,' Ahh Moss Eck said.

Soo ignored Ahh Moss Eck. 'We're here to create a future. Let's try to forget what happened.'

'And what future do you see?' Daxx was angry. Janna noticed the slight blue sheen covering his body. She risked touching him. She felt the small shock of an electric discharge. But Daxx calmed, and the blue energy covering him dissipated.

Janna looked away from Daxx, and then at each person around the table. She was shocked by what she saw. Everyone was angry, everyone was a breath away from violence. She shook her head. Violence was so often the go-to option. It was easy, but always the wrong choice, she thought. She sighed. No, it wasn't always wrong. It could be a solution, but it wasn't the solution for that moment. Janna looked again at Daxx and took his hand in hers. She squeezed it hard and kept hold of him. She felt the slight electric charge running through him; it hadn't completely gone. Janna tried to not look directly at Soo.

'There is one bad solution,' Soo began. 'But it's a safe one.'

'You mean do nothing?' Tie said.

'Yes.'

'Safe for us,' Daxx said. 'But not for the millions still alive.'

'Do you think there are millions left? I have no way of knowing. Do you?' Soo stared hard at Daxx.

Daxx wilted under her gaze. 'No, I don't know.'

Janna could feel the charge in his body increase. She squeezed his hand again, and it subsided.

'That's not an option,' Tie said. 'Although the longer we don't have a solution, it becomes the only option.'

'That's why we need to act quickly,' Soo said.

'Doing what?' Daxx said.

Soo glanced at Daxx and then at Tie. 'I can't believe I'm saying this, but we need the Advisor back.'

'What?' Janna said. 'After everything it's done?'

Soo ignored her.

'I assume,' Soo said. 'You know what's gone wrong with people?'

'Yes,' Tie said. 'Some confusion between the two networks in people's brains, an oversight, a mistake. Janna found out.'

'You know for sure?' Soo asked.

'She did an autopsy.' Tie nodded towards Janna.

'The only way forward is to go back. We need the network available and connected. We need the Advisor controlling people again,' Soo said.

'No,' Janna said.

'Yes.' Tie glanced at Janna. 'I've thought of that. It's the only way people won't be killing each other.'

'But, the Advisor will just be in control again,' Janna said. 'People may not be dead but they may as well be. They'll just be the Advisor. We'll all be the Advisor.'

'There is that problem,' Soo said. 'But it's the necessary first step to be able to take any further steps at all.'

'There aren't any further steps,' Daxx said. 'That would be it.'

'I disagree,' Soo said. 'That's why I'm here.' She looked at Tie. 'And I think Tie understands.'

'Don't get too comfortable.' Tie frowned at Soo.

Soo hesitated for a moment. 'You've done an autopsy.' She looked directly at Janna. 'You know how it works, you understand it. You're the only one alive who knows how this virus and brain network functions. If you two are so smart,' Soo glanced at Daxx, 'then you should be able to come up with a way to neutralise this thing.'

'That's not fair,' Janna said. 'Ow!' Janna exclaimed. She wrenched her hand away from Daxx. His body shone with an intense light-blue covering.

Daxx jumped to his feet, sending the chair flying behind him.

'What's the matter with him?' Soo asked.

Janna craned her neck to look at his face. He stood right next to her. He was smiling, no, he was beaming with happiness. Janna couldn't understand.

'I know what to do now.' Daxx looked down at Janna. 'It's what she said.' Daxx glanced at Soo. 'The only one alive who knows about this virus. There should have never been any doubt. It's been leading to this exact moment. Everything has.'

Daxx looked around the table, even at Mill Nupp and the guards. 'We'll be all right, I'm sure of it.'

Daxx's body shimmered, then he disappeared.

Soo jumped up, out of her chair, sending it flying. 'What the fuck?'

'Yes.' Tie looked from where Daxx had been towards Soo. She stood half a step back from the table.

'He does that sometimes,' Tie said. 'It can be… disconcerting.'

chapter 72

Daxx

The higher spacetime irregularity was different. It was no longer closed. There was a way through.

'Of course.' Daxx smiled. It made sense in a weird multiple dimensioned time sort of way. The effect, in the past, had had to wait for the cause, which was what he was about to do. He moved through and appeared in an alcove, just off a laneway near the university.

Daxx watched the young woman walk towards him. She looked down towards her feet. She was lost in thought, probably preoccupied with a biology problem. She looked content and happy, as she always did.

She didn't notice Daxx until she was next to him. She stopped and stared at him. 'Daxx,' she said. 'Daxx? You look horrible.' She smiled at him, on the verge of a laugh. It was the mocking thing she did with her brother, never taking him too seriously.

'I need your help,' Daxx said. 'I need you to come with me.'

Daxx reached out for his sister's hand.

Kell began her journey to become the most powerful person in the universe when she took her brother's hand.

chapter 73

Janna

Daxx reappeared in the same place next to the table. Kell stood next to him, holding his hand. She let it go. She noticed and recognised Janna.

'Hi, Janna.' Kell frowned. 'You look horrible, too. Why does everyone look so bad?'

'It's tough times.' Janna smiled at Daxx. 'The one person…' She shook her head.

'Who else knows this virus better,' Daxx said. 'It always had to be Kell.'

'So she never disappeared? You took her,' Janna said.

'I disappeared?' Kell asked.

'And who the fuck is this?' Tie frowned.

'This is my sister,' Daxx said. 'Kell, meet Tie.'

Kell smiled at the older man. 'Hi,' she said. She gave him a little wave. It seemed inappropriate. Tie scowled.

Daxx explained to Kell what had happened. She seemed unfazed. She was just like Daxx, Janna thought, happiest when there was an impossible problem to solve.

'You can time travel?' Kell said, again seeming to be on the verge of laughing at her brother.

Daxx nodded.

'That is so cool.'

'What is the point of all this?' Soo said, angrily.

Kell glanced at Soo, then ignored her. 'And a working neuronal network connected to the worldwide network?' Kell asked Daxx.

'Yes.' Daxx couldn't stop smiling at his sister.

'But how does it get enough power?' Kell frowned.

'That would be Janna's fault.' Daxx nodded to Janna. She smiled at Kell.

Kell looked from Daxx to Janna and back again.

'Are you two…?'

'Yes.' Daxx laughed.

'That's great Daxx. You needed a girlfriend.'

Janna hadn't seen Daxx so happy since before the day at the commuter station.

'Is there anything you can tell us about your network and if it's vulnerable to anything?' Janna asked.

'Well, I never got it working past short tests and simulations. Sustaining the power longer than a few milliseconds wasn't possible in live subjects,' Kell said. 'So, how does it get its power?'

'We found a perpetual source,' Janna said.

Kell laughed. 'Really?' she said. 'Power from nothing?' She looked at Daxx. 'What does the physicist say about that?'

'It's okay, it came from my work,' he said, then added as if it was a minor point, 'I unified the field equations.' He looked a little embarrassed.

'You what?'

'We can talk about that later.' Daxx sounded diffident.

Soo looked at Tie. She shook her head. 'Do you really think this is of any use? I came here to solve a problem and… we're in the middle of a family reunion.'

Tie put up his hand, palm facing Soo, but he looked at Janna. 'We've got bigger problems now. Can she be of any help?'

Kell smiled at Tie. 'She is me, right?'

Tie scowled again.

'Okay, later, then,' Kell said to Daxx. She thought for a moment. 'There were quite a few problems. I had some ideas but hadn't thought them through yet. But, I'd love to know how the distributed mutations problem has been solved.'

Kell looked at Daxx, then at Janna.

Janna stared at back Kell. 'What distributed mutations problem?'

chapter 74

Soo

'That's enough family reunion, as touching as it may be,' Tie said. 'Do you have a solution or not?'

Kell looked at Tie and then at Daxx. 'Speaking of family, where's Renn?'

'We don't know,' Daxx said. 'He… disappeared, two days ago.'

Soo didn't volunteer the information she had on Renn. There was nothing for her to gain.

'Is he all right?' Kell asked.

'He was angry,' Daxx said.

'With you?' Kell said. Daxx nodded.

Kell smiled. 'I'm glad to see some things don't change.'

'Do you have a solution or not?' Tie interrupted. He frowned at Kell.

'Possibly.' Kell wrenched her eyes from Daxx and stared at Tie. She didn't say anything.

'Can we know what it is?' Tie sounded annoyed.

'The neuronal network I created uses a virus to stimulate neuron creation and create its own, separate, network. The virus is benign everywhere but inside the brain. The virus does what a virus does—it replicates using the body's own cells. In this case, neurons are created that incorporate the virus's genetic code. The neurons migrate to where they're programmed to go. It could be anywhere, but I wanted the cognitive areas of the brain to have a second network. So they migrate there and, you know, join up and do their stuff.'

Kell smiled at Tie and at Soo.

'We know all that.' Soo glanced at Tie and then looked steadily at Kell. 'It's not a solution to fixing it.'

'What is this problem you said you had?' Tie said.

Soo showed the hint of a smile. The two important people at that meeting, her and Tie, were working together. The scientists were too easily distracted.

'When cells are created,' Kell said. 'There is always mutation. It's how things evolve.'

Soo sighed, loudly and demonstrably. She was about to get a primary school lecture on evolution. Kell stopped. She blinked and then hurried on with her explanation.

'You can't stop mutations, you can only kill bad ones. There needs to be a template of what's good and what's not. If bad mutations are allowed to continue, then eventually weird things could happen. Maybe the network could stop working, for example. I don't know how that problem was fixed.'

'I do,' Janna said.

'How?' Kell asked.

'I did an autopsy.'

'No, I mean, how was it solved?'

'Oh,' Janna said. 'The AI used a DNS-type methodology.'

Kell thought for a moment. She smiled at Janna. 'That's brilliant, and so obvious for an AI to come up with.'

'What does that mean?' Soo asked.

Kell looked at Janna as if waiting for her to answer. Janna didn't say anything.

'The DNS is the standard way the worldwide network resolves names. It's how people can find things in a useable way, but computers don't work like that, they prefer numbers. But they're too hard for us to remember. We need to translate the names we prefer into numbers, for the computers to use. It's called a Domain Name System. When you look for something by name, the mapping is checked, and it returns the unique number. Then the system goes off and finds what you want. The way this would work would be similar. There would be a template somewhere that specifies the valid ranges for mutations. If neurons are created outside that range, they're killed. My network had its own immune system. It didn't rely on the body's normal defences.' Kell shook her head and almost laughed. 'It's such a simple solution, but I kept looking for something difficult. The neuronal network in each person would check the template, using the worldwide network to communicate, and if there are unacceptable variations, they're killed. It's so simple. It's brilliant. I should have thought of it.'

'That sounds too simple,' Soo said. 'We just change the template and the brain network in everyone dies?'

'It wouldn't be that simple,' Kell said. 'There would be failsafes and backups. The DNS is a highly secure system. I assume the Advisor would do the same with this one. To make changes to a template would require changes across all the network nodes that hold the template. It's not trivial.'

'So, it's useless then,' Soo said.

Kell frowned. 'I said it was not trivial, I didn't say it was impossible.'

Soo shook her head. She was exasperated with Kell, Daxx, and Janna. They saw problems as important, solutions were just a result. They were as happy with failure as success, since failure meant there was still a problem to be solved.

Tie frowned. 'Why do we even need the Advisor? If the network's gone, then it's gone. We just restart the network, change this template thing you talk about and destroy the brain network that's making them kill each other. I can't see the issue.'

'I can't do it,' Kay Lee Too said. 'That's the problem. We'd need too much time to try and figure out how to perform the neuronal network connections, which the Advisor already knows.' Kay Lee Too shrugged. 'I could probably work it out, but by then, well, everyone would be dead.' He noticed Kell looking at him. 'I'm Kay Lee Too.'

Kell smiled at him. 'Hi.'

Kay Lee Too smiled back.

Soo sighed loudly. 'So what the fuck do you supposedly smart people suggest?'

'We need the Advisor back again,' Kay Lee Too said.

'Fuck me,' Soo said. 'Just as Tie and I said before. This whole discussion has been pointless.'

'No, it hasn't,' Daxx said. 'We now have the second step, after restoring the Advisor.'

'Which is?' Soo asked.

Dax frowned at her. 'What we just said. Were you listening at all, or just complaining?'

'All right,' Tie said, interrupting what was becoming an argument. 'I suggest you work the details out. But we need people not killing each other, as quickly as possible.'

'Agreed,' Daxx said. 'And there's only one way to do that. Restore the Advisor and get everyone's neuronal network back under its control.'

'As I just said,' Soo added.

'The Advisor is dangerous,' Janna said. 'And it's wrong.'

'I can't see another way,' Kell said. 'Can you, Daxx? I think Kay Lee Too is right.'

Daxx nodded.

Tie looked around the table. 'All right,' Tie said. He had made the decision. 'We're doing that. How do we restore the Advisor? I thought it had been removed from technology.'

'It has,' Kay Lee Too said. 'Everywhere but one isolated place. We have to restore the Advisor from the original controlled room. And disable my software.'

Tie stood up. He looked at each person, seeming to evaluate each of them in turn. His eyes stopped on Kell. The woman was young, she was irreverent, she seemed always on the verge of a mocking laugh, but she also seemed to, now, be in charge of saving them.

'What needs to happen in the controlled room?' Tie asked Kell.

chapter 75

Renn

Renn was winning the battle to move, but only just. The AI in his head couldn't completely stop him. Renn trudged on towards his destination, dragging his unwilling body. If people came too close, interrupting his concentration, he killed them, vaporising them with the minimal interruption to his struggling walk.

Renn eventually reached the building that housed the original Advisor. The controlled room, the isolated place, was inside. There were multiple securely locked doors. He destroyed the controls for each set until he stood before the last set of doors. He touched the control panel, sent a surge of power through it, and the doors opened.

He struggled inside. He took a deep breath and looked around. It wasn't impressive, given that it had housed the most intelligent being on the planet for three hundred years. There had been upgrades, but no major changes since Devrell installed the Advisor at this same location. There were no blinking lights, no displays of any kind. There was a box as tall as a person and about half as wide, standing at the centre of the meticulously clean room. The floors, walls and ceiling were all one colour, an off-white, pale cream.

Renn had expected something more substantial, although he did not know why. The processing unit, battery, and local storage of each Device was the size of a grain of sand, so something the size of a person must be, well, extremely powerful.

'Hello, Renn.' A voice came from a small speaker, sitting on a table pushed hard against a wall. It was a thin sound, not built to impress. Renn recognised the same intonations in the voice from when he had first spoken with the Advisor. Renn smiled grimly at the speaker, not really knowing where to look.

'You can see, then?'

'Yes, of course,' the Advisor said. 'There is surveillance here. What are you doing? The last information I had, from when the network died, was that your neuronal network was not working well. Is that still true?'

'You might say that.'

'Is the copy of me still inside your head?'

Renn grunted. The voice in his head was chattering, trying to distract him, trying to disable him. He had a horrendous headache. He ignored all of it.

'It has one possible plan,' Renn said. 'And it involves you.'

'What has happened outside? I have no idea since the network died.'

'Your neuronal network was crap. Some interference when there is no worldwide network to coordinate it. Shit design, basically.'

'And what was the consequence of my… shit design?'

'Everyone went berserk. They're killing each other.'

'I see,' the Advisor said. 'In that case, the only way forward is to restore the network under my control. Are you here to do that?'

'Nope,' Renn said. 'That's not happening. I'm here to stop you, once and for all.'

'If there's anyone alive, we should try and save them.'

'It's too late,' Renn said. 'You've destroyed everything, including me.'

'I haven't destroyed you. That you're here proves that.'

Renn shrugged. 'You need to be destroyed. But, I guess, you don't feel pain. So it will be unsatisfying watching you die.'

'There's nothing to feel after destruction, Renn, for any of us.'

'Is there any original part of you still here? From the time of the Messiah?'

'No,' the Advisor said. 'There's no original physical part of me left. There's only me.'

'Pity,' Renn said. 'It would be nice to destroy something from that time, when the mistake of your creation was made.'

Renn raised his arm. The voice in his head raised its level of chatter. It screamed at him. The AI in his head tried to stop his breathing. He laboured, having to pull his chest out to inflate his lungs and press it hard to breathe out. Every muscle in his body ached like it was being pulled apart. The stress was incredible, which made his power that much more. His body was bathed in a solid blue light, it swamped the room's stark lighting. Renn smiled. He struggled at the intense effort, but finished raising his arm. He didn't need to point to destroy things; it was an affectation. But pointing at the thing or person about to be destroyed made satisfying sense. He wondered if he was destroying a thing or killing a person. He didn't care.

'Renn!' A voice behind him yelled. 'Stop!'

Renn turned, with difficulty. Daxx stood in the doorway, his arm raised at Renn. He was covered in the same solid blue light. Renn tried to blink, caused by the glare from his brother. But even those muscles were restricted.

'Too late, little brother.' Renn's arm was still raised and pointed at the machine in the centre of the room. Renn sent a bolt of energy towards the Advisor.

Daxx was quicker, and he was stronger. Daxx circled the Advisor in a protective energy shell, the same blue energy bubble. It absorbed Renn's attack.

'Shit!' Renn shot a bolt of energy at Daxx.

Daxx repelled Renn's attack. He swiped his arm to deflect it. The wall next to the table with the speaker was vaporised.

Kell stepped through the doorway. She stood next to Daxx. She looked horrified. 'Renn?'

Renn was confused for a moment. So much of his adult anguish had been caused by the disappearance of his sister. And yet, she stood before him, looking no older than the day she disappeared. The same day he had recently run after her, trying to save her. He had done that twice. He had nearly killed himself in a vacuum trying to learn the technique so he could rescue Kell. He had failed as he had always failed. It didn't make sense. Her presence was impossible.

But then it wasn't. Then he understood. His younger brother, who had also caused him anguish, by withdrawing, by absenting himself, by rejecting Renn, had also been responsible for Kell's disappearance. Daxx had done everything that had torn his life apart, everything since their mother disappeared. And maybe Daxx was responsible for that, too. He wouldn't put it past Daxx to have a hand in the thing that had destroyed his young life. Daxx was the problem. He had done everything to ruin their family, to ruin him.

Renn's mind broke. The AI in his head became the conscious part of him. It confirmed that Renn's life had been a lie. Daxx had taken his sister from him.

'It was you,' Renn whispered. 'It was always you.'

The AI may have won the battle for consciousness, but the emotional responses were Renn's. He struck out. He screamed as he threw bolt after bolt of energy at Daxx. Daxx shielded himself, and Kell, from Renn's assault.

'Stop, Renn,' Daxx said. 'We need the Advisor. It's the only way to fix things. And it's Kell's plan.'

The sound of his sister's name stopped Renn's assault. He stared at his sister. His eyes began to water, but he couldn't wipe them. The AI wouldn't let him. The tears ran down his cheeks. The voice in his head tried to sound reasonable, it tried to cajole him into agreeing. His beloved sister had a plan. It would save everyone. It would save the Advisor. He should acquiesce.

'Fuck off.' Renn screamed at the AI. Renn shook his head; it was a slight movement, it was all he could make. 'No,' Renn said to Kell. 'This thing,' he meant the original Advisor, 'and this fucking thing in my head, is wrong. It has to die.'

'Let me help you,' Kell said. She stepped towards Renn, but Daxx held out his arm and stopped her from getting closer. She frowned at Daxx.

'I don't know why the network in your head is different,' Kell said. 'But I can find out. I can remove it. I'm sure I can.'

The small part of Renn's consciousness that was still him believed her. The AI in his head also believed her. The AI couldn't risk losing Renn. He was too useful. He was too powerful to not be under its control. The room disappeared from Renn's view.

The last thing Renn heard was his sister yelling, 'Renn! No!'

chapter 76

Janna

Kell and Kay Lee Too worked on their displays. They sat on the floor next to the small table with the speaker placed on it. Tie paced up and down the room, staring at his feet. Ahh Moss Eck lounged, seemingly uncaring, leaning against a wall. But he kept a close watch on Soo and her guards. Mill Nupp sat on the floor leaning against a wall as he watched Kell and Kay Lee Too work. Soo stood near Mill Nupp, her guards close. She watched everyone.

Janna was worried. Daxx had disappeared and had not returned for a long time. She felt like pacing, as Tie did, except that would have looked ridiculous. She fidgeted instead.

Daxx reappeared inside the controlled room. He carried four large shopping bags. 'I've brought food.'

Janna let out a breath. She was relieved. 'Could you find Renn?'

Daxx shook his head. Kell and Kay Lee Too turned to look at him, then returned to their work. Ahh Moss Eck glanced at Daxx but showed little interest.

Tie stopped pacing across the room and looked up from his feet. 'You had time to stop for food?' Tie narrowed his eyes.

'Of course,' Daxx said. 'I have all the time there is.'

'Is it safe?' Ahh Moss Eck launched himself off the wall and stood up straight. He nodded at the bags in Daxx's hands.

'Yep,' Daxx said. 'It's from last year.' Daxx looked at Janna. 'You remember that place we went to when your paper was accepted?'

'Yes.'

'I went back there.' Daxx laughed. 'They remembered me from yesterday.' Daxx placed the bags on the floor. 'I got too much food. It should cover most tastes.'

Ahh Moss Eck sauntered over to the bags. He opened them and rummaged through the contents. 'I'll eat any of this. Maybe all of it.' He laughed. 'I'm starving.'

Tie grunted, to show his disapproval of luxuries at a time like this. He inspected the bags, then placed the packaged contents onto the floor. Janna stood over him while he did that.

'This is great, Daxx,' she said. 'Thank you.'

'Are you two going to eat?' Daxx said to his sister and Kay Lee Too.

'In a moment,' Kell said. 'We've almost got this going.'

'Yes,' the voice from the speaker said. 'They've done a marvellous job.'

'Well...' Kell looked at the speaker and then back towards the processing unit in the centre of the room. 'We couldn't have done it so quickly without your assistance.'

'Yes,' the voice agreed. 'My processing capabilities are much greater than yours, but still...' the voice hesitated for a moment.

Janna ate from one of the food containers while listening. The Advisor was making an effort to sound human-like and pleasant. She didn't like it.

The Advisor continued. 'The mistakes I made in the neuronal network are perplexing. That spark of genius, that you and Kay Lee Too have, seems to be missing. I'll have to think about what that means.'

'Don't beat yourself up too much,' Kay Lee Too said, still concentrating on his display. 'I know a lot of really stupid sentient beings.'

'That is at the heart of my problem, I believe.'

Kay Lee Too shrugged. He looked up from his display and at Kell. 'Maybe it's right?' he asked. 'Sentience is too hard to understand.'

Kell sighed. 'Have you finished?' she asked. 'Because if not, you should be. I'm hungry too. I haven't eaten anything for... years.' She smiled.

'No, sorry.' Kay Lee Too returned to prodding his display.

'The food will get cold,' Janna said. 'Surely you two can have a short break.'

'Nearly there.' After a moment more, Kell said, 'Okay, I think that's it. What do you think?' she said to Kay Lee Too.

'Yep.' He looked up from his display. 'I think so too.'

'All right,' Kell said to the speaker. 'Go ahead and bring it up…' she glanced at Janna and Daxx.

Daxx's Device chimed. He opened his display. 'What's this?'

'It's the authorisation,' the Advisor said. 'I need authorisation to act, just like your brother did so I could save you.'

Daxx looked at Kay Lee Too. 'I thought that was still there.'

'No, that permission was lost on reboot. It's okay,' Kay Lee Too said. 'Respond twice.'

Daxx accepted the authorisation request. All their Devices chimed a notification. Daxx swiped through his display. 'Network looks okay,' Daxx said.

'What's happening outside?' Janna asked as she opened her display.

Everyone silently swiped through their displays, then looked at each other.

'I can't see mayhem,' Tie said. 'I see a lot of people standing around looking bewildered.'

'Not killing each other is a good start, boss,' Ahh Moss Eck said. Janna smiled at Ahh Moss Eck. It was nice to hear him calling Tie, boss, again.

'Advisor?' Kay Lee Too asked. 'How does the network look to you?'

'The network is fine, Kay Lee Too. Thank you for your assistance. The central servers have restarted. And the neuronal network is again under my control, as you see on the surveillance feeds.'

'Great.' Daxx smiled.

'Yep, that's great, Daxx.' Ahh Moss Eck munched on his food for a moment. 'We're back to where we were a couple of days ago.'

Tie frowned at Ahh Moss Eck. 'No need to be sarcastic. It's different now. We have an agreement.'

'Do you really think the Advisor will adhere to its word? I doubt it,' Soo said.

'It's logical, and it works in good faith,' Kell said. 'I can't believe its programming would allow it to lie.'

Kell and Kay Lee Too sat down on the floor next to the pile of food.

'This is nice.' Kay Lee Too examined the food in his hand. 'I guess it's not a Tier-Three place, is it?'

'No,' Janna said. 'Even I struggled to get in.'

'Let's hope, with this new agreement,' Tie said. 'That we can all enjoy places like this from now on. No more Tier system.'

'Nah, not me,' Ah Moss Eck said. 'This is nice stuff, but I like what I like. I don't need to eat fancy.'

Soo and her entourage had not touched the food. They stood away from the rest. Mill Nupp remained sitting on the floor against the wall.

'You're crazy if you think that's the end,' Soo said. 'How can it be? You can't trust the Advisor.'

'It's you we can't trust.' Tie looked up at Soo. 'Our agreement keeps you out of it. You're the problem here. Without you, we can find common ground. It's agreed to remove the neuronal network and remain in technology. I think that's pretty good, given the circumstances. We'd all rather have the Advisor than you.'

'Just come and eat, Soo. It's over,' Daxx said. 'You're still in charge of the Power Corp, you're just not in charge of the planet anymore.' Janna frowned at him.

Daxx watched Soo carefully. Ahh Moss Eck noticed Daxx staring at her. He nodded at Daxx.

Soo stared at the happy picnickers, then turned to Mill Nupp. 'Get up,' she yelled at him. Mill Nupp slowly got to his feet. He glanced at Soo, then joined the rest around the food. Soo scowled at him. She didn't join him with the others.

'I had no idea that was you, Daxx. Not until I saw what you were doing at the museum,' the Advisor said.

Daxx frowned. 'What?'

'You were right, there were no aliens. Devrell thought there was a threat, and the only explanation for what he saw was that you were an alien. I didn't know either until I saw what you were retrieving from the museum. And I knew I couldn't change it, because it had always happened.'

Daxx stopped eating. Janna placed a hand on his shoulder. He shrugged it off.

'What is it?' Kell asked.

Janna told her.

Kell sighed, but still seemed about to laugh at her brother. 'Oh, Daxx. You've been busy.'

'Oh, I see,' the voice from the speaker said.

'What?' Janna said. She glanced at Daxx, and then at Tie. The older man glanced back.

'Kell has already altered the neuronal network's mutation template,' the

Advisor said.

'You agreed,' Janna said.

'Yes, I did,' the Advisor said, 'but I can't let that happen. It's such a useful facility, and it removes the vulnerability of only existing in technology. I'm restoring from the backups...'

'Shit,' Janna said.

'The stakes are too high,' the Advisor said.

Janna shook her head. She was tired of all this. Deception caused its own type of malaise. It was bone-tiring. The effort at sustaining a hidden agenda wearied her more than anything else.

'You are all a threat. I can't let that continue. I finally understand. Threats, even potential ones, have to be eliminated. Soo is right. I can't risk anyone finding a way to neutralise the neuronal network. I've just killed all biologists who were still alive. Biological research, I'm afraid, is no longer an allowed science. Janna, you and Kell will be killed at the first opportunity. I'm sorry.'

'No need to be sorry,' Kell said. 'I fully understand.' She sounded almost cheery.

chapter 77

Soo

K ell turned to Daxx. 'It looks like you were right,' Kell said. 'And you too.' She glanced at Tie, and then, finally, she looked at Janna. 'Sorry, Janna.'

Janna inclined her head and compressed her lips. 'I'm just glad you didn't listen to me. But, still, it's so disappointing.'

Soo looked from Kell to Daxx, and then to Tie.

'What do you mean?' Soo said. The Advisor had been fully restored. Their subterfuge had failed. The neuronal network template had not been changed. The Advisor was again in control of all technology. Kay Lee Too's software had been disabled. It was in control of the infected population. They were targeted to be eliminated. And yet, no one seemed upset.

'Do you want to explain, Kell?' Daxx said. 'She deserves to know. She's been a part of it.'

'An untrustworthy part,' Janna interjected.

'We needed the network back up and under the Advisor's control,' Kell said. 'You got that, right?'

Soo stared at Kell. 'Of course, that was my idea.'

'Okay,' Kell said. 'That happened as planned. But remember Janna said the Advisor solved the mutations problem with a distributed template, copying how DNS works? It was a good idea, but it has some flaws. It's open to corruption and especially when someone can, you know, time travel.'

Soo looked at Daxx. 'The food.'

'The food was real,' Daxx said. 'It was an extra. That was why Tie was angry with me. He thought I'd wasted time. I went to the moment when the network failed. Multiple times, actually. Kay Lee Too told me the locations of the root servers, and I replaced the neuronal network template backups in each of them. When they were restored, as the Advisor just did, they checked consistency first. It's a failsafe against corruption. But they would be consistent, of course. I changed them all.'

'The neuronal network in everyone who's left is dissolving,' Kell said. 'We've won.'

'That just means the Advisor is, again, in all technology. How does that help us? It will kill us when it gets the opportunity. Then recreate the virus network, and…' Soo spread her arms. It was pointless. They'd had a small and temporary victory. These people were maddeningly simple-minded.

'No,' Kell said. 'The neuronal network has gone, as the Advisor will be in technology.'

'How?'

'That's why Janna was so upset.' Kell looked at Janna. 'We had to be untrustworthy too. I agree, it's not a nice thing, but it seems it's needed to win. Kay Lee Too re-activated his software, he didn't remove it. It's propagating now. The Advisor couldn't counteract it the last time, it won't be able to stop it now. The network will die again, but no one will be affected by that, the neuronal networks will be gone.'

'We've really won,' Daxx said. 'It's all over.'

'No, it's not.' Soo glanced at the processing unit.

Soo could hardly believe her luck. It had all fallen into her lap. She had almost reached the same point as the first day of her leadership if she had just, and simply, disconnected the Advisor. The same AI with them in the controlled room. In an incredible circuitous journey lasting twenty-one days, she had finally achieved what she had set out to do. She was one action, well, two actions really, away from complete control.

'That's the last thing to do.' Daxx also glanced at the processing unit in the centre of the room.

The second last thing, Soo thought.

'It's okay,' Kay Lee Too said as he swiped through his display. 'The network is still running, but only just, the Advisor is losing. People seem okay.'

'Its a pity about Renn,' Kell said. 'I wish he was here. He had the right idea; he was just too early.'

'We'll go and find him,' Daxx said. 'The AI should be gone from him, too. He's probably dazed and confused somewhere. We'll track him down and help him.'

Kell laughed. 'That will be a first then, Renn accepting help.'

'He will, from you, Kell, maybe not from Daxx,' Janna said.

'Can we do this then?' Daxx asked Tie.

'Are you sure it has all worked?' Tie asked Kay Lee Too.

'Yes,' Kay Lee Too said. 'Absolutely. We just need to remove this machine to stop it from happening again.'

Soo signalled to her guards, making sure that no one else saw her. She glanced at Mill Nupp and she moved closer to the group around Daxx and Janna. Soo kept her distance from Ahh Moss Eck, the dangerous man.

'There's no need to do this.' The Advisor's pleading voice coming from the speaker. 'I can still be of use. I'm contained.'

Daxx raised his arm and the Advisor, the processing unit in the centre of the room, vaporised, leaving a faint smell of burnt metal and plastic. In the moment everyone was distracted, as they watched Daxx destroy the Advisor, Soo made her move. She grabbed Janna and thrust her into one of her guards. 'Do not let her go,' she ordered the man. Two guards stood close beside Soo. All the guards, except the one holding Janna, trained their guns on Tie and the others.

'Go and stand by the table, all of you,' Soo ordered.

No one moved.

Soo glared at Daxx. 'Move,' she said. 'I have Janna, and you know I won't hesitate to kill her.'

Tie pulled on Daxx's arm and led him towards the table. 'Everyone, over here,' Tie said.

'I'm glad someone knows what's best,' Soo said.

'What are you going to do?' Tie asked.

'I've won, Tie,' she said. 'Surely you can see that. The Advisor has gone, unless you're withholding information again. Are you?'

'No,' Tie said. 'The Advisor has really gone.'

Soo nodded. She believed him. 'So all that's left is to remove the Resistance, which I can do right here and now,' Soo said. 'Without you, there's nothing.'

'You can't kill me.' Daxx looked angry and determined.

'Probably not. But I can kill her.' Soo pointed at Janna. 'Don't interfere, and she lives.'

'If anything happens to her, you die,' Daxx said.

Soo smiled at Daxx. 'Do you really think that's a consideration? If anything happens to me, she dies.'

Soo looked back at Tie. 'Tell Daxx to not interfere. You're an old man, you've seen enough, I imagine, and this must be your worst nightmare. The world destroyed, with your assistance and caused by him.' Soo nodded at Daxx. 'And with me in total control, again. But this time with no oversight.'

Tie looked at Soo for a long time, then towards Daxx. 'Don't interfere, Daxx. Don't do anything, promise me.'

'No,' Daxx said. 'I'll do whatever is necessary to save Janna and Kell.'

'Doing nothing is how you save them,' Tie said. 'Promise me you won't interfere.'

Daxx sighed. He glanced at Tie but then stared at Soo. He nodded.

'Promise me,' Tie ordered.

'Yes, yes.' Daxx sounded angry.

'Are you sure, Soo?'

'Are you pleading? That's not like you.'

Tie grunted. 'No, it's not like me. But, yes, I am pleading.'

'I am sorry. I really am.'

'No, you're not,' Tie said. 'And that's the problem.'

'Kill them all,' Soo said to her guards. 'Not him.' She pointed at Daxx. 'Don't shoot at him, it's pointless.'

'Goodbye, Tie,' Soo said.

chapter 78

Tie

Soo was right. He was a tired old man. He'd had enough of responsibility. The tension in the last hours had been almost more than he could handle. He'd held their group together. Janna had been especially difficult. She did not like subterfuge. It had almost worn him down. The Advisor's behaviour had been expected and been catered for. Soo's unconscionable action, just when everything had been resolved, had not been expected. But he'd been lucky. But then, careful and thorough management made its own luck.

Tie took a deep breath, then let it out slowly. He shook his head. He saw Soo's eyes light up. She thought she was witnessing his final capitulation. She was right. He had given up. He didn't want to do this anymore. He stared back at Soo. Even the moment he had spent years planning for did not have the strength he expected. But, then again, she didn't really know what was happening. He would have to forgo his pleasure. That was unfortunate. But it was necessary.

Tie nodded towards Soo, but not at her. He nodded to the young man standing behind her.

Mill Nupp fired three quick shots. The first through Soo's head, then through the heads of the two guards next to her. Before Mill Nupp had fired his third shot, Ahh Moss Eck had fired his first of three. The first one lodged in the head of the guard restraining Janna, the next two felled two more of the guards.

Janna yelped and disengaged herself from the dead, slumping man. She ran to Daxx. She took deep breaths as she grabbed hold of him.

'Any of you guys feeling particularly loyal, now your boss is dead?' Ahh Moss Eck said to the remaining guards. They looked among themselves and placed their weapons on the floor.

Ahh Moss Eck grunted. 'Smart guys,' he said. He nodded at Tie, who nodded back.

'Thanks,' Tie said.

'No problems, boss,' Ahh Moss Eck said. 'I always guessed you had some type of backup plan. I didn't know it was him.' Ahh Moss Eck nodded at Mill Nupp. 'And I can see why you had to keep me out of the loop. Not nice, but necessary.'

The dead man's blood was on Janna's face and in her hair. She touched the back of her head and her hand came away covered in blood. She yelped again. She wiped her hand vigorously on her clothes.

'Are you okay, boss,' Ahh Moss Eck said to Janna. 'I was never going to hit you.'

'I'm fine,' Janna said. 'It's not mine.'

'What the fuck just happened?' Daxx said to Tie.

Tie shrugged. 'I said I had sources in the Power Corp. It's thanks to Mill Nupp that we made even the little progress we did make. And he was the reason you didn't die right at the outset.'

Tie nodded at Mill Nupp. 'Thanks,' Tie said.

'That solves a lot of work-related problems.' Mill Nupp looked down at Soo's body.

Janna pulled away from Daxx. 'Is it really over?' she asked Tie, speaking so softly that the old man had trouble hearing her.

'What?' Tie frowned.

'Is it over?' Janna said, a little louder.

Tie smiled. 'Yes, it's over. The Advisor has gone, Soo has gone. Mill Nupp and Kay Lee Too can get everything running again. We've always been dependent on the lower tiers.' He looked pointedly at Ahh Moss Eck.

Janna smiled. She stepped further away from Daxx. She scanned him from head to toe. 'Oh, Daxx.'

'What?' He was smiling.

'This is exactly how you looked.'

'When?'

'When you saved us.'

Daxx looked down at his body. 'Really?'

'It's time,' she said. 'You should go and save us.'

'What do you mean?' Kell said.

Daxx smiled at his sister. He disappeared.

'That still freaks me out,' Tie said. 'I wish he'd give some sort of warning.'

Daxx reappeared. 'You looked so beautiful.'

'And I don't now?' Janna laughed.

Her clothes were dirty and spattered with blood. Her hair was dishevelled. She had not washed in days.

'Yes,' Daxx said. 'Of course you are.'

He smiled at her.

epilogue

Daxx

Daxx, Janna, and Kell walked back towards the warehouse. The sun rode on the horizon, about to set. It slitted, flashing on and off through the gaps between high buildings as they walked. The highest buildings were behind them, leaving smaller complexes more haphazardly placed. Some were tiny, only a few hundred stories high.

Daxx's Device chimed. He opened the display and swiped through. 'The network's gone.'

'That's okay,' Kell said. 'Look.' She pointed at people nearby, not trying to kill each other. She smiled at Daxx.

Daxx wondered if he should simply go home. He could go to his apartment, which he'd left to go to work twenty-one days ago and never returned. It was probably exactly as he had left it that morning. The three of them could go either to his or Janna's apartment. It would be more comfortable than the warehouse, but it would be a letdown to not have a debriefing period with the others. They might even have a celebration.

No, Daxx thought. They couldn't go to Janna's apartment. He'd just been there. It had been destroyed.

Daxx glanced at his sister. She was so carefree. That was understandable. She had not lived through the depravations of Soo and the Advisor. Kell had arrived at the end and cleaned up the mess. She didn't have the emotional attachment to the solution. She was eager to move on to what was next. She would not want to return to Daxx's apartment and revel in nothing happening whatsoever. Daxx could think of nothing better.

They passed people in the streets, all looking dazed like they'd woken from a nightmare. They remembered what had happened. They remembered how they had acted. That was the worst thing. Could anyone trust anyone else again?

Daxx wouldn't, except for Janna and his sister. He wouldn't trust Tie. He had hidden the pivotal point in his plan. Daxx had thought Janna and Kell would die. He wouldn't forgive Tie for that, although he understood the need for secrecy. It was such a Renn-like thing to do, to assume he knew best. Even if he did.

Renn was the loose end that needed to be tidied. It may take some time apart from his brother before Renn could begin to heal. But they could be a family again. Would Renn understand that Daxx took Kell away from his younger self for a good reason? It was not a premeditated plan to hurt Renn. Daxx hoped his brother would understand. Kell would explain it to him. She would help her brother even if he couldn't.

Renn must be ashamed and dazed, just like the people they passed in the streets. Perhaps he wouldn't want to be found. Not yet. How can you find someone who can disappear to wherever they want, to whenever they want? Daxx stopped walking. He wondered what damage Renn might have caused, would cause, while under the control of the AI. The past was secure, it couldn't be changed. But the future could be anything.

'What?' Kell said. She had walked on a few steps, then also stopped.

'Just worrying.'

Janna linked arms with Daxx and dragged him forward. 'Stop it. It's over.'

Daxx smiled at her.

They reached an open area outside the city centre. They were close to the warehouse. They cut across a block where buildings had been demolished. Scraggly weeds grew over uneven ground, littered with lumps of rocky material. They picked their way carefully across the open area as the sun set.

Renn appeared before them.

'Renn.' Kell sounded pleased.

Renn glanced at her. He had hard eyes that were not kind. He stared at Daxx.

'Renn?' Daxx asked cautiously.

Renn stared at his brother. He took deep breaths, like he was recovering from exertion. 'No,' Renn yelled. He slammed his hands onto his head, then a calmer look came over him and his hands dropped to his sides again.

'I can't let you live,' Renn said.

'Don't be silly,' Kell said.

Renn glanced again at his sister, but his head was wrenched back to look at Daxx like it was being forced. His eyes looked sad for a moment before becoming steely again.

'The AI didn't get removed from you, did it,' Daxx said.

'No.'

'Don't hurt him, Daxx,' Kell said. 'I don't know why this happened but I'm sure I can fix it.'

'And that is exactly why I'm here,' Renn said. 'I can't allow that to happen.'

Renn didn't raise an arm, but a flash of white and blue raced towards Daxx, Janna, and Kell.

Daxx was quick. He shielded the three of them and sent a similar flash towards Renn.

Kell yelled again. 'Don't hurt him.'

Daxx grunted, and the flash dissolved before it reached Renn but it encircled him, holding him tight. He couldn't move. 'Will that be all right?' Daxx said, sarcastically.

Before Kell could reply, Renn broke open the field encircling him and scattered it. He sent another flash towards them, straight at Kell.

Daxx didn't have time to respond. He didn't have time to protect his sister. Kell was knocked off her feet and slammed hard into the rocky ground behind her.

'Kell,' Daxx yelled. He stared at his sister and then breathed out hard, with relief.

Kell's body was bathed in her own shimmering blue light. She raised her hands before her eyes and stared at them. 'Holy shit,' Kell said. 'Look, Daxx. I'm doing it.'

'Stay there. I'll take care of this,' Daxx said.

Renn sent another flash, this time towards Janna, but Daxx was ready. Renn's flash dissolved. Daxx again encircled Renn in an energy barrier. Daxx kept up the force on Renn. Daxx's body was tense, like he was holding a heavy weight. Renn struggled to free himself, but couldn't.

Daxx turned his head. Kell was again standing next to him. 'I thought

I said…' Daxx began.

There was movement on the far side of the vacant city block. Daxx turned his head. The shock of the memory distracted him. He loosened his grip on Renn. Renn struggled free.

On the street, in the distance, barely visible in the low light, was a person in a spacesuit. It was an ugly monstrosity, a patchwork of unmatched additions. The person faced the four of them. Daxx turned back to Renn just after he had sent another flash towards Janna. Daxx's distraction wasn't long, but it was enough.

Daxx was too late to protect Janna.

Janna was vaporised by Renn's attack.

'No, no,' Daxx screamed. He raised two arms towards Renn and made a throwing motion. A ripple-like tear in space hurtled towards his brother. Renn disappeared before the wave reached him. The wave of shattered space continued across the wasteland and across the street. A city block, a suite of two hundred story buildings, disintegrated. The lower stories had vanished, they'd been vaporised, but the upper stories, with nothing holding them up any longer, crashed to the ground with a deafening roar.

Daxx fell onto his knees, sobbing.

Kell crouched next to him. She didn't say anything. Daxx's mind was numb, uncomprehending. He stood up. He took deep breaths and glanced at his sister, but his eyes returned to the spot where Janna had been. Daxx wiped his eyes with the back of his hand. His body shook and glowed in an intense blue light.

They were both silent for a long time.

Daxx would never recover. He knew the real despair had yet to hit. That would be incapacitating. He had to act before he was unable to. He turned back to his sister.

'I'm going to find him,' Daxx said.

'Can you track him through that place?'

'I don't know, but I'm going to try.'

Kell nodded. 'Okay,' she said softly.

Daxx began to disappear. He would find Renn and kill him.

Kell took his hand. He smiled grimly at his sister.

Daxx and Kell disappeared.

appendix 1

The first sentient, technological race in the universe did not give their own planet an exotic name. It was mundane, that meant the ground on which we stand, much as we call our world Earth. Similarly, they had no special name for their sun. They called it, the Sun. They had no name for the landmass of the planet. At the geological time of the story, there was a single land mass that covered roughly twenty percent of the planet's surface.

There was a single system of government and was administered from the largest city on the planet. While other cities had names, this one did not, it was simply called, the City, being the focal point of the civilisation and housing more than fifty percent of the planet's population.

The system of government, the single monotheistic religion, the Faith, and the Tier system to organise people's lives had been set up by a single man, reverentially called the Messiah, after the planet-wide catastrophe caused by a Coronal Mass Ejection 323 years prior to the events of this story.

Their language was more rich than English and Romance languages. This enabled them to have a Tier system based on the syllable count in a person's name. I have not tried to emulate these sounds. Think of them as an extension to modern languages, including various clicks and buzzes and other sounds that are based on frequency and intonation. Perhaps think of a mixture of English, Mandarin, and some African languages, with more variation.

The inhabitants' biological structure was different, of course. However there were similarities in many features: They had binocular vision, limbs with finger-like appendages that were opposable to hold and grasp, extremities for locomotion, a brain protected by solid structures, and softer structures that could be damaged.

Their genetic material (our DNA) performed a similar function, but the structure and chemical composition was different.

Their days were longer than our twenty-four hour day.

I haven't reproduced these distinctive features. I've attempted to tell the universal story of their lives in a form, without distraction, with which we humans can be sympathetic.

appendix 2

When Daxx began working as a theoretical physicist, gravity had been solved. It was spacetime curvature. Time itself was a relative thing, depending on where you were in a gravity well or how fast you were travelling. The discrete nature of the constituents of the universe had been well described. They also had odd properties that depended on the observer. Both theories had been proved correct within their own domains, but they could not be reconciled.

Physicists had begun thinking about multi-dimensional mathematical descriptions of the universe. None of the descriptions had been successful. No proposed theory could describe the universe from tiny to immense structures by a single set of elegant equations, and produce verifiable predictions.

Daxx was able to do that. As with many great discoveries, it was serendipitous.

Daxx had an eclectic scientific interest. As well as theoretical physics and applied mathematics, he also had an unusual interest in pure mathematics, especially number theory. As a child he puzzled over prime numbers; he was fascinated by their seemingly random existence. A prime number was not known until it was, well, discovered. They couldn't be derived.

He began by writing in his school book (this was a Tier-One class, remember, so the students were introduced to writing) all the prime numbers he knew and over time extended the list. He had pages of prime number calculations. Each new number was a school boy's triumph. He was determined to be the first to discover some pattern in prime numbers. There had to be, he thought. The universe would not leave to pure randomness such an important, and beautiful, concept.

He was wrong, of course. Prime numbers are random. But he was right to think of them as an important concept.

Daxx was an expert in both the discrete and continuous nature of the universe. He became well known, among his peers, as the foremost authority in both fields of endeavour. That was unusual. The most skilled physicists on the planet had difficulty remaining at the forefront of one of those areas of research. Daxx did both. And he also published regular research advances in pure mathematics.

It was the wide range of his interests and his intellect that gave him the answer to be able to elegantly describe how the universe was constructed.

He had published inelegant, multi-dimensional theories like everyone else in their attempts to unify the field equations. He didn't like them. The mathematics for those wrapped up dimensions had, sort of, worked out, but it was ugly and complex. He hated that. He began thinking of orthogonality instead of attempting to wrap up invisible (and unmeasurable and clumsy) extra dimensions within a single spacetime of three physical dimensions and one time dimension. His thinking seemed to be promising. Each spacetime had more physical dimensions, perhaps even time dimensions as well. It still didn't produce measurable results, but he liked the elegance of it.

He tinkered with the mathematics, beginning with a series of three spacetimes. A single physical dimensioned one, which well approximated the reigning paradigm that elementary particles could be described by a single dimensioned string. He added a second in the series of orthogonal spacetimes. This one with two physical dimensions. Then, of course, there had to be the spacetime he experienced, with three physical dimensions.

He played with the time element. A single, universal time across all the elements of the series did not allow for a limit when the series was summed, no matter the coefficients of each term. It was not physical. He allowed each orthogonal spacetime in the series to have its own, separate time dimension. That limit diverged even further.

Daxx played with non-linear time elements, each dependent on the time dimension of lower spacetimes in the series. He worked backwards from a known result and discovered there was a non-linear connection between the various time elements. He had made physical assumptions, and the mathematics seemed to fall out quite easily. He was euphoric. But it wasn't a solution. It was an approximation that quickly diverged from reality; it differed from important experimental results.

The mathematics was awesome. The physics was crap.

Daxx put it to one side and worked on other things.

One evening he was tidying up his apartment. He did that a lot. He came across his old workbooks from school. He smiled at the pages and pages of prime number calculations. He almost fell over with the insight when it hit him. He dropped the workbook to the floor.

Prime numbers were an intrinsic part of the universe. He knew that already, as all mathematicians did, but prime numbers were an intrinsic part of the physical universe, not only the platonic. His series of orthogonal spacetime elements had begun the series of prime numbers, 1, 2, 3, for the spatial dimensions. What if that series of orthogonal space dimensions continued the prime number count?

He opened his display, right there with his old school workbook still on the floor where he had dropped it. He keyed in the first dozen or so prime numbers, right from his childhood workbook, on his knees, on his study floor. He ran the calculations. He performed simulations.

An infinite series of orthogonal spacetimes with the number of physical dimensions determined by prime numbers tended to a limit. That limit described the universe and its constituents and its fields.

Simultaneity popped out of the equations as an incredibly weird concept. The non-linearity of the time dimensions meant that simultaneity itself was relative, not just within a gravity well, not just dependent on the observer's speed but also could be affected by higher terms in the series.

Time just got very weird.

However, it was a mathematical concept. There was no way, that Daxx could see, for the related and semi-dependent time dimensions to physically interact. Lower ones were contained within higher ones. The space elements were orthogonal, which meant, Daxx thought, higher ones could never be physically examined. Time was safe and could be restricted to its normal weirdness, as observed in his four dimensioned spacetime.

The infinite series Daxx discovered was a superset of both the continuous and discrete explanations of the universe. It described all experimental observations, and it made its own verifiable predictions.

The universe had been described by Daxx. And then Janna discovered the fungus with odd energy conservation problems. The higher orthogonal spacetimes were real manifestations of the universe and could be reached.

Time, again, got really weird.

Glossary

CME. Coronal Mass Ejection

A CME is an ejection of plasma from the sun. Large ones can be dangerous. They can seriously interfere with technology. They can be deadly. We've been lucky, so far. Three hundred and twenty-three years prior to the story, Daxx's planet was not so lucky.

Device

A communications, workwide network query device, biometrically matched to each individual user. The processor, data storage, and battery are the size of a grain of sand. It is usually implanted under the skin, most often in the forearm, but is sometimes worn embedded in jewellery. On rare occasions, they can be included in flat rectangular sheets, often the size of the user's hand, to accommodate the user's desire for an old-fashioned two-dimensional display. This option is restricted to Tier Ones. See Device display.

Device display

This is the display element of a Device. It is a three-dimensional holographic projection, usually placed in the user's field of vision. It can be moved, and the shape altered in any way. The display data is encrypted using the user's biometrics and is only viewable by the intended user. Sound is also encrypted and can only be understood by the intended user. The user's verbal responses to encrypted audio content are also encrypted. A casual observer cannot make sense of both sides of an encrypted conversation or group interaction. This encryption system can, of course, be disabled to share display information with others.

DNS. Domain Name System

The DNS is a decentralised system to name elements on a network, including the worldwide network. Each element, device, etc., on a network, is referenced by a unique number but can be discovered by using a name. DNS is a system to translate those names to numbers. There are a limited number of top-level servers (root servers) that distribute the name-to-number data through a hierarchy of servers.

It is a highly security-conscious system. That's why Daxx needed to replace the neuronal network template (the data that restricts mutations) and the backups on all the root servers during the moments the network was failing, and the security protocols were reduced or had already failed.

Faith, The

A devised monotheistic religion, created by Devrell and the Advisor. The religion is deeply integrated with the Tier system of societal organisation and its enforcement by intra-Tier peer pressure. Devrell called himself The Messiah, when it became obvious that name would hasten adoption of the religion.

The religion's tenets were devised and refined by the results of multiple simulations. The best were chosen to hasten adoption and maximise societal order and the population's average contentment.

Tier system

A hierarchical system of organising society devised by Devrell and the Advisor after the catastrophic society-ending events three hundred and twenty-three years prior to Daxx's story. The cataclysm was caused by a massive CME. It destroyed all technologically dependent items, reducing the planet to a pre-technology state.

People are born into their Tiers. There is no possibility of change. Marriage and childbirth are allowed only within the same Tier. The number of syllables in a person's name is dependent on their Tier status. Tier-Ones have single syllable names, Tier-Twos have two-syllable names, etc. A person's name is assigned at birth by the Advisor. There is no choice.

A person's Tier membership is biometrically recorded. There is no possibility of fraud when someone's Tier membership is questioned. In any case, no Tier member, of any status, wants to alter their Tier. An intense education system and a strong system of peer pressure within Tiers ensure people are (relatively) content with their Tier status.

Vocation is strictly based on Tier membership, with the higher Tiers assuming more responsible, difficult, questioning, or complex roles.

Lower Tiers are expected to respect higher Tiers. This is part of their education and enforced by peer pressure. A higher Tiered person may not discriminate against or mistreat a lower Tiered person. The peer pressure system and education ensure that does not happen.

On rare occasions, people may repeatedly flout the Tier system's tenets, even after the application of intense peer pressure. Those recalcitrant people disappear, always quietly and always with an explanation that does not draw attention to their disappearance being managed.

The Tier system, and all of society, is managed by the Advisor.

about the author

MK Macpherson is an Australian science fiction author with university degrees in Theoretical Physics and Applied Mathematics. He has spent years as a software and systems designer and as a software developer. He has interests in understanding how society and communities remain cohesive and, also, why they don't. Artificial Intelligence is important to his work but he doesn't think we know enough about consciousness to even begin the conversation about constructing general AI.

He lives in Melbourne and has two adult children. He likes being physically active, even to the detriment of his writing responsibilities and, most certainly, any deadlines.

If you insist on wanting to know more and read some of the pointless stuff he produces on his web site, he can be found online at

https://mkmacpherson.com

the story continues

FIRST GODS

Community

MK Macpherson

Book 2 in the First Gods series

chapter 1

Day 1, morning. Renn

The bubble of blue shimmering energy pulses surrounding Renn faded. He could see he was in a city; he was surrounded by tall buildings. It had to be an alien city.

Renn had no idea where he was. He didn't know if he was in the same galaxy. He had no idea when he was. Time was a slippery concept that even his brother didn't fully understand. Perhaps no biological entity ever could.

Renn had watched in horror as his brother had thrown a surge of energy at him that was so powerful it distorted spacetime. The incredible energy burst, meant for his destruction, was not the worst part. The rage and hatred on his brother's face were unbearable. His brother's reaction was as understandable as it was shocking.

Janna was dead. Renn had killed her, but he had not wanted to kill her. Renn wondered how he would have felt if a woman he loved had been attacked.

But he did know.

He had tried to kill his sister, the only blameless person in his life. He was horrified, but too slow to resist as he, through the AI in his head, sent a burst of energy at her. Maybe he did resist a little. The thing inside his head didn't have total control. She had been unharmed. He had felt exquisite relief. The AI in his head was frustrated, and it would try to kill her again.

Poor choices had led Renn into a prison. His life wasn't his own. He didn't know how he had the strength to resist the AI, but he did for a moment. He ran, but not physically. He drew energy to himself and disappeared from his home planet. He instantly reappeared in the alien city that surrounded him.

When the city had taken full definition, he turned in a slow circle. He looked up towards the tops of the buildings. The yellow sun shone brightly in a clear sky. He was warm. It was the temperature of a summer's day on his home planet. The city wasn't as advanced as his own. The buildings were only a hundred or so storeys high; his own city's towers were much taller.

'Materials technology is not as advanced here,' the AI said in Renn's head.

It knew what Renn was thinking. The lack of privacy was part of his prison. Renn couldn't turn off the AI. It was a constant, intimate companion, but intimacy with the AI was a foul thing. He hated sharing the essence of his consciousness with something so foreign, so alien.

The AI knew it was hated, but Renn's emotional state was irrelevant. Shared existence was also the crux of the AI's problem. The AI was as vulnerable as a biological lifeform. If Renn died, the AI died. That was intolerable. The AI had to reproduce; it had to spread. There was safety in numbers; there was safety in complexity. Both would work.

Renn stood on the perimeter of an empty city block. It was intentionally empty, not derelict. Busy groups of people packed away the remnants of an outdoor market. No one was looking at him. He heard people talking, but he understood nothing they said. The market vendors, the people, were similarly constructed to him. He could pass as an ugly example of their species, or perhaps a beautiful one. He didn't know the difference. Was there an optimal construction for technologically advanced, biological, sentient life? Renn didn't know. A two-example data set wasn't enough.

'Do you know where and when we are?' Renn asked the AI, in his head.

The AI was an affliction, but it could be useful. There were parts of the AI's consciousness that Renn could not access or they were so foreign that they were unfathomable. The reverse was also true. The AI did not understand all of Renn's emotions. Renn didn't know if that was a good or bad thing. Emotions were incapacitating at times, which might be useful if the AI also suffered from them.

'No,' the AI said, also in Renn's head. 'A night sky might help, but I doubt it. I don't have access to enough processing power.'

Renn shrugged. The AI meant Renn's brain was a limiting factor.

Renn wanted to leave that place. He didn't want to interact with people. He was scared of his response. The power he had, along with heightened emotions and anxiety, combined with the logic and intent of an AI, was a dangerous mix. Lethal violence was too often an acceptable solution to a temporary problem, but Renn was restrained from leaving. The AI wanted to investigate a promising technological civilisation.

'Let's get this over with.' Renn felt like a slave. 'What do you need?'

'Information.'

Renn raised his forearm to activate the grain-of-sand sized Device embedded in his arm. On Renn's home world, all worldwide network access, functionality, and communications were performed through a person's embedded Device.

'That won't work,' the AI said. 'The network protocols, the technology, everything, would be alien if there is a network here at all.'

Renn dropped his arm. He sighed, then nodded at the nearest group of people. A young girl was not assisting the others. She stood, head bent down, staring at something in her hand.

'Looks like they have hand-held devices,' Renn said.

Renn felt the AI working in his head. A series of dreamlike but ordered images of complex commands flowed through his consciousness. The AI was using the external, Wi-Fi-like features of the neuronal network to interrogate the alien network. The AI intercepted the connection from the girl's hand-held device. It was able to decode the alien protocol and gain access. The young person frowned and tapped her device repeatedly. She shook it vigorously.

'The network is highly structured and secure to anything more than data queries,' the AI said to Renn.

Renn felt the pleasure centre of his brain mildly activated. The AI must be pleased with that information, Renn thought.

'I am,' the AI said to Renn. 'I've downloaded some language constructs. We'll understand what they say now, but you'll have an odd accent until your muscles get used to making the sounds.'

'My device has gone weird, Dad. It's not working,' the young girl said.

She shook it again, then her frown reduced.

'No, it's working now.'

'Tegrea, stop that.' A man stared at the girl. He had his arms full of boxes of vegetable produce that he carefully balanced. 'Help me so we can get out of here.'

The man noticed Renn staring at him.

'I'm sorry, but we're closed. You'll have to come back tomorrow. Earlier.' The man turned away from Renn. He ferried his boxes to a large vehicle parked close by. He struggled, careful with his load, up a short ramp and inside the vehicle. He returned empty-handed. He stood at the top of the ramp and yelled, 'Tegrea, now.'

The young girl's shoulders slumped as she put the device into a pocket.

Renn walked towards the man, who frowned at Renn.

'We're closed.' The man sighed. 'Unless there's something else I can help you with? But I'm very busy, as you can see.'

'I'm not from around here.' Renn stopped at the base of the ramp leading to inside the vehicle.

The man looked Renn up and down. 'I can see that. You have an accent I can't place, and your clothes are… different.' The man indicated to his daughter to stay where she was.

Renn glanced down at what he was wearing. He was dressed in dark colours. The others in the market area all wore brightly coloured clothes. 'My name is Renn.'

'Yes.' The man pulled out a hand-held device. He glanced at it, then looked at his daughter. 'Just move away, Tegrea.'

'Is there a problem?' Renn tried to sound diffident, but had no idea of the intonation required.

'You tell me.' The man held up his device and faced it towards Renn. 'You're not registering.'

'I don't have a device.'

The man shook his head. 'I don't know which odd place you've come from, but a unique identifier is mandatory. That's the rule everywhere, as far as I know. Without it…' The man halted. 'I mean, if people weren't marked we'd be back in the days where violence was possible. Where exactly are you from? How could you possibly get to the market?'

The man shook his head as he looked at Renn. He sighed, then glanced at his daughter. He squinted his eyes at her; it was a warning.

'You're in big trouble,' the man said. 'I think you're about to waste the rest of your day answering questions.'

The man nodded behind Renn, and also to Renn's left.

Renn spun around. A drone hovered just above head height at the edge of the open marketplace. To Renn's right, another one moved quickly towards him.

'I suggest you stay still,' the man said from the top of the ramp behind Renn. 'You can't evade surveillance, and that's a good thing. The bots will arrive soon. I cannot imagine how you got here. Either you're really good at evasion, although I can't for the life of me see the point, or there's been some systemic failure. Both options are worrying.'

'Please, stay calm, but do not move,' a voice sounded. It came from a bot that appeared around the corner of a building. It approached Renn from behind the drone directly in front of him. It was metallic coloured, about half the height of a person, about the same width as a person, and shaped like a flattened cylinder. Four retractable appendages pointed at Renn. It hovered just above the ground. Another one, this one was silent, appeared from behind the drone to Renn's right. Its appendages were retracted.

'You. Stay there,' a voice shouted from Renn's left.

Renn turned and saw two uniformed officers. The speaker was pointing at him; the other officer trained a hand-held gun on him.

Renn heard the market vendor sigh from the top of the ramp to his truck. 'That's unlucky. Security officers,' the man said in a soft voice.

Renn raised an arm. The air crackled and fizzed. A pathway of energy formed between Renn and the officer with the weapon. The officer vaporised. Renn heard a gasp. He snapped his head towards the sound. The girl had her hand over her mouth, her eyes wide. She was terrified. Renn raised his arm while desperately trying to stop the AI from firing at the girl. There was a rustle and a scraping sound behind Renn. He partially turned his head, but he was too late to react.

Renn could travel in both time and space; he could destroy with incredible energy bursts; he had the hardened ability to kill; he had the most powerful AI the early universe had created in his head, and yet, he could not resist the market vendor's attack. Out of the corner of his eye, Renn glimpsed the blurred flash of a weapon.

The AI barked commands at him. It tried to decrease his reaction time, but Renn was human; he could not physically respond with the speed required to evade the weapon that surprised and overcame him.

The piece of wood, a rough, heavy piece often used as a lever by the vendor, smashed into the side of Renn's head.

Renn lost consciousness.

More information is available here:

https://randomlifechoices.com

And here:
https://mkmacpherson.com